HE FOUGHT HIS FEAR

There was something important down here in the cave, and he had to find out what it was.

He finned forward. Unease vibrated here, screamed out at Buddy to turn around and swim for the cave's mouth as fast as he could.

And then he saw it.

Or, rather, he saw *them*. The first was a scrap of white on the cave floor. Abandoned, discarded, it seemed oddly familiar, something he had seen many times before.

And the other thing . . .

Bile poured up into Buddy's regulator, and he swallowed it down, choking on bitter acid.

God. The other. It was big. *Big.* It came at him out of the murkiest depths of the cave, a great spotted, undulating mass, sinuous of tail and fin, with a great underslung mouth blankly open, and black fathomless eyes which looked right at him . . .

Also by Julia Grice
* *The Passion Star*
Wild Roses
Daughters of the Flame
Emerald Fire
Lovefire

* *Published by*
WARNER BOOKS

Cry for
the Demon

by Julia Grice

WARNER BOOKS

A Warner Communications Company

All characters and incidents in this book are completely fictitious, as is the fictional beach where the body of Karen Weeks is found, and the village of Makai itself. The author has taken geographical liberties which come out of her imagination only.

WARNER BOOKS EDITION

Cover design by Gene Light

Cover art by Paul Alexander

Warner Books, Inc., 75 Rockefeller Plaza, New York, N.Y. 10019

Ⓦ A Warner Communications Company

Printed in the United States of America

First Printing: December, 1980

10 9 8 7 6 5 4 3 2 1

This book is for my friends, for all the people I love and whose caring helped me through a hard time. It is for Lee Butcher. It is for Margaret Duda and Roni Tripodi and Elyse Rogers and Douglas Alden Peterson and Cecilia Morneau and Toni King and Ann Hellie and more, many more of you. How lucky I am to have you. If friends are worth more than purest gold, then I am rich, rich, indeed . . .

I lived in Hawaii seven months to write this book and fell in love with Maui's sweepingly beautiful scenery, and with the warmth of its people. I would like to offer thanks to those who assisted me with my scuba diving and with ocean lore: Kent Fletcher, Linda Kowalsky, Steve Harris. Al Akkerman told me the fascinating true story of the dog who appeared in smoke, and Barbara Young, R.N., helped me with medical data. I would like to thank Jacques-Yves Cousteau and his son, the late Phillipe, for writing their book, *The Shark: Splendid Savage of the Sea,* and also for the wonderful television specials which sparked my interest in the ocean. I am also grateful to my literary agent, John K. Payne, without whom I would be lost.

The tiger shark is easily identified by the indistinct vertical bars and spots along its sides. It is probably the dreaded *niuhi* of Hawaiian legend. Polynesians and Hawaiians endowed most sharks, especially the large maneaters, with supernatural powers. Due to their dependence on and familiarity with the sea, they were well aware of the awful power of the large, hungry shark, and so they came to see the shark as a god in disguise . . .

Gar Goodson, in *The Many-Splendored Fishes of Hawaii.*

The blue tranquility of his form surrounds me with the sensation of a web of murderous and yet beautiful force ...

Phillipe Cousteau

His skin is creased with a thousand silky furrows at every movement of his body, emphasizing each pattern of incredible muscle. The crystalline water has ceased to exist; he is there in the unbelievable purity of the void and nothing separates us any longer ...

Phillipe Cousteau

Cry for the Demon

Prologue: June 8, 1974

They were at Lani Beach.

Jerome McCann, clopped over the tufted grass in his Hawaiian foam-soled thongs, which cut at the tender area between his big and second toes. "Dammit, Joey, we'd better hurry. Your Mom's already packing. Why'd you want to come out now, so early, when we'll barely have time to get the sea water off before we have to leave for the airport?"

He was carrying mask and snorkel and swinging fins from side to side against his thigh. The flippers were still crusted with sand glued to the rubber surface with salt.

"I dropped my goodie bag," his son said. "By the coral, that big bunch of coral. I lost it yesterday when I got the water in my nose and had to go in."

"Goodie bag," snorted the father. "Damn fool name for a net bag."

"That's what they call it here, Dad. Goodie bag. That's what the man in the shop said. Dad, I got to get the bag. I put three good shells in it, and I want to take them back home. It isn't deep there, only about twelve feet, and I remember right where it fell, by some rocks and stuff."

"If the shells have live animals in them, you aren't taking them anywhere. They'll die inside and stink to high heaven. Besides, you can't bring shells back to the States, not like that."

"But I want my goodie bag."

The boy trotted to keep up with his father's angry flip-flopping as they cut across the grass and around the picnic tables to the sandy patch that sloped downhill to the beach. The father's legs were spindly; the boy's were lean and quick and brown.

"You'll have your damned goodie bag then. Just quit bitching about it, will you? And don't go falling all over with your flippers this time, Joey. Remember Tuesday, when the surf knocked you over and I had to pull you out?"

But the surf would not knock anyone over this morning. It was calm and lacy-curling and lappingly contemplative. To their right, a spit of lava rock jutted out from the sand and probed into the sea. It was a favorite site for snorkelers.

Jerome McCann narrowed his eyes at the outcropping of rock. He put one hand to his forehead to shade his eyes. There was a speck of white on the rocks, down low at the waterline, as if something had been washed in.

A beach towel, perhaps, or an old T-shirt? Everyone wore T-shirts here; it was practically the Hawaiian uniform, for those under forty, at any rate.

Or—he narrowed his eyes still further—*was* it a towel? Well, whatever it was, the waves were picking it up and tossing it gently, and he could tell that it was thicker than a towel and bulkier. A beach cushion then.

Abruptly his mood grew less impatient. It was a beautiful morning. The sea lay before them, its blue mirroring the sky.

"Well, come on, Joey. Let's go to it and get that damned bag before your mother has both of our hides for breakfast."

The boy giggled. They waded out into the water. Waves curled around their ankles, then their knees. The water was cold at first, and Jerome McCann shivered and looked longingly at the shore. But Joey urged him on, and then they were both in waist-deep water, squatting to pull on the flippers. It was a stork act to yank on the awkward fins. Joey grabbed onto his father's forearm to keep from losing his balance.

They both put the snorkel tubes into their mouths. Jerome McCann bit down hard on his mouthpiece, nervous about water entering his snorkel tube. Although he had not admitted this to his son, he'd had trouble all week with it, and more than once had inadvertently sucked in mouthfuls of gagging, choking sea water. And having seen *Jaws,* he feared that while he was snorkeling along the surface, a huge gray bulk, ferocious with teeth, would flash out from beneath him. He had not admitted that to his son either.

But the sea was calm this morning, so cresting foam-tops would not crash over the top of his snorkel tube today. Jerome McCann began to relax as he floated face down on the surface, He started to kick diagonally toward the rock spit. Fingers of the reef underlay the surface, bright with coral formations and exotic fish. He was absurdly grateful that none of them was larger than a trout.

They finned along, looking for the goodie bag, which was blue, eighteen inches square, and closed with a double metal bar.

They passed a moray eel, a small one, waving its blunt head from a crevice in the coral. Its teeth snapped menacingly. It was miniature savagery, too raw for this calm morning. But the eel was fifteen feet below, and Jerome McCann had no intention of going any closer to it. He kicked on by.

Joey paddled over to his father and raised his head out of the water while taking the snorkel tube from his mouth so that he could talk.

"Dad, it isn't here. I'm going over there to search those other rocks. I don't remember exactly where I dropped it, but I know it's somewhere near here, it's got to be."

"Unless it got washed ashore."

"The surf wasn't that high last night. Maybe it just got caught on some rock, Dad. I want that goodie bag, it's mine."

"All right, all right."

Drifting parallel with the surface rocks, Jerome McCann turned to get his bearings. There were submerged reefs near here, and he was nervous about getting washed into one of them. Coral was sharp and could lacerate the skin. His eyes followed the sweep of lava rock, idly looking for the speck of white he'd seen earlier.

It was still there, the beach pillow or whatever it was, hooked on a low ledge and almost draped around a jut of rock. It was wrinkled-white, except for broken pieces of pinkish material hanging from parts of it. A swirl of dark hair waved as idly as seaweed in the casual push of the water. Hair. Pubic hair. God help him, it was pubic hair, and then a tangle of more hair higher up—

Jerome McCann clenched down so hard on the mouthpiece of his snorkel tube that his teeth and jaws hurt. His throat convulsed as he struggled not to throw up. He swam toward Joey and grabbed at his left flipper, jerking hard at it and then violently motioning his son toward shore.

"In? Go in? Aw, please, Dad. Not yet. I haven't had a chance to dive. I've got to look for my bag. It's the only way I'll ever—"

Joey, turning in aggrieved protest, faced the rocks now, too. He stopped in the water, gulped, choked, and pushed his mask up onto his forehead.

"Dad. What's that?"

Jerome McCann managed to get his snorkel tube out of his mouth. "It's nothing, Joey. Nothing. Go in to shore, I tell you. Go in!"

"I want to see what it is."

"Joey!"

But the boy had already pulled on his mask again and was finning toward the rock, wiry brown legs propelling him so rapidly that Jerome McCann could only follow his son, choking and gagging again into his snorkel tube and praying that he would not vomit, for if he did, he was sure he would drown.

"Dad— Dad, it's a woman, a woman lying on the rocks, and—" A cough from Joey, a breathy rising of the voice. "And she hasn't any clothes on, Dad, and she hasn't any legs, and she— She—"

Something drew Jerome McCann closer . . . drew him despite the vomit pushing up the back of his throat and his pumping heart, which slammed inside his chest like a whale trying to get out. Drew him kicking and fearful in the direction of the rock until he could see clearly for himself the form lying there.

The woman's naked torso was leached white. Her nipples had turned purplish; the pubic triangle was beaded with foam bubbles. Grotesque scrapings marred her thighs and mons pubis as if she had been entered—God help her—by something jagged and rough and monstrously big. Chunks of flesh trailed from the jagged stumps of her upper thighs, where the legs had been taken off, the bulk of what was left floating just beneath the surface.

Then, hideously, a bigger wave rolled in. It lifted the body and half turned it, revealing the fish-white back with its strange, blurred marking, like a tattoo.

Jerome McCann realized that his bladder was emptying into his bathing suit and from there into the sea, into the sea that could take everything—blood and flesh and terror and vomit and urine—and assimilate it all.

"What's wrong with her bottom?" Joey was asking now in a voice gone high and babyish and sick. Now even he was backing away, choking. "Something's cut her, something's scraped her. And she hasn't any legs."

"Nothing. Nothing's wrong. Don't look, Joey. Dammit, don't look."

As they swam away, their flippers churning the water, the woman-thing rolled again. Still caught on the rocks, she was rising and falling softly with the waves, her hair fronding the water like seaweed, her purplish nipples turned upward to the morning sun.

Chapter 1

They had a window view of great sweeps of blackness—vast and impenetrable, as if they were flying through deep space.

They were aboard Hawaiian Airlines flight 806, en route to Maui from Honolulu, and below them was the night sea.

They had seen the sea after Los Angeles and Ann knew that if it had been daylight, she would be viewing foaming breakers pockmarking the water, visible even from 10,000 feet. Lines of white as if giant fish were broaching, school upon school of them, or perhaps a thousand white whales, skimming the water. It was hard for a Michigander to believe that those white lines were huge waves, to believe how big the sea was, to accept the fact that the breakers could go on and on and on, whether or not anyone was there to see them, or to care.

Great eons of water, Ann thought. *Primordial, savage.* And in the midst of that wilderness of waves, the Hawaiian Islands. Paradise made miniature and easily missed.

Ann Southworth shifted in her cramped seat. She put aside the Laurie McBain romance she'd brought with her to read on the plane—she'd barely started it—and picked up her needlepoint again. As she did so, she glanced across the aisle, where her son and daughter sat together.

Kristal, fifteen, peered out of her window with rapt attention. Buddy, his long, sixteen-year-old legs folded awkwardly in the seat space, was bent over a book titled *Easy Diver.* He was scowling.

The young woman in the seat next to Ann unexpectedly turned to her and remarked, "Say, your fingers really fly over that needlework." She had been napping much of the way. "I noticed that when we left L.A."

"Oh!" Ann was startled. "Why, yes, I suppose they do." She felt uneasy then and looked down at the work she held in her lap. It was a large white mesh canvas, twenty by twenty, with random patches of color filling the mesh only in places, as if the artist did not yet know what the final picture was to be.

The woman also stared at the canvas, her lips pursed.

"I never saw anything like it before, all those dark, ugly colors. So gloomy. Did you buy it in a shop? I didn't know they made kits like that."

"It isn't a kit."

Annoyed, Ann let her fingers flip the needle under two threads so rapidly that the eye could not see exactly what she did. She pulled the yarn tight in two swift motions. The yarn—the finest of Persian wool—was a deep, sea-green gray. In Ann Arbor she had searched two shops for exactly the right shade.

The sea. For days she had been thinking of the sea, even dreaming about it. And now it was coming out in her work, its deep fathoms of underwater gloom and quiet menace. Ann's fingers continued to stitch. She didn't even like this canvas, she thought. Not really. But it was as if she were obsessed by it.

"Your hands move like lightning," Ann's seatmate observed.

"I suppose. I've been doing needlepoint since I was eight."

It was true. Her mother had taught her, along with knitting and embroidery and crochet, all of the skills she had thought Ann would need for the prosaic life that lay before her. College. Marriage. Children. The standard things.

"If it's not a kit, does that mean you're making it up?" the woman asked as if creating something yourself were somehow a crime.

"Yes." Ann took two more rapid stitches, trying to suppress her irritation.

"But you don't have any lines marked on the canvas to follow. How do you know what the design is going to be?"

"I don't. Not yet."

"Then—" The woman made a fluttering, rejecting gesture. "I don't see how you can do it. How can you know what to put where? What tells you?"

For the first time, Ann smiled. She looked up from her canvas at the earnest, plain woman, who appeared to be about twenty-five. Her seatmate had muddy skin, a sprinkling of old acne scars, and the unlipsticked lips. She wore a little gold cross at the neck of her prim white blouse, and a plain brown cotton skirt—like a nun's—covered thick legs.

It was, Ann thought wryly, a decided contrast to her own size 10 jeans and hand-embroidered blouse, to her blonde hair, sleek and blunt cut, blown dry. No nun was she.

"Oh, I suppose the devil made me do it," Ann remarked, laughing. "At least, sometimes I'm beginning to wonder."

It had been a joke. A poor one, perhaps, but since Bob's death, most of Ann's jokes had been lacking. It was as if all of her humor had to be forced up past some huge choking knot that was lodged in her throat.

Seventeen years of marriage, she thought dully. Gone like dirty water down the drain. Over and done. And worst of all, in a horrid, secret way, she had been relieved.

"The Devil," the young woman said. "I wouldn't wonder. Those colors!" She moved her knees closer together then, her hand fumbling at the cross she wore about her neck. The plane bumped through some light turbulence, a drink tray rattled, and two Oriental stewardesses, beautiful and lustrous, giggled together near the galley.

"Have you found Jesus?" the woman asked Ann abruptly.

"Jesus?"

"Well, it's obvious you haven't, or you wouldn't be doing needlework like that. You made a joke, but don't you see that it wasn't a joke? Don't you realize that you are doing work that is ungodly and unclean? You have opened up your mind to the powers of darkness, and you are letting things in."

Ann tried to smile. "I don't know about that. Actually," she explained, "I'm Kristal-Ann Designs. I make needlework kits. If this turns out well, I'll repaint it in acrylics on canvas, count out the yarn requirements, and sell it to the shops. It's a business, that's all."

Her fingers still flew, pulling yarn in and out of the mesh, faster than she had ever worked on any other canvas before. She found herself talking, explaining to this odd woman why she and her two children had come to Maui. Ann's husband, Bob Southworth, had died in November of a heart attack after being mugged in a shopping center. Ann had decided impulsively to take Buddy and Kristal out of school a week early and come to Maui over the Christmas holidays. They planned to rent a house for a month. She had already promised her son that he could learn to scuba dive. As for Kristal, her daughter was lured by the prospect of photographing beaches and tidal pools and sunsets. Kristal was a camera buff. She'd won a prize once in the *Detroit Free Press* photography contest with a photograph of her own toes.

"Her toes?" The girl glanced across the aisle, inspecting the teenager's fragile blonde beauty.

"I suppose *she* hasn't found Jesus yet, either. Don't you know that Satan is always there, waiting for us to do something that will let him in? We can let him in with a camera too. Taking pictures of your own toes, what sort of thing is that to do? That's not a picture, that's—"

"Letting in the devil," Ann supplied.

"Yes."

"Well, my Kristal is a very good, very sensitive girl, and I'm sure she wouldn't let in the Devil on purpose." Ann heard herself go on. "As for religion, we do go to Church—the Free Unitarian Church in Ann Arbor. It's a very liberal church," she found herself explaining with angry pleasure. "They're very big on discussions and retreats."

"*They* don't believe in God." The woman stiffened, and her fingers clutched the cross at her throat. "And you think that coming to Maui is going to make you forget your husband's death and your other sins?"

Her other sins—daydreaming, making up a man who wasn't Bob, who was tender and passionate . . .

"Why, I— I don't know . . ." Ann was taken aback.

The plane bumped and lost altitude, slanting downward.

"Hawaii won't make you forget. Only God can do that. God and our sweet Jesus. They are the only ones who can ease your sorrow and guilt—not needlepoint or cameras or vacations or any of the work of the Devil. Satan wants to use such things only to get inside us and use us for his own aims, his own dark pleasures."

"The only dark pleasure this family is going to have is the pleasure of getting the best suntan in the Hawaiian Islands," Ann snapped, rolling up her canvas. "We're going to get ourselves as black as the Coppertone ads, and then we're going to go home and be the envy of everyone on our block."

"Oh—"

"And now," Ann said, "if you don't mind, I'm going to look out of the window."

"Oh, you can't see anything at night but some lights. I've been here four times and I know. It's nothing to look at from the air at night, nothing at all."

The woman's hands played with the cross, turning it over and over, compulsively.

The trauma of the night Bob died had been spreading ever since like acid across Ann's days, poisoning each of them. She supposed that was an over-dramatic way to think of it, but, God, it was true.

They'd gone to Washtenaw Mall. It had been Friday, a night when Ann Arbor families did what Ann thought of as recreational shopping—strolling, looking, maybe buying. The Southworths had come to buy a new recliner for Bob to use while he watched television.

The upholstery in his old chair—the one he regularly fell asleep in by ten o'clock every night—had finally given way to frayed holes revealing crumbling foam rubber.

Ann, perfectly capable of doing the reupholstering herself—thanks to her mother, she could sew anything, from men's suits to puff pillows—balked this time. She was tired, she announced, of sewing things for the house. She wanted more time to spend on Kristal-Ann Designs. She was selling her kits in Michigan and Ohio, making real money, and she had hopes of expanding.

So Ann and Bob had arrived at the shopping mall with tension simmering between them. Buddy had come along, but Kristal was staying overnight with a girlfriend. Bob resented Ann's work, which had grown to take up more and more of her time and thoughts. She resented his resentment. She knew there wouldn't be any sex tonight, for whenever Bob was angry at her, he fell asleep in the damned chair and slept there all night, leaving Ann to lie alone in their bed, fantasizing a misty dream lover who spoke tender words and stroked her nipples with his fingertips as he kissed her.

Huge parking lots surrounded the shopping center, stranding it in asphalt. They had to park at the back, near the access road. A movie theater near the J. C. Penney store offered four pictures.

"Well, damn," Bob complained, "I knew we should have gone in the Sears side, Ann. I don't know what's playing, but they've taken all the damned parking spaces again."

Bob never knew what was on at the movies. It was one of the things that separated them.

"It's all right," Ann said, sighing. "Let's just park here and walk. It isn't that far."

"You never even looked for a place any closer," Buddy said. "I bet there were dozens."

Healthy sixteen-year-old that he was, Buddy loved the game of looking for the closest parking space. As a brand-new driver, he took pride in mastering all the skills of the road.

They got out of the car, locked it, and huddled up their jacket collars against the fine, misty November chill. The three of them trailed out in a line, none of them walking together as they started toward the mall entrance. Buddy loped ahead in the lead, then came Ann, and finally Bob, who had stopped to double-check the door lock on Ann's side of the car.

Ann jammed her hands into her pockets, letting the strap of her leather purse hang unencumbered from her shoulder. The air already smelled like the snowstorms and slush and sleet to come. Ahead, the entrance to the mall gleamed yellow, and she could see silhouetted people going in and out. Then she heard a muffled sound, half grunt and half cry. Bob's voice? It was his and yet not his.

She turned. Three figures struggled in the dark. They uttered choked exclamations and panting noises, half-animal. Someone was gagging, the retch tearing harshly at the air. At first Ann could only stand there frozen. Two men were punching her husband. They grabbed at the lapels of his good suede jacket and rammed their hands into his pants pocket, pulling him forward so that his knees buckled and then yanking him upright as if he were some rag doll.

Bob. Her husband, Bob, was getting mugged while Ann stood paralyzed, unable to move, unable to open her jaws to scream.

Voices muttered. The muggers were saying something to Bob. He cried out. Her husband was being shaken back and forth, faster and faster, like a marionette controlled by a palsied hand. Ann could not see anything distinct of the two muggers. Were they young or old, black or white, short or tall? She could not seem to comprehend anything. She wanted to scream but couldn't. She couldn't even move. God held her, she had turned to stone.

"Mom?" Buddy had at last turned. "Mom, what's the—" He saw, then whirled and came running back toward them, shouting and yelling, his booming sixteen-year-old voice surprisingly loud on the moist cold air.

The muggers let go of Bob and ran. They raced back through the angled cars, dodged into the next row, faded into the night and were gone.

Bob had collapsed onto the pavement, and still Ann could not move.

"Dad? Dad, are you all right? They're gone now." Buddy bent over his father anxiously. "Dad, did they get your wallet? Dad, what's wrong? Why aren't you saying anything? Mom!" Her son's eyes accused her. "Mom, don't just stand there!"

It was Buddy who ran into J. C. Penney and made the phone call, Buddy who came racing back out to the parking lot to throw his ski jacket over the prone body of his father and tuck it in carefully . . . as if that would make a difference, as if that would make any difference at all.

All Ann could do was to stand there, her hands still pushed down into her pockets, and think that there wouldn't be any sex tonight or any other night. There wasn't any need for a chair now, no need to fight any more, no need at all.

Bob was dead before the ambulance arrived.

"Damn you, Mom, why didn't you *do* something, anything?" Buddy demanded of her at the hospital, his eyes red-rimmed and puffy with tears. They had taken Bob away and were doing whatever hospitals do under such circumstances.

"You just stood there, you didn't even scream out, you didn't touch him, you didn't do anything, not one damned thing. Mom, what's the matter with you? Mom, if you'd just screamed out earlier, yelled out anything, anything at all, maybe those guys would have run away. Or I could have saved Dad. He would have been all right, he would have lived. Mom, they killed him, and you let them. You let them, Mom. Did you want my dad to die, Mom? Did you?" Buddy screamed at her. "Did you?"

They were met at Kahului Airport by Susan Rogers, Ann's first cousin, who was renting them the top floor of her home in Makai. They descended the ramp from the plane onto bare cement and walked outdoors through moist, cool tropical air toward a low building.

Ann had a brief impression of palm trees and black sky overhead. Then they were inside, and her cousin Susan was dropping a white lei over her shoulders and hugging her.

"God, Ann, you're finally here after that long flight from Michigan. Isn't it a pisser? And I mean that literally. The last time I went to the mainland the big recreation from Honolulu to Chicago was standing in line at the can."

Susan and Ann, inseparable as young girls, were now almost strangers.

"A lei," Ann cried. "A real lei! It smells wonderful! I thought they only did that in Hollywood movies."

"No, it's all part of the Hawaii bit. I bought these right here at the airport. These are Plumeria blooms," Susan added. "Don't they smell strong though? Perfume, ugh!"

Ann laughed, and drew back to look at her cousin. Susan was thirty-nine, a year older than Ann herself, with a round, vaguely discontented face, tanned almost to leatheriness. She had a thick, athletic figure, and wore a pair of cutoff jeans and a Navy T-shirt, far too large for her, which said *Seatec,* whatever that was. Blue thongs with thick, multicolored soles completed her outfit.

"Oh don't mind the way I look," her cousin said, noting Ann's glance. "We're very laid-back here. Everything moves on Hawaiian time. At first it drives you bananas, but after a while you learn to live with it. Cliff and the kids are home glued to the TV set," she chattered on. "I didn't think there'd be room for all of us in the car, what with your luggage and all."

As Kristal and Buddy moved closer, Susan uttered a shriek and said, "My God, Ann, what have you done to these two, given them growing pills? The last time I saw Kristal, she was in a Brownie uniform, for God's sake, baking cookies or whatever it is Brownies do. And Buddy was running around in a baseball cap with dirt all over his knees."

"He still does that," Kristal piped up. "The dirt part, anyway."

Buddy looked indignant. "I'm going to learn to scuba dive while I'm here. And I'm going surfing too. Mom's going to buy me all the gear. I've already been checking the dive catalogs, and I know just what I want."

Nearby, a Hawaiian family converged, brown-skinned father, plump dark-haired mama, and four toddlers all wearing shorts, T-shirts, and miniature versions of Susan's thongs. A tourist couple was quarreling about their luggage. The wife was afraid the bags had been lost; the husband was assuring her they had been checked through; both looked hot and tired and anxious.

The terminal had no walls, Ann realized, and a tree was growing up through a hole in the roof. More people crowded through a side door, wearing plastic name stickers and identical leis. A tour group.

"Well, enough of this shit," Susan said. "Let's go and get the luggage over with, and we'll see whether two women and two teenagers can manhandle it all into a Toyota."

Half an hour later they had retrieved the last of the suitcases and had loaded everything into Susan's white Toyota. Buddy and Kristal were wedged in the back seat among some of the smaller pieces of luggage, while the cousins sat in the front. Ann still clutched her needlepoint bag, afraid that her fragile canvas might get ruined in Susan's trunk, which, as Susan's flashlight had revealed, was full of sand and ants and smelled like fish.

Darkness flowed over the car and covered it like black water. Only the headlights of the oncoming cars gave the impression they were moving at all. The air, Ann noted with indrawn breath, seemed incredibly clear. She could look out of the window and see lights twinkling far away in the stark blackness. There was no moon. They passed under a grove of trees oddly shaped and closing in over the top of the road like dark, looming umbrellas.

"Monkey-pod trees," Susan explained. "This road we're on is called Puunene." _Poo-oo-nay-nay,_ she had said. "You're going to have to learn how to pronounce all the Hawaiian names. Almost all the street names are Hawaiian here—except for Bobbie Lane up in Makai Heights," she added with a laugh. "Somehow that one slipped through."

Ann sat up front wondering what Buddy and Kristal thought of their nonstop guide, and what the house would be like, and whether, after all, she had done the right thing in bringing them here. The moonless Hawaiian night was dark, darker than she had ever dreamed it possible.

They drove through tall, waving grasses higher than a man's head.

"Cane fields," Susan explained. "Sugar cane. They grow _pakalolo_ in these fields, too," Susan added casually. "The locals do. Their own private crop, if someone else doesn't get there first."

"_Pakalolo?_" Buddy asked from the back seat.

"Crazy tobacco. Hawaiian buds. Marijuana. We're all very laid-back here," Susan said. "By the way, that's Makai up ahead. The hotels and so forth."

She had pronounced it *Ma-Ky*.

A crescent of lights glittered ahead of them, and Ann could see buildings with yellow windows, clear and tiny and perfect, and miniature car headlights. She leaned back and let her eyes flutter half shut, and thought about the dark Hawaiian night and about the grayer night at Washtenaw Mall.

Chapter 2

"A hundred eighty degrees of ocean view," Susan explained with pride the following morning. It was Sunday, December 10. Susan had herded Ann, still in her bathrobe, out onto the lanai, a cup of morning coffee in hand.

"A volcano out back, if that impresses you, and in front of us three other islands and sometimes four. That's what you pay for, and that's what you get."

Ann could only stand silent, awed by the vast sweep of blue ocean marked with wind patterns and cloud reflections. They were high on a hill on the flank of Haleakala, the world's largest dormant volcano. A long crescent of hotels was strung out at their feet, like miniature matchboxes. To the right bulked the West Maui Mountains, mist-folded in blues and greens. On the horizon loomed four islands, three of them crowned with masses of white clouds. The three were Kahoolawe, Molokai, and Lanai. The little one, a speck of an island riding in the lee of Kahoolawe, was Molokini.

"It's nothing, really, but a pile of rock and a lighthouse," Susan said. "But the diving and snorkeling there are superb. There are sharks, of course, but they never bother anybody, and the water is incredibly clear."

"You dive, too?" Ann questioned.

Susan grimaced. "God, yes, the whole family does, except for Cliff, and all he does is bitch and pay the bills. Cliff is good at bitching."

After she had dressed in shorts, Ann walked outdoors to look at the house in which they would be living for the next month. It was what Susan called a pole house, and it was exactly that—a big house on stilts. Wedged on a steeply sloping lot, it was a massive chalet-style rectangle finished in caramel-colored siding with a shingle roof. There were protruding beams and wood and glass everywhere. Both the top and bottom floors had wraparound decks—lanais, they called them here. A flight of stairs connected the top lanai with the lower one.

She headed downhill and around the house. The space beneath the house was high enough to walk under, its floor paved with dried grass, bare dirt, small lava rocks, and assorted household junk. A driveway curved down steeply from the road, its angle so precipitous that it could never have existed in snowy Michigan.

The side yard was lush with tropical foliage. In back the grass deteriorated to scraped red-brown dirt and clumps of ragged palms. Evidently this was still in the process of landscaping, for a small Massey-Ferguson bulldozer sat unused, and a huge pile of lava rocks had been pushed to the back of the lot. There were abandoned buckets and rakes, a stack of empty twenty-five-gallon drums. The whole effect, Ann thought, was somehow tired and discouraged.

They ate breakfast at the Rogers' house, for, as Susan explained, "I filled your fridge at Superette, but I didn't know what the hell you people eat, and I probably bought all the wrong things."

Breakfast consisted of scrambled eggs, chunks of fresh pineapple, and a glass of thick red juice, which young Lisa Rogers assured them was guava nectar.

"Are you going to dive?" Lisa asked Buddy. She was fifteen, a thick-waisted girl who had inherited her mother's build. She had small eyes, lusterless hair, and puppy fat blurring her facial features. Looking at her, Ann felt proud of Kristal's fragility, her blonde good looks.

"Oh, yes, Mom promised! I was going to take a scuba course in Ann Arbor, but Aunt Susan wrote I could get one here at a shop, and that's what I'm going to do."

Buddy was nearly jumping up and down at his seat in Susan's breakfast nook, his big, awkward knees banging the underside of the table. "I've been reading all about it. I shouldn't have any trouble with the class, I don't think."

"Oh, they'll teach you at the dive shop. Kam'll teach you."

Lisa was offhanded. Her brother, Mick, sixteen, stubby and dark-haired, began to talk knowledgeably of sharks and cave diving, and "diving the back side of Molokini," most of which made Ann uneasy but seemed to impress Buddy greatly. After a while the four teenagers went out on the front lanai.

"Diving," sighed Susan. "It's all they ever think about, the little bastards. They spend a fortune on air and equipment, and they're ruining the trunk of my car with their damned tanks and regulators."

"They don't realize how hard money is to come by here on Maui," Cliff said heavily. "They think it grows on kiawe trees or washes up with the tide."

Cliff Rogers was stocky and thick too. He had a big, wide mouth, a leathery suntan, and a dour expression. He was assistant manager at the Hoku Maui Hotel, and his wife was the accountant there. Four nights a week, Cliff moonlighted as night deskman at another hotel. They rented out the top floor of their pole house to tourists.

But, as Cliff explained, the mortgage payments were high. A lot alone here in Makai Heights might cost $150,000. There was a housing shortage. People had to scramble on Maui to survive, he told Ann sourly. Anyone who thought it was easy to live here in paradise was sadly mistaken.

Ann felt uncomfortable. Luxurious poverty with a sweeping view. It was hard to imagine.

"It seems so lovely here," she said lamely.

"It is, for the tourists." Cliff's voice was flat. "They've got time to go to the beach in their bikinis and eat in all the fancy hotels. Me, I don't. When I get some time off, the car needs fixing or the yard needs work. It's taken me eight months to get that far on the backyard. The earth is so dry it's like cement, and the lava is everywhere. This whole damned island is a rock."

Even before she entered the shop, Ann knew that she was going to buy scuba equipment for herself as well as for Buddy. Perhaps, unconsciously, it had been in her mind all along.

The Ocean Divers shop was located in a hotel arcade, sandwiched between a sandal and shoe store, and a delicatessen. Its windows featured shiny blue tanks, an array of wet suits in blue and orange, and a fish net hung with dried lobsters and seashells.

As Ann and Buddy opened the door, a bell jangled.

A man was standing behind a glass counter looking off into the distance, his attitude fixed, as if he saw something no one else could see.

For an instant after Ann and Buddy had entered, he did not move. Then, abruptly, he smiled and said, "Can I help you with something? A snorkel rental? Or an air refill?"

"Yes. I— That is, we want to buy some equipment and sign up for a class."

"A scuba class?" His accent seemed vaguely eastern to Ann—Boston, perhaps? There was something old-fashioned about the way he spoke, she decided. It was not so much in the words as in the way he said them. Yet the total effect—coupled with a deep baritone voice of rich timber—was striking.

"Yes," she said quickly. "A scuba class is what we want. You see, I promised my son—"

She faltered. Seldom had she seen a more good-looking man. His eyes—dark brown, nearly black—were fixed on hers with alert interest. He was tall, more than six-four. His body was built for bulk and power, with wide shoulders that strained the yellow T-shirt he wore. His hair was black, his eyes dark, his skin tan, and Ann wondered briefly what his heritage was. Surely there was a flavoring of native Hawaiian, a touch of Oriental, perhaps Samoan. Yet the nose was hawklike, the jaw line arrogant with a deep chin cleft. He looked as if he could have been an ancient king.

Or—Ann caught herself swallowing hard—he looked like one of the heros in a Laurie McBain romance novel. Yes, she thought. That was exactly it. A dashing, arrogant, beautiful hero who would gallop up on his fiery horse to sweep the heroine up into the saddle with him, kidnapping her to his aerie, where sparks would fly between the two before—deliberately and deliciously—he took her . . .

Ann caught her lower lip between her teeth, flushing. For an instant she felt an odd awareness of danger. A light *frisson* of fear rippled across her heart. Then it was gone. Buddy was nudging her. His voice, she could tell, was annoyed.

"Mom? Mom, go on, ask him about the classes, will you? And my air card. I want to get certified and get my card."

"That's easily accomplished here."

The man's smile revealed white, even teeth. He leaned against the glass counter, his body in perfect, relaxed repose. "We have a five-day certification course. The cost is $120 and includes all gear and transportation. I recommend it."

Again Buddy elbowed her. "But we're going to be getting all our own gear. My Mom said—"

"That's right," she put in hastily. "We'll be buying our own equipment."

"Both of you." Somehow it was a statement, not a question.

"Why, yes—"

Beside Ann, Buddy stiffened. The man's dark eyes held hers. Ann found that she was trembling slightly, that her breath was not quite even.

He smiled at her, then looked at Buddy. "I only thought you might be afraid of sharks. They are fond of eager young men sometimes."

Her son glowered. "I'm not afraid of any sharks."

"Shame on you! A statement like that coming from a diving instructor!" Ann kept her voice light.

He gave her another smile, a brief mock bow. "It was only a joke and, I gather, not a very funny one. Actually, most of the sharks here on Maui are white-tipped reef sharks. They aren't very aggressive and have little interest in human beings. We are not their natural food, you know."

Buddy was fiddling with a pile of printed brochures stacked on the counter top. *"Maui No Ka Oi,"* the leaflets announced in large blue letters.

"Maui No Ka Oi," Buddy interrupted, sounding out the syllables. "What's that mean?"

"Maui is the best." The man smiled and extended a hand. "I am Kam Smith. If you take the diving class, you'll be seeing a lot of me. I'll be your instructor."

"Oh." Buddy was still scowling, Ann noticed. "Well, I guess I'm signing up."

"I'll sign up, too," Ann said.

Now Buddy's scowl was turned on her. "But, Mom—"

"I'm taking the class, too, Buddy. I'll buy gear for the two of us. And for Kristal, if she wants it."

"She doesn't," Buddy said sullenly. He wasn't looking at her, and Ann realized with dismay that this was something her son had wanted for his very own.

A little spurt of anger flared in her. How dare he? She was young, and physically active, too, and she needed this, God, how she needed it. Bob had died and it was her fault. Now she had to do something she was afraid to do, to battle the cowardice within herself. Her son's words to her that horrible night came rushing back to her now. *Mom, what's the matter with you? Mom, if you'd just screamed out earlier, yelled out anything, anything at all . . .*

"We'll both sign up for the class," she said firmly. "We'll take the first two openings you have. Since we will have our own equipment, I hope there'll be a discount."

"I think that can be arranged."

Her natural efficiency, the ability that was building Kristal-Ann Designs into a growing concern, had taken over.

"And this morning I'd like to get us both suited up, or whatever you call it. We'll buy whatever we need."

"Mom—" Then Buddy's last protest died. He walked to the back of the shop, where a row of wet suits hung from a rack, and began riffling through them.

Kam smiled at Ann again, and she noticed the pleasure displayed in that expression did not wholly touch those black and compelling eyes of his.

"Well," he said, "you seem to be lucky this week. We're starting a class tomorrow and you and your son happen to be the only ones who've signed up."

"Good."

"Class starts here at the shop at 9:30 in the morning. We stop for lunch, make a dive in the afternoon, and we're back here by 3:00 or 3:30. The sea is beautiful beyond all imagining, Ann. I'm sure you will find it so."

He had called her Ann. How had he known?

Ann looked at him. For an instant she thought of deep water and muted sea colors and something with teeth, darting, lunging. Then, with an effort, she pushed away the fancy. He had known her name. But, she assured herself, Susan or Mick Rogers had probably already been in the shop and had mentioned that they were coming. After all, wasn't it Susan who had recommended the dive shop in the first place?

"Good," she repeated. "It sounds fine to me. I've been thinking about diving for weeks now. I'm even doing a needlepoint seascape. Not my usual style, but I'm just getting myself prepared, I guess." She tried to smile. "Actually, I'm a little nervous."

Fear. It had always been with her since earliest childhood. A bee swooping down on the porch where she stood with her doll, to sting her on the chest. Big boys shouting at her in the alley, chasing her toward school, until she cried and wet her pants and was scolded by her teacher.

Her Uncle Tom picking her up by the feet and dangling her off the diving board, then dropping her, screaming with terror, into the water.

Then, later, the phobias, the ugly sneaking fears that she constantly fought. A fear of heights. Panic if she were riding an elevator that jiggled erratically, or came to an unexplained stop. A dislike of flying. And the fears of the unknown. Not wanting to drive to Detroit's inner city for fear of rape or mugging or worse. Fears of getting lost, of leaving Bob, for what would she do on her own without him?

Fear. And all of it she had fought with a savage self-hatred and shame. She did walk to school again the next day, in spite of the big boys. She did learn to swim and do it well. She did ride the elevator, and she drove to the inner city.

Now she would take scuba diving lessons. And she would stop thinking about a night in Ann Arbor, a night filled with blurred, struggling figures . . .

It took more than two hours to buy the equipment. Kam gave them the full tour, answering each of Buddy's many questions in detail. Endlessly Kam and Buddy discussed the merits of steel versus aluminum tanks. Did they want to buy an octopus regulator with an extra air port in case of emergency? Did they want to spend $250 on a B.C. vest with an automatic inflator that fed from the air supply, or did they want the standard fifty-four-dollar variety?

Buddy and Ann struggled into the awkward wet suits, pulling them on over their clothes, a process that reminded Ann of fighting her way in and out of a full-body girdle.

"That one felt like a tourniquet," she told Kam, panting, after she had stripped off the fourth suit. "And it made me look like a pancake," she added.

Kam was grinning. "Nothing can make you look

bad, Ann. Not even a wet suit. And if I were you, I'd forget the women's suits anyway. All we have in stock right now are the ones with the crotch straps, and those will bind you underwater. Try a men's small. It'll fit you better—you're tall—and be more comfortable."

The men's small didn't have the molded mounds for her breasts and would probably squash her flat, but—

"Anything," Ann said in exasperation. "Anything at all. Just let me out of here and get me to the beach before I suffocate to death on all this neoprene."

She ended up spending more than a thousand dollars. Kam stuffed all of her purchases into two red canvas gear bags, except for the tanks, which were too heavy. She paid for it all with her Visa card. There was insurance from Bob's estate, a percentage from the law practice in which he had been a senior partner, and income from Kristal-Ann Designs. Money wasn't lacking.

If money couldn't buy happiness, it could still purchase a pretty good imitation. And Buddy had already forgotten his sullenness and was expanding with enthusiasm, a child let loose in a toy shop. She wanted to see him happy, wanted to see the accusing look wiped from his face and replaced by normal boy-emotions.

Damn, she thought, *his father would have wanted him to have a little fun.*

In the rental car, with the gear stowed in the trunk and Buddy sprawled beside her in the front seat, Ann pulled out onto Makai Road and turned right in the direction of the beach where they had left Kristal.

"Well, we're certainly a lot poorer now," she said gaily. "That stuff cost me an arm and a leg, and half the other leg, too."

"Yeah."

"We'll go and pick up your sister, and then let's find us a restaurant," she went on. "We'll stuff ourselves on *mahimahi* and steak and pineapple and coconuts, or whatever this place can offer, and we'll get so fat nothing will sink us."

Buddy propped his chin on his hand and stared out the window at a girl in a bikini top that barely covered her loose breasts.

"Buddy? Bud, is something wrong?"

"No."

"Then why the silent treatment? I should think you'd be happy to have a full set of scuba gear. God knows, we've heard nothing else from you for the past month. Isn't that what you wanted?"

"Yes."

"Then what? What's wrong?"

"I don't like him."

"You don't like who?" She kept her voice casual, although she knew.

"You know. Kam. That man in the shop, the one who's going to be our teacher. I just didn't like him."

"And why not? I thought he was very patient with all of your questions. He certainly spent a lot of time answering every one of them."

"Sure. With all the money we spent in there, Mom, what else could he do? I didn't like him, that's all. He was too— I don't know. He looked at you too much. And he made that joke about not going in the water or a shark might get me. What sort of joke was that to make? Even I know that's not what a dive instructor should say. It wasn't right."

"He was only teasing."

Ann's voice rose a little. All of this was ridiculous, she told herself. Buddy was piqued because his mother was joining him in the class. He was upset too because a man who wasn't his father had shown some interest in his mother. That was all this was.

"Teasing. Yeah, I guess." Buddy slid down on his spine, his eyes swiveling to the shoulder of the road, where a female hitchhiker in track shorts was trying to thumb a ride. "All the same, Mom, I didn't like him. I'll take the class, and I'll be polite, because I want my card. But I'd watch out for him, if I was you."

Chapter 3

After lunch at the Kona Wind, hamburgers, after all, and a strawberry daiquiri for Ann, the three of them spent the rest of the day at the beach. They sat on the sand on woven beach mats until the wind came up and began to whip the fine, sticky sand into their hair and faces and between the strands of Ann's needlepoint.

"Mom, what's it going to be?" Kristal asked as they were packing up. "I've never seen you do a canvas like that before, without even a sketch. It's so weird, just a lot of lines and shapes. And the colors... This isn't like you."

Ann frowned. "I know, baby, I know. This one is just different, I guess."

This afternoon she had progressed a bit on the design. The space to the bottom left of the canvas was now beginning to take shape as a rather free-form scuba diver. The diver's body was recoiled backward, almost as if in alarm.

"Well there's something depressing about it, that's all," Kristal insisted. "Do you really think all those women who use kits are going to buy something like that?"

"I don't know. I don't even know if *I* like the damned thing," Ann said. She scooped up her towel and shook the sand off it. "Grab your suntan oil, girl, and let's get going. I should stop at that supermarket—Superette, or whatever it's called—and pick up some meat for dinner. Did you get good pictures, Krissie?"

"Oh, yes. In the morning I did. The tidal pools were nice then. And the rocks. I love the rocks here, they're just like sculpture. I could sit looking at rocks for half the day."

"As, no doubt, you did."

"Yes, and now I've got to find a camera shop and get my film developed. I hope there's a good shop here."

"Oh, there will be. Tourists take a lot of pictures, don't forget. It's the main activity of vacationers."

They walked over the grass to the parking lot and loaded everything into the car, which was smoldering hot inside from the sun. An ice cream truck was parked in the lot—"Frozen Explosion" its sign read—and Buddy bummed three dollars from Ann. Without consulting anyone, he went to the truck and returned with three enormous sticky creations of cake, nuts, and strawberry ice cream. Ice cream dripped down the stick and onto Ann's hand.

"Jesus!" she said. "Buddy, you have the appetite of a Cub Scout. Of six Cub Scouts. This thing belongs at a den meeting, for heaven's sake."

Buddy licked at his ice cream. "It's good, though. Even if it does give me zits, it's worth it after lying out there in the sun all afternoon. Sun makes me hungry."

"Everything makes *you* hungry," Kristal announced.

She took one delicate bite of ice cream, then let the remainder slide off the stick and fall at the base of a coconut palm.

"There," she said in satisfaction. "Strawberry short-cake. Very nourishing. Help the coconuts grow big and strong."

They rode back to Makai Heights. On the way back, Ann's skin began to itch unbearably. Sand had stuck to her feet, and she could feel it in the crotch of her bathing suit and even (she decided) in her teeth. She could hardly wait to get back to the house and take a long hot shower.

Dinner was steaks broiled in the oven on aluminum foil, for, as Ann discovered, there was no broiler pan in the oven, and she did not want to complain to Susan.

After dinner came the sunset, vast spectacular sweeps of orange and red and purple-blue. Kristal prowled about with her camera, experimenting with the light. She balanced precariously on the railing of the lanai in order to get a better angle. She brought out a Polaroid, took some more shots, then laid them in a row on the lanai carpet to develop. One of the pictures, Ann noted, was spoiled. She saw her daughter frown at it in puzzlement.

Then came television in Hawaii, where, Buddy learned to his great disgust, programming ran a week behind mainland schedules, and he had to watch the same *One Day at a Time* he had seen the previous week in Ann Arbor.

By ten o'clock Ann was cold, and it dawned on her that she had been hearing, for at least two hours now, the sound of wind whistling past the house. It shrieked past the cracks in the jalousied windows like a Michigan April blow. The windows weren't air tight. And, Ann noted with dismay, there wasn't any furnace. Evidently that was not considered a necessity here in Hawaii, at least not in rental pole houses. Another thing, she thought wryly, not to complain to Susan about.

It was three o'clock in the morning when she was awakened by the sounds coming from Kristal's bedroom. They were soft, agonized little moans, as if her daughter were once again five years old and caught in the grip of some boogie-man nightmare.

Ann lay in bed a few minutes longer, hoping the moans would stop. They did not.

At last she threw back the bedcovers—she'd had to use both the blanket and bedspread to keep warm—and crawled out of bed. She padded past the sliding door that opened onto the lanai, seeing the slit of moon. Its reflection spilled down in a swathe of silver on the flat ocean. Down the hill, a few hotel lights gleamed. It all looked stark, vaguely surrealistic. Even the night view was like a dream, she thought dazedly.

"No . . . no . . . God, no . . . Oh, God . . ."

Ann entered the bedroom where her daughter slept. Kristal too had a sliding glass door with an equally spectacular view of stark moon and sea.

Ann stopped, her shortie nightgown rustling. She drew in a deep breath. There was a smell here in the room.

An odor of . . . what?

Sea things, she thought uneasily. Rotting sea creatures and seaweed and shells and fish and sand and slime. Had Kristal brought up a shell from the beach that was turning rancid?

"God, it's hurt, it's injured, it's thrashing in the water, I hear it, I feel it. I know it, I know it . . ."

Kristal's moans were louder now, muffled. "It's a message," she groaned. "It's food, and it tells me . . ."

It's food, and it tells me.

Ann started toward the bed. Unease cramped in her gut. What, in the name of God, sort of nightmare could

Kristal possibly be having to say such an outlandish thing? *It's food, and it tells me.*

As she neared the bed, the sea smell got stronger. Kristal lay on top of the covers, looking absurdly childish in her pink ruffled baby doll pajamas, more like five than fifteen. And her voice was five, too—high, thready, terrified.

"It's waiting . . . and now I'm coming . . . coming so fast, so very fast!"

"Kristal!" Ann pounced upon her dreaming daughter, shaking her awake with unnecessary violence. "Krissie, for heaven's sake wake up, will you? You've been having a nightmare."

"What? What?" Kristal's blue eyes popped open. They stared at Ann wildly, as if she did not even recognize her.

"I said you've been dreaming. Wake up!"

"Dreaming?"

"Yes, dammit. Wake up, honey, and sit up in bed. I'll go to the kitchen and get you some hot milk or something. Maybe some hot chocolate."

It had been the medicine for nightmares when Kristal was five, and now Ann fell into the solution automatically.

"Cocoa," Kristal whispered. Her eyes blinked and then resumed an expression of normality. Her mouth was trembling. "Haven't had that in a long time." She sat up, clutching at her mother, her ash-blonde hair wispy about her face. "Mom— Oh, Mom, it was horrible. Awful. My dream—"

"Yes? Tell me, honey."

Something made Ann not want to know, but she had always listened to the contents of nightmares.

"Oh, Mom, I was under the sea. It was dark down there, but I didn't care, it was beautiful, all muted in a thousand shades of green and blue and gray and purple—" Kristal had always dreamed in colors. "But I didn't notice that. I mean, I did, but I didn't."

She stopped in confusion. "*I* noticed it, but I, the thing that I was, didn't . . ."

Kristal was trembling violently, her whole body shaking.

"You're all right, honey. You're all right. Just cold." Ann felt cold, too. She pulled a blanket over her daughter's shivering form. "December in Hawaii, what a surprise, eh? We'll all have to take lots of blankets to bed with us, won't we? Come on, honey, roll under the blanket. I'll be back in two shakes with something hot for you to drink."

"Mom!" Kristal clutched her. "Mom, don't go yet. Not yet. It's cold— And the dream . . . oh, you can't imagine. There was . . . something struggling in the water. Something that I knew about somehow, but I don't know how I knew it. It was just a . . . a feeling or something. Then I was going toward it, swimming faster and faster, feeling it all through my body. The power. I was strong, so strong, Mom, and it felt good, going through the water like that, my fin—"

She stopped, gulping. She made a little gagging sound deep in her throat. Then there was an abrupt silence in the bedroom, so profound that Ann could hear Buddy snoring in his room, the distant rumble of a car motor starting up, a repetitive clicking sound coming from the water heater in the utility room.

Never had Kristal dreamed a nightmare even remotely like this one. The sea smell was fading. Whatever it had been, its stench was nearly gone now.

"Well—" Ann pushed back a sudden, sick feeling. "—you'll feel better when I get your cocoa, if I'm lucky enough to find some in that kitchen. Somehow I don't picture Susan buying cocoa at the supermarket, do you?"

"I guess not." Obediently Kristal snuggled under the

covers to wait, exactly as the five-year-old Kristal had done after she had dreamed of bears and wolves.

On the way out the door, Ann's bare foot skidded in something wet. It was a puddle of wetness on the carpet, and something, some dark atavistic night impulse, made her stoop down to feel the extent of the puddle.

"Did you spill something, baby?"

"No, Mom. Why?"

"Oh, I was just wondering."

Ann's finger probed the small pool of water already soaking into the fiber of the carpet, noting that it seemed oddly gritty. Sandy, almost. Yet Kristal was a fastidious girl, not in the habit of spilling things.

Her forefingers tested the cool moisture. Then, without her consciously planning it, her finger went up to her mouth. Ann tasted the end of her finger.

Salt. The spilled wetness was salty.

Ann managed to get to her feet. She went out into the hall and switched on the light. Blinking her eyes at the brightness, she stumbled into the kitchen, where she opened all of the cabinet doors looking for cocoa or chocolate syrup, and found none. At last she poured a pint of milk into a saucepan and heated it.

She was trembling all over.

Chapter 4

"So you're going to make the first big dive today," Susan said as she lifted up her coffee cup to drain its contents. She had climbed up to the Southworths' lanai and rapped on the sliding glass door, bringing with her four fat yellow-orange papayas from her own trees.

"Hope you can eat these, we're sick to death of them. Good luck, m'dear," she added. "I hope everything goes swimmingly . . . and that the fucking fish don't eat you."

"Thanks," Ann said dryly, still somewhat groggy from a night of little sleep caring for Kristal and heating milk.

It was eight in the morning, December 11, edging toward Christmas. From the lanai, the ocean lay spread before them in a thousand shades of muted blurred blue.

There were smooth trails of wind currents sketched across its surface.

Morning sounds drifted up to them—chiefly the noises of construction and birds. The bird calls were liquid: cuk-*oo*, cuk-*oo*, one cry answering another one. There was also the warning beep beep beep of a big construction grader, the whine of a chain saw, the staccato bang of hammers on a house under construction.

"In a month or so, the whales will start coming," Susan went on. She was dressed for work in brown polyester slacks and tailored blouse.

"Whales?"

"Oh, yes, the humpbacked whales come here to Maui every winter to mate; it's quite a tourist attraction. Sometimes we can stand right here on the lanai and see them."

Whales. Volcanoes. Islands. Air so clear it made everything seem unreal. Hawaii, Ann decided, was a place of extremes. She took a swallow of coffee and felt her stomach reject it.

"Not hungry?" Susan was grinning. "Well, that's all right. You shouldn't eat too much before diving anyway. You don't want to get any gas in your intestines, or it'll bother you when you're down. The pressure does funny things."

"Great."

"But you don't have to worry. Kam'll take care of you. That's his job. Just remember not to hold your breath when you're making your ascent, or you'll probably embolize. The air expands inside you. It's a gruesome way to die, air pops out in your lungs and expands them, and these little air bubbles speed all through you doing terrible things, and you get air pockets in your chest cavity and even in your neck—if you live that long."

"Susan—"

Susan grimaced. "Well, sweetheart, just thought I'd

encourage you a bit. Now I'd better get my ass to work before they take it into their heads to fire me. That would be financial disaster here at the Rogers', I can tell you that."

God, Ann thought, after Susan had trotted back down the outside steps to her own lanai. Why, she wondered, had Susan tried to scare her like that? Maybe she and Buddy could return the equipment? And then she saw Buddy's accusing face and knew that no matter how dangerous the diving was, it was better than the looks he would give her if they didn't.

Kristal stirred beneath the covers. A spasm of terror coursed through her muscles, as automatic as an electric shock. *Fins cutting through the water . . .*

She stirred again and moaned; slowly the terror drained away. It was morning. A bar of sun as warm as if it had come from a furnace spilled across the blanket. She flung back the covers, stretched like a cat, and sat up.

From her bed she could see the ocean, an incredible sheet of blue jello. The view of hazy islands and fissured West Maui Mountains was so sweeping that she despaired of catching it with her camera.

A tanker moved like a toy boat across the horizon, its progress measured in millimeters. Kristal blinked her eyes and thought of last night's dream. There were things she had not told her mother, because there were no words for them: the abject horror of being trapped in something's body; of seeing with alien eyes and thinking alien thoughts; of being a predator, a killer for whom death was electric, orgasmic pleasure. . . .

She heard a chirping cry, as if made by some small bird or animal. Kristal's eyes left the view and swung back into the bedroom. She looked around. Her milk cup from last night sat on the night stand. Her jeans were folded on a chair. And near the chair, a lizard about four inches long, scurried up the wall. It was flat and tan-colored, with round black dots for eyes.

Kristal sat and watched the lizard with interest. After a while she slid off the bed and went to get her Canon and quickly changed the lens. As she focused, she felt her bare feet touch grittiness. Sand. Black, pebbly sand. How odd. Had she accidentally tracked in sand? But it hadn't been here last night, she remembered. She was sure that she would have noticed if it had been.

She scraped up the sand with her fingers and threw it into the wastebasket. Half an hour later she emerged from her room dressed in cutoffs and a worn T-shirt that said "Huron River Rats" and with half a roll of film devoted to the gecko.

In the kitchen she found a note from her mother taped to the refrigerator: *Buddy and I are at the diving class. Food in fridge, help yourself. Susan said Lisa going to the beach later, will give you ride. Don't forget suntan lotion. Love, Mom.*

Kristal grimaced. She didn't like Lisa Rogers and had no intention of going anywhere with her. She opened the refrigerator and poked among its contents until she found the papayas. She took one out and sliced it in half with a paring knife. She scooped out all the small black seeds with a spoon and then, thoughtfully, ate both halves of the fruit as if it were a cantaloupe. It tasted, she decided, like flower blossoms.

Her breakfast finished, she searched in the kitchen until she found a Maui telephone book. She skimmed down the Yellow Pages list of camera stores. Fuji Photo Film, Kutsunai Photo Studio, Makai Camera, Perriera Camera, *Overnight Work Our Specialty.*

Ten minutes later, her camera case slung over her shoulder, she was walking briskly down Palivli Street. When a blue Datsun came barreling over the crest of the hill, she stopped and stuck out her thumb. The car immediately pulled to the side of the road with a squeal of tires.

"Need a ride?"

The driver was about nineteen, with straw-blond hair, his bare chest tanned a rich chestnut. In the back seat was piled an untidy litter of bathing suits, damp towels, pop cans, and potato-chip wrappers.

"Yes, to the Makai Road. I'm going to Perriera Camera. Is that on your way?"

"Yeah, I'm going to Mahini, that's practically across the street."

"Mahini?"

"Yeah, it's a beach. Mahini-peopeo, that's the full name. Also, there's Lani One and Lani Two. Good snorkeling."

She opened the right-hand door of the Datsun and got in.

"You on vacation?" he asked her, gunning the motor again.

"Yes."

"Like it here?"

"Oh it's beautiful."

"Taking a lot of pictures?"

"A few."

She fingered the camera case thoughtfully for a moment. She had taken along the spoiled Polaroid and put it into one of the storage pockets, along with the other pictures she had taken . . . the normal ones. She had never taken a picture like it before, and she wanted to ask someone about it. How could a photograph of the sunset come out with the outline of a shark etched among the clouds as if by acid, its huge body twisted, its mouth slung open, its eyes glaring? Especially when all of the other shots taken immediately before and after this one showed nothing of the kind?

"Well," the boy said, "I'm going to be right across

the road at the beach if you want to get together after-
ward. I've got a couple of joints too, the best Hawaiian
buds. It's a trip, man, gettin' high on the beach. Really a
trip. Nothing like it."

"I guess." Kristal said it vaguely while her hands
kept playing with the black vinyl camera case.

She could not get that shark picture out of her
mind.

"Yeah," said the boy in the camera shop, "that's
some shot, isn't it? One of a kind."

He was tall and gangling, with big hands and feet
that promised size and power when he finally grew into
them. His face was thin and dark . . . intense, and his
horn-rimmed glasses gave him an owly look. Kristal felt
somehow as if she knew him already. Back at Huron
High he would probably play first chair in Band and
belong to the Chess Club and the Math Club. Here on
Maui he sold cameras.

Kristal laid the other pictures down on the glass
counter in a row. "See these? Just plain garden-variety
sunsets. Your regulation pinks and oranges and yellows.
Nothing to get excited about, right? And then this one."
She gestured toward the renegade picture. "Different."

Different. Yes. Here in the artificial light of the
camera shop, the shark outline was even clearer, its
mouth more savage. Its eyes burned toward the camera.

The boy studied the photo, his lips pursed. A
customer—a plump tourist of fifty—came in to drop off
some film. He excused himself to wait on her, then
returned.

"Dad'll kill me if I don't keep the customers happy,"
he explained to Kristal. "I'm Donnie Perriera. I work
here nights and vacations and Saturdays—Dad says he's
going to make the shop Perriera and Sons when I get out

of high school. He's trying to get my brother to go in with him, too, but my brother says no way."

Donnie began to stare at the Polaroid shot again, as if something in it both puzzled and alarmed him.

"You're not going to college then?"

"I'd like to, but it'll probably be Maui Community College. Mainland schools aren't cheap, and we don't make all that much here—just enough to get along on. I'll probably end up running the store anyway. . . . it's what Dad wants."

"And you?"

Donnie Perriera was silent. As he adjusted his glasses and scowled down at the photo, Kristal was aware that she had trespassed.

"About the picture," she said to change the subject. "What do you think?"

"Do you really want to know?"

"Why else would I ask?"

"I'll tell you what it reminds me of. When I was about nine, I had this thing about model rockets. I was always making them and setting them off, begging Dad for new rocket kits, making myself pretty obnoxious, I guess."

Donnie laughed self-consciously. "I had this pet dog, Maka her name was. She was just a *poi* dog really, but I loved her. And one day I was fooling around with one of my rockets and my pocket camera. I got out a stepladder and I lit a match and set my rocket on fire. Then I climbed up on the ladder to get a picture of it burning. You know, like in a real crash, an exciting shot full of action?"

Kristal nodded.

"Just as I was snapping the shutter, I heard the squeal of car brakes. I dropped the camera and ran out into the frontyard. And there she was."

"Maka? Your dog?"

"Dead. She'd been hit by a car and died instantly."

"Oh—"

"The next week I finished the roll of film and Dad took it into the shop to develop it. When I got the pictures back, I could hardly believe my eyes. There was the rocket burning away, giving out this big cloud of black smoke. And in the smoke was the outline of a dog. My dog Maka . . . all bent over in agony, as if she were dying. Only . . . she hadn't been anywhere near my camera at all. She'd been out in front of the house being hit by a car."

Donnie Perriera regarded Kristal with unsmiling eyes. "Do you believe that?"

"Yes."

"Most people don't. They tell me I'm crazy. They look at the picture and tell me I'm reading too much into it, that it's my imagination working overtime."

"You still have the picture then?"

"Sure, I've saved it. I've got a couple of others too. I'll show them to you sometime. And I've got a book—"

"Here at the shop?" Kristal was being persistent. It was one of her bad habits, Ann had told her once. To zero in on someone and not stop until she had learned everything she wanted to know from them.

"No, the book is at home. But the picture—yes, I've kept it. Do you want to see it?"

"Yes," Kristal said, and Donnie turned and went into a back room.

He came out with a worn manila envelope. Carefully he riffled through its contents until he had found a small black-and-white snapshot. "There," he said and laid it down on the counter. "Look at that, and tell me if you don't see a dog in that smoke."

Kristal caught her breath and stared. It was a crude photo, crooked and slightly out of focus, exactly what might be expected from a nine-year-old boy standing on a stepladder. It showed a stretch of earth littered with small lava rocks, among which a model rocket lay on its side, a funnel of black smoke rising from its flank. And bunched in among the smoke was the twisted form of something . . .

Kristal narrowed her eyes. Yes, it was a dog. She was twisting in an awkward position, her hind leg bent forward as if she were convulsing in the last rictus of death.

A shiver iced up Kristal's arm. She had experienced the same sort of gut-freezing chill in Ann Arbor when, driving to a football game with Buddy, they had come upon the body of a dead jogger just seconds after he had been hit by a car. Death. Death in the air. Quickly she backed away from the picture, a sudden perspiration sheening her forehead.

"Wow," she said. "That's a dog, all right." She stared at Donnie Perriera. "What made the picture come out that way?"

"Who knows? God, maybe, or the devil. Things happen sometimes in pictures, things we can't explain. We get shots of things we can't usually see, or shouldn't be able to see, or don't want to see."

Inside the camera shop it was dark and cool. The rows of film, the booklets and straps, the lenses and accessories were all arranged in orderly precision.

Donnie and Kristal stared at each other a long moment before Kristal picked up the Polaroid shot of the sunset and thrust it back into her camera case. "I'd like to see that book of yours sometime," she said. "Just for the fun of it."

Again they looked at each other.

"Do you want to go over to the beach?" Donnie asked. "I get an hour for lunch. We'll walk down to the Makai Burgers and pick up a couple of burritos or something. They make pretty good burritos there."

"All right," Kristal said.

Chapter 5

The sea was choppy, full of whitecaps, and the surf swept up on the sand, washing it in massive semicircles. A dog ran along the water's edge, chasing the Frisbee Buddy had hurled to him. Kristal was padding about barefoot with her camera, intent on her work.

Kam Smith sat beside Ann on her towel, the tanks and gear piled beside him. "Now, Ann, surely you aren't afraid. You can't be, not a woman like you."

"A woman like me? Now, what's that supposed to mean? God knows I haven't any special qualities. I'm just like everyone else."

"No, you are not like anyone else. Not at all."

Kam touched her arm. Again Ann felt the electric tingle, the thing that had been growing between the two of them all day. Attraction? Magnetism? Raw sex? She wasn't sure what it was. Only that it existed. There was something about Kam Smith that drew her, helpless, into his orbit.

"You have special qualities," Kam repeated. "*You* are special."

"Oh come on, Kam," Ann said and laughed.

She tried to relax. All around them on the beach, people were frolicking. Girls in bikinis strolled, old people waded in the surf. A few yards away a naked baby boy toddled toward the water, his dimpled buttocks flashing. Ann wondered if he would get sunburn on his minute-sized pecker.

They had been snorkeling, had practiced clearing the mask and inflating the buoyancy-control vest. And now, as soon as she had warmed up, they were going back in the water again to make a real dive, using the air tanks. Ann had not believed that she could be so tense.

"Yes," Kam was saying, "your eyes, they're special. And that hair of yours is like sunlight. Here on Maui most of the *kamaaina* women have black hair. Blonde hair is out of the ordinary."

"I touch it up with hair coloring."

But Ann could not help preening herself a bit, stretching out on the beach towel until her body showed to best advantage. For thirty-eight, she looked pretty good, she told herself. Her breasts were small and uptilted, her belly was flat and her thighs were sleek.

Beside her, Kam sat still and controlled, handsome in his yellow T-shirt.

"You're beautiful, so you don't have to be afraid," he went on, as if this were logical.

Ann forced another laugh, her unease returning. "My looks? What does that have to do with being able to dive?"

Kam's eyes fastened on hers. "Because the sea loves beautiful women and takes care of them. You'll see. Someday I'll take you diving deep, and then you'll know the beauty, the real beauty. You will experience something known to few women . . ."

Somehow she felt he was talking about more than just diving. Something hung between them, something breathless . . .

The dog had run off with the Frisbee and Buddy came trotting back to them, all energetic male adolescent.

"Mom! Kam! What are we waiting for, the tide to turn? We've got a dive to make. Let's do it!"

"I wanted your mother to have time to rest and warm up. She got cold."

"Well, it's been an hour, hasn't it? Mom, you're warm enough now, aren't you? I want to dive."

It was a different world. Wholly and totally. A world composed of nothing more than the regulator mouthpiece, upon which Ann had clamped her mouth so tightly that her teeth hurt, for through that tube came air, life.

Water pressed down on her, cool and green-blue. She swam doggedly on Kam's left side, Buddy on his right. She kicked her flippers frantically to keep up, wishing she could grab onto Kam's hand like a three-year-old.

They were swimming over sand as bare and clean as a desert in Saudi Arabia. Its surface was rippled and pocked with swirling eddies like miniature dust storms. All around her it looked the same. Bare sand, eddied in currents and clouds. There were no directions, no way to get her bearing. If Kam and Buddy were to disappear, she would be lost, totally and forever. She could swim on for eternity over this trackless sand—

With enormous effort, Ann pushed away the fantasy. Her breath, she noticed, was drawing in with almost frightening ease, as if a hose-full of air were somehow trained directly on her mouth, whooshing oxygen at her.

Was it supposed to do that? Was it supposed to feel

as if air were flooding her lungs, as if she couldn't really even get her breath? And why did Kam and Buddy swim along so calmly when panic was beating in her own lungs like a trapped sparrow?

They could be no more than fifteen feet under here, but to Ann it felt fathoms deep. She felt as if she were stranded light-years away from the air, weighted down and trapped by the heavy tank and the countless belts and fastenings that bound her at waist, shoulders, and crotch.

God, if there was an emergency, she was supposed to unstrap the weight belt and drop it. She had read that in the *PADI Dive Manual,* in class. But where was the damned buckle?

Blindly she fumbled at her waist, feeling the alien objects there. Webbed roughness of a belt. Metal. The stiff lower edge of the buoyancy-control vest. One of the belts, she knew, belonged to the tank backpack. One was the weight belt, strung with ten pounds of lead weights. The B.C. vest had a waist strap, too, but that was underneath all the rest of it; she'd put that on first . . .

Jesus, oh, Jesus. Beside her, Kam was gesturing, pointing to his own mask, then to hers. What did it mean? Why didn't he notice her agitation and do something to calm her? But—she sucked air more rapidly—what could he say underwater? How could she talk to him?

God, she thought. The signal. There had been a two-page spread in the dive manual about signals. But now she couldn't remember any of them. Besides, this had only been going to be an introductory dive. "Your plain, basic dive," as Buddy had put it. "Ho-hum. Routine."

She was breathing faster. Air seemed to speed into her throat as if being blown there by some pumping machine. Was it supposed to do that? Her mask felt strange, too. Instead of being tightly sealed, its edges felt flaccid, loose. Water was seeping inside and had begun to pool half-way up the glass.

Salt water stung her eyes. Ann stopped finning and began to fuss with her mask. She drew a snorting breath with her nose and water bubbled and stung into her nasal passages.

Panic stabbed her. What if her mask filled completely with water? If it completely filled and she were to breathe in that water . . .

She clawed at the mask. Her breath gasped at the regulator, her lungs pulling it for more air. Dimly she remembered something Kam had said in the class about clearing the mask. *Tilt your head back and look up. Hold the mask at the top, but loosen it at the bottom, just a crack. Blow air out through your nose.*

She had given up all pretense of swimming now. Beside her, Kam was turned toward Buddy, making some sort of signal to him. Water had flooded into Ann's mask, burning her eyes. She could barely see. Frantically she sucked air. The sea pressed down on her. She was alone. Isolated.

Mom, what's the matter with you? Mom, they killed him and you let them. You let them, Mom . . .

Air hosed down her throat, pumping in full tilt so that she could barely force it out again. Something was wrong with her air. Even she knew enough to know that. Something was terribly wrong. The mouthpiece tasted of rubber and salt and she could feel her throat work with sobs.

She grabbed again at her mask, clawed at the belts around her waist, kicked toward Kam and grasped his hand, pulling on it violently.

Through an air pocket in the mask, she glimpsed him, hovering effortlessly in the water, making no useless motions. Were air bubbles even coming from his regulator? She didn't see any. And then she did see some bubbles flashing silver—her own—and she was jerking again at Kam's hand. Her jaw ached from clenching the mouthpiece, and air sprayed down her throat, gagging her.

Dropping Kam's hand, Ann kicked for the surface, breathing in great, gasping, aching wheezes like a drowning victim.

They made a surf exit so ignominious that, later, Ann could only recall being pushed by waves so powerful that she was like a little chip of balsa wood. She was lifted and tossed and then rammed, tank and all, into the sand.

Her face dug into the sand. She tasted sand. Her knees scraped grit. Water backed and sucked at her legs, and she fell onto her side, made top-heavy by the tank. Hands grabbed at her. Kam's hands. She looked up and saw that a group of people on the beach had come forward and were staring at her.

"Jesus, Mom, what in the hell happened to you? Kam signaled you about a dozen times, didn't you see him?" Buddy put his thumb and forefinger together in a circle. "That means okay, don't you remember? And you're supposed to do the same thing, and that says you're okay, too. Weren't you even listening to one thing he told us in class, Mom?"

"Y-yes . . ."

Ann's teeth were chattering. She sat huddled on her towel still wearing her wet suit, which was coated with sand, trying not to see the anger darkening her son's face. He was furious because the dive had been aborted, and it was her fault. *He* had been all right, he wanted her to know. He had wanted to stay down longer. He, Buddy, still had 1500 pounds of pressure in his tank. He wanted to go out again.

"Go out, in that?" Ann pointed to the surf.

"That's nothing!" Buddy said contemptuously.

"Mom, babies can play in that surf. What was wrong with you?"

Mom, damn you, why didn't you do something, anything?

Buddy stripped off his new wet suit, peeling it away from his skin. He maneuvered the damp neoprene with harsh motions exactly as if he had been a grown and furious man.

"I . . . I panicked," Ann admitted.

"You sure did!"

Buddy threw the wet suit down on top of the clutter of flippers, tanks, and backpacks, and marched toward the water's edge. His back was rigid.

Ann fought not to cry. "I . . . I'm sorry I panicked," she said to Kam. "My air, it wasn't coming in the regulator right. It felt as if it were being hosed down my throat—spraying at me."

"You were hyperventilating. Sucking air."

"And my mask. It was loose. Water kept coming in it."

"You were breathing out through your nose, Ann. That's why your mask didn't have a tight seal. I was trying to get you to come to the surface so I could tell you. Didn't you see me signal?"

"No . . ." Her voice was small and forlorn, like a child's, and she hated it.

"You have to breathe in and out only through your mouth, Ann. Slowly, deeply, and calmly. You never breathe in through your nose, ever. The only thing that you do with your nose is to blow to clear your mask, and of course when you're clearing your ears, you pinch your nostrils and blow against them."

"Oh . . ."

Her whole body was shaking now. She sat huddled and miserable on the sandy towel, failure beating in at her. Sand was pasted to her legs, caked on her feet and on her cheeks and in her hair. In front of them the ocean looked exactly as it had when they went in.

Kam reached out and touched her shoulder. "It's not uncommon for people to panic when they make their first dive," he told her. "It's my fault, really, I should have taken you more gradually, prepared you more. But you did so well snorkeling. And the sea cares for lovely women. It takes care of them."

He'd said that when he had promised to take her into deep water. Ann wasn't sure she wanted to go into any water. The sun baked down on them, and Ann grew warmer. The sand on her feet was drying. Beside her, Kam sat very still, his eyes narrowed at the horizon, where the pineapple island of Lanai was shrouded in afternoon clouds.

"Well," Ann tried to say it lightly, "I guess today was a corker, wasn't it? I mean, I nearly drowned."

Kam said nothing.

"A grown woman," she said. "Panicking like a little baby. Don't you think I'm silly?" It was as if the words came dragging out of some deep recess within her. "Well, tomorrow is going to be different. Tomorrow—"

Chapter 6

They showered at a public beach faucet, rinsing their equipment of the corrosive sea water as Kam instructed. An hour later they were sitting poolside at the Hawaiian Beach Maui Hotel, watching as a young, sunburned mother tried to teach her two-year-old to float in a pool as blue as an Arizona turquoise. In the water Buddy was doing the butterfly.

Ann toyed with her drink. A Chi-chi, it tasted like a milkshake laced with coconut and pineapple and tiny ice crystals. She could feel its rum warm her veins.

Two bikinied girls strolled past them, casting frank stares in Kam's direction. He was handsome in his tan shorts and Hawaiian shirt, wildly, darkly so, his face hawklike and mysterious. Ann felt a self-congratulatory pleasure: Kam was with her and not one of those pool beauties.

His eyes, focused on hers with dark intensity, had not left her face since they had entered the lush hotel courtyard.

"I really do plan to keep on diving," she told him firmly. "Do you think I'd give up just because of a little scare?"

His eyes admired her. "No, I knew you were serious. You're destined for the sea, Ann. I've felt that from the beginning, very strongly."

Ann laughed. It was easy, she found, to laugh now, when she was safely dressed in her white terry jump suit, her diving gear stored in the trunk of her car.

"Destined? Oh, I think you're making it sound a bit dramatic, don't you? My husband died last month. He was being mugged and I froze. I couldn't even scream or do anything to help him. Maybe I'm taking this scuba course now to prove something to myself, I don't know."

"Are you trying to prove you're no longer afraid?"

"Yes, do you think that's so wrong?"

Kam said nothing; his eyes were approving though.

Without her quite knowing how it happened, she found that she was telling Kam about herself and Bob, things she had told no one else.

"The marriage wasn't good," Ann said. "I was even thinking about a divorce. And then his dying like that—" She shivered. "And since then my life has been strange, disjointed. I wake up in the morning exhausted, as if I hadn't slept a wink all night. And my work has changed. I do needlepoint originals and sell them as kits to shops. I'm doing a canvas now, a picture of the sea . . ."

"Do you like the sea, Ann? Does it fascinate you?"

"Yes! No! I— I don't know."

She toyed with her Chi-chi, turning the wide-mouthed goblet around and around until it made wet marks on the table top. Across from her, Kam's Manhattan was untouched.

"I've been thinking of little else," she admitted. "And I can't understand it. Why should I, a woman living in Ann Arbor, have this odd obsession with the ocean? This canvas I'm doing now, this underwater seascape, it keeps growing somehow. It's almost as if it were working itself, as if I didn't have anything to do with it at all."

Kam looked at her. "Odd."

"Yes. Sometimes I feel as if I've been working on the damned thing in my sleep. One morning I did wake up with needle marks in my fingers and there was a six-inch square that wasn't there when I went to bed." Ann's laugh was hollow. "After that, I went to the doctor and he gave me some Valium, which, it turned out, I couldn't take. Tranquilizers do funny things to me."

Kam nodded. "Maybe I can suggest something for you to take then."

"You? What could you suggest?"

"There are many plants growing here on the island that have beneficent effects if taken properly. I've been studying the arts of the *kahunaanaana*," Kam told her. "They were the old Hawaiian magicians—masters of the black-and-white arts—most interesting. Do you know they could actually pray a person to death if they chose?"

Ann pantomimed the beating of a drum. "Do you mean like a witch doctor?"

"Don't make fun, Ann. The *kahunaanaana* are taken seriously here in Hawaii, at least in some quarters. They are even in the law books. Did you know that you can be fined up to $500 if you are caught practicing *hoopioio, hooanaana,* or pretend to have the power to pray a person to death?"

Ann shivered. In the pool Buddy was doing the crawl now, his stroke smooth and effortless, his wet back flashing in the sun. The smell of coconut oil drifted toward them, to mingle with the smell of frying fish and hamburgers from the restaurant kitchen.

"Those Hawaiian names," she said quickly, "they're a mouthful, aren't they? As for praying people to death, isn't that something out of the nineteenth century? People are too sophisticated for that sort of thing now. I mean, we have television now, and *Mork and Mindy*. This is 1980, not the Dark Ages."

"Is it? They have done studies, Ann. It is a well established fact that there are men who have been able to gain control over their involuntary muscles—"

"You mean biofeedback."

"Well, yes. In India men have been able to show this control to such a degree that it's said they have actually defecated through the mouth. They've been able to slow the beating of their hearts to one pulse a minute or even less. As for the mind, that too, Ann, can be a very powerful instrument. For instance, telepathy. What if impulses can be transmitted from one brain to the unconscious center of another? What if that second brain could be told to tell its muscles to slow down, or even to mutilate its own body?"

Ann shifted in her deck chair. She was uneasy, although she could not have said exactly why.

"Well, I think it's just nonsense, that's all. It's sensationalism! Why would any normal person want to do such things to anyone else? Why not just—oh, tell your enemy off? Or sue him in a court of law? The standard legal things?"

Kam's smile was slow, his teeth even and white enough to be used in a toothpaste ad. "You are a very practical woman, aren't you, Ann Southworth? A very down-to-earth person."

"Yes, I suppose I am. Kristal is the dreamer in our family, not me."

"Perhaps here on Maui you'll dream. Hawaii has that effect on some people."

"Maybe."

"I'm going to make you into a skilled diver, Ann. The best there is." Kam's voice was soft, and his hand had reached out to clasp hers. She could feel the magnetism that leaped between her skin and his, like an electric jolt.

"Oh, Kam, I don't think—"

"You are a woman of rare courage, Ann. You don't see that yet, but I do."

Was there a strange look on Kam's face, a look of dark grieving, as if he knew something she did not? Ann decided that she had been mistaken.

"How can you feel so certain that I'm going to be a good diver? My son certainly doesn't think so. Buddy is already convinced I'm half crazy for buying myself all that expensive gear."

"I know more than you think, Ann. My ancestors have lived here on Maui for many hundreds of years, and there is much I know that can't be written in books or tabulated by any scientist on his charts and graphs."

Another girl in a bikini slid by their table, her breasts bobbing under flimsy cloth. Kam's eyes did not even flicker in her direction.

"You don't have to worry about anything, Ann. Not so long as you are with me. Just trust me. Trust me."

Moonlight slanted onto the bed where—that night— Kristal Southworth stirred and moaned in her sleep. As always, the dream started out slowly. At first it was nothing but a field of color. Flat. Soft-washed, misted with floating specks of plankton and down-slanting sunlight and reflected wave shimmer. It was a primordial blue, implacable and cruel, a color the like of which Kristal had never imagined could exist, for she saw the blue, that incredible sheet of living color, through two pair of eyes: her own and the shark's.

Slowly, in the sweep of blue, things became visible.

Specks were suspended in the water, tiny bits of life. Fish swam at the limits of her vision, sensed a new presence, and darted away. A larger form angled to the left and disappeared. But these were normal fish movements, the usual, predictable panorama of the sea. There was nothing to jar sensory receptacles, nothing to disturb.

And, dreaming, Kristal inhabited a body sculpted a hundred million years ago. It was a sinuous body. The nose was pointed, the jaw massive, the body itself powerful, long and sleek. The triangular fins were planed for speed, the sweeping tail constructed with a high, graceful split. It was thirty feet long. The skin, with its dulled tigerlike stripes, was covered with denticles. These were harsh scales that could cut and rend and abrade, and were equipped with delicate sense organs. With her skin, she could taste the floating specks of matter in the water, even the most minute speck of blood.

Her nostrils were set wide apart, and as water flowed through them, she could detect differences in the concentration of an odor. Afterbirth from a female dolphin. Garbage thrown from a ship. A rotten side of beef jettisoned from a trawler. Like the most indefatigible of hunting dogs, she could follow a scent across miles of ocean and arrive unerringly at its source. She could smell, and the next instant be there.

She could hear perfectly. The slap of a swimmer's hand against the surface, an anchor dragging against coral, the roaring, whistling, squeaking, grunting song of the humpbacked whale. Pressure, vibration—she knew these too, could sense them with a radarlike line of sensory canals running along her flank. Instantly she could detect the floundering of a creature wounded or frightened or dying.

Now, with all of her sensory equipment, she surveyed the blue, reading it perfectly. At present all was normal. As usual. But somewhere in the vast primordial blue was food. As Kristal shivered in her dream, she knew that all she needed to do was to wait, her powerful thirty-foot body slicing through the water, until food indicated its presence.

For surely it would . . .

Chapter 7

It was December 12. To the east, Haleakala brooded, the massive bulk of the dormant volcano obscured now by dirty-white late-afternoon clouds. The air had gone chilly. In an hour the sun would set.

Ann Southworth parked her car in the parking lot of the Makai Town Center and headed toward the low, stucco-covered shopping mall. Shops caught her eye. A T-shirt shop. The Beach Bum, wall-to-wall wicker and straw hats. A bathing suit shop featuring, in its window, a crocheted maillot with solid areas to cover only the nipples and pubes.

The Stitch'n Time Stitchery was located next to an ice cream shop. It was a well-appointed store, relentlessly modern, with needlepoint and crewel kits tacked to every wall surface, including those along the stairs that led to the second-floor loft.

Kit heaven, Ann thought wryly. Many were kits she had seen before, but most were Hawaiian—myna birds and the Iao Needle and Diamond Head, whales and seashells and Plumeria, each canvas painted in bright acrylics so that the buyer needed only to fill in the proper areas.

Ann made up her mind to bring in her own portfolio of Kristal-Ann Designs to show the owner. Meanwhile, she edged toward a rainbow wall where yarns were stuffed into small square boxes. She felt drawn to the muted greens and blues, the heavy, sinister violets. Her fingers itched to pull wool through canvas. *Sinister,* she thought. Now, why had that word come into her head?

Light rays, traveling through the water, got diffused and lost, Kam had told them today in the diving class. Some colors went sooner than others. The name Roy G. Biv expressed which colors were lost first. R was red, the first shade to be sucked away into the sea. Then came O, for orange. Y was yellow. Then green, blue, indigo, and violet. If you bled at 100 feet below the surface, your blood would flow out green.

"Is there something I can help you with, ma'am?"

"Yes. I— In a minute, I guess. I'm trying to match a color."

Ann said it in confusion. She was still thinking about blood coming out green. Flowing out from the body in soft, feathery fronds as beautiful and impersonal as a sea anemone . . .

She shook away the thought and took out her canvas, which she had brought with her in a red tote bag, and unrolled it. The unfinished mesh seemed to leap up at her, and she frowned at it. Why did she feel as if there were something evil about the canvas, something frightening?

"Is that your project?" the clerk asked. She was a sixtyish blonde, wearing a blue Angora sweater. She herself had been engrossed in a white-on-white pillow, bland and intricate.

"Yes."

The woman frowned. "Funny—"

"What's funny?"

"Why, your canvas. It really almost makes me shiver, as if a cat had just walked over my grave . . . although I can't imagine why it would do that. It's just a bunch of colors, really, isn't it? Modern art?"

"Modern art."

Ann agreed, nodding. She gazed at the canvas. Weren't there more stitches in the upper-right corner today than there had been last night? She must have worked on the canvas more than she had thought.

"Well—" The clerk was bored and wanted to get back to her own work. "Well, if you need any help matching colors, let me know. I'll be right here."

"Yes. Yes, of course."

Ann went to the box that held the purple group. There were deep blue-violets, grayed and muted. Cold. Evil.

Evil? Skeins of Persian wool?

Ann caught her breath. Inside the air-conditioned shop, with its wall-hung kits of whales and flowers and mushrooms, she had begun to shiver uncontrollably.

Night, and dinner, and all of them tired from a day spent touring the crater of Haleakala.

"Kristal," Ann questioned. She had been dusting the living room—grudgingly, for this was supposed to be a vacation. "Krissie, what on earth is this, this picture you've taken?"

"What picture?"

"Why, this odd one. Is it a double exposure? I've never seen anything like it. Did you get it when you took all those shots of the sunset that first day?"

Kristal spoke quickly. "Oh it's just a bad one, that's all. One of my goofs. I don't know how it got out here in the living room. It must have fallen out of my shoe box."

Ann looked at her daughter. Was she mistaken, or were there faint smudges beneath Kristal's eyes, as if she hadn't been sleeping well?

"Mom? Those are my things," her daughter said. "I wish you wouldn't touch them."

"Honey, I was just straightening the living room before we went to bed. You must have forgotten to put your things away."

"I guess I did."

Kristal, wearing cutoffs, her slim legs bare, moved to retrieve her camera and pictures. She shuffled the odd shot among the others, almost as if she didn't want Ann to see it.

The days were marked off by the routine of the dive class. Each day Ann crawled out of bed, fighting exhaustion, and threw on a T-shirt and a pair of shorts over her bathing suit. Then she drove down to the dive shop for the session with Kam, Buddy drowsing beside her.

In the mornings the air was clear. You could lean out of the car at the bend in the road and see the four smokestacks of the Puunene Sugar Mill, twenty miles away. Then, walking into the shop, they would be caught up in the ambience of diving, of water depth and volume and pressure, air squeezes, PADI activities, and dive tables.

There was a coffee machine, and at noon they would eat lunch from the deli or, once, Big Macs brought back to them by Gordon Begrin, the shop owner, a lanky man of forty who was perpetually clad in purple bathing trunks and the yellow Ocean Divers T-shirt.

In the afternoons they dove.

On her second dive Ann walked into the sea wearing full gear and holding on to Kam's hand so that she wouldn't be tumbled over by the surf. They swam under the waves, mouthpieces clamped in their teeth, Kam still gripping her hand Blindly, trustingly, Ann followed him. She clutched his fingers tightly, her attention more on him than on the water itself. As long as Kam was there, she was safe . . .

By the third dive Ann found that she did not need to hold Kam's hand, but could fin along beside him, sucking deep, regular breaths from her regulator and making a conscious effort to blow out her air. Breathe in, blow out. Breathe in, blow out . . .

Concentrate. Sit on the bottom. Put on her tank in the water as Kam had showed her, ducking it over her head almost as if it were a shirt. Clear her mask. Clear it again. Take the regulator out of her mouth, making little humming sounds into the water so that her airway would be kept open and she would not embolize. She sang a sea song and tried not to think about her lungs popping or air bubbles perking lethally through her veins.

"I knew you could do it," Kam told her when they surfaced. He was smiling, his black eyes intent on hers. "You'll be an excellent diver. Just take it slowly, Ann, one step at a time, and don't let all those fears build up in your mind. There is nothing to be afraid of, not while I am with you. The sea takes care of beautiful women. It will take care of you."

"Sure, sure," Ann said, but she was pleased. She *was* doing better.

Even Buddy admitted that. Her son looked at her with more respect now, and he kept his promise to be polite to Kam, though he obviously did not approve of the attention the teacher paid to his mother.

"Most of the sharks here are white-tips and not too aggressive," Mick said, waving his arms. "You know, chicken shit. You can dive around them, and they'll just swim up and look you over like a dog does. Some dog! The little ones are more dangerous than the big ones, though. That's because they're more curious, I guess."

Mick Rogers had a lot to say about sharks. Short, just a shade over five-seven, with a solid body like his father's and the same wide mouth, Mick could talk diving incessantly. He'd been diving for two years, he boasted to Buddy, and had dived as deep as 200 feet. He had once seen a great tiger shark, at least thirty feet long, come boiling out of a cave near the lava flow. It had lunged out of the cave entrance, arrowed off along the edge of the coral, and was gone, scaring Mick into peeing into his wet suit.

That was last year. No one else had seen the Tiger, except for Mick, and some of his diving buddies, even Kam, accused Mick of lying, claiming they'd never seen or heard of a shark that big. But Mick knew he'd seen it.

"God," Buddy said enviously. "God, I wish I'd seen it. I'd take my old spear gun and pop—right in the brain. I'd kill that sucker dead."

"Not a big mother like that one, you wouldn't. You aim a gun at a shark that big, you'd damn well better kill it," Mick said. He took a drag off the pipe, then passed it to Lisa, who was still coughing from the last toke she had taken. The three of them were sitting in the dirt underneath the lanai, visible to no one except a couple of myna birds squawking like bratty children, and a gecko clinging to one of the poles.

"A wounded shark, it's a bitch," Mick said. "They're murder. They'll snap at anything, they don't care what. Metal, a boat, a spear, another shark, you, me, what the hell do they care? Me, what I do diving and I see a shark, I take out my knife and cut diving buddy into little pieces. Then the shark eats him and leaves me alone."

"Ha." Lisa said it hollowly. She talked around the big breath of smoke she held in her lungs. "Ha, try that just once with me, and I'll slice you up into bacon. Shark bacon."

"Yeah, yeah, not if I get you first."

"You won't," Lisa said. She sat with plump bare legs apart, one hand loose between her thighs. Buddy's eyes followed that hand. "You won't, because I can swim faster than you can. I'll be twenty feet away while you're still crapping in your wet suit."

"Yeah, sure you will," Mick said.

Buddy waited for his turn at the pipe, his throat dry and burning from the last pull he had taken. Sexual thoughts were beginning to flood his mind. Vivid images of himself burying his head in Lisa's full thighs, nuzzling his nose right up until he could smell the funky, pungent odor of her . . .

And he didn't even think Lisa was sexy. It was just that she was female and this *pakalolo,* it was really good, the best Hawaiian buds, just as Mick had promised. It had been worth the $50 he'd lifted from his mother's purse.

"Cave diving," Mick expounded, the expert. "That's where it's at, man. You got a light? A good underwater light?"

"No," Buddy said. "Not yet. But I'm getting one. For Christmas. I've already asked Mom."

"Yeah, you need a good one; you don't want one that leaks because that would be a bummer. One time I saw this shark down by Ohia Beach, and it swam out of this cave, and man, all I did was take my light and shine

.... that sucker's eyes, and it just finned away. Man, ...ed into the coral and it was gone . . ."

Buddy took a drag from the pipe and held the smoke. He sat fuming, fighting back his envy. Damn, it just wasn't fair that Mick should live here in Hawaii and be able to dive whenever he pleased, just dump his tanks into his mother's car and go, while he lived in landlocked Ann Arbor and had to beg his mother for everything he wanted.

Damn, damn her anyway for taking the class and spoiling things. Why did she have to dive? She'd probably insist on going with him everywhere, just as if he were still four years old. Or she'd lecture him about safety. God, she'd already done that, telling him not to hold his breath or he'd embolize. Christ, he knew that, he'd read it in the diving books, he'd known that for months.

She thought she knew everything after taking a couple of lousy classes. Well, it was that Kam Smith, crawling all over her with those wet dark eyes of his and telling her she'd be a great diver someday. What bullshit. He, Buddy Southworth, was a far better diver right now than his mother could ever hope to be even if she took lessons for ten years.

Three figures, wrestling and groaning in the misty November night. His mother, standing there rigid, her hands jammed into her pockets. And the terrible expression on her face, as if she'd been turned into a goddamned frozen statue, as if she couldn't move and didn't even want to . . .

"One of these days," Mick said, accepting the pipe Buddy had handed to him, "One of these days we're going to go out together and I'll show you that damned big Tiger and then you'll know what I'm talking about. It's big, man. Big. And it's got teeth. Jesus, has it got teeth. It could swallow Lisa with one bite."

Buddy grinned. He forced his eyes away from Lisa's

crotch. "God, not Lisa, not her. No shark in the world could take her with one bite. It'd have to be at least two, maybe three."

"Up yours," Lisa said calmly. "Both of you."

Chapter 8

"You here mont' vacation?" Mary Tanaka asked.

"Yes. A month."

Ann was in a fever to shower and change for her date with Kam, who had invited her to dine with him at his beach house. But Susan had suggested hiring a maid—she said she knew a woman, Mary Tanaka, who really needed the work. Recklessly Ann had agreed; she didn't feel like spending her holiday housecleaning.

"I do your maid work, t'ree t'irty an hour, yah?"

"Yes, that's fine. I think if you'll come twice a week, on Tuesday and Friday mornings, that will be best. Just light cleaning, nothing heavy."

Mary Tanaka was part Hawaiian and part Japanese. She was a hugely fat woman with enormous brown arms and legs bursting out of her sleazy polyester shorts and top. She had black hair pulled into a frizzy knot at the nape of her neck, pitted brown skin, and—she told Ann—three children and no husband. She lived upcountry in Makawao and drove an ancient Ford. She once had held a job at the Mahini Beach Hotel as a maid but lost it when she had slipped on a wet floor and broken her ankle.

"I too fat, I fall ladiz room," she explained cheerfully.

Ann nodded. The woman was hard to understand. Her voice was rapid and indistinct, the syllables poorly pronounced. This abbreviated dialect—pidgin English—was spoken by many of what Susan termed the locals.

"I come Friday?" Mary Tanaka questioned. In her big moon face, sharp eyes regarded Ann.

"Yes, that would be fine."

"And Christmas coming, *Mele Kalikimaka,* you know?"

"Christmas?" Ann was puzzled. Then she remembered the three children. "Oh— Yes. There will be some gifts for your children, Mary, if you come here every time and do good work for me."

The woman nodded. "Yah. Yah."

"Now, if you'll excuse me, Mary, I really have to go and shower now. I've been diving, and I'm all covered with sand and salt."

"You good *haole,*" Mary Tanaka said unexpectedly. Her wide smile revealed two broken teeth. "I hope you don't have bad mont'. *Mele Kalikimaka!*"

Christmas, Ann thought as the woman left. Good god, it was nearly the holidays already. She must get some shopping done. There was Buddy and Kristal, and a few things for the Rogers, and then the little Tanakas, of course. They were small girls, Mary had said—three, five, and seven. It would be fun to buy toys for little children again.

Half an hour later, she was in her car jolting along the Kaunoa Road toward Kam's beach house. Late afternoon sun washed onto the reddish dirt of the road. Ann frowned as she concentrated on the job of driving. The road, full of spectacular bumps and dips and rock-strewn gullies, was like an obstacle course. She veered around a rock as big as her head, then pulled sharply to the left to avoid an outcrop of kiawe thorns. She bumped and rattled, nearly fracturing her skull on the roof of the car. The bottle of wine she was bringing rolled onto the floor. Ann started to lean over to retrieve it, then changed her mind. This road demanded all of her attention.

The road wound 'round and 'round, giving glimpses of rocky beaches. There was a field full of giant, scraggly prickly pear cactus. A huge, rounded hill loomed to her right—it was a cinder cone for the volcano.

Kam's house was almost the last one on the road before you reached the old lava flow, he had told her. The driveway was to her right, a rutted path partly covered with crushed rock. She drove in. The beach house, set among kiawes, coconut and banana palms, and a mass of Hawaiian shrubbery, presented a face of redwood and glass. As she drove up, Kam came out of the back door of the house to meet her.

"Ann—I'm glad to see you made it here!"

She got out of the car, remembered the bottle of wine, and reached back in for it. "Oh God, I made it, but I don't know how. That road! I swear I drove by a mud puddle deep enough to sink the car in."

Kam was smiling. His black eyes met hers, and a little charge of energy leapt between them. "Well, it isn't just anyone I invite to brave Kaunoa Road all the way out here, but I think you will find it has been worth it. I have a small and very pretty black sand beach."

"Black sand?"

"Yes, indeed; it was a gift from the volcano. Come on and I'll show it to you. Watch your step."

The house had a lanai on two sides, and Ann followed Kam to the left, going down six steps and then pausing in awe.

The view was kingly. Spread in front of them like a travel poster was the ocean, late sunlight glittering on whitecaps, surf washing up over tumbled rocks. On the horizon loomed the military island of Kahoolawe, its flanks marked by tiny white surf lines. To the right, Ann could see the coastline she had just driven, Kaunoa Beach a stripe of yellow dotted with small black specks that were bathers. And in front, down a rather steep incline, was indeed a small curve of dark sand.

"Come on down," Kam ordered. "But mind the chicken wire—that's to give you footing on the hill."

A length of chicken wire had been laid flat on the sand from the lanai downhill to the beach. Gingerly Ann traversed it. The beach was tiny and private, tumbled heaps of rock blocking it off on either side from intruders. And the sand, she observed, was almost black. It was rather coarse, much of it consisting of small, gritty pebbles.

"It's lovely!" she cried in delight. "Oh, just gorgeous. I'm so envious! To think that you're lucky enough to have all of this to yourself—"

"Yes. I inherited this land from . . . an ancestor. If I hadn't, I couldn't afford to own it today. Do you know that there's a house down the road very much like mine that rents out to tourists for $5,000 a month?"

"Really?" Ann was shocked. "Do you use the beach much?"

"Every day."

Did Kam's well-carved, almost arrogant mouth seem to tighten? But Ann decided that she had been mistaken.

"Your house is beautiful, too," she told him. "May I see it? Oh—and I forgot, there's a bottle of wine. You said something about steaks, so I brought red, I hope that's all right."

"It is."

He brushed close to her as they climbed the path back up to the house, and Ann could feel a quickening of her breath. Perhaps it had been wrong for her to come here, perhaps . . . After all, Bob had been dead only a month. In the olden days wasn't a woman supposed to wear black for a whole year? But it wasn't the olden days anymore, she reminded herself and forced back a feeling of choked excitement.

Ann had not known what she expected from a house owned by Kam Smith—what, after all, did she know about him other than the fact that he taught scuba diving, had attended the University of Hawaii, and, other than that, had lived on Maui all of his life? Yet, obediently she followed him through the house, admiring the ocean view that pushed in through nearly every window of this sparsely furnished dwelling to provide its main decor.

The place looked as if it had been furnished by a store, and, she decided, it probably had been. A lamp still bore the label *C. S. Wo*. There were a few pieces of good-quality rattan, a table or two, a lamp. There were no books, no magazines, no television set, no memorabilia or plants, although a storage room off the kitchen held diving gear neatly arranged on wooden pegs. There was a fiberglass sink for soaking the gear.

"Very handy," she remarked. "As for your view, it's super. You must really enjoy it."

"I do. But to me, it isn't a 'view.' It's just the sea out there. Home."

The sea. Home. It was an odd way to put it, but Ann supposed it was true. She herself was new to Maui, full of wide-eyed tourist enthusiasm. But to Kam, of course, this wasn't vacationland, this was home. Each rock, she felt sure, was so familiar to him that he barely saw it.

When she put the bottle of wine into the refrigerator to cool it, she saw there the making of their dinner: tossed salad neatly arranged in a monkey-pod bowl, frozen peas ready to heat. A steak. Period.

"Good grief, Kam," she cried, amused, "don't you ever eat? Your fridge is so empty! What on earth do you do if you wake up in the middle of the night and want a snack? Or if somebody drops in for a beer? Or if you wake up hungry for a big breakfast?"

Kam laughed. "I don't snack, I don't encourage people to drop in unexpectedly, and I don't eat breakfast. I've been a bachelor for a long time, Ann, and I prefer to eat out. It's easier."

They talked a while longer, that odd excitement simmering between them, and then Kam suggested that they go for a short swim before eating. Ann went into a bedroom to change. Was it Kam's room? she wondered, for the room was furnished so impersonally that it was impossible to tell who slept here, or, indeed, if anyone slept here at all.

She stared at her reflection in the mirror over the white dresser. Her cheeks, she decided, looked flushed. Would she, Ann Southworth, sleep in this room tonight, or in one of the other rooms of this strangely barren house?

I don't know, God help me, I don't know. She narrowed her eyes at the pretty blonde woman who gazed back at her. *I don't know if I'm ready, I don't even know if I want to. I don't know what I want. All I do know is that I did want to come here. Very much.*

Kam met her in the corridor, wearing blue nylon swim trunks and a blue mesh tank top that showed off the powerful curve of his shoulders. Ann could not help noticing what a big man he was. And there was about him an aura, a kind of energy that seemed to crackle.

For a moment his eyes held hers, and she felt drawn, almost sucked up into the darkness of his gaze. His eyes, she felt, looked as if they had suffered pain. And now they searched her own, as if looking for something.

There were times during her fifteen years of marriage to Bob Southworth when Ann, in her most secret fantasies, had imagined a man like Kam. A man whose eyes were full of gentleness and pain.... Quickly she shook away the fancy.

"Does the surf come in high here?" Ann asked to break the silence between them as they walked down to the beach. She touched her hands to the side seams of her yellow bikini bottom, feeling the satiny sheen of the fabric. Kam's eyes had lingered appreciatively on her body. He was drawn to her, she knew. He liked her looks. Liked her.

Kam began to tell her about the ocean, about the channels that ran between the Hawaiian Islands bearing such melodic names as the Pailolo Channel, the Auau Channel, the Alalakeiki and the Alenuihaha.

They waded into the water, Kam not bothering to take off his tank top. Ann stepped gingerly around the large round rocks that dotted the shallow water. When the water reached her waist, she dove forward and began a fast crawl.

The water, she noted, quickly got deep, almost as if part of the little beach area had been scooped out by a giant underwater bulldozer. There was the surge and wash of current, the splash of the foam-topped waves. She kicked on ahead of Kam and lost herself in the sheer physical joy of swimming.

Pausing to tread water and to catch her breath, Ann thought she saw a great, grayish shape loom in and out of her field of vision. It moved so quickly that she was not sure she had seen it at all. But it had been—she panted for breath—as big as a boat, for God's sake.

She began swimming back toward Kam.

"Kam! Kam, where are you?"

Nerves, she thought. *Or a cloud shadow. Or a big reef, perhaps, just under the surface of the waves.* But she hadn't been wearing a diving mask, so she hadn't been able to see clearly.

"I thought I saw something," she told him, laughing, as he surfaced from an underwater dive, his black hair plastered to his skull and giving him a planed-down look, like a warrior in a dark helmet.

"What did you see, my beautiful Ann?"

He seemed jocular, excited, touched as she was by the curious excitement of the late afternoon swim.

"God, I don't know. Something big. A whale, maybe, or a big rock? Are you sure you don't have a sea monster or two here on your very own secret beach?"

"Not a one," he told her. His white teeth flashed in a smile. "Well, maybe just one or two . . ."

And he was chasing after her, splashing and laughing, and when they raced for the shore, he held back just enough so that Ann could be the triumphant winner.

As they were grilling the sirloin steak on the small barbeque that Kam had set up on the front lanai, Ann thought of Mary Tanaka.

"Kam? There's something I've been wondering. You don't speak as most of the people do who were born on Maui."

Kam looked at her. "It's a shame that such bastardization of the language had to occur. Yes, Ann, I can speak pidgin English when I wish, just as a Detroit black can speak the street language when he chooses to do so.

"Members of my family have been speaking the

King's English for a hundred years. My great-grandfather was a servant of one of the missionaries in Lahaina, Josiah Faulker. Faulker thought that pidgin English was an abomination. He insisted that his servants receive proper training in the use of the language. His wife, Sarah, instructed my grandfather in reading and speaking English."

Kam's eyes, looking over the edge of the lanai railing toward the ocean, seemed distant, almost brooding.

"A hundred years," Ann said. "Missionaries. All of that seems so far away now."

"Does it? Time is flexible, Ann. A hundred years can pass as quickly as a heartbeat, or it can go as slowly as the time the sea takes to round off the sharp edges of a rock."

"I suppose." Ann frowned at the cooking sirloin. "How do you like your steak?"

"Medium rare."

"Then I think it's ready." It was; pink and juicy.

"Tell me about the missionaries," Ann said.

"What is there to tell? They lived in Lahaina. It was a whaling port, rough and lusty and full of sailors ashore to take their fun in whatever way they could. It's a tourist attraction now, of course. You must visit it one day. There are many shops."

"But the missionaries?" she prompted.

"Josiah Faulker had a small church on Front Street, ministering to the seamen and converting what natives he could. His wife, Sarah, ran a little school and taught English. She was very beautiful."

Again Kam's dark eyes seemed to brood.

"And what happened?" Ann asked curiously. "Did any of the sailors ever come to church? Were there many converts?"

"A few. Most of the sailors preferred their own brand of pleasure. But Faulker never gave up; he was a hard worker. His wife, Sarah, was killed in an accident in 1875, but he stayed on at Lahaina until he died."

"Accident?" Ann's interest was piqued by the woman who had been—according to Kam—beautiful.

"Yes, it was most tragic."

"But what happened to her?"

"She was killed by a shark." Kam's expression was distant. "She loved to swim and handled herself very well in the surf; it was most unusual for that era and for that type of woman. One morning her body was found on the rocks . . . what was left of it."

"Oh . . ."

The sea cares for beautiful woman, Kam had told her. The phrase seemed to jump into Ann's head, to spin there perilously. The sea hadn't cared for Sarah Faulker.

After they ate, Ann rinsed the plates, then loaded them into his KitchenAid dishwasher. They walked back onto the lanai. The sun had dropped below the horizon, leaving only a melancholy violet to light the sky.

"A memory," Ann said, looking at it. "That's what that glow in the sky reminds me of—a memory of a sunset rather than the actual thing."

A curious mood of sadness had crept over her.

"Yes, the sky is lonely tonight." Kam was leaning over the porch railing. Some trick of the dusk emphasized the blunt bone structure of his face, the carven cheekbones and deep hollows of eyes that gave him the look of an ancient king.

"Lonely?"

"Yes, Ann. If you had watched as many sunsets as I have from this rocky beach, you would have a different feeling about the passage of time. The sea wears away at a rock, Ann. It rolls it over and over, washing sand in to grind away at its edges. Lifetimes flash by while that rock is slowly wearing away. People live and love each other and die, and still that rock is there, and its changes cannot even be seen.

"Can you imagine the loneliness of a rock, Ann? The deep, abyssal loneliness? It must always go on, for nothing can stop it. And it will be there at the end of the world, long after the last love is gone . . ." Kam stopped. The afterglow had faded to deep purple and night crept toward them.

"I can't imagine that kind of aloneness," Ann said finally. "I can't even comprehend it."

"Most people can't. You've no idea, Ann, no possible idea—"

Kam again stopped, and she could sense an agitation in him, a quickening in the vital energy that surrounded him.

"Let's go for another swim," he suggested abruptly.

"A swim? Now? But it's dark already. And I'm sure it will be chilly. Besides—" Ann hugged herself, "besides, our bathing suits are wet, and I told my son and daughter I would be back soon. They'll be wondering where I am."

"You did not tell them you would be out late?"

"No, I— I didn't—" She didn't know why, but her mood of excitement had somehow evaporated. It was too dark now to see Kam's face, but she sensed his presence next to her, could hear his deep breathing.

Any minute now he would turn to her, take her in his arms.

And she— She didn't want to go for a night swim. She loved the water, but she knew that at this moment she didn't want to go into the sea with Kam Smith. Every hair follicle on her body was prickling, and there was a knot in the tensed pit of her belly.

A moment hesitated between them, a breath of time. Something connected them, something as real as the night wind that now was blowing up from the sea. Then it was gone.

"It's all right, Ann," Kam said. "Another time then. I'll see you tomorrow at the dive shop. I want to go over the tables with you, just to make sure you and Buddy understand them. You'll be taking your test, you know."

"Yes," Ann said.

She drove away from the beach house thoughtfully. Whatever was between them wasn't finished yet, and both of them knew it.

Chapter 9

The dive shop was clean and modern, with its tiled floor and wood-burned signs: *Masks and Snorkels for Rent. No smoking. We are filling tanks with compressed air. Mahalo.*

Free-standing shelves held diving accessories: surf mats, diving boots, underwater lights, first-aid kits. A row of regulators hung from a pegboard. There was a wall for flippers, another one for masks. A rack held books for sale: *PADI Dive Manual, Seashells of Hawaii, The Edible Sea, Easy Diver.*

There were two back rooms. One was a classroom; the other held the big air compressor machine, with its dials and gauges, and the tub where the tanks had to be cooled in water before filling. A second tub of water was used to soak diving gear, and above it was a row of pegs where wet suits, masks, and fins could be hung to dry.

There were wheeled racks filled with aluminum tanks, a desk littered with papers, a coffee machine. A yarn mop leaned in a corner.

Kam's world, Ann thought. *Another part of it, anyway.* She swallowed dryly, trying to keep her burning eyes open. She hadn't slept well. Part of it had been Kam, and part of it had been—

"Well, Mom, you ready for the test?" Buddy was asking her. He regarded her warily, as he sat in the classroom perched on the edge of a cabinet, wearing cutoffs and a T-shirt carefully chopped off just below the armpits to reveal his bare, muscular boy-chest.

She tried to smile. "Yes, Buddy, I'm ready. I think! I studied late last night and right now my head is spinning with formulas—Boyle's Law and pressure and charts and graphs . . ."

"Oh it's easy, Mom—if you know what you're doing."

Meaning she probably didn't.

Ann went into the classroom and sat down on a folding chair. She thought about the needlepoint canvas. Stirring in bed at 3:00 A.M., she had opened her eyes to see moonlight spilling into the room. The canvas, which she had left on a chair, was covered by shadows, cast by the dresser, perhaps, or the hanging plant by the sliding door. But whatever had caused it, some trick of the moonlight made it appear as if the canvas had been . . . worked on.

Yes, Ann had thought, that was exactly it. In the upper-right corner of the canvas, some freak of light made it seem as if two figures had been stitched there. Flexing her fingers, she stared at the needlepoint. One of the figures was very large; the other was smaller and more curved, straining away from the bigger one, which seemed almost to engulf it.

Odd. Ann caught her breath. She was sure she

hadn't yet filled in that area of the picture. Then suddenly, irrationally, a poem had popped into her head. It was a poem she had read in college, in a class in modern poetry. She couldn't remember who had written it.

How can those terrified vague fingers push
The feathered glory from her loosening thighs?

Jesus, Ann had thought, turning over in bed and burying her face in the pillow. What a stupid thing to think of at this hour of the night. A poem I read nearly twenty years ago, a few lines of verse meaning nothing, really. She had been a young girl when she'd first read that poem, a girl waiting for womanhood and for Bob Southworth, for all of the other things that were to fill her life. Still, she did not remove her face from the pillow, and it was a very long time before she could fall asleep again.

"Ann?" Kam came into the classroom. His voice was resonant, almost tender as he touched her arm. "Ann, you look so tired. Are you sure you want to take the test this morning?"

"Of course I want to take it."

She looked at him, at the brown, boldly carved face, the fathomless black eyes. Her heart had begun to pound slowly, thickly. Her mouth was dry.

"Mom—" Buddy was impatient. He thumped down the empty can of Pepsi from which he had been drinking. "Are you two going to keep staring at each other, or are we going to take the test?"

Ann flushed. "We'll take the test, Bud. And mind your manners."

Kam gave Buddy a long look. Then he carefully placed the boy's empty pop can on a shelf.

Three hours later, both Ann and Buddy were the possessors of temporary cards, entitling them to the rank of Basic Scuba Diver. Buddy was jubilant, waving his card about and giving it mock kisses, abruptly a little boy again.

Ann held her own card in suddenly moist hands, feeling herself tremble.

"Now you're ready to begin learning about the sea," Kam told her. "I have much to teach you."

His voice was deep, sonorous.

"Can we make a boat dive now, Mom?" Buddy begged. "I want to go to Molokini, and Lanai too. You can get charters, Mick says. Charter a dive boat. And the sub! Mick says he's dived the sub, it's a World War II sub, sunk in about 200 feet of water, and—"

"Give yourself a little time, young man," Ann said. "You've had your card how long? All of four minutes?"

"But we're only staying here a month, and—"

"Hush, Buddy!" Ann's irritation was a sharp surge of acid. "You're a scuba diver now, not a little boy who must have everything right this minute."

Her son glared at her resentfully. "Aw, Mom, do you have to spoil everything?"

That afternoon, Ann and Kristal drove to Lahaina along the curving road that hugged the seacoast. Buddy said that he did not want to go with them. He and Mick and Lisa were going body surfing, he announced. Mick was going to show him how to ride some waves.

"But wouldn't you like to see Lahaina?" Ann began. "It's supposed to be an old whaling port, very colorful—"

"A tourist trap," Buddy told her, getting that sullen look again. "Mick and me and Lisa, we'll catch it later."

Ann sighed. "All right. But be careful in that surf. Are you sure you'll be—"

"I'll be all right."

Lahaina. Once it had been a whaling village, roisterous and wild, ministering to the needs of ships and sailors. Now, like an uneasy combination of Dodge City and Tijuana, it catered to the tourists.

Ann and Kristal strolled along Front Street, jostled by girls in T-shirts and bikini bottoms, longhaired men in canvas pants, middle-aged women with the look of Michigan's Grosse Pointe wealth.

Front Street, crammed with shops, grabbed greedily for the eye. There were opened doors, alleys leading back mysteriously into recesses, upper windows where (Ann imagined) brown-skinned prostitutes must once have beckoned the seamen.

You could buy a frozen yogurt here. You could buy T-shirts and sarongs and oriental jade and scrimshaw. You could buy paintings by Maui artists, diving gear or condominiums or a frondlike branch of black coral plucked from the sea at 250 feet. You could sit in the Lahaina Broiler and look out over the harbor with its schooners riding at anchor.

Ann and Kristal poked among the shops. They examined lithographs of humpbacked whales. They marveled at metal sculpture, intricately detailed, showing dockside scenes complete down to a miniature spilled bucket of paint.

"Honey . . .?" They were in a jewelry shop, and Ann was trying on pink coral rings. She was rummaging in her billfold for money with which to pay for one of the rings. "Krissie? Do you know, I think I'm missing a bit of money from my purse. Either that, or I was shortchanged at the supermarket the other day when I was shopping."

Kristal did not look at her. "I'm not the one who took it, Mom."

"Why, honey, I didn't say you were. I was only mentioning—" Ann stopped, chagrinned. "Of course I don't think that either you or Buddy—"

Or did she? Hadn't Buddy been resentful lately,

distant from her, absorbed in his sudden new friendship with Mick and Lisa Rogers? When Buddy had been eight or nine, she'd caught him once, pilfering from her purse. She supposed she ought to ask her son about it, but she didn't want to . . . not now, with his father's death fresh in his mind. They had come here to Maui to forget, to relax—not to tear at each other.

Just off Front Street they discovered a two-story frame house hidden behind a tangle of bougainvillea and a green-painted picket fence. Its decaying upper and lower porches had wooden railings and worn plank floors that spoke of days long past when women in long skirts sat in rattan chairs sipping pineapple juice and gazing out at the sea. There was a smaller frame building to the right. It looked to Ann as if it might once have been a small school.

"Look—" she began.

"Oh, look at that house!" Kristal exclaimed at the same time. "Oh, who do you think lived there? I'm going to take it."

She began fiddling with her Canon, while Ann leaned over the fence, staring at the house.

A man wearing nothing but a pair of track shorts came around the corner of the house, holding a rake. Seeing Kristal's camera, he paused and grinned.

"Can you tell me who owned this house originally?" Ann called to him.

The man wiped his face. He was about thirty, with a gingery, ragged beard, and looked as if he could have been a graduate student somewhere.

"Why, it was a church once, I think. The missionary lived here in the house and held services in the parlor. Nobody lives here now, though; the place is falling apart. I live in that building over there. That used to be the school. I take care of the place."

"Do you know the name of the people—the missionaries?"

"I think it was Faulker, something like that."

Josiah and Sarah Faulker. They had lived here. She could almost picture Sarah Faulker walking across that porch, her step strong and graceful, for she had been a capable swimmer, good in the surf. She had been beautiful. But the sea had not taken care of her . . .

Kristal moved to the left along the sidewalk in order to get a better camera angle. Her intense young body was concentrated on only one thing, the picture she was about to capture.

She snapped four shots, then exclaimed to her mother, "Gee, it's great here. This old house, it's so old, I can feel it. Spirits or something!"

"Someday they're going to restore this place," the caretaker was saying. "Bring in all the old furniture and open it up and charge admission, the way they do at the Baldwin House. A shame to let it go like this."

"Yes . . ."

The man returned to his yard work and Ann waited for Kristal to put away her camera. When the house was restored, she wondered, would it still contain its ghosts? A stern Josiah, and the man who had been Kam Smith's grandfather?

When she thought of Kam's grandfather, she kept seeing Kam's face instead, his disturbing black eyes. Or was the ghost that of Sarah Faulker?

One morning her body was found on the rocks . . . what was left of it.

Ann swallowed hard against the lump that had risen to fill her throat.

Food.

In the dream it came, indicated itself as a change in

the vast blueness of the water, a thrumming along nerve endings. Something sick or wounded was thrashing erratically. And in her dream Kristal Southworth turned and twisted, beginning to moan as the shark's urgency took possession of her, and she began to arrow toward her prey. How strong she was, how sinuous the twist of dorsal fin. She was a killer. And yet—

In the dream Kristal began to cry out in soft breathless gasps, for it was more than just killing. There was something else, too. Something that had been slowly building, as real as the black cloud that had hung that day over the dead jogger in Ann Arbor.

Loneliness. Deep, primordial, eternal loneliness. God, oh God, the despair of it, the agony of being trapped in this primitive killer-body speeding through blue toward prey.

Alone for millenia. Burdened by aloneness, crushed by it, by the isolation from all that was warm and human. Laughter. Soft whispers after the fire embers had burned low. Embraces. Soft wet sweet giving.

She knew about these things and longed for them ... had experienced only a taste of them, a few brief moments spaced over the terrifyingly long span of centuries.

Kristal sobbed. She twisted under the sweat-soaked sheets, jerking her knees up and writhing, unable to escape from the terror of the dream. The loneliness was terrifying, like being trapped in hell. To be a shark, a primitive killer and fully that, and yet to be more. ... Something that could feel, something that could yearn for human love and caring.

But the food still sent out its urgent message, and the shark body that was more than a shark lunged toward it because it had to, because it must. And it took Kristal with it because that too was something it must do.

Messages. If food sent out messages, then so did the

shark. Broadcasts to whomever could receive them, in whatever way it could be received.

I am lonely. God, God, I am so lonely. I ache with it. I agonize with it. I must stop it. I need . . . I need . . .

But it was the arrival at the food that made Kristal scream out in her sleep, a whisper scream rasped out in a voice gone dry from terror. She writhed and arched her back under the blanket and momentarily lost control of her bladder. Hot moisture trickled down her thighs to puddle on the sheet.

Food. It was a grouper, blunt and thick-bodied, flopping through the water half on its side, finning erratically. Tags of flesh hung out in strings from underneath its dorsal fin, for it had already been wounded by a moray eel. Now it made nervous, quick movements. Panicky.

It all happened fast, in a lash of huge dull-striped, darting power. She was at the grouper, *at* it, savaging it, rending it, tearing it off in twenty-pound chunks. The water clouded up with bits of flesh, chunks of bone and spurts of body fluid and soft, wet gobbets of flesh and skin. There was the snap of massive jaw, the razoring of swift teeth on bone . . .

And Kristal felt it all—the lunging satisfaction of gorging, the bits of flesh in the water exciting her even more, so that it was like an insanity—this enormous throbbing joy of slaughter.

But still, at the back of it all, she felt loneliness, she felt *alone.* Alone before these islands had ever finished forming out of the fiery earth. Alone while the lava erupted and spewed out its red-hot bombs, alone while it cooled and hardened and formed land. Lonely when the first men came, and alone again after that . . . save for a few times.

A woman. Water washing her face, laving the pliable lovely naked beauty of her. The wet, velvety softness. A

*moment of wild, plunging ecstasy before it was all torn
away . . .*

In the dream Kristal uttered low, choking shrieks.
"Mom— Mom, oh, god, Mom—"

"Honey, Krissie, are you all right? My God, I heard
you screaming and came right away. Were you dreaming
again, honey?"

Ann was beside her daughter's bed, her hair braided
for sleep, looking almost Kristal's age in the yellow eyelet
shortie gown she wore.

"Mom—" Kristal clung to her mother, weeping.
"Mom, make me stop dreaming, make it go away. I don't
want to dream anymore."

Chapter 10

During the day Kristal's dreams seemed to recede, to become unreal. Twice she had hitchhiked down to the camera shop with film to be developed. She and Donnie ate lunch at Lani Beach, where Kristal amused herself with her Polaroid, snapping the fattest, bulgiest ladies in bikinis she could find. There were plenty.

"Tourists," Donnie said. "You can tell 'em a mile off."

"How?" She was giggling. "I'm one, how can you tell?"

"Oh, a hundred ways. Nobody but a tourist gets so red. And the shoes." Donnie pointed to his own Hawaiian flip-flops, which were half-buried in sand. "The lady tourists wear fancy sandals and fancy beach jackets and hats. Nobody but a tourist wears a hat. And they mispronounce everything. Makai. Lahaina." He imitated. "And if they see you on the beach, they ask you the same old questions. 'Oh, you live here? You really live here? How do you like it here? Don't you think you're lucky?' "

Donnie hoisted a handful of sand and sifted it through his fingers. "I guess I'm not so lucky. Maui is like a ghetto, Kristal. Some people never get off the island, or if they do they only get as far away as Oahu or the Big Island. Me, I want to go farther. I want to go to the mainland. I want to see what's over there. And someday I'm going to do it, too."

"You can come visit me in Ann Arbor. That's a ghetto, too," Kristal said thoughtfully. "Every place really is, I guess."

"I guess."

Two days after they had been to the beach, Kristal came to the shop again with a new picture to show Donnie. He was alone in the shop; his father, he told her, had driven to Kahului to buy a Rototiller for his garden.

"Jesus," Donnie said as he handled the Polaroid shot carefully by its wide edge. "Where'd you take this one? Lani?"

"Yes. Day before yesterday, when we were there . . . you know. I was fooling around this morning, looking at everything, and—"

The picture, at first glance, did seem ordinary enough. Behind the plump tourist was a view of water-washed rocks, surf boiled at their base, forming lacy embroideries of spray.

It was only at second look that you saw the mist hanging over the rocks, as if a patch of fog had somehow settled there. And it was at third glance that you saw, dim and indistinct, the swirlings in the cloud shaped like something washed up at the base of the rocks.

Something . . . dead.

"You took this on a sunny day?"

"Yes, you know I did. You were *there,* Donnie, it was at Lani Beach."

"No fog? No clouds? Good weather?"

"Donnie! You were—"

"And your film, it was new? You bought it here at the shop?"

"Yes."

"Well, it's not a double exposure, I can tell that," Donnie went on. "I know things like this can be faked, but I don't see any reason for you to fake a picture like this." He brandished it. "I mean, why should you? You're only a kid, a tourist, and you don't have to impress anybody. At least not me."

"I know."

A little silence fell between them. Donnie was frowning, two lines creasing his forehead over the owlish glasses. Kristal leafed through the envelope of pictures she had picked up today. These were the Lahaina batch: wharf shots, the harbor, a group of shop fronts, the Faulker house.

"There!" she cried suddenly. "I knew it, I just knew it! I had a funny feeling about that house!"

"What is it?"

"There." She pointed to a picture. "Look. Just look at it, will you? Up there, over the fence, to the right. See it?"

Donnie reached for the photo and examined it carefully. His glasses glinted in the overhead florescent light of the shop. Then he caught his breath. "It . . . looks like a shark. See, there in the clouds? You can spot him plain as anything. His head and halfway down his body. Look—the dorsal fin—"

Kristal was shivering, hugging herself. "Then you see it, too. Those eyes . . . God, staring out at us like—like black holes!"

She felt as if she could not get warm. "I don't like this, Donnie. I don't like it at all, and I don't understand it either. Why am I getting pictures like this? I never took any like them before, not in Ann Arbor. I never even wanted to."

"Maybe you're sensitive," Donnie said thoughtfully. "*A* sensitive," he emphasized. "Maybe there's something in you—some force, some psi ability that we don't know anything about yet. Something that makes it possible for these pictures to happen."

"Oh, no—"

"Have you ever seen a ghost?"

"Well, once." Kristal ran her fingers nervously up and down the side seams of her cutoffs. "I was twelve, I guess. We'd bought this old farmhouse in Saline, back in Michigan, and one night I was coming back from the bathroom and I saw this lady on the stairs. She was wearing a white dress and looked so sad. I smelled her perfume too. But there wasn't any lady in the house, there wasn't anyone at all except the family. Dad and Buddy made fun of me. They said I was telling stories, trying to get attention. But I wasn't."

"No, you probably weren't."

Kristal's eyes were focused on the shop door, upon which hung a set of Indian bells. "And then last year, that jogger killed by the roadside. That man was dead, Donnie, and I knew it. I didn't even have to look at his body to know it. Death was in the air. I know that sounds funny, but it's true. It was a cold, ugly black cloud, almost a *thing,* hanging there in the road over him. I'd never felt anything like it before, so horrible. And when I tried to tell Buddy, he laughed. He said I was crazy. But I'm not!"

"You're a sensitive, all right. There's a book I want to show you, Kristal. Come on, I'll get it. It's in the back room."

The shop had a small, cluttered back room, crammed with cabinets, a formica table, sink, and refrigerator. Hanging plants were everywhere, and three calendars from seed catalog houses hung on the walls. Another door led to a darkroom and bathroom.

Donnie went to a drawer and pulled out a hardcover book with a glossy black-and-green cover. He handed it to Kristal.

Ghosts in Photographs was its title. She flipped it open at random, reading the captions of pictures. *Mrs. Lincoln with spirits of Abraham Lincoln, taken by Mumler, circa 1865. Spirit extra of a deceased father, taken by Mrs. Deane, circa 1921.*

"Weird," she said. "Donnie, this stuff is weird!"

"Spirit pictures. A lot of people believe in it, though. And there were dozens of witnesses to most of these pictures, responsible guys like doctors and lawyers who swore they were there when the photos were taken and that there wasn't any trickery."

There were old-fashioned photographs of stiff people sitting for portraits. Other, blurrier faces were superimposed on their bodies, or floated off behind their shoulders.

"These pictures," Kirstal marveled, turning a page, "they really make me shiver."

"And this is only one book on spirit photography," Donnie told her eagerly. "I've seen others, with even better pictures than these. A man named Hans Holzer did a really good book. He had pictures taken at an abbey showing monks who had died hundreds of years ago."

"It's scary, that's what it is."

"Yes, and listen to this." Donnie began to read aloud.

Wyllie had been psychic from childhood. The 'extras' that appeared on his plates . . . threatened to interfere with his serious portraiture. Like Mumler, he at first did not seek to record these spirit extras. Eventually, when he realized the true cause of these disturbances, he settled down in his enforced role of psychic photographer and produced some very remarkable and highly distinctive results . . .

Donnie looked up. "Does that make you think of anyone, Kristal?"

"Me!" She was scowling. "But, Donnie, I don't want to take crazy pictures, I don't *want* them! I want to be a real photographer, I want to take good pictures, I don't want creepy things interfering!"

Donnie was playing with the two pictures she had taken, jiggling them up and down in his palm. "Funny. Funny what these make me think of. You say you never took any shots like these before you came to Hawaii?"

"No, never."

"Then why do you suppose you're getting them now?"

"I— I don't know! Donnie, how would I know that?" Kristal grabbed the two photos from Donnie's hand and flung them to the floor. "If I knew, I wouldn't have to come here and bug you, would I? God, I—" She stopped. "Jeez, Donnie, I'm sorry. I shouldn't take it out on you."

"It's all right, come on." He bent over, picked up the two pictures, and tossed the book back into the filing cabinet. "Let's go to the beach. I'll lock up for an hour or so; Dad'll never know. Besides, he locks up once in a while, too. It gets boring here sometimes."

Ten minutes later they were seated on an old resort towel staring out at the blue sea, where a freighter inched toward Lahaina.

"Now, let's talk," Donnie said. "There's more, isn't there?"

Kristal moistened her lips. "Yes," she said. "My dreams."

"I thought so."

Unconsciously Kristal reached for the corner of the resort towel and pulled the terry cloth up over her bare legs to warm herself; she sat shivering in the hot sun.

"Nightmares," she said. "Terrible ones, Donnie, so awful that I wake up practically screaming. Mom knows I've had a couple, but she doesn't know that I have them every night. If she did, she'd drag me off to the doctor or fill me full of sleeping pills or something."

Donnie listened intently.

"But that isn't even the worst of it," she went on, shakily. "I find things. I find sand in my room the next morning, Donnie, and I don't even know how it got there. And sometimes the sand is *wet*."

"Sand? Are you sure you didn't bring it up from the beach yourself?"

"Of course I didn't!" snapped Kristal. "Don't you think I'd know it if I brought back a whole handful of sand? Besides, the sand is . . . black. I don't even know where to get any black sand."

"Black?" Donnie pushed back his glasses, flipped a cowlick of dark hair out of his eyes. "I know some black sand beaches. Do you think your brother is doing it? *My* brother, he's an asshole, he'd do anything for a joke."

"No. I asked him. Buddy's a turkey, too, but that isn't his kind of humor. Besides, he's too busy running around with Mick and Lisa. My cousins," she explained. "Second cousins or something like that."

"And it isn't one of them?"

"No, why should it be? Donnie, we lock the house at night. And why would they do a dumb thing like that anyway? Put a centipede in my bed—now that's something Mick might think of. That's about his speed."

Donnie hesitated. "Okay. What are your dreams about, Kristal?"

There was a long pause. The blonde girl sat huddled in the beach towel, her eyes focused unseeingly toward where a flat blue line of sea shimmered up to meet the sky.

"A shark, Donnie. I dream of a huge shark slicing and swimming through the water. Only— Only I don't just dream about him, I *am* him. Does that sound crazy to you? But I am that shark, Donnie. I'm a killer, I feel it, I feel exactly what it's like to aim myself through the water and chop and slice at something."

Kristal's voice had faded almost to nothing. Her body was caught in a shudder.

"It feels good to kill," she said in a monotone. "God, oh God, it feels so good, I'm in a frenzy, almost. I *am* that shark. *I am him . . .*"

It was the morning of the 18th. Ann sat with her cup of coffee in the dining ell of the pole house, staring out of the back window at the morning view of the volcano, and wondered why she felt so tired. She felt dragged out, as if she hadn't slept a wink all night. And, oddly, her fingertips were sore, as if she had pricked herself over and over with the blunt end of a tapestry needle.

Haleakala, she saw, was almost free of its lowering clouds this morning, its slopes blue-green. The flanks of the volcano, Susan had said, were used as pasturage for beef cattle. Once, taking a walk late at night, Ann had heard a steer lowing plaintively.

The slopes had looked inviting for climbing. But Ann had overheard Mick telling Buddy that he shouldn't explore the hills immediately above Makai Heights. Some of the locals, Mick said, grew their private crops of *pakalolo* in hidden places among the fields. They would kill anyone who blundered into their spot. People had been known to climb into those hills and disappear.

It was nonsense, of course. Such things didn't happen on a civilized, tourist island. Still, could children's gossip be entirely discounted? She was no longer sure of anything. Exhaustion gripped her in a vise.

Kristal came out of her bedroom, buttoning a white blouse. She was rubbing her eyes.

"Good morning, Krissie. Want some breakfast? There's toast and some of that pineapple-guava jam I bought. And orange juice. Or you could have guava. I think there's some left."

"I'm not hungry."

Her daughter's skin was golden brown, dusted with a sprinkling of freckles. But, Ann thought, her eyes looked dulled.

"Sure you're hungry, sweetheart. You always eat breakfast. Try a piece of toast," Ann persisted.

"Okay." Kristal did not look at her mother. She walked to the table, fished a slice of Pali honey-wheat bread from the package, and thrust it into the toaster. She stood staring down at the filaments lighting up red inside the toaster, as if she had never seen such a phenomenon before.

"Krissie? No more bad dreams? You've been sleeping all right, haven't you?"

"Oh yeah. Sure. I'm fine, Mom."

"Sure?"

"*Yes!*"

Her daughter's assurances did not satisfy Ann, but she herself felt too tired to pursue it further. She hadn't been sleeping well either. There was Kam—odd, disjointed dreams of him, of the dark eyes that could fix on hers with such intensity. Energy, simmering between them like nothing Ann had ever felt before. What *was* it, that force that hovered between two people, connecting them?

And then there was the needlepoint. She was beginning to hate that canvas. Even in her sleep, its unfinished shapes and colors haunted her. She kept dreaming about a dark-stitched hole in which something lurked. And a pair of figures entwined at the upper right of the canvas, the big one nearly engulfing the smaller one.

How can those terrified vague fingers push . . .

Ann shivered.

"What are we doing today?" Kristal asked. She had put the slice of toast down, untouched.

"Well, a week from tomorrow is Christmas. I thought we'd round up Buddy and get in the car and do some shopping. We can go to the Makai Town Center, and Susan says there's a good shopping center in Kahului. I sort of promised to buy some things for Mary Tanaka's kids."

Her daughter's eyes did not light up, and Ann rushed on. "They're small, the oldest is only seven, and it'll be fun buying for little ones. And maybe we'll see something we'd like for ourselves. Souvenirs, and all that."

"Okay." Listlessly Kristal reached for her glass of orange juice. She held it in her hand and stared at it.

Ann sipped coffee silently. *Souvenirs.* She hated herself for saying the word. Was she trying to buy their forgiveness? Was that why she had spent so much money on diving equipment, why she had brought her children here to Maui in the first place? To buy what they would not give freely?

"Morning."

It was Buddy, his hair rumpled and sticking up in patches, his pajama bottoms baggy. He padded out of the bedroom looking young and rangy and uncomfortably like his father.

"I smell toast. Where's the egg? Doesn't anyone ever fix eggs around here? Or bacon? I'm hungry!"

Christmas had come to Maui in a display of outdoor lights strung among tropical blooms. Plywood Santas and reindeer flew over papaya palms and bougainvilla. A mailbox was draped with tinsel.

They drove down Paliuli Street toward Kapa Street, past the pole houses and imitation Spanish castles. In one driveway a small brown boy riding a tricycle stared solemnly at them. He was wearing a bathing suit and sandals.

"Tacky," Kristal said as Ann negotiated a corner. "It just doesn't seem like Christmas here, that's all. I'm sorry, but Christmas isn't Christmas without snow."

"They set off firecrackers here on New Year's Eve, too," Buddy put in. "Mick said so. It's just like the Fourth of July. Firecrackers and screamers and pinwheels."

"*Mele Kalikimaka,*" Kristal read aloud. "I guess that means Merry Christmas. The Christmas trees here are weird. They're so skinny they don't look like real Christmas trees at all. Not like Michigan pine trees, anyway."

"Christmas is more than a pine tree," Ann said, immediately hating herself for it.

They drove to Kahului, exhausting the subject of tropical Christmas and then settling into silence. Ann wondered what her son and daughter were thinking. Did they miss their father? What *did* they think about?

According to the tourist brochures, the Kaahumanu Shopping Center had been named after Queen Kaahumanu, the favorite wife of King Kamehameha I. It was the only shopping center Ann had ever seen with a fabulous view. Silhouetted behind it, framing the Sears store in remote beauty, were the West Maui Mountains, tall, scored by eroded valleys, almost mystic. But the center itself was prosaic enough. They could almost have

been back in Ann Arbor, for there was the standard
record store, the photo studio, and bookstore, even a few
of the same chain stores she had shopped at Washtenaw.
There was also Shirokiya, a Japanese department store,
and shop windows bright with Hawaiian shirts and long,
gaudy dresses.

It was at Garfunkle's Dunkin' Donuts that Ann saw
the girl who had sat beside her on the Hawaiian Airlines
plane when she had first arrived on Maui.

Buddy and Kristal had both wandered off—Buddy
to poke in the record shop, Kristal to browse at Shirokiya.

The young woman emerged from the shop with a
greasy bag tucked under one arm. She looked just as Ann
remembered her—plain, intense, thick-bodied, wearing a
green polyester outfit intended for a woman thirty years
her senior. As the woman headed toward Ann, her stride
wide and rather masculine, her eyes lifted.

Automatically, Ann started to speak a greeting, but
before she could get the words out of her mouth, she saw
the other's expression change from recognition to surprise, then to a sort of startled horror.

"*You*," the woman hissed. "It's you, isn't it?" Her
voice had risen. A man passing in the other direction
glanced at them.

"Why, yes," Ann began. "I—"

"It *is* you! Don't you know that I can tell what
you've been doing? I can tell, do you hear me? I can see
it on you, the Devil's dirt!"

The girl's voice rose with surprising strength, fire
and brimstone here among the holiday shoppers. Two
boys of fifteen had craned their necks to goggle.

Ann stopped, shocked. "Please, I really think—" she
began.

"It's disgusting! I can see it, I can *smell* it! It stinks
on you, you reek of it! Oh, yes, you're an evil one, an evil

woman who has opened her heart to Lucifer! God lets me see, God lets me know. You have the mark of the devil on you, the devil's very Godforsaken mark!"

Ann could not believe it. She stood frozen in the concourse, her heart pumping madly.

The woman stood rigid, her mouth working, her neck muscles corded, hands clenched into fists.

More people gathered. Buddy appeared in the door of the record shop. Shock then anger showed across his face as he started in their direction.

"Oh yes, the Devil's mark!" The woman's body shook as if seized in some powerful fit, and menacingly she took another step toward Ann. "You have it, his mark, *his!* The Devil, Beelzebub, oh my God, yes. He comes in many forms, my lady. Fish forms and fire forms and eel forms and slime, with fangs and claws and teeth and ugly, ugly! And when he puts his mark on your back, then you are his. *His!"*

Someone called out, but the righteous one was beyond noticing. She was screeching now. "Ugly and vile and putrid! His evilness, his disgusting body has touched yours—"

Buddy slammed his way through the crowd, and without breaking stride he snatched his mother's arm and yanked her off down the length of the shopping center so fast that Ann had to run to keep up with him. She could smell perspiration coming from her son—man-sweat, a man's odor.

"Thanks," she began. "That woman, I think she was the one I sat next to on the plane—"

"Jesus Christ, Mom, what were you doing talking to a freak like that? What got into you? Everyone was looking at you! She was raving crazy! Can't you handle anything? Can't you handle the simplest goddamned thing?"

Chapter 11

The military was bombing Kahoolawe. First came a low, rolling rumble that shook the floor of the lanai. Then puffs of red-black smoke rose from the island. Dirty clouds hung over the island, and after a while Ann, squinting, could see the tiny dot at cloud base that was the strafing bomber.

Exhausted, she sat on the lanai with a glass of rosé wine over ice. The trip to the shopping center had been a total disaster . . . that frantic woman shouting at her, Buddy's face adult with anger. *Jesus Christ, Mom, what were you doing talking to a freak like that? Can't you handle the simplest goddamned thing?*

This trip wasn't going right. Not at all. Perhaps it had been a mistake to come here.

She got up and walked along the lanai toward the sliding glass door that opened into her own bedroom.

There was still an hour before she had to start the fish she had bought for dinner. She would find her needlepoint and do some more work on the canvas. She padded barefoot around her bedroom, looking for her work bag. She was sure—well, nearly sure—that she had left the tote bag beside her dresser, on the floor.

"Have you seen my needlepoint?" she asked Kristal, who was in the living room engrossed in a book. It was a large hardcover and the girl seemed oddly furtive about it, holding the shiny cover so that the title was obscured to Ann's view.

"No, Mom. Haven't."

"Are you sure? I could have sworn I left it in my room—"

"Sure I'm sure. Do you think I get into your things and snoop? Well, I don't. I never would."

Kristal turned a page, absorbed in her reading.

"A new book, Krissie?"

"Just something I borrowed from Donnie, is all."

"Donnie?"

"Donnie Perriera. Didn't I tell you about him? He works at the camera shop. I go down there sometimes, and we eat lunch on the beach. He's a senior, he goes to Baldwin High over in Kahului."

"Oh—" Ann was about to ask the title of the book, then bit off the question at the last moment. She wondered how long the defensive stage lasted with teenagers. "Well, if you see my canvas... I don't understand what happened to it. I'm sure I left my bag right there in my room. I remember putting it there."

She was beginning to be irritated.

"Mary was here cleaning yesterday," her daughter suggested. "Maybe she moved it somplace."

"Mary Tanaka? Oh, yes, I suppose—"

At dinner Ann questioned Buddy about the canvas.

"Aw, Mom, what would I want with that stuff? Listen. Mick and Lisa and me, we're going to the movies, okay? Mick's driving, he's got the car. It's an old Bruce Lee flick; they're big on karate stuff here."

Ann was convinced that Buddy had had nothing to do with the missing canvas. Like his father, he held little interest in her work, discounting it.

After dinner she paced around the house again, going through the living room with its supply of old magazines, its big flowerpots filled with spider plants and ferns that Susan had provided as decor. She checked the kitchen, the small utility area, all of the bedrooms. Finally, in her closet, on the floor behind a long evening skirt, she found the canvas bag with all of its supplies: extra yarns, scissors, acrylic marking pen, tapestry needles, strapping tape, quilting templates. But the canvas . . . was missing.

Well, damn, Ann thought. She walked outdoors to the driveway and went through her car, then knocked on the Rogers' door and questioned Susan.

Her cousin laughed wearily. "Oh, God, Ann, do I look like the sort who'd bust her butt on needlework? Jesus, I've got all I can do right now to get my ass to work every morning, let alone put up with that husband of mine and those crazy kids. Maybe you'd better call up that maid you hired. They like pretty things; she probably picked it up to look at it and then put it back someplace else."

"I don't know," Ann said. "I hate to . . ." But she went back upstairs, searched for the little scrap of paper on which she had written Mary's telephone number, and dialed.

The phone, it appeared, belonged to a neighbor. Ann had to wait nearly ten minutes for the fat woman to come to the telephone.

"Lo?" The voice was thick with island patois.

"Mary? This is Mrs. Southworth, Ann Southworth. You came to my house to work for me ... ."

Was there a brief hesitation?

"Yah?"

"Well there's something I've been looking for, a needlepoint canvas. I can't find it. It was all rolled up in a long roll and put inside a red canvas bag. I don't suppose you might have seen it yesterday while you were working?"

Silence came from the other end of the wire. Ann could hear the sound of fat-woman breathing. In the background a child shrieked.

"Canvas?" Mary Tanaka said at last.

Patiently Ann repeated what she had said.

"Don' know. Don' know nothin' no canvas. I clean, that's all, yah?"

"I know that, Mary, and I know that you're honest—" Ann was embarrassed. She should never have made this call. "Of course you wouldn't have taken it, Mary. It's just that I can't find the *canvas*. You didn't see it, did you, while you were vacuuming?"

Another silence broken by heavy breathing.

"Eh, yah," Mary Tanaka said at last.

"You mean you did see it?"

"No."

"Then—" Ann began in exasperation.

"You wonder where that thing go," Mary Tanaka said suddenly. Her voice was very far away down the long tunnel of a faulty telephone line. "You think, Mis' Southworth. You think. You know that man, he might take it, he do things. He do things. We hear about him, we know ..."

"What man?" Ann asked impatiently. "What are you talking about, Mary? I can barely hear what you're saying. The phone line must be going bad."

" ... shop. We know, we hear things."

"What things? Mary, I can't hear you clearly. There must be something wrong with the telephone."

" . . . ask him. Ask him, Mis' Southworth. Ask him why he never take off his shirt."

It didn't even make sense.

"What? Mary, I can barely hear you . . ."

A snatch of voices came from the other end of the line, a louder volume of children screaming in the background. Then a click and the line went dead.

Slowly Ann replaced the receiver.

"Mom?" Kristal called from the kitchen. "Mom, did she know where it was?"

"No, she didn't. And I never should have called her. Now she probably thinks I was accusing her of stealing."

"Oh, well. Anyway, why are you getting so uptight about it? It'll probably show up. After all, where could it have gone?"

Ann said nothing. The canvas was not going to show up. It was not in the house at all. She felt very sure of that.

Kristal was getting ready for bed. Carefully she began the ritual—the new procedure she'd started within the past week. First she undressed and pulled on her shortie pajamas, carefully adjusting the narrow ruffles at the neck and at the hem of the panties. Then she tied back her blonde hair into two little-girl pony tails. She stared at her own face in the mirror. She looked scared. That was it. Scared. She was frightened of the dream she was going to have, the nightmare that would pursue her sleep until it had caught her.

She gazed at herself, at the blue eyes that were reddened, at the dark smudges under them attesting to the fact her sleep had been disturbed night after night.

Jesus, but she didn't want to go to sleep. Couldn't

bear it. She turned away from the mirror and picked up the stack of books she had bought at the Huki Lau Newsstand. She got into bed, pulled the sheet up, and opened *These Golden Pleasures* to the first page. Then she hopped out of bed again and popped a Nodoz into her mouth. Truck drivers used them, she'd heard, to stay awake on long hauls across the country. They'd keep her awake, too.

But sooner or later you'll still fall asleep, a little voice in her head mocked her. *You can't stay awake forever, Kristal Southworth. And if you let yourself get tired and rundown, won't it weaken you? Weaken your resistance so that more can get in?*

Well, she wouldn't think about that possibility. She'd read and she'd take the pills and she'd pinch herself black-and-blue if she felt the slightest urge to nod off. She refused to sleep!

Kristal had read ten pages when she remembered the doors. She had to jump out of bed again. First she went to the lanai sliding door and carefully closed and locked it, testing the latch. Good. It was secure. Nobody could get in that way, not even a gecko. They'd have to cut the glass first, and she was a light sleeper; she'd wake up and hear it.

Then she fixed the door to the hallway. It locked, too. But she had bought a roll of Scotch tape and a spool of thread at Island Pharmacy. Now carefully she taped the thread to the door frame at about hip level. If anyone walked through the door in the dark unbeknownst to her, they'd break the thread, and then she'd know.

For extra insurance she took the green plastic wastebasket and set it right in front of the door, filling it with any old junk she could find in the room. A plastic hairbrush, an alarm clock, an empty shampoo bottle, a couple of painted coconuts she'd bought to mail to Trish and Sue, her two best friends back home. If anyone tripped over the basket, it would fall over and rattle like hell. Then she'd wake up and she'd *know*.

She stopped in the middle of the room to survey everything. The lanai door was locked. The other door was guarded as well as she could manage. The top of the dresser was clear, except for the clothes she had taken off, the shorts and T-shirt neatly folded. Reluctantly Kristal climbed back into bed. She had left the bedside lamp on, and it cast a dim yellow glow. One lone moth flickered around the light, making her think of Michigan summers. She reached for the romance, opened it again, and grimly focused her eyes on the print.

Beautiful girl, handsome man. Dear God, was she going to dream again tonight? Was she?

She was like a sheet of paper on which messages were being written. But always it began with that sheet of primordial blue, floating with specks of living matter. Then, after a time, Kristal would find herself a part of that blue, twisting sinuously through it.

Sometimes she would be after food. At other times it would be . . . other things. Horrible things.

Tonight the blue changed, grew lighter, stippled with sun-glitter, and she realized that she was nearing the surface. She was on top, cutting through troughs of choppy waves. She had a sense of day . . . of air, sky, sun. A spit of rocks jutted forward into the sea, and behind them was a yellow beach, flanked by palm trees and more tumbled rocks.

The woman sunning herself on the rocks was naked and brown. She was about thirty years old, with waist-length, shiny black hair. She lay with her belly up, legs spread slightly apart to reveal the black tuft of pubic hair, the jut of hipbone, ripple of supple ribs. Her back was arched, small, perfect breasts tipped apart. Her eyes were closed against the glare of sun.

It could have been any day, any century.

And he . . . *he* cut through the water close to the base of the rocks where the surf boiled up. The loneliness, the wanting, the needing, was a geyser in him now. It was a force as strong and uncontrollable as the lava that once had burned out of the volcano and down to the sea.

Powerful tail muscles flexed. Fins cut water as cleanly as teeth sliced flesh. In her sleep Kristal moaned and gagged a little, drawing her arms and legs together in the fetal position.

The woman on the rocks sighed in her sleep, too, spreading her brown legs further apart in order to find a more comfortable position on the rock. She was beautiful, in the full prime of her womanhood.

I am lonely. I ache with it. I want, I need . . .

Kristal stirred under the blanket, feeling the hot weight of the morning sun across her body. She kicked away the covers, caught her breath in a childish, sleepy gasp. She sat up in bed, her heart hammering. Then she forced herself to look around the room. The bedside lamp was still on. The moth that had been circling it was dead now on the night stand, its wings dusty. Beside her lay the book, its pages wrinkled where she had rolled on them during her sleep.

She didn't remember falling asleep. One minute she had been reading, desperately turning pages. The next she had been caught in fathomless mist-blue water inside the mind and body of a shark.

She swallowed hard. Fearfully her eyes continued to survey the room. The lanai door was still locked. The other door was as she had left it, too. The thread was still taped across the threshhold, and on the floor the waste-paper basket was as she had arranged it, full of its pathetic assortment of junk.

No one had entered her room last night. No one human. Dreading what she would see, Kristal's eyes went reluctantly to the top of the dresser . . .

Her clothes from yesterday were still there. Only ...
only they were wet, soaking wet, as if a whole bucketful
of sea water had been poured over them. And smeared on
the top of the T-shirt she had worn yesterday was a whole
handful of black lava sand, most of it in coarse granules
the size of dried peas or coarse sugar.

She was standing in front of the dresser now, looking
downward in mute horror at that pile of sand. Black sand
out of the ocean, still moist from the sea water that had
washed it. Sand she hadn't put there. Sand nobody had
put there.

Kristal bit down hard on her knuckles, choking back
a cry.

Chapter 12

It was just after breakfast, December 19, and the smell of fried eggs filled the dining room. Ann had picked a bouquet of bougainvillea from the tangle of bushes by the driveway, and the blossoms—bright magenta, bright fuscia—clashed gaily. In the utility closet a gecko chirped.

"Mom? Have you been in my room?" Kristal asked.

"Your room? Sure, honey, about ten minutes ago. I just put some clean sheets in there. I wish you wouldn't bring up so much beach sand, Kristal. You know it makes it hard for Mary to clean."

Did Kristal seem to freeze?

"I— I'm sorry, Mom. Did you come in my room last night? After I was asleep?" There was a curious urgency to her question.

"No, Krissie. You had the door shut tight, and I

figured you're a grown girl now, and if you keep your door shut, it's a signal you want your privacy. So I didn't come in. Anything wrong?"

"No. Nothing's wrong."

"More nightmares?"

"I'm fine!"

"Sure? You look—oh, I don't know. Like maybe you might be coming down with something. Are you having a good time here on Maui?"

"Yes, I'm having a great time. It's beautiful here."

"Is there anything you want for Christmas, Krissie? I still haven't finished all my shopping, and I guess there's still time if you want to add a few things to your Christmas list."

"I'm a bit big to make out a list for Santa, Mom."

Ann laughed. "Yes, I suppose you are. Funny, I can still remember all of the Christmases we used to have. Remember that Christmas in Saline when it didn't snow all day and you'd gotten the new skis and you kept pressing your nose to the window about every half hour, and at last it did snow? By seven in the evening we were in the middle of a blizzard. You'd gotten your wish after all."

"Yes. I remember that Christmas."

Kristal's voice was brittle. She turned around and went into her bedroom and closed the door.

Ann remembered that she and Bob had decided to let the skis be a present from him; the warm ski sweater Ann had made carried the tag from her.

Another day, the 20th. The ocean lay flattened before them, wind paths scrawled at random on its surface. Susan had climbed upstairs with another handful of papayas on her way to work.

"Haven't you found that accursed needlepoint yet, Ann?" she asked in response to Ann's query.

"No. And I've looked everywhere for it. It just isn't here. And I can't understand where it could be."

"Buddy? Kristal? None of the kids has seen it?"

"No, and neither did Mary Tanaka. It's just among the missing, that's all. Maybe some gremlins got it."

"Hawaiian gremlins? You mean the *menehune*." Susan was grinning. "Listen, don't worry, it'll show up. Lost pennies and all that."

"I suppose." Ann took the papayas and thanked Susan listlessly. Again, she had not slept well, and once she had thought she heard moans coming from Kristal's bedroom. But when she had gotten up to try her daughter's door, it had been locked.

Also she could not help recalling the odd telephone conversation she'd had with Mary Tanaka. The Hawaiian woman, since that time, had gone about her work silently. She had not mentioned the canvas again, nor had Ann.

You know that man, he might take it, he do things. He do things.

Kam Smith? Was he the man to whom Mary had been referring? *Kam?* Yet, try as she would, Ann could not imagine the diving instructor being fascinated enough by her needlework to bother to steal it. Why would he?

True, she had mentioned the canvas to him in her conversation several times, and she had even brought it along once to the diving class.

"The sea." That day, Kam had fastened his eyes on the canvas, something in them widening and contracting in a small pulse of energy. "You are painting the ocean in yarn, aren't you, Ann? And what do you see?"

"I— I don't know yet. The canvas isn't finished."

"As you learn more, the canvas will be completed."

"I guess."

But their conversation had passed to other things, and Ann had lost herself in the fascination of being with the man. Kam could talk endlessly about the wild creatures and plants of the island, Kipahulu, the volcano's rain forests, its exotic cinder cones, the lava tunnels which riddled Maui. And when they were not talking, silence filled the air between them with a curious vibrating power.

Bob Southworth, in fifteen years of marriage, had never made her feel like that, not ever.

"So what are you doing today, Ann?" Susan was asking now, bringing Ann back to the warm December morning. "The kids tell me you've been seeing a lot of Kam Smith."

Kam.

"Well . . ." For some reason, Ann was flushing. "Actually, he invited me to go out to Molokini today with him. Buddy is wildly jealous, but we're going to make a dive."

"A dive? Don't you think you're seeing a bit too much of the man? Dives, lunches, dinners, swim dates. Christ, I don't mean to barge into your business, but— Okay, I'll barge. I mean, it's been such a short time since Bob—"

"It's just a friendship," Ann said sharply.

Susan grinned. "Ann, Annie, why so defensive? Did I say there was anything wrong in your having a boyfriend? Enjoy it, girl. Enjoy. Except—"

Ann felt her lips smile. "Except what?"

"Well . . . be careful, that's all. Don't let yourself get carried away. After all, this is only a vacation. You know what I mean."

"I told you, Susan, he's just a friendship, nothing more. I'm a big girl now."

"That's good," Susan said. "Because— Oh, I don't know how to say it. Maui is small, everyone knows everyone here, and I see Kam at the shop every time we get our tanks filled. He's a loner. Really and truly a loner. That's what puzzles me."

"Puzzles you?"

"That he'd take an interest in you."

"And what's wrong with me? Have I got my face screwed on backwards?"

"Of course not, and don't get in a fucking uproar. It's just that you're a *turista*. He had a girl before—one girl—but it was nearly four years ago, and she lived here in Makai, she worked at the travel agency. Do you realize how many attractive women walk into that dive shop every day?" Susan frowned. "And he's had only one serious girlfriend in four years. There's got to be a reason, Ann."

Angrily Ann thrust her hands into the pockets of her shorts. "What are you trying to say, Susan?"

"Nothing. Not exactly. Women feel these things, and I know he's . . . well, straight. Sexually, I mean. It's not that. But, Ann, what makes him so standoffish with women? I tell you, it takes hard work to live on Maui all this time and not have women, especially when you look like he does. Think about it. He's a beautiful man, Ann. I suppose he's almost too good looking. He looks the way a man might if he'd set out to be deliberately attractive to women."

Ann snorted. "A man can't help being born with his looks, Susan! Kam certainly didn't request to be handsome, for heaven's sake."

"No. I guess not. But, Ann, there are whispers. The local people gossip about him."

But before Ann could question her further, Susan shrugged. "Oh, fuck. I talk too much. Go on out to Molokini, Ann, and enjoy. It's gorgeous out there, you'll love it."

"You're beautiful, Ann, a beauty today. And do you have your suntan lotion? You're going to need it, the sun'll be hot out there."

Kam Smith was cheerful as he helped Ann to stow her gear bag into the back of his Toyota pickup truck. As he hoisted the bag, his big shoulder muscles rippled his yellow T-shirt.

Half an hour later, they were in the small catamaran, the sandy, hotel-lined shore slowly receding from them. The red-and-yellow striped sails filled up with wind.

"Oh, it's like another world out here," Ann exclaimed. "God, that sun feels good. I feel about a million miles away from Ann Arbor."

He smiled at her. Ann felt a slow, delicious turning in her belly as Kam reached out to cover her hand with his own.

"In some ways we are a million miles away. And I'm glad you are sharing this with me. Ann, there is so much I would like to share with you. If only you could know."

He had been a bit too intense.

"We'll be sharing lunch in a while," Ann said briskly, fighting the feeling that was in her. "I packed ham sandwiches and Maui Wowee potato chips. Buddy says they're like no potato chip you can buy on the mainland and insisted I stock up on some."

Kam's arm slid around her. She felt his nearness almost as a blow to her viscera. *Dear God,* she thought disjointedly. *I can't believe this is happening. All he has to do is touch me and I start shaking. And when he looks at me with those black eyes of his . . .*

The little island of Molokini was no more than a half-moon of exposed rock—a sunken volcano crater, Kam said—covered in places with green undergrowth. A lighthouse perched on its summit, circled by one lone bird. Sea birds, Ann had noted, were rare on Maui, and she watched this one with interest, as did Kam.

"Alone," he said suddenly, in a voice so low that she almost didn't hear it. "Just that bird and all that rock and sea."

"Do birds really think much about things like that?" she said. "Loneliness is peculiar to humans, I would think. Do deer or mountain lions or even fish think about being alone? No, they don't even know what such a thing is."

"Don't they?"

Kam busied himself with anchoring the catamaran, near where forbidding rock cut sharply down to the water.

"Look," he said after he had done so. He reached into one of the boat's hatches and withdrew a plastic bag filled with dried bread. "Food for the fish. Watch."

He tossed some bread into the translucent blue water. Almost instantly the surface popped and bubbled. Things splashed. Ann cried out in astonishment. Fish had come to gulp at the bread, rather large creatures, some of them two feet long.

"Oh, they're voracious things," she cried out, laughing. "Look how they fight over that piece; why, it's a bread lust!"

Kam smiled and handed her a slice of dry white bread. "Here. Feed them yourself. And we'll take some down with us for our dive. There is a big rock where the butterfly fish come—you'll like that."

Ann did like it—the plunge into cool water with her tank and gear, the effortless sinking into misty blue, the panorama of tumbled coral and rock spread below them, painted in hundreds of bright hues. She finned through the water beside Kam, breathing slowly and deeply into her regulator as he had taught her. For the first time, she felt at home in her environment. The air came sweetly, the feel of the rubber mouthpiece was comfortable between her teeth.

Kam reached out and gave her hand a squeeze, and Ann squeezed back, a rush of happiness filling her. Even underwater, the magic between them existed. They began to swim, angling over the coral growths, sculling upward to avoid a high outcrop of rock, then cutting down again. It almost felt exactly like flying, Ann observed with delight. You could go up, down, around, exactly as you please. You *flew* . . .

They swam downward to where a half-moon opening split the bottom of a coral mound. A three-foot white-tipped shark lay sleeping, motionless under the overhang. Ann drew a quick breath into her regulator, but Kam made the okay gesture and then they swam on.

At a round outcropping he stopped and handed the plastic bag to Ann. He had ripped one of the corners, and water had begun to seep into the bag, moistening the bread. Ann pulled out a chunk of the soggy dough, and then the fish began to come, great butterfly swarms of them, yellow reef fish as bright in color as a child's crayons. There were larger, gray fish too and a long thin creature that darted in among them, all of them fearless.

Ann let out a little cry into her regulator. The fish had surrounded her like a cloud of golden butterflies. They darted toward the bag. They swam between her arms and the bag, stared curiously into her mask, investigated her fins, did everything but touch her. They were exquisitely perfect, and all of them possessed goggle eyes and small, opened mouths filled with teeth.

An hour later they had made a second dive, eaten the lunch Ann had packed, and were sunning themselves on the deck of the catamaran.

Ann awoke from a vivid dream in which she was being grasped by something and hauled toward the mouth of a cave, where a creature with sharp, strong teeth and a raw sexuality waited for her . . .

She stirred and sat up. The boat was rocking. The

sun burned hot on her skin, and perspiration ran in rivulets between her breasts.

Beside her, Kam still slept, his yellow T-shirt dried to his skin now, its fabric stretched tightly over the powerful bulk of muscle. He had worn it underneath his wet suit for both dives. Why? Ann wondered. He had also worn it in the water for each of the diving classes, that evening at the beach house, and on several other occasions when he had taken her to Lani Beach.

Ask him why he never take off his shirt.

Kam stirred slightly in his doze, and she could see the even rise and fall of his chest. Asleep, he seemed curiously vulnerable, with almost a little-boy look to the curve of his mouth.

He stirred again, rolled over onto his belly.

Ann watched him for a long time. Then she surprised herself by reaching forward. She grasped the lower hem of Kam's shirt and pulled it upward to reveal his bare back.

She didn't know why she had done it, or what she had really expected to see. He had smooth, hairless, brown, beautiful skin, each muscle clearly outlined and moving slightly with his breathing.

But superimposed on that fine skin, like an ugly violation, was a scar. It was more than a scar, it was almost a tattoo. It started below the man's neck and curved downward almost to his waist—bold, ugly, violent. Its shape was—Ann hesitated, trying to find something in her mind with which to compare it. A horseshoe? No, that wasn't it, for a horseshoe had an open end, and this scar was a complete circle.

Yet it wasn't a circle either. It was too curving half-moons, really, attached to each other and swinging open like a bite mark in an apple. A bite mark.

Ann caught her breath at the fantasy that came to her, that of Kam being caught in the jaws of some giant creature, crushed and mangled in its teeth until the mark of upper and lower fangs was etched onto his skin.

Slowly she released her breath, barely aware now of the rocking of the catamaran and the wash of surf against the nearby island.

The scar. She had never seen anything like it, for it was peculiar in another way. Its color was bluish black, discolored by some inky substance, as if Kam had submitted himself to the needle of some primitive tattoo parlor. In places the skin was puckered, and the tattoolike effect was uneven.

What on earth could have done such a thing to him? she wondered, but whatever had caused it, whatever accident it had been, it must have been a dreadful sight. Blood must have gushed down that handsome back. It must have been terribly painful, like being flayed with a whip—

"Have you had enough of looking?" Kam asked.

Ann jumped. "Oh! You startled me!"

"You deserve to be startled. Do you always peer under men's shirts while they're sleeping, Ann?"

Ann felt herself flush crimson. What she had done was extremely rude. There was no excuse for it. What was she to say?

"Kam. I don't know what possessed me to do such a thing. Really, I don't. I had no right, no right at all—"

Kam sat up, pulled the shirt back down over his back and adjusted it. He looked at her.

"I can't blame you for being curious," he said at last. He sat very still, arms wrapped around brown, muscular legs, every muscle, as always, in iron control. Yet, surely Ann could sense a tension in him, stretched taut.

"A man sunbathing in a T-shirt, as if he had something to hide," Kam went on. "Of course you would think it strange."

"No, I didn't think—"

"You did think it. You wondered. Otherwise, why would you have pulled my shirt up?"

"Well— I suppose—"

Kam's face was expressionless. "The explanation is simple enough. About seven years ago, the tourist trade here on Maui got slow, and I took a temporary job with a welding shop in Kahului. We had a contract to do some of the sugar cane harvesting equipment, and one day when I was working I slipped and fell into the machinery."

"Oh!" Ann recoiled. "Oh, I'm sorry. It must have been painful."

"Yes."

"And the . . . the tattoo effect?" she could not help asking.

"The machinery was coated with oil and debris. It caused some discoloration of the wound."

"Oh." Ann felt like a fool, an intrusive fool. Kam had never mentioned working in a welding shop. But, she reminded herself, why should he have? He was not obligated to fill her in on every facet of his life before he had met her. After all, as she had insisted to Susan, they were "only friends."

Still, it bothered her.

"Kam," she started again, hesitantly, "you don't have to be ashamed of your back. I mean, you do have a scar, but that's nothing to be shy about. Lots of people have scars."

Kam looked away from her. his beautifully carved face in profile.

"You are a tourist, Ann. You don't know Hawaii."

"Of course I'm a tourist! What does that have to do with your back?"

"You don't understand," he insisted.

"What don't I understand? Everyone on Maui goes out in the sun—fat people, old people, wrinkled old women with legs like baggy parchment—"

"Never mind the reasons why, I don't care to reveal my back to public view."

Kam had put a distance between them, creating discomfort that seemed to hang in the air, separating them. Yet before the catamaran was halfway back to Makai, he smoothed things over with a swift reaching out to her, and a sudden, hungry kiss.

"Ann, oh Ann, do you know how good you feel to me? How very good?"

In spite of herself Ann felt herself responding to him. "Kam," she whispered, "I'm really so sorry I was nosy. I won't be that way again."

"It doesn't matter."

"But—

"I said that it doesn't matter, Ann."

He was kissing her again, catching her up in something frighteningly exciting. His mouth demanded, his lips seemed almost to devour her, the excitement pulsated between them like a laser.

"Ann, you are beautiful. Do you know how lovely? Do you even know?"

Kam murmured things to her, strange, choked things that seemed to erupt from deep within him. They sought each other, their hands demanding, receiving. Ann had the feeling that she was being pulled closer and closer to something powerful, overwhelmingly and totally sexual. Yet it was more than sexuality. It was a force wholly beyond her understanding.

At last, almost by mutual consent, they pulled away from each other. The wind had picked up, filling the sails. The waves were choppy. Ann felt weak, drained of all emotion. Something had interrupted them. She wasn't quite sure what it was.

Ahead loomed the profile of the island of Maui, with its two summits, Haleakala and the West Maui Mountains.

"Ann," Kam said at last, "you don't understand, do you? You don't know me at all."

"I . . . I'm not sure what you mean."

"One day you will understand me. You will know me, Ann. It's a promise."

Chapter 13

"Wait a minute, hey, wait a minute, you guys, I gotta pee!"

Lisa Rogers thrust a paper bag full of mushrooms into Buddy's hand. Giggling, she raced on ahead of the two boys, her buttocks jiggling. She ran zigzag across a corner of the pasture toward a row of bushes that formed a windbreak. Dimly she could be seen through the bushes, squatting, and after a moment Buddy turned his gaze elsewhere.

It was the 24th. They were what Mick referred to as "upcountry," about halfway up the side of the volcano in one of the pastures used to graze Maui's beef cattle. Somewhere nearby a steer groaned plaintively, as if protesting their intrusion into its territory.

This pasture, Buddy decided, didn't resemble the

Great West. The small plot, tipped against the volcano's shoulder, was strewn with *kiawe* trees, bushes, hummocks, rocks, and cut by washes where water flooded from the heights during the winter rains.

On the way up Lisa had insisted they drive past Oceanview School, a private high school she had attended for a year.

"Until they kicked me out, that is. Oh well, who cares? Bitches and bastards, all of them yap-yap-yapping at me all the time about my grades. You'd think that was all they could find to do with their fucking time. Well, I told them they could take their damned English and their damned math and shove both of them up their behinds, that's what I told them."

"Sure you did, Lisa. Sure." Mick scoffed.

They had driven Susan's Toyota up the curving driveway, deserted because of Christmas vacation. Buddy gaped at the view the school commanded—a sweep of faded-blue ocean and misty islands so awesome that he, who had grown used to the view from his aunt's pole house, still had to catch his breath.

"Jesus!" He said it involuntarily. "Look at that view. Look at that. That must be what God sees when He looks out."

"God?" Lisa's titter was malicious. "Oh, Buddy, you're a fool of a tourist, that's all. God wouldn't even bother to look up here at this bummed-out old drag of a school."

Flushing, Buddy looked around at the scattered, gracious outbuildings, the careful plantings and shaded paths, all of it tilting downward toward that incredible godlike view.

"It's like a country club up here," he said, wishing he hadn't said that idiotic thing about God. Mick and Lisa were going to think he was an asshole.

"Country club?" Lisa snorted. "Prison is more like it!"

They roared out of the driveway in a screech of rubber and gravel and headed uphill again through groves of eucalyptus.

"Here," Lisa instructed at last. "Park here. The barbed wire's easier to get through here. I guess the kids from school have worn it all down."

Buddy was ashamed of himself for the feeling of dismay that was pushing through him. What would his Mom say if she knew he was here, about to start looking for magic mushrooms, whatever they were?

Well— He tightened his lips. Let his mother think anything she wished. He didn't care anymore, he was through with her. She'd just stood there while her husband collapsed on the cement, not even bothering to call for help. Making him, Buddy, do it, when he himself was so scared, he had almost wet his pants right there in the parking lot at Washtenaw Mall.

He'd gone to get help, and when he got back, Dad was already dead, his face screwed into an agony of pain, his opened eyes accusing Buddy, who was standing there with his father's $20 in his pocket.

Well, he'd meant to put it back in his father's wallet, and he would have. He only borrowed it. But Dad had died first, and Buddy hadn't had the chance to put the money back, and that made him a thief. Stealing from a dead man—how low could you get?

You couldn't get any lower than that, not unless you were his mother, who had let his Dad die. Ever since she started that business she had stopped caring about them. She wouldn't even cover Dad's chair. He hated her. God, he hated her.

"Come on," Mick said impatiently, "let's not just stand around. What are you guys waiting for? Afraid the barbed wire's going to rip the seat of little boy's pants?" His voice got high and mocking.

Buddy said nothing. He closed his mouth into a thin line and crawled between two rusty strands of wire, grazing himself on one bare knee. A little trickle of blood ran down his right leg, but he didn't say anything. He just stood there looking around him at the lush cow pasture. It made him think, somehow, of *Heidi,* and his mother reading aloud to him, the two of them curled on the couch in front of the fireplace.

"Hold up the wire for me now," Lisa commanded. "I don't want to rip my shorts."

"Get over it yourself, you cow." Mick was already forging ahead toward one of the piles of cow dung that were scattered about the pasture.

But Buddy stopped to help his cousin, holding up the top strand and trying not to stare as she wiggled her ample behind through the wire.

"There," she said with satisfaction. "Well, look, Buddy, I brought up a couple of paper bags for the mushrooms. You'd better come over to me and show me what you get before you put it in your bag, though. I don't want you poisoning us with the wrong kind."

Buddy accepted a crumpled brown paper bag. He looked out at the pasture. A wind had come up and was blowing the grasses and the little wildflowers caught in them. Two more steers bellowed, and somewhere a bird called. It was all very rural and beautiful, although Buddy would have bitten his tongue out before he would have admitted such a thought to either Lisa or her brother.

"Where do you find the things?" he asked quickly.

"They grow near the piles of cowpoo. Right on top of them sometimes. So all you have to do is look for the cow crap. They like damp, shady places too."

"Great. Just look for the cow pies."

Buddy did as he was told, wondering aimlessly over the field, turning to stare as the other two bent over, exclaimed, then began picking.

Ten minutes later Lisa was finished. "We found some big ones, and a lot of them," she explained. "Sometimes the mushroom patches get all picked over. The kids from school all come up here and take everything. Some guys I know have their own secret patches and they won't tell anyone else where they are."

"This is our patch," Mick said commandingly. "Don't you tell anyone, not even that sister of yours. I don't trust her."

"Okay," Buddy said.

"She's a funny kid, your sister. Fooling with that camera all the time."

"Yeah."

Mick was stuffing a handful of mushrooms into his sack. They were smooth, 'tan-purplish, most of them about the size of the canned button mushrooms that Ann bought at the A & P to put on pizza.

"Are we going to cook these things?" he could not help asking.

Lisa laughed gaily. "Oh, we've got some bread in the car. We'll make sandwiches. Mushroom sandwiches. That way they'll go down better, and they won't taste so bad. And it'll be worth it, you'll see."

Back in the car, Lisa pawed through the mushroom harvest, separating out the largest.

"We'll eat these now," she announced. "The rest of 'em we'll take home and hide in the refrigerator."

Lisa spread one of the bags on her lap and arranged the mushrooms on top of the brown paper. Buddy stared at her soft hands working the mushrooms which had taken on a bruised slick from the handling. His gorge rose a little. They looked fungoid and ugly, like the sort of lunch a Walt Disney witch might serve. He looked around for the bread but didn't see any.

"How many of these things do we have to eat?" he asked warily.

"Oh, a lot, actually. About this many." Lisa stirred the whole batch and with a forefinger separated out a pile amounting to about two-thirds of a cup.

"All those?"

"Sure, they taste terrible but you just gag 'em down any way you can, and after about half an hour, man, you won't *care*."

Ugh. What would Mick and Lisa think if he suddenly rushed out of the car and off to the side of the road to barf? They'd think he was a fool, a babyish, fucking idiot. A tourist.

Uneasily Buddy eyed the pile of mushrooms that Lisa had set aside for herself. A whole double handful. And he too was expected to eat that much. Had to ... or they'd laugh at him.

"We ought to go make a dive after we're stoned," Mick said loudly, grabbing for his share. "Man, it's a trip, it's like nitrogen narcosis; only you don't even have to go deep. You just swim along and laugh like a fool into your regulator and watch the fish fly by acting crazier than you are." He was laughing. "A trip, man. You swim around in circles, you toot along upside down and chase your own bubbles, take off your regulator and hand it to a fucking fish—" He stuffed a handful of mushrooms into his mouth and started to chew.

"Hey," Buddy said, "leave some for me."

He reached out toward the paper bag and selected the largest one he could find, the biggest and darkest of all.

Eighty-one degrees, Ann thought. Could you believe it? And the sky washed as clean as Monday's laundry. She was sunbathing on the lanai, enjoying having the house to herself. Both kids were gone. The romance novel she had started on the plane lay open beside her to a torrid love scene. *Christmas tomorrow,* she thought. *I hope I get through it.*

The afternoon sun beat down intensely, baking her skin.

Ann fancied she could see all her worrisome thoughts rising like smoke in the hot air. That night at Briarwood. Poof! Buddy's hostility to her, that went flying upward, too. The girl at the shopping center, screaming out those terrible things. The puzzle of Kam Smith . . . That one was a little harder to be rid of.

Was she really deeply attracted to the man? Or was it all, as Susan insisted, only a vacation fling? She found, now that the opportunity presented itself, that she was not as comfortable with the fling idea as she had been when it was theoretical. Ann turned over on her belly, pushing aside the book. Unwillingly she began to think about the scar on Kam's back. It had been bothering her ever since she had seen it.

She frowned. Once, on vacation, she and Bob had visited an anthropological museum in New York City. There had been an exhibit on tattooing, with a facsimile of a human leg covered with fanciful scrolled designs. The pictures, the display card said, had been marked on the skin with bird-bone needles dipped in a pigment made of soot.

Ann remembered standing there in the museum staring at the little display and thinking about standards of beauty. To some people, a suntan was sensational. To others, beauty was a bone through your nose.

Now, she moved so that the sun would brown her back more evenly, thinking about that scar.

Ask him why he never take off his shirt.

She had thought Mary Tanaka was speaking nonsense, but now the woman's words swirled in her mind uncomfortably. It was shame, of course . . . shyness, fear of humiliation. That was why people usually hid disfigurations.

But what had caused the scar in the first place? Suppose it *hadn't* been a welding shop accident. Suppose it had been something else instead, something creepy that he didn't want her to know about.

What about some other sort of accident? If not at the machine shop, then somewhere else, somewhere Kam hadn't wanted to talk about.

Ann let her eyes pop open again, to focus on the blindingly blue Maui sky. She couldn't think of any other kind of accident that would be so mysterious as to cause gossip, or cause Kam to be so secretive. A war wound? Something dreadful and bloody received in Viet Nam? Torture? The mark of some Satanistic voodoo cult?

Ann laughed to herself, sighed, and gave up. A welding shop accident was a better explanation than any of those, wasn't it? Certainly it sounded far more plausible. And yet . . .

A car pulling up the driveway interrupted her thoughts. The motor was a noisy one, and Ann sat up to see who the visitor was. The car was a white '70 Ford, its fenders bleared by rust and red Maui dust. Its back bumper was loaded with ancient stickers. *I'd Rather Be Riding a Mule on Molokai. Stop the Bombing. Keepa You Hands off, Mafia Staff Car.*

A lanky boy was at the wheel, and beside him sat Kristal, her face set.

Was it her imagination, or had her daughter lost weight since they had arrived here on Maui? She was so intense lately . . . withdrawn, almost.

Ann got to her feet, starting guiltily. Bob. My god, Bob. She had nearly forgotten him. Of course Kristal had every reason to look somber and thin. She'd lost her father little more than a month ago. In the name of God, how could a widow and mother have forgotten that? What was wrong with her?

Buddy was not really certain how they had gotten down to the dive shop. The drive had been wild, crazy. Careening around blind curves and through the little one-horse, falling-apart country villages. Laughing, giggling, stopping at a little store somewhere—the Pukalani Superette, was that the name?—to buy Pepsis.

They had drained the cans and tossed the empties out of the car window. Lisa sat in the center front seat, her fat legs thrust apart, self-appointed guardian of the mushrooms, which she kept doling out to Mick as he drove.

Buddy too kept on eating. *Why not?* he asked himself. *Why the hell not?* When they stopped in Makai at the Standard station to buy gas, they were all laughing so hard that the dark-skinned girl attendant there paused to goggle at them as if they were all crazy. That made them laugh all the harder.

At the dive shop Kam Smith filled their tanks, staring at them out of those uneasy black eyes of his, until Buddy felt nearly sober. Kam didn't like him. Buddy was sure of it. Somehow, that made him shiver a little, as if a dog had peed on his grave.

"How is your mother?" Kam asked him.

"Oh, she's all right, I guess. Getting her Christmas shopping done." Buddy's words came out crazily, and he wondered if they even made sense. Mick and Lisa were laughing.

The shop's owner had decorated it for the holidays. A little artificial tree sat on the glass-topped counter, hung with tinsel and seashells. Underneath it had been placed pictures of scuba gear cut out of catalogs. It was Christmas Eve, Buddy remembered with a great spasm that seemed to start in his gut and flood up through him like a garden hose being turned on.

Christmas Eve on Maui without snow and without Dad. He felt the laugh coming, a huge, monstrous, unstoppable laugh, and he let it pour out of him.

Then somehow they were out of the shop, and he was sitting on the curb by the walk in front of the door. He was throwing up onto the grass, throwing up all those mushrooms and the Pepsi he had drunk, and Lisa was standing above him, her fat brown legs like two columns. He thought maybe she was holding his head, but he wasn't sure, he wasn't sure of anything at all . . .

After he had thrown up, Buddy felt different, not so high as before. He said little as Mick lugged the heavy air tanks to the trunk of the car and shoved them in. Their diving gear was ready in the trunk—his own, too, he noted with surprise. Evidently Mick had loaded it all this morning before they had left for the mushroom pasture. Had he planned to make a dive all along? He probably had. He and Lisa probably did it all the time, diving high.

They all piled into the car again, heading out past Makai toward Kaunoa Beach. Mick swerved the car until the tanks in the trunk rattled and clanked against each other. They narrowly avoided hitting an old Ford pickup with two little brown children sitting in the bed.

If they had hit that truck, those two little kids would have gone splashing all over the road, Buddy told himself, but somehow that fact didn't seem to have meaning, seemed only to be a part of the hot, late afternoon, the pitiless blue sky.

Lush greenery seemed to grab at them as they hurtled past it. It was so green that it wasn't even real, it was

all artificial, manufactured in Taiwan and stuck in the
ground with wires and masking tape. Maui. Maui on
Christmas Eve. Maui without Dad.

Oh, God. Oh, damn, damn, damn.

Chapter 14

They drove out to the old lava flow and parked the car in an area that looked as if a bulldozer had come along and crushed all the lava rock to tin can-sized rubble. There were car tracks where four-wheel drive vehicles had been through. Ahead Buddy could see the lava flow itself—black, contorted rock like something from another planet.

"We gotta haul our tanks quite a ways," Mick said, laughing as if he had said something terribly funny. "You up to it, Buddy, old guy? Easier to suit up, do it on your back."

"Do it on your back? Tee hee . . ." Lisa bent double with her mirth. She leaned forward in the front seat, her long hair scraping the floor.

"Come on, you asshole, come on." Mick poked his sister with his elbow. "We'll show Buddy boy what diving is all about, yeah? Show him a thing or two, right? Show him some caves."

"Caves, yeah."

They opened the trunk, which stank of decaying seashells, and began dragging out the gear.

Ten minutes later they were ready, hot and perspiring in their wet suits. The weight of his tank dragged at Buddy's shoulders. Something, some strap or other, was caught at the small of his back. It dug into his skin like the head of a red-hot nail, but he wasn't about to ask Mick or Lisa to help him with it. They'd laugh at him again, call him a tourist.

Lisa, he noted, looked as bulky as a man in her gear. Her shorty wet suit was neon orange and flattened her tiny bust to nothing. Sweat ran down her face, and a drop of moisture hung from the end of her nose.

"Jesus Christ, let's go," she kept saying, fooling around with the mouthpiece of her regulator. "Hope to Christ this damned thing works. I got sand in it last week at Ohia Beach and old Kam was messing with it at the shop."

Mick began to lead the way down the path. Their feet slipped and slid in the loose stuff. Lisa was next in line, and Buddy lurched after them, staggering under the weight of his equipment. His heart was pounding until he thought it would burst right through his wet suit.

The path cut toward the sea, where the surf swept in. Each time it dragged and sucked back out again, it caused a stony rumble of the loose rocks that lined the shore. Sweep . . . rumble . . . sweep . . . rumble.

It was wildly beautiful. The huge blue sky, the rocky promontories jutting out. As they walked, the lava field grew wilder, more torturous. Buddy craned his neck, staring at the pinnacles and spires of frozen blackish rock. He wondered when all that red-hot lava had come pouring down. Legend said you weren't supposed to take a piece of lava away from the island or Pele, goddess of the volcano, would cause bad luck to fall on you.

Here, underneath a brutal blue sky and surrounded by bombed-looking rubble, Buddy thought it seemed very possible.

They walked until Buddy thought he couldn't stagger another step, and still Mick kept going, as if his tank were growing lighter with each step instead of heavier.

"You got to watch out for the currents here," he kept saying back over his shoulder. "Ever dived in current, Buddy, old boy? Got to wear your gloves and hang onto the coral or you get swept away, swept away, man . . ."

Mick's words grew breathless as he navigated a rock step-down. "There's places along the coast of Lanai where the surge is so strong it can sweep you right in and out of a cave. Man, if a diver ever got caught in that current, he'd be pulled right into the mouth of that cave whether he wanted to go there or not . . ."

Mick's laugh was a cackle. Buddy shivered. Surge. Current. Didn't Mick's brain even connect the fact that *they* might be going into danger here, too, that they were all high, stoned out of their goddamned minds?

"So this is Donnie Perriera. I'm glad to meet you, Donnie."

Ann pulled the beach wrap over her shoulders and tried to look dignified, like a mother, instead of a perspiring, sunburned woman clad in a barely decent bikini.

"I'm glad to meet you, Mrs. Southworth."

He was a tall, lanky boy, with dark skin, horn-rimmed glasses, and a thick head of black hair. His hands and feet were too big, giving him a half-grown-puppy look. *He might even be a good-looking man one day,* Ann thought. If he ever filled out. Under his right arm, Donnie carried a stack of paperback books.

A brain, Ann thought, remembering her own high school days. Boys like this had been interested in electronics or math. They could tinker or do equations, play chess in tournaments. Kristal would be safe with him.

"Doesn't your father own the camera shop in Makai where Kristal goes to get her film?"

"Oh, yah. Yes," the boy corrected himself, eliminating the trace of Maui accent. "We've been doing all her film," he explained. "My Dad develops it."

Ann rattled off some small talk, the first things that came to her head. The weather. The beauty of Makai's beaches, the geckos and mongooses she had seen. The boy's replies were intelligent and alert. He reached out to her somehow, although she was not quite sure why. Maybe it was the sensitive features, the level brown eyes, the care with which he spoke.

"Donnie's been showing me some of his pictures," Kristal was saying excitedly. "He's good, Mom, really good! He's won contests. He won second prize in that photography contest that *Natural History* has. It was beautiful, a time study. He brought some things to show me ..."

"Oh, I'm not so great, Mrs. Southworth," Donnie said. "Kristal is the good one. She's a natural-born photographer. I just brought some books to shown her, that's all."

He was holding the paperbacks, Ann noticed, with their titles down, so that she could not read them.

She sighed. "Well, you two can have the lanai, then. I'm going to go take a shower, and then I guess I'll make some lemonade. Would you guys like some?"

"Lemonade'd be great, Mom."

Kristal and Donnie walked to the railing and stood looking out at the view, neither of them saying anything. Ann had the uneasy conviction that they were waiting for her to leave.

"Lemonade'd be good, Mom," Kristal repeated. "This hot dry air makes me thirsty."

"Will do." Ann said it cheerfully. As she opened the sliding door and started toward the bathroom, she wondered what these two were going to talk about while she was gone.

"You're going to think I'm crazy, Kristal. Plain gone crazy from too much *pakalolo* or something." Donnie shifted the pile of books under his right arm. "But it's true. Or it could be true. I swear to you it could be."

"What could be true?" she demanded.

They stood staring out at the sweep of sea and mountains and islands, neither of them seeing any of it. To their left, a pair of myna birds squabbled, and in the house they could hear the running of Ann's shower.

"This idea of mine," Donnie said. "It could be true. Tell me about your dreams again."

"My dreams? But, Donnie, I—"

"Tell me. All of it."

"Well—" Kristal frowned. She pushed at her blonde hair, lifted it up from her neck, then let its weight fall on her shoulders again.

"Well, I told you, I dream I'm a shark. I'm down there in the ocean and I'm swimming fast, I'm swimming up to my food and I want to kill it. I do kill it. I— Oh, Donnie . . ."

"Go on, Kristal. Keep talking. Don't stop."

"It's terrible. Donnie, you've no idea, you just can't. Oh God, but it's awful and I'm caught in it. I'm there in that shark's mind and I can't get out."

Donnie's brown eyes examined her. "Maybe he sends out thoughts and somehow you're able to pick them up and that's why you dream."

Kristal stared back at him.

"*He?* What are you talking about? Donnie, all I do know is I'm scared. I don't want to go to bed at night anymore, I'm afraid to. I lie there and read and I count sheep and I look up at the ceiling and I pinch myself to stay awake. And then, somehow I'm asleep anyway and it's happening again, and I can't stand it, Donnie, I can't stand it another night!"

"Shh," he warned. "Don't let your mother hear."

"Oh. Yeah—"

"What more about the shark?" he prompted.

"Oh . . ." She hesitated. "I can't explain it exactly. It's as if he's more than just a shark, it's as if there were part of a human being in him too. He feels pain, Donnie. I know he does. He's lonely, so lonely that it's agony for him; he's been all by himself for thousands of years. Except—" She drew a quick breath.

"Except what?"

"I . . . that's the part I don't like to think about."

"What part? Come on, Kristal."

"Well, there are some bad parts. The parts when he's not alone. There are places in the dream where—"

"Where *what,* Kristal?"

"There are girls." She said it with difficulty. She felt cold. "Girls. Women. And he . . . he finds them and he . . ."

Donnie was staring at her.

"He *hopes,*" she went on. "No, it isn't exactly that, he . . . he yearns. He longs for them, he dreams for them, like a man on a desert island thinking about a glass of beer or a thick steak. Like someone who's starving. Only . . . only it's awful, it isn't like *that* at all, it's *terrible* . . ."

She made a fluttery little gesture. "I don't want to talk about it. I don't want to think about it."

Donnie pushed his glasses up on his nose. He put the books down on the lanai and then he sat down cross-legged. It was a position that made his knees look bonier and lankier than ever.

Kristal sat down, too. "But the worst part of the dreams," she went on in a flat voice, "is that they don't end when I wake up. I find things in the morning. Beach sand, Donnie. Black beach sand. And puddles of sea water. They weren't there when I went to bed at night, and I don't know how they got there."

"There could be explanations," Donnie said, "for that."

"Sure. Like what? My brother, playing tricks on me?" Kristal scoffed. "I know nobody got into my room. I locked the lanai door and I taped a piece of thread to the other door."

"And?"

"Nobody came in the room. No one. The next morning, I got up and there was sand all over the dresser, like it had been dumped there. And my clothes, they were soaked."

Donnie was fingering one of the books. He looked thoughtful.

"And then there are the pictures," Kristal went on in that expressionless voice again. "Those terrible shark eyes looking at me as if. . . as if they'd like to—" She stopped, swallowed. "Donnie, before I left the house today to see you, I got out all my pictures and I went through them again. And I found some more that are— Well, look for yourself."

Kristal reached into the pocket of her shorts and pulled out a small stack of snapshots. She arranged them on the floor of the lanai in a neat row.

"Look. Look at these. They aren't as clear as the others, that's why I missed them the first time. But it's in there, all right. *He* is. Just look."

Cool water slid in through all the openings in Buddy's wet suit, making him shiver once before it warmed up to his body temperature. He put the mouthpiece of his regulator into his mouth, drawing on it and hearing the faint wheeze as air traveled the hose to his lungs. He floated on the surface, looking down.

Water surrounded him: blue, mist-washed. Sunlight slanted down to illuminate the humps and outcroppings of coral and tumbled lava. Reef fish darted in flashes of color. Wave reflections undulated in a shining web of light. It was a landscape so colorful and strange that it might have come from a dream. Or a nightmare.

The thought slipped uneasily into Buddy's mind. Beautiful this setting was, and yet what *was* the difference between dream and nightmare? Sometimes, not much.

Now, why did a thought like that pop into his head? Buddy began to fumble with his B.C. vest. As he did so, he made a complete revolution in the water, surveying his surroundings on all sides. Reconnoitering.

Nothing, he thought. Nothing out there. He could feel sweat begin to ooze out of his skin beneath the wet suit. There was nothing out there at all but water and coral and reef fish.

To his left, Mick and Lisa were beginning their descent. *Everything fine,* Buddy assured himself as he too went down, spiraling to the bottom. When his flippers hit the small patch of sandy bottom, he succeeded in puffing a small amount of air back into the vest, enough to float him a little higher in the water. He didn't want to drag the bottom, he wanted to be suspended weightless, an underwater astronaut.

He made another complete revolution, peering out through his mask at the reef. The bright sea colors were dyed as true as his mother's Persian wool. A small, spotted fish delicately picked its way through the coral fingers, completely at home here.

Mick was signaling him now, indicating that he should follow. Obediently Buddy finned after the other two. It seemed to him that Mick swam aimlessly. He paused to dart through a narrow passageway between two mounds of coral, yanking off a red sea urchin from a ledge and then tossing it below him, as if it were garbage.

Then Mick stopped to turn a slow somersalt. Silver air bubbles plumed up behind him in a trail. To Buddy's left, Lisa had curled herself into a fetal ball, knees drawn up to her chest, black flippers sticking out ludicrously. She kept plucking at her orange wet suit, as if she would like to tear it off and swim naked.

Stoned, Buddy thought dully. Both of them. He was down here with people who were bombed out of their minds, even he was not wholly normal; he could feel that.

Everything seemed remarkably clear and plain, as if there was some enormous secret of creation and he was on the verge of discovering it. He felt as if someone had blown him up with laughing gas. He wanted to hump through the water in the dolphin kick. He felt like whirling madly up to the surface, then plunging down again. Flying, dammit. Flying!

But some tight little instinct in him wouldn't let go of reality. Buddy glanced at the gauge that hung from the hose to his left and saw that they were at a depth of 40 feet. His air pressure was already down to 1400 pounds.

Funny. He didn't remember swimming that much. Where had all the air gone? Did Mick and Lisa feel the same way he did, soaring, yet tied to reality at the same time? What had they all been doing to use up that much air?

But Mick kept swimming deeper into the coral forests, and Buddy had no choice but to follow, unless he chose to dive alone, and he didn't. The thought of being down here alone was horrifying.

Buddy's tank was down to 1300 pounds of pressure when he spotted the cave. It was located in a huge, mounded structure of rock that had tumbled downslope from the lava flow. The cave mouth was a wide, horizontal fissure, a half-circle of dark, oozy blue, beetled over by rock. Its effect was somehow sinister.

Yes, Buddy thought. *Sinister.*

The opening was darker than the surrounding water but still light enough to see into. Buddy knew that the cave was big, that it was riddled with other, small openings that helped to light it. Its area, he surmised, filled nearly the whole of the big coral-covered hump. One of the tourist guidebooks had talked about lava tubes, tunnels made by escaping molten lava.

Was this one of those? Buddy drew a sharp, short breath into his regulator. It could be. God, anything was possible here on Maui, anything at all. The underwater world was a strange one, maybe not even following the same rules . . .

Mick had seen the cave, too. He finned rapidly toward the entrance, making annoyed gestures with his hands. Somehow Buddy understood what he meant. They didn't have a light. Somehow, in all of the driving around and packing and hauling of gear, they had forgotten to bring an underwater light.

The cave was light enough to see anyway. And now Mick and Lisa were swimming toward the mouth. Then Mick stopped and jumped a little and finally pointed toward something.

Cautiously Buddy swam closer. It was a moray eel Mick had found, a large one, its thick body protruding from a crevice in the coral. Its head was nearly as large as a small melon, its beak snapping open and shut savagely. The small, angry eyes glared.

Buddy edged backward, his heart pounding. The eel seemed to be glaring directly at him, undulating its thick neck out of the crevice as if it intended to go after him at any moment. Eels could bite savagely and chop an unwary diver's hand off. They could also leave their lairs to swim freely. He tried to imagine that hideous, fat, spotted body snaking through the water, coming after him. The moray was guarding the cave mouth. Strange that he should realize that. Yet he was sure it was true.

He kept backing away from the eel, and it was then that he felt the sharp pain dig through the back of his wet suit. He whirled about, choking back a scream.

Another moray eel occupied a crevice on the other side of the cave mouth. A second guard. This one was even bigger than the first. Its tooth-filled beak snapped again, viciously read to take another bite of neoprene.

Fear pumped into Buddy. Somehow, in jumping to avoid the second eel, he had broken the seal of his mask. Cold, salty water was now stinging his eyes and clouding his vision. He clawed at his face. His rear end was throbbing.

Mick had started to laugh. He hung suspended just outside the cave mouth, safely away from both eels, floating there in the sunlit water, and he shook with laugher. Beside him, Lisa was bent over at the waist with her mirth, pointing derisively at Buddy, the buffoon, the fool, the tourist.

Mick pointed down to the seat of his own wet suit, making an insulting gesture there. And Buddy knew what had happened. The moray had ripped his suit, had bitten him in the goddamned ass, and there wasn't a thing he could do about it. It had happened, and Mick and Lisa were laughing. At him.

Gasping, almost sobbing, Buddy sucked in a huge lungful of air. Then, without really knowing that he was going to do it, he finned forward. He swam gingerly between the two eel guards and then downward, under the coral overhang and into the mouth of the cave.

He should've had a light. He should've had one.

That was Buddy's first thought as he swam forward; and his second one, as his tank scraped coral, was *My*

God, I'm too high. Hastily he angled downward to make room for the bulky aluminum tank on his back to pass under the overhang. Then he was inside.

The cave was big. It was even bigger than Buddy had thought, a huge, cathedral-like structure taking up what surely had to be the entire inside of the coral head. Its walls stretched off into shadow, into dark and murk. Yet the cave was not entirely dark, for there were holes, mostly in the upper reaches, that gave access to the open water. Through these apertures sunlight streamed down in triangles and shafts of light, giving an eery vision to the cave.

The ceiling was mostly coral growths, the floor of the cave was sand, and all of it was creepy. Terror began to pump through Buddy, a slow throbbing tuned exactly to the beat of the blood in his veins. Something was wrong in here. *Something was wrong.*

In his agitation Buddy had begun to sink toward the cave bottom, forgetting his buoyancy. His flippers landed on the sand and kicked it up in swirling, dusty clouds. Instinctively he kicked to raise himself higher. The last thing he needed was to stir up the bottom. If he clouded up the water, then he wouldn't be able to see, and he had to see, *had to—*

But what did he have to see? What was wrong? Some feeling seemed to vibrate in the water around him, electrifying every mote of water, every droplet. *What was it?* God, if he only had a light, if only Mick was beside him to point and laugh and make everything seem normal. If only he could see clearly what was in here.

Something had to be. He could sense it; Jesus, he could *feel* it. His body was covered in huge goosebumps that prickled his skin . . .

Buddy looked down at the gauge again. He had only 1000 pounds of air now, and it was going fast. His fear was making him gasp it up; he had to get out of the cave fast. If he ran out of air while he was still inside the cave, he might not be able to get out in time, not unless he swam up through one of the holes. But they might not be big enough. He could drown in here, he could suffocate . . .

He fought his fear, forced himself to breathe slowly and evenly, to draw in measured amounts of air. Because he had to stay here a few minutes more. There was something important down here in the cave, and he had to find out what it was.

He finned forward and a little to the left, where the light was brighter, and one small reef fish darted in a shaft of sunlight, as if everything were perfectly ordinary. But it wasn't ordinary. Unease vibrated in here, as though someone screamed at Buddy to turn around and swim for the cave mouth as fast as he could. Get out while he still had time . . . before it was too late.

And then he saw it. Or, rather, he saw *them,* the two things simultaneously. The first thing was a scrap of white that lay on the sand bed of the cave floor just past the bar of sunlight to his left. Abandoned, discarded, it seemed oddly familiar . . . something he had seen many times before.

And the other thing . . .

Bile poured up into Buddy's regulator, and he swallowed it down, choking on bitter acid. God. The other . . . was big. *Big.* It came at him out of the murkiest depths of the cave, a great, spotted, undulating mass, sinuous of tail and fin, with a pointed nose, great underslung mouth blankly open, and black fathomless eyes that looked right at him.

Carefully Donnie Perriera examined the pictures that Kristal had arranged in a neat row for his inspection. It took him several minutes, during which his breathing became slow, absorbed.

At last he pointed to one of the pictures. "This one. This one of your mother and Kam Smith going into the water. When did you take it?"

"When Mom and Buddy were taking that class. I went down to the beach with them one afternoon to watch them dive. I took a whole bunch of pictures, and this is the only one that came out funny. At first I thought it was just a cloud shadow over their heads, but it isn't. See?" Kristal pointed.

"A shark's head," Donnie whispered.

For a long time both of them stared at the photograph. Neither said anything.

"And look," Kristal added, "look at this funny line on Kam's back. When I first looked at the picture, I thought it was just part of his equipment. You know, all those straps and tanks and things that they wear. But it's not that at all. It's . . . funny. A big circle almost. But it's not a circle either."

"It's a jaw," Donnie muttered.

"And this one." Kristal went on. "I took this one of Mom sitting in her chair with her needlepoint. You know, the canvas she's been looking all over the house for and hasn't been able to find. Well, look. This picture really gives me the creeps."

"Why?" Donnie peered. "I don't see anything."

"That's because you've never seen the real canvas. I have. See, there? Those funny-looking lines and shadows? It's as if someone had sketched in *the way that canvas would look when it was finished.*"

"I still can't see."

"Right there," Kristal said impatiently. "Look at the upper right. I know she didn't have that part done. There's something there, something that was never there before. It looks like a . . ." She caught her breath. "I don't know . . . something bad. If only the picture was bigger, maybe if it was enlarged a bit."

Kristal and Donnie stared at each other.

"*I* could enlarge it," Donnie said. "Dad lets me use the darkroom whenever I want."

Kristal hesitated.

"Are you afraid?"

"No . . . not exactly."

"Then what?"

"All right, I *am* afraid. You'd be scared, too, Donnie, if you'd dreamed the same dreams I have, and if you took pictures like these."

"Okay."

The myna birds were still squawking, and in the house Ann's shower had shut off.

Kristal took the stack of photographs and shuffled them, her eyes somber. "Well, those are the pictures. Come on into my bedroom, and I'll show you the sand."

"Do you want to know what I think?" Donnie asked ten minutes later. His eyes, behind the horn-rimmed glasses, had begun to light up with eager fire. He and Kristal were back out on the lanai, their shoulders close together. In the kitchen Ann was clinking glasses now, and they knew they'd have to hurry. In a minute or two she'd be out here with them, dispensing lemonade and good cheer.

"Yes, I want to know what you think. I've been waiting to hear it." Kristal's voice was sharp.

"Okay, I'll tell you. Did you ever hear of a shark god?"

"A *what?*"

"A shark god."

Kristal gave a sudden burst of nervous laughter, and Donnie cut her off. "Listen, Kristal, the old Hawaiians were really a religious kind of people. I've read a lot about them, you study it in school, you know, and I go to the library a lot. They had all kinds of gods. Gods for everything. In one book there was a big long list of them—gods for fishermen and *Kapa* makers, gods of the volcano, and ghosts and spirits of all kinds. One kind was called *aumakuas*. These were ancestral gods, and people worshipped them.

"One of these was a woman lizard god named *kiha wahine*. She was like a mermaid with long, flowing black hair, the body of a woman above, and the shape of a lizard below. Sometimes she was supposed to come on land in the form of a beautiful woman. The native Hawaiians are afraid of lizards, you know, and when smallpox and leprosy came to the islands, some people thought that *kiha wahine* had caused it. She was supposed to have given the people *puha*, that's ulcers, and *alaala*, a bad skin disease here in the trophics."

Kristal stared at Donnie. "But all of that is just superstition. Myths, legends. None of it's *true*. A lizard god didn't make people get those diseases. Germs did."

"Germs? Did they?" Donnie's eyes were quizzical. "Well, listen to this. Some of the 'lesser gods,' as this book calls them—" Donnie waved an orange paperback. "—were sharks. Ukanipo. Uhumakaikai. Kamohoalii. Each place along the coasts of the islands had its own shark god, and its people who worshipped it. They'd bring gifts to the god like a pig, a chicken, or some food. And the shark, he'd do his share by protecting the people, guarding them from any danger. If a man was upset in his canoe, the shark god, if he felt in the mood, might come to his rescue and pull him back to safety.

"See?" Donnie flipped open the book. "It says right here that a lot of people today still believe in shark intervention. People still talk about things like that, the native Hawaiians, anyway. I have friends at school who say that there's still a shark god living down off Kaunoa Beach."

The air on the lanai, hot, clear, seemed to shudder slightly as if some force had passed through it. Kristal felt a coldness creep over her skin, and she forced a little incredulous laugh. "But, Donnie, none of that is real. It's just stories, superstitions made up by people who don't have any education and . . ."

She faltered, and Donnie's lower jaw thrust out grimly.

"Some people," he told her, "think this kind of thing is real enough. It says right here in this book that the largest of the Hawaiian shark gods was Kuhaimoana. He was huge. His mouth was supposed to be as big as a grass house, and the channels around the islands of Maui and Oahu were too small for him, so he had to spend most of his time in deep water. And there was Kamohoalii. He lived right here on Maui. He was supposed to be the older brother of the volcano goddess Pele . . ."

"I don't believe any of this!"

Donnie ignored her. "There was a weird thing about these shark gods. They were supposed to have the power to assume human form and walk around on land disguised as a man, a good-looking, strong young man. Nobody knew who they were, nobody could ever guess, not unless they saw the young man's back."

"His *back?*"

"Sure. There was supposed to be a mark on his back, the outline of a shark's jaw. Some stories say it was like a tattoo, and the other stories say it was more like a real shark's mouth. Anyway, that was how you could tell that he wasn't really a man but a shark. And—"

"Stop, Donnie. I don't want to hear."

Donnie's laugh was nervous. "There are legends about that, too. Sometimes the shark man would go up to people, and he'd make a little joke . . . warn them not to go in the water or a shark might get them. Well, sometimes the people he warned would ignore him and go in the water anyway. Then the young man would shrug and walk away, disappear along the beach somewhere. After a while there would be a terrible accident. Someone swimming in the surf would be attacked and eaten by a shark . . ."

Kristal's shiver was violent. "Ugh! Donnie, I don't want to hear about it anymore. It's too horrid. After those dreams I've had—"

"You've got to think about it."

"I don't! I don't have to!"

"What if you've somehow gotten mixed up with one of those shark gods? What if he's causing your dreams, Kristal? What if he's the reason why those pictures you've taken have come out so strange?"

"Oh good grief!" Kristal cried impatiently.

"Well? You told me yourself you're a sensitive. You've seen ghosts before, you've seen *things*. Certain people can attract stuff like that to them. They can tune in to the spirits."

"And you think I'm like that? You think I'm . . . like those people in the book you showed me, the ones who took the weird pictures?"

"Yes . . . I think you are. You do tune in. You're like a . . . a tape recorder or a video tape, something like that. You record things that other people can't see or hear."

The coldness still oozed over Kristal's skin, a chill as icy as the cloud of death that had risen over the dead jogger in Ann Arbor. The dreams. The pictures. The black sand she had found in her room.

"Donnie, I don't believe you!" Her voice rose, quivered at the edge of hysteria. "I just don't believe you at all!"

A shark. Jesus, it was the biggest shark Buddy had ever imagined or thought of or seen pictures of. Its length was terrifying, dwarfing Buddy and dwarfing the cave too, as if the shadows it came from were barely large enough to contain it. The big form was evil in its grace, the undulant writhe of muscle and tail and fins. It twisted toward Buddy, aiming directly at him so that he could see the mammoth blunt head, sense the raw, primitive force.

The eyes glared at Buddy balefully.

Jesus, Jesus, those black eyes knew him, could look right at him, deep into his soul and know all the things about Buddy Southworth. *Eyes. Black.* Almost human, brooding at him, sucking at him, angry, full of dark pain.

And then the huge beast rammed at him, so close that the rasp of its skin scraped Buddy's wet suit like a huge file, tearing at the neoprene as if it had been crepe paper.

Power in the water, shock and vibration. The shark twisted away toward the depths of the cave again. Buddy's jaw was clenched down on the mouthpiece of his regulator so hard, he could feel the pain deep in the sockets of his teeth. A dull pain numbed his leg. Was it bleeding? Blood, he remembered with a raw, gagging choke, attracted sharks. Only a few droplets could cause them to go into a feeding frenzy. A spasmic orgy of slaughter.

Was he bleeding? *God, was he?* But he dared not look down at his leg now. The animal had turned and was making another pass at him, glaring at him with those terrible eyes.

Fear flashed in Buddy's mind. *Those eyes knew him.* He was sure of it. Knew him and were filled with smouldering fury directed at him alone, at Buddy Southworth. But how could that be?

The shark lunged past with a giant slash of its tail that pounded the water beside Buddy and sent him reeling into the wall of the cave, his tank slamming into rock.

Those black, baleful eyes. They reminded Buddy of someone. His heart pounded sickeningly inside his chest as he clung to the coral cave wall, waiting for the shark to make another pass at him.

Kam Smith. Buddy's breath came in quick wheezes. That's who those eyes were like. Kam Smith, with his black, fathomless eyes that looked as if they had seen the worst in the world, as if they had suffered for hundreds, thousands of years, and were suffering still.

There was a flash of something dark at the cave mouth. Was it the shark going out? Buddy hoped so. His teeth were clenched down on the rubber mouthpiece so hard that he thought he had bitten through it. In his terror he had forgotten again about his buoyancy, and now he was sinking downward once more. The tips of his flippers scraped sand again, kicking it up in sluggish yellow clouds.

Buddy glanced down at the cloud of sand, and for the second time his eyes saw the white object. Now that he was closer, and the shark was gone, he knew what it was . . . his mother's needlepoint.

Jesus Christ, it was his mother's needlework canvas, and it was lying here on the floor of a lava cave forty feet under the surface of the ocean, and *how had it got here?* In the name of God how, and why did the shark have Kam's eyes and . . .

Buddy glanced again at the pressure gauge. He had only 100 pounds of air left. God, he was almost out, he had almost nothing left. He had to get out of the cave. But was the shark still at the entrance?

Buddy, Buddy, don't think of that. Don't suck air. Just relax . . . relax . . .

Biting down on the mouthpiece until his jaws ground with pain, he started toward the cave mouth, forcing his breath to go in and out shallowly. *Breathe, exhale . . . That's it. That's it, Buddy . . .*

As he kicked over it, he glanced down involuntarily at the canvas again. Through the air space of his mask, he glimpsed the design. Someone had stitched in the missing yarn.

An obscenity it was, almost Oriental or Indian in flavor, the big shape and the smaller curved one. And what they were doing was— Buddy gasped and gagged. What they were doing was monstrous. God, he had never seen anything like it, or thought of such a thing, not even in his most lustful fantasies.

Two figures, wound together, penetrated together, and one was . . . one had . . .

Buddy cried out into his regulator and fled toward the mouth of the cave.

Flat, blue water, empty. Mick and Lisa were nowhere in sight. They must have scrammed as soon as the big shark boiled out of the cave. *Scared,* Buddy thought raggedly. Mick had been scared shitless after all. That figured.

He pulled on his regulator and got nothing, nothing but tightness and the taste of empty hose. Air. No more air. He was out.

Somehow he managed to remember the routine he had learned in the dive class. Toss the regulator out of his mouth. Rip off the weight belt and throw it away from him so that he couldn't be caught in its webbing. Start finning rapidly upwards, then fling himself on his back to slow down his speed, ride upwards on his back so that his belly would be the first part of his body to break the surface.

And above all, keep humming.

Ooooooo mmmmmmmm ooooooooo. Don't stop humming, or all that compressed air he'd breathed at forty feet would keep expanding in his lungs until it exploded his cells, burst them apart, little air bubbles perking like soda pop through his blood and brain.

The surface came toward him. It was sun-tossed,

wave-washed, and it was Jesus beautiful. Buddy reached it alongside his own bubbles, and he still had enough air to let his belly break the surface first. Then he was treading water and had enough presence of mind to inflate the B.C. vest so that it would float him like a life jacket.

Perfect. Just as he had been taught in class . . . by Kam.

Sun splashed down and, remembering the shark, Buddy drew his flippers upwards toward his chest. He thought about the movie *Jaws,* which he had seen three times. He remembered the expression on the face of the swimming girl as the big maneater began to work on her legs.

A shout reached him.

"Buddy! Buddy! Jeez, did you see it? Did you see that big mother? A tiger it was, the one I saw before! It must've been a fucking twenty, thirty feet. I told you, I told you!"

Mick and Lisa were already on shore by the rocks. Both of them were jumping up and down and waving at him, shading their eyes so they could see him better against the sun glare of late afternoon. Lisa had already taken off her tank and set it down on the rocks.

They had gone off and left him. After all his big talk about caves, Mick hadn't even dared go in this one, and he and his sister had both panicked at the sight of the big shark. They had swum off and left him to be eaten. The bastards. The dirty bastards.

Buddy began swimming toward shore, in his fury forgetting everything except what he was going to say to Mick.

But he didn't say anything to Mick, as it turned out. When he had reached the rocks, he was too tired, and the surge was tossing him about like a cork. He needed Mick to help haul him out of the surf, and by the time he had dragged himself onto the wet rocks and Lisa was stripping the tank from him, he had already started to feel sick.

Sick somewhere deep inside him, an ugly, shaking feeling that was like a thousand cases of the flu all rolled up into one. Every pore of his skin ached, and his gullet was one long tube of agony. His last thought before he collapsed at Lisa's feet was of the shark's eyes.

Human and inhuman all at once, burning with pain and loneliness and fury. Kam Smith's eyes. The eyes that looked at his mother in ways Dad's never had.

Chapter 15

Buddy was aware of being half dragged, half carried the long way back up the lava path to the car, where he was shoved into the back seat amid a litter of diving gear.

As the car swayed back and forth on the rough Kaunoa Road, he could hear snatches of Mick and Lisa's conversation.

"Jesus, that path, I thought I was going to die, that kid must weigh a ton. And what happened to him, do you think he embolized?"

"Shut up, Lisa, shut up, you little shit. He didn't embolize, how could he, he was all right when he came up, he waved to us, there wasn't a thing wrong with him."

"But he's sick, Mick. There is something wrong with

him. Maybe it was those mushrooms, maybe they did something to him—"

"Shut up, I said!"

"But, Mick, Mom's going to blow her mind when she finds out what we did. She said we were never supposed to dive without telling her, not after last time when you— And the mushrooms, Mick . . . what if Buddy tells her? You know what she said about dope, you know what she'll do. God, we shouldn't have taken him there." Her voice whined. "It was your idea, Mick, not mine. You wanted to show him— Now they'll blame us—"

"They won't blame us if you keep your stupid trap shut and don't say anything."

"But, Mick—"

"Shut up, Lisa, just shut up, and keep him quiet, too. It's bad enough he's sick, don't make it worse. Or I'll take you back under and I'll feed you to that damned big tiger shark, see if I don't."

"You wouldn't. You didn't even dare go up to it, Mick Rogers, you just turned and ran like a scared rabbit. I bet you even peed in your wet suit."

"Shut up! Shut up!"

Buddy let the words pass over him. He slouched against the seat, his backbone feeling like Play-doh. A gear bag slammed into him as the car swerved around a bend. Those eyes. Those terrible shark eyes.

He couldn't get them out of his mind. A shark with eyes like Kam Smith's. Jesus, what was he thinking? He was crazy. A shark with human eyes? With the eyes of one particular human being, a man who happened to teach scuba diving in a dive shop in Kihei, Maui? It was ridiculous, fantastic, weirder than any science fiction story he had ever read. God, he really was sick to think such a half-assed thing.

Buddy twisted on the seat, choking back a groan.

Pain had begun to radiate all through his body now, torturing his nerve ends. In fact, thrusting out one bare forearm, he could almost see the pain, gouging up on his skin like a welt.

What had happened to him down there? *Had* he embolized?

No, he felt pretty sure that he hadn't. For one thing, he had hummed religiously all the way up. He hadn't been down long enough or deep enough to have the bends, he knew that too. It had only been as Mick was pulling him out of the water that he started to feel sick.

Sick . . . Jesus, he felt terrible. Was he coming down with something awful? He felt as if he were one throbbing, burning boil . . .

"We'll get him in the house somehow," Mick was saying in the front seat, "and tell his mom he's coming down with the flu or something."

"But the dive—"

"Oh, shut up," Mick said impatiently. "We'll take care of it, we'll think of something, don't we always? And get rid of those goddamned mushrooms, will you? Throw them out the car window. The last thing we need is for her to catch them on us. She'd really kill us then."

"Yeah," Lisa agreed gloomily. "She'll send us to school over in northern Minnesota or Wisconsin or somewhere, and it'll be a military school; my God, we'll be prisoners."

"No, we won't be," said Mick. "So just let me drive, will you and quit your bitching?"

In the house Buddy was only half conscious of the television set on and his sister curled up in front of it, watching dully. Her face looked kind of white and funny. A woman on the television set was singing a jingle about lipsticks. His Mom wasn't there. Out shopping, he supposed, buying stuff for Christmas Eve. Or maybe she was on a date with Kam Smith.

Kam Smith. Jesus, those dark terrible eyes that burned at you, accused . . .

Kam Smith's eyes belonging to a shark? It was a crazy dream brought on by the mushrooms, that was it. He'd had a bad trip, a delayed reaction from all those sickening mushrooms he'd forced himself to gag down.

He tried to hold back a groan as Mick walked him past the television set in the direction of the hallway and his own room.

"What's wrong with him?" Kristal asked as they went by.

"We were at the beach, is all," Mick answered.

"He looks terrible to me."

"Well, he's not. Are you, Buddy, old guy?" Mick jabbed him in the ribs so hard, Buddy had to gasp for air. The red-hot poker in his gullet seemed to pierce him even further, to sear right down into his solar plexus.

Inside his own room Buddy fell face first onto the bed. Behind him, he could hear Mick closing the door. He lay where he had fallen, smelling the clean, linty odor of the chenille bedspread.

"Listen . . ." Mick's face was right by his, square, grim, mean. ". . . listen, you asshole, you better not say one word to your mother about what we did today. I mean the mushrooms or the dive at the lava flow. Get that?"

"Mmmm, yeah . . ." Buddy was past caring what Mick said to him out of that twisted mouth.

"Because if you dare squeal . . ." Mick's hands gripped Buddy's shoulders, pinching like flames. "I'll take you back to the lava flow and drag you down to the rocks and throw you in the water. And I'll cut your legs first so you'll bleed a lot, and I'll slice you up into little bites and feed you to that big damn tiger shark, do you hear me?"

"Fuck you," Buddy managed to say with the last

breath left in him before he let his face roll into the bedspread. Then he was unconscious.

Dusk had fallen, and the spectacular Maui sunset filled the sky with a hundred shades of salmon-pink, orange, red, fuscia, purple.

"Mom?" Kristal said as Ann came in through the door, her arms filled with grocery sacks and packages. "Mom, there's something wrong with Buddy. He's sick, I think."

"Sick?" Ann thrust the bags onto the dinette table and righted one that had started to tilt. "How sick?"

"I don't know. Mick brought him back here about two hours ago, and he just sort of staggered past and went to his room. He's there now. I went in twice to look at him, but he's sleeping. He groaned a little in his sleep. I tried to bring him a glass of water, but he didn't want it."

"Okay, honey. You did all you could. I'll go look."

Briskly Ann walked toward her son's room and pulled open the door. He lay sprawled face down on the bed wearing nothing but a pair of cutoff shorts. Pink shades from the sunset had seeped through the lanai door, giving everything, including the prone Buddy, a roseate tint.

"Buddy? Bud, are you all right? Krissie said you were sick."

Buddy stirred. Slowly, with enormous effort, he turned over. Then he opened his eyes. For a second their expression was blank, focusing on the wall behind Ann. Then gradually a normal expression crept into them.

"I'm all right, Mom. I'm okay now." Was there a frightened look on her son's face? "I— I just felt kind of funny this afternoon for a while, is all. I might be coming down with the flu."

Buddy touched his own right arm, staring down at it

with a look of puzzlement. Then Ann saw him glance down at his leg. He swallowed experimentally.

"The flu?" Ann was worried. "Let me feel your forehead. Damn, I wish we had a fever thermometer. I guess I can borrow one from Susan . . . or I'll run down to the drug store and get one. You'd think you could go on a vacation without having to bring things like thermometers . . ."

All the while she talked, she was feeling the smooth, damp surface of her son's skin. "Nope, no fever. You're just as cool as Grandma's cucumber salad. Any sore throat?"

Buddy swallowed again. For the second time, his face looked bewildered.

"No . . ." He said it slowly. "I thought . . . this afternoon, Mom, my throat felt different, like somebody stuck an old hot poker down it. And my skin was all hot and burning."

"Well, you look fine now." She stared sharply at her son. Actually, she thought, his eyes looked glazed, as if he had seen something terrible, as if he had witnessed a dreadful accident, or had seen a ghost . . .

"Better just rest tonight," she told him, "and take it easy. It's Christmas Eve already, did you know that? I bought some eggnog at Superette and some chips and dip. I thought we'd all wrap our gifts and put them under the tree."

"Tree?"

"I bought a little tree too. Really, it's a terribly small one, and it's artificial, but we can't have Christmas without a tree, can we, even if this is Hawaii?"

"No, I guess not."

"And tomorrow," Ann went on valiantly, "tomorrow we're having a big Christmas dinner. I bought a turkey, and we're going to have that, and we're getting together with Susan and Cliff and the kids, and I invited Kam Smith too. He said he'd come."

"Kam Smith?" Buddy's eyes seemed to flick with alarm. "Aw, Mom—"

"Don't *aw Mom* me," she snapped. Unaccountably her voice was shaking. "I know you don't like him, but it's Christmas, Buddy. We're going to have a nice Christmas, a good one, do you hear me? And I don't want you to be sick. I want you to fight it, I want us all to be—"

Her voice broke off. *Happy,* she had almost said. *I want us all to be happy.*

Buddy looked at his mother as if he knew and loathed the word that she had almost blurted. His face looked ravaged or was it only the glowing pink light from the sunset, streaming in to wash the gold bedspread with its color?

"What were you doing today?" something made Ann ask.

Buddy hesitated. "Diving."

"Where? With Mick and Lisa?"

"Yes, with Mick and Lisa, damn them."

"I thought they were your friends. I thought you liked them."

"Well, I don't."

"I suppose you'll make it up with them tomorrow. You'd better, it's Christmas. Anyway, Buddy, you'd better tell me before you dive again next time. Okay? I don't like you going out without me knowing. Remember what Kam said about—"

"Okay, okay." Buddy's lips twisted. "Listen. Did you ever find your needlepoint, Mom?"

"What? My needlepoint?" For an instant Ann stared at her son. A little alarm was thrumming through her, although she couldn't say exactly why. Something was wrong, though. She could feel it.

"Your needlepoint canvas. The one you lost." Buddy wouldn't look at her.

"No, I haven't found it. Do you know where it is?"

"Nope. Just let me alone, Mom, will you? I don't want any eggnog, I don't want anything." Buddy turned his face to the wall. "I just want to go to sleep."

It was Christmas Day. Ann had gotten up early to stuff the turkey, a job not easily accomplished in the small, unfamiliar kitchen that was not very well equipped. She searched all over for skewers with which to fasten shut the dressing cavity and finally stitched it shut with undyed Persian wool.

It just didn't seem like Christmas, she thought as she hurried about. It was too sunny, and too hot, and there were papayas ripening on the kitchen counter, vivid Hawaiian blossoms in a vase in the center of the dining table. The small tree she'd bought and hastily decorated seemed out of place.

There had been a satisfactory assortment of gifts under the tree, Ann had seen to that. Buddy got a new Chronosport dive watch, a diving light, and a boogie board to use in the surf. Kristal got a new lens for her camera, a deluxe book on photography, and a delicate salmon-pink coral bracelet that Ann had bought at the Makai Town Center.

From Kristal, Ann had received a lacy nightgown and peignoir set (for whom was she supposed to wear it? Ann wondered), and from Buddy a statuette of a humpbacked whale.

The unwrapping of the packages had taken only minutes, all three of them grimly tearing off paper as if to get it over with as quickly as possible. Neither Buddy nor Kristal mentioned their father, but his spirit seemed to haunt them all, and it was with relief that Ann finally bundled up the last scraps of holiday wrapping paper into a garbage bag and set it outside the back door.

Well, that's over, she thought. *Thank God we don't have another Christmas for twelve months.* She immediately felt ashamed of herself and went back into the house to hug her daughter and pat her son's shoulder affectionately.

"You're pretty good kids, did you know that?" she told them. "Not into too much trouble, good mannered, fun to be with, and easy to get along with—most of the time, anyway! Not very many parents are as lucky as I am, I guess."

"Aw, Mom," Buddy said. He still looked pale, and he had dragged out of bed this morning to open his gifts as if that act required all of his strength.

Kristal said nothing, looking at her mother with eyes that were wide and blue and distant.

"Well—" Embarrassed, Ann patted her daughter's shoulder, then went back into the kitchen. She hoped that the arrival of Mick and Lisa in an hour or so and the distribution of presents to Mary Tanaka's three youngsters would cheer things up. Otherwise she was sure it was going to be a very long, long day.

Mary and her children—three slim brown-skinned little girls who tore into their gifts with almost manic enthusiasm—had finally left. Susan Rogers, clad in a long and garish blue muumuu, ignored her glum husband to sail into Ann's kitchen. She carried a tray laden with holiday goodies.

"Pies!" she cried. "Two cherry and one apple. None of my family can stand pumpkin or mince, what about yours? And I baked some Christmas cookies too. They were out of a package, but what the hell, a little green food coloring and no one knows the difference anyway. Fuck all those fancy chefs."

Susan, it seemed, had already been enjoying some Christmas libation at home. She plucked Handi-Wrap off the plateful of cookies, tasted one, and then slid the plate onto the dining table by the hors d'oeuvres Ann had prepared.

"There," she said. "Let the cockroaches feast on this if they dare."

Ann poured more eggnog, mixed Scotch and water. She got out cokes for Mick and Lisa and Buddy, fruit juice for Kristal.

Somehow the day began to inch along. The four teenagers escaped to the lanai as soon as they had made their obligatory greetings. Susan and Cliff and Ann all sat with their drinks, waiting for Kam Smith to arrive.

Susan's talk flowed nonstop. She repeated hotel gossip, carped at Cliff because he had not repaired the small bulldozer sitting in their yard, and told a story about a female tourist who had had hysterics when she saw a gecko run up the wall of the hotel dining room.

"Christ, this is the tropics, for God's sake, what do people expect? The poor little geckos are harmless things —we've got three of them living on the outside of our bedroom window and two in the mailbox, and do I have hysterics every time I see one? No, I do not. If I did, it'd get to be damned boring."

"The damned things crap in all the cupboards, though," Cliff put in sourly.

Susan ignored him. She swirled the ice around in her drink glass, frowning at it. "People," she went on. "What asses they can be. Remember that movie, *Jaws?* Remember when that came? Nobody'd go down to the beach, they all thought they were going to get—"

Susan's voice broke off as the sound of a car motor rumbled up the driveway. She looked questioningly at Ann.

"It's Kam Smith," Ann said.

Susan made a loose, teasing face, an expression that told Ann she had better consider Kam only a harmless flirtation. "Your handsome beach boy, kiddo? God knows, you can pick em."

"He's *not* a—"

"Isn't he?" Susan's eyes had gone vaguely glazed. She hoisted her drink to stare at its melting ice cubes. "Besides, I was just talking about sharks and all. Kam can tell you about that. It was his girlfriend who was the last known shark incident around here."

"What?"

"Sure. Sure, didn't I tell you? She got it in the water just like that silly girl in *Jaws*. Some unlucky tourist and his boy were the ones who found her. Out looking for a goodie bag and found another kind of goodie instead."

Susan leaned forward, giggling.

Chapter 16

"Hello, Ann. Thank you for inviting me. I hope you have a good holiday." Kam leaned forward to kiss her, and Ann's heart began its swooping flutter.

She imagined that his entrance into the living room caused a subtle change. Once Kam's big muscular body crossed the threshhold, everything inside seemed smaller somehow, darker and more cramped. The plants Susan had hung about seemed suddenly silly.

Susan shifted about on the love seat, recrossing her legs and adjusting the skirt of her muumuu. Cliff Rogers stared at the newcomer sullenly.

As for Ann, she felt her blood begin to pound in quickened rhythm. What *was* it about this man that could capture her so? She struggled to understand it. His looks? He was handsome, no one could deny that. There was a magnetism about him, a force that seemed to radiate, crackling, into the room. He wore beige pants and a faded Hawiian shirt open at the throat to reveal brown skin and a faint beating pulse.

Carefully Kam greeted everyone. He walked out on the lanai to speak to the four teenagers who sat perched on the railing with their pop cans.

"A drink, Kam? What will you have?" Ann asked when he had returned. "There's bourbon, Scotch, and eggnog spiked or unspiked. And of course, I've got soft drinks too, and some fruit juice, passion orange, I think . . ."

"A bourbon and water will be fine."

"Well, Kam Smith, diving instructor," Susan began when he had sat down on the love seat opposite her. "We were just talking about you— Well, almost."

"Talking about me?"

"I was telling Ann here about shark attacks on beaches and about that girlfriend of yours who got it— what was her name?"

"Karen Weeks."

It seemed to Ann that she could feel a change in the air around Kam, a chilling. His eyes were hard black stones as he stared at Susan. But Ann's cousin continued, unabashed.

"What happened to her anyway? People said some really funny things. They hushed it up, nobody'll talk now, nobody really knows. As for those people who found her, I feel sorry for them. I mean, I heard the poor little kid practically upchucked into his snorkel. It was not your average tourist day at the beach . . ."

Ann sat frozen. Kristal, she noticed, had come in from the lanai to sit curled on the floor by the sliding glass door. Her daughter's face looked drained of all color.

"It was an unfortunate and tragic accident," Kam said quietly.

"Oh, hell yes, it was really tragic to get gnawed in half by a shark. Do you know the damned things can take a twenty-pound bite out of you?"

Susan tilted up her drink and took another long sip. Something was eating at her, Ann realized. Did it have something to do with that squat, glum husband of hers, or the two children who, Ann had gathered, were a bit wild and definitely a headache?

A little silence had fallen into the room, echoing against the walls. Kam—there was no other word for it—was glowering.

"Look, let's change the subject, shall we?" Ann said brightly. "This is Christmas Day, and isn't it a gorgeous one? Sun on Christmas, and just imagine being able to go swimming after you've eaten your turkey dinner. That seems amazing to me after Michigan, and I can't get used to seeing palm trees on Christmas . . ."

She kept on chattering, saying anything that came into her head, for there was something in the room, something dark and wrong. Susan sat huddled over her drink, her expression drunk and angry and discontented. Beside her, Cliff would not look at his wife. Kristal had begun to stare out of the window, her mouth bleak.

But most of all, the wrongness seemed to center about Kam himself, in the way he sat, his body held unnaturally still, every muscle in perfect control. It was only his eyes that were not under control. They stared outwards, through the sliding glass doors toward the sea, and their expression seemed almost to burn.

For Buddy, Christmas Day passed on caterpillar feet, inchingly slow. He had awakened feeling drugged and dull and apprehensive, although he wasn't sure of what. He'd had to spend the whole day pretending.

First had come the Christmas gifts. He had to act as if he enjoyed opening them, act like a damned kid again, ripping off paper and throwing it on the floor just as he'd done last year, and the year before. Like he had when Dad had been alive.

This year Dad wasn't alive. This year they were here on Maui, and he was opening presents he didn't deserve. He was a thief, a dirty father-robbing thief, and he should've got nothing. There should've been coal in his stocking instead of a dive watch.

But he had forced himself to pretend to like the watch, and, really, it was a nice one. Big, easily readable, with a nice bezel that he could use to set the time when he started to make a dive. Besides, his mother had bought it for him, and he'd been painfully aware of her eyes fixed on him as he opened the package. She wanted him to like it. She wanted him to be delighted with his gifts, happy with today, to have everything just as it was before.

Didn't she know things couldn't be like that again? What was wrong with her, anyway? There were times when Buddy felt himself vastly older than his mother, times when he felt almost a pity for her. Did she think she could buy back his love and regard? Did she think a goddamned trip to Maui would do it? Or diving gear, or a watch, or presents, or putting her goddamned arm around him, or anything . . . anything at all?

At Ann's request he helped Mary Tanaka's little ones with their gifts, a glum Santa Claus. He watched them all drive away in Mary's ancient car, feeling sad. He was still sunk in misery when the Rogers arrived and Mick and Lisa dragged him out on the lanai.

"Did you tell?" Mick whispered at once, pulling him off into a corner by the railing where there was a small plastic-topped table and two yellow chairs.

"No, I didn't," Buddy snapped. "Besides, she didn't ask much, and I was feeling a lot better by the time she got home anyway."

He wasn't feeling all that well now, though, he noticed. His hearing seemed funny, as if sounds came from a very long distance down a tunnel. And his arms itched. Not much, but they itched Absently he scratched.

Mick looked relieved. "Well, you didn't embolize then. What was wrong with you, too much playing around with your own dork?"

He nudged Buddy, and gave a cackling laugh that sounded amazingly like his father's. A surge of dislike went through Buddy.

"We've got some more *pakalolo*," whispered Lisa. "Want some? You've gotta pay $25, though, that's your share. Mick and I got the car last night and we picked it up in Lahaina. From a friend of Mick's." Her eyes were glittering in her round face, and she wore a pair of new polyester slacks that were too tight around her bottom and showed the elastic of her bikini panties.

"Sure," Buddy said sarcastically, "sure I want to smoke some more dope after those great mushrooms we ate. Maybe I can get sick again. I'd really like that."

"Yeah, yeah, yeah." Lisa made a face. Yesterday could've happened a hundred years ago for all it mattered to her.

Kristal prowled the lanai, taking pictures with her new wide-angle lens. She asked the three of them to pose. Safely away from visibility of the house, Mick clowned around, giving Kristal the finger and pointing obscenely at Lisa's rear end.

It was then that Kam Smith arrived and walked out onto the lanai to greet them.

"Hello, Buddy." He spoke in that stuffy Eastern accent that Buddy didn't see how he could have gotten on Maui; it just didn't fit the island or Kam. It was only one more strange thing about Kam Smith, whom he had decided he didn't like at all.

And especially now, he didn't like Kam, for the man was staring at him. Staring. And his eyes—Jesus, they were just like two black coals, fixed on Buddy, burning at him, sucking at him, as if they could draw Buddy's soul right out and hang it up to dry. *Those eyes knew*.

Buddy stood with his back against the lanai railing and felt as cold-stone scared as he had ever felt in his life. Jesus, it was as if Kam Smith *knew what Buddy had done yesterday*. Knew how he had swum down inside that cave, had seen the needlepoint with its obscene nightmare picture, and had seen, too, the evil, sinuous grace of the shark that had Kam's eyes . . .

Or did Kam have the shark's eyes?

It seemed an eternity that Buddy stood pinned there, caught by the burning intensity of the dive instructor's look. But it could have been only a second or two, for Kristal was already sliding in front of them to snap a picture of himself and Kam.

Abruptly Kam stirred. "Don't take any more pictures of me."

"Why not?" Kristal was nervously defiant. "It's Christmas, isn't it?"

"I am not photogenic, and there are many other things to capture with your camera. Go down to the sea and photograph the movement of the surf. The waves are beautiful, Kristal. They are always changing, yet ever the same."

The four teenagers stared at him. The adults they knew did not talk like this.

Abruptly Kam turned and went through the sliding glass door and back into the house again to join the adults.

"Weird, man," Mick said.

"Yeah," Lisa agreed.

For some reason Buddy's eyes met those of his sister, and the two exchanged a look.

"I'm going to take some more pictures of him," Kristal said softly.

And—although he wasn't quite sure why—Buddy felt a quiver of fear in his gut. His throat was beginning to hurt again, too, as it had yesterday. The skin on his arm felt itchy and funny. He guessed he must be coming down with the flu, after all.

Kristal too found the day full of unease. She had been frightened when Kam Smith tried to stop her from getting his picture. But she had taken it anyway—what could he do to her here in her own house with her mother and Aunt Susan and Uncle Cliff right here? How could he possibly hurt her?

Still, she wished that Donnie Perriera had been here too. At least he'd be somebody she could talk to. He wouldn't laugh at her, as Buddy often did, and he wouldn't call her a baby.

They ate dinner, the large Norbest turkey that Ann had spent the day roasting. It came out perfectly, its white meat moist and succulent. Everyone raved about the turkey and said how good it tasted, but Kristal could not help noticing that no one seemed to be digging in with much gusto.

Buddy, for example, spent most of the meal pushing the canned cranberry sauce around on his plate with his fork. Canned cranberry sauce. It was really symbolic of this holiday, Kristal thought, with its artificial tree, the hot sunlight, and the garish bougainvillea for a centerpiece.

Aunt Susan, she saw, had had too much to drink. The word *fuck* had crept more and more into her aunt's conversation. But evidently she used the word a lot, for nobody paid it any attention, at least not sour old Uncle Cliff, who spent most of the meal complaining about the high cost of living here on Maui. Mick and Lisa were talking about diving again. They wanted to go out on a charter boat called the *Odysseus.* It operated out of Lahaina.

Sharply their father informed them that he couldn't afford it. Did they think he was made of money like the lousy tourists who could afford to blow $20 apiece over at the Makai Golf Course just to play eighteen holes? He, Cliff, liked to play golf, too, but he was damned if he would pay $20 just to bat a ball around a course.

After dinner they all went in the living room again and sat around talking some more. Ann told everyone not to worry about the dishes, she and the kids would do them later. Talk buzzed in the room like sleepy bees. Kam sat near her mother and kept devouring her with those black eyes of his.

Kristal tried not to look at the way her mother's hand accidentally brushed Kam's thigh, the way Kam seemed to talk only to her. There was electricity between the two of them, she decided uneasily. Did anyone else in the room notice it? She thought her Aunt Susan did, the way Susan kept looking at the two of them. But Cliff was too busy talking about high prices at the grocery store, and Buddy was morose, saying nothing to anyone. Mick and Lisa, as usual, were absorbed in themselves.

"Show off your pictures, honey," Ann said suddenly, during a lull in her conversation with Kam. "I've been telling Kam how good you are, Krissie. He wants to see what you've done."

"Oh, Mom—"

"She *is* very good, you know," Ann explained to Kam. "She's taken some gorgeous shots while she's been here, good enough to go on a post card or on a calendar, if you ask me."

"*Mom—*"

"Yes," Kam said. "Go and get your pictures, Kristal. I'd really like to see them."

So there was no choice but for Kristal to go into her bedroom and get out the shoe box in which she was temporarily storing her work.

Hesitantly she took out the first photograph, one of the sunset shots, and held it up.

"Another fucking Hawaiian sunset," Susan put in, her drink tilting dangerously. She peered at the picture. "Sunsets are as common as sand here. Every fucking day another one, and another one after that . . ."

"You're the one who wanted to come here," Cliff said.

"Sure, I wanted to come to paradise, who the fucking hell wouldn't? But there isn't any paradise, Cliff, old boy . . . ever notice that? All there is is bills and more bills and bitching and moaning and cockroaches in the kitchen and mice in the drawers. And the goddamned fucking sunset that keeps coming every goddamned night whether you want it or not, and whether or not you can afford to pay for it . . .." Abruptly Susan was crying into her drink, and Cliff was staring into space.

Kristal stood with the shoe box, embarrassed. 'Here," she said to Kam in the silence that filled the room. "Here are my pictures, you can look through them if you want. I took a lot down at the beach. I was trying to get some of the rocks and stones in the tidal pools. Rocks are beautiful, don't you think? I love them. All the colors and textures . . ."

"Yes." Surprisingly, Kam was agreeing with her. He leafed carefully through the loose photos. "You should have this one enlarged," he commented, holding one up.

Kristal nodded. A small, curious fish, darting among perfect, round rocks. Yes, it was certainly one of her best. Beautiful enough to appear in *National Geographic*, or *Natural History*. She subscribed to both. Perhaps she'd ask Donnie about it.

"What's this one?" Kam asked, holding up another photograph.

Kristal leaned forward to look at it. "Oh, that. It's just one of my goofs." She reached forward, intending to take the picture from him, but Kam would not release it, and now he began to examine it carefully.

Kristal felt alarm twist in the pit of her belly. It was no goof that Kam Smith held in his hand. It was the shot she had taken at Lani Beach, the one that showed the clouds hanging over the rocks and, beneath them, the strange white object that looked exactly like a woman's naked dead body.

"Please," she begged. "That— That's one of my bad pictures. I didn't mean to put it in with the good ones, I don't know how it got there."

"What's that cloud?" Kam was scowling. "There, to the right."

"That's overexposure or something."

"And this." Kam pointed. "This down here, on the rocks. It looks like a woman."

Kristal snatched at the picture, thrust it back among the others. "Somebody swimming in the water," she said quickly. "It didn't come out right. I hate this picture."

Kam was looking at her. His black eyes lifted from the shoe box to stare into her own, searching her out.

And then Ann rescued her daughter by reaching into the shoe box and pulling out another shot, exclaiming over it.

"Very beautiful," Kam said. "I think, Ann, that your daughter does indeed have ability. Talent, perhaps, of the most unusual sort."

That night—Christmas night—the dream began for Kristal as usual, with a field of misty blue water floating with tiny specks of plankton. But this time she seemed to get into the shark's mind even faster than usual. She twisted and writhed under the covers, crying out as the dream began.

Sunlight flooded down into the water, making glittering chains of reflections on the sand and coral bottom. *He* arrowed through the water. Proud muscles flexed, gloried in the feel of their own power.

But tonight there was something different. Not a food frenzy tonight, nor the abyssal loneliness that always caused Kristal to weep in her sleep. Tonight there was purpose, a reason for the powerful slice through the water, a destination. And in a few short seconds Kristal saw what it was.

They were finning up toward shore, toward a place where a deeper channel cut toward the beach. Clouds of sand were stirred up by the surge, to plume back and forth, forming ridged ripples. Then, suddenly there she was. A woman diving out from the rocks, her bare brown body lithe in the water, as sinuous in her own way as the shark was in his. She was utterly naked, her black hair streaming out from her as she swam.

And, Kristal saw with horror, her swim, too, had purpose. She was swimming to where the shark waited for her in the deepest channel. Oh yes, surely that was her intent . . .

In the shark emotions boiled. Swelled up in him like a huge tide, engulfed him like the feeding frenzy, frantic, urgent. *I want . . . I want . . . I'm lonely, so lonely. I need, I must have . . .* Something was happening within the shark's body—an engorgement, a stiffening, a readying . . .

Kristal tossed and turned more violently now. She groaned aloud as the shark's powerful form lunged to-toward the swimming woman, making a pass so close to her that the sandpaper hide abraded soft skin. Soft, her skin was, dear God, how soft, and when the shark's skin scraped it, it bled raw red fluid into the water.

Yet still the woman, as if possessed by some dreadful compulsion, kept swimming, her naked legs kicking, her pubic thatch plainly visible. Now she was diving beneath the water, and he . . .

He swam to meet her.

The woman twisted in the water, arched herself like the most fragile of flower blossoms. Naked, she was, and ready . . .

The shark lunged toward her, bending snakelike. Kristal hadn't believed that the long, powerful, spotted body could be so dextrous, could wrap itself so ardently around anything, could clasp . . .

Clasp.

Dear God, dear Jesus!

What was it? What was happening? What was happening?

Thrusting. Thrusting into softness, into bleeding orifice . . . grinding, orgasmic joining. She gripped him, her strength like steel, her head flung back, agonized, and she was coming . . .

AND HE . . . HE . . .

DEAR GOD. OH, GOD . . . GOD . . .

Chapter 17

Kristal shrieked in terror as she ran out of her bedroom, pajama top flying, to her mother's room.

"Mom! Mom! Mom!" This time Kristal didn't care about the thread she had left to bar the doorway, or the sinister things that might appear on her dresser in the morning, or the fact that someone might laugh at her, call her baby. She had to get out of that room, had to escape the obscenity of that underwater scene.

Kristal's mind could not encompass what she had just experienced. It was all she could do to yank open the door of Ann's room and stumble to where her mother, curled on her side, slept heavily.

"Oh, Mom! Wake up, Mom! It was terrible, terrible! Oh, he—" But already Kristal could not remember exactly what had happened, what the dream had been about.

Ann stirred and mumbled sleepily. Kristal pulled

back the bedcovers and climbed under them, burrowing up against the warmth of her mother's body.

"Krissie?" Ann mumbled.

"Mom— I had a nightmare—"

"Another one?" Ann sat up and switched on the bedside light.

"Awful, it was awful, Mom, the worst one of all, I can't tell you, I can't explain—"

"But, darling—"

Helplessly Kristal cried and felt her mother's arms go about her and was ashamed of being so easily comforted. As long as she was in her arms, it hadn't happened at all, she hadn't been in *his* mind and seen the— The shudder shook her whole body.

"Honey, honey, it was just a dream, that's all," Ann's voice soothed. "Just a bad dream."

Kristal drew back a little, to stare at her mother. Ann's face was softly beautiful in the lamplight, her cheekbones delicate, blonde hair falling to her shoulders. Her skin was bare under the nightgown Kristal had given her today for Christmas. Yes, her mother's body was as soft and lovely as the woman's in the dream . . .

A knot of horror stiffened her. She felt cold with the shock of it. For it wasn't hard to imagine her mother's form in the place of that brown woman in the water. Her mother, nude, twisting gracefully through the water to meet that long, powerful shape . . .

"Krissie? Krissie, is anything wrong?"

"Oh, Mom—" Kristal's voice choked. She stared at her mother, unable to speak. What was there to say? *I saw a terrible thing in my dream, I saw a shark and a . . . a naked woman. The woman could have been you, Mom. I think it might be going to be you . . .*

"Krissie, honey, I want you to stop this right now. I want you to calm down. Dreams aren't real, surely you know that. Dreams are only little pieces of thought that your unconscious plays around with, rearranging them in different ways, cleaning out your mind almost."

Was her mind that dirty? Kristal wondered jaggedly. Was it her *own* mind that had thought up that terrible scene? *Where were her dreams coming from?*

Ann's voice was soft, almost a croon. "See? You're relaxing a bit now, aren't you, honey?" She smoothed back Kristal's damp hair. "Lie back, Krissie. Let it all slide away. It was a dream, a bad dream. By morning you'll have forgotten it all. You won't remember a thing. I promise."

Kristal lunged forward, pushing back the soothing hand. "I will remember! I will!"

"Now, honey. How about some hot cocoa? I did remember to pick some up at Superette. You just lie here in bed like a good girl, and I'll—"

"Hot cocoa!" Kristal's voice was a shriek. "Mom, what good will that do? It was terrible, *terrible!* I don't want cocoa, I don't want anything at all. All I want to do is to leave Maui. It's wrong here, Mom. Everything, everything!"

"But—"

"My pictures, they show it. The . . . the other things. Mom, we've got to change our plane tickets and leave!"

"Leave?" Ann was bewildered, alarmed. "But we've paid for a whole month, darling, and Susan and Cliff need the money. We can't just clear out of here; we promised them we'd stay. Besides, it's a vacation for all of us, and Buddy's been looking forward to the diving for so long. I promised him today that he could go on the *Odysseus—*"

"Diving! I don't care about diving! Mom, don't you see, it's wrong here, *there's something wrong,* and we've got to leave Maui! Before it's too late!"

"Krissie, Krissie, darling . . ."

"Leave! Leave Maui, Mom, leave tomorrow. Promise? Promise!"

Kristal awoke the next morning in her own bed, feeling as if she had walked long miles in her sleep or done tremendously exhausting work. All of her body ached: arms, legs, back, hips. Pain squeezed in her temples exactly like the "before" case in a television ad for headache remedy.

She crawled out of bed and padded into the bathroom. It was early, probably 7:30 A.M. she estimated from the looks of the sun streaming in the window. No one else was up. Silence shimmered in the house, broken by an occasional moan coming from Buddy's room as her brother stirred in his sleep. Funny. Buddy was not usually a sleep moaner. A snorer, maybe, but she had never heard him groan in his sleep before.

She used the toilet, then fumbled in the medicine cabinet until she had located a bottle of Extra Strength Tylenol. She spilled three of the capsules into her palm and took them with tap water. Ugh. But at least she had got them down, and maybe after her bath her headache would go away and she would be able to think.

Leave Maui, Mom, leave tomorrow!

Dimly she remembered saying that, screaming it, into her mother's shocked and disbelieving face. But now it all seemed unreal. She could barely remember the dream now—it seemed very far away, blurred.

Trembling, Kristal stared at her face in the bathroom mirror. Exhaustion shadowed her eyes. Her mouth was quivering. She turned away from the mirror and slid out of her shortie pajamas. She let them drop to the floor in a heap and stood naked, gazing for a moment at the tub, where a grit of beach sand had dried in a swirl near the drain. Ocean sand, she had learned, did not flow naturally out of a tub, no matter how hard you tried to wash it away. You had to push it out with your fingers. She wondered just how many tons of beach sand got swept down Maui's drains every year. A lot, she was sure.

She stepped into the tub and adjusted the flow of water to the searing hot temperature she preferred. Water began to thunder into the tub, sending up moist, comfortable clouds of steam.

When the water had filled up to the level of the drain knob, Kristal reached for the cake of blue soap and a washcloth. Carefully she began to soap herself. Shoulders first, her arms, then her chest and neck and breasts. Something on her left arm felt sore, just below the elbow, and when the washcloth touched it, Kristal winced. She turned her arm up for inspection. Odd. There was a rash on her arm. It looked almost as if she had scraped herself against something rough, up against the coarsest grit of sandpaper maybe, or asphalt, or even a cheese grater.

Carefuly she examined the wound. It looked fairly fresh, as if she might have received it in the last hour or so. Except, of course, that that was impossible. She'd been sleeping.

Kristal caught her breath, expelled it in a sigh, and continued to soap herself. On her left thigh she discovered a similar scrape.

Where had it come from? She was sure it hadn't been there before she went to bed last night. And this one—she ran a fingertip over its surface—this one was actually still bleeding a little, tiny droplets of red oozing up to the surface of the skin to seep away in the bath water.

Even her throat felt as if something had scraped it. Kristal swallowed, testing the rawness there. Maybe she was coming down with something awful—beriberi or trench mouth or strep throat.

Uneasily she soaped, rinsed, soaped again. Her bare knees rose like flesh-colored islands out of the bath water. The dream. The woman twisted in the water, arching herself like the most fragile of blossoms. Her own voice, screaming. *It's wrong here, Mom. Everything! Everything!*

She pressed her lips tightly together, swallowed against rawness, and began the final rinsing. As soon as she was out of the tub and dressed, she would wake up her mother and tell her everything, all she could remember about the dream.

But what could she remember? It was all fading now, erasing itself from her memory like disappearing ink. All she could see now was water and a powerful body twisting, undulating through flat blue . . .

Tell Mom everything, Kristal thought feverishly. That was what she must do. She would beg her mother to go back to Ann Arbor, and they'd go. They would throw everything into their suitcases and jump into the car and head for the airport. They could rearrange their flights later, but they'd be safe at the airport.

They must leave. At once, as soon as they'd had breakfast. Or maybe, Kristal planned jerkily in her mind, they wouldn't even wait for that.

It was then that it happened. The moving.

The moving. That was all that Kristal could find in her head to describe it. Something, some invisible thing, picked up her naked, dripping body from the bathtub and flung her against the tiled wall.

One minute she was sitting in ten-inch deep soapy water, staring down at the mounds of her wet knees, and the next she was flying, legs gangling and apart, arms flailing, against the wall. Power vibrated in the steamy air of the bathroom. Raw energy, like the subliminal rumble of some enormous munitions factory. Her nose smashed against porcelain, arms and legs fighting it. For an instant she seemed to hang there against the wall.

Then the force was gone. It had seeped away. Kristal's wet, naked, slippery hips slid back down the tile wall and over the porcelain lip of the tub back into the water. She landed with a splash. Water sprayed on the wall, the floor, even the mirror. Kristal's buttocks skidded on the tub bottom. And in the bottom of the tub, among what was left of the water, her scrabbling fingers met grit.

Sand. Black lava sand, granules and pebbles and grains of it, exactly as if it had been picked up from some beach in handfuls and flung into Kristal's bath water.

Except, of course, that that was impossible. It could not have happened. The . . . the *moving* could not have happened. It was not possible. Not logically, not rationally.

In what remained of the bath water, Kristal sat rigid.

Ann too awoke with a feeling of unease so strong that she sat up in bed immediately and reached for the filmy pink nylon peignoir.

She had thought—lying there just climbing to the edge of awareness—that she'd heard something. Was it a scream, a muffled shriek, coming from the bathroom? Or maybe it had only been a part of some early morning dream, because the house was quiet enough now. There were only a few soft moans coming from Buddy's room, as if her son were fighting demons in his sleep.

Ann got up and went into the hall. *Damn,* she thought quickly, as she walked. Kristal's nightmare of last night had been disturbing. The girl had actually been in hysterics, begging to go home. Evidently her father's death, and the stress of Christmas, had affected her much more strongly than Ann had suspected.

Well, maybe they would go, Ann thought as she headed toward the closed bathroom door. If both youngsters agreed they wanted to leave, and if they could figure a way to do so without hurting Susan's feelings or causing the Rogers financial hardship . . .

She reached the bathroom door and rapped on it.

Silence.

She knocked again. "Kristal? Krissie, are you in there? Is everything all right?"

And then her daughter's voice, slow and tired and taking a long time to reply: "Yeah, Mom, I'm fine."

"But I thought I heard a noise . . . something—"

A hesitation. Then an uncomfortable small laugh. "I slipped," Kristal said. "Slipped in the tub. Banged my hip and gave myself a scare."

"Oh." Ann stood outside the door, wondering why her unease did not subside. "You're all right then? Not hurt?"

"No." Ann could hear scraping sounds against porcelain and wondered what her daughter was doing. Cleaning out the tub?

"Well . . . I guess I'll go put on a pot of coffee then. God knows, I could use a cup. And Buddy wanted to go to Lanai, maybe I'll make some phone calls, see if I can get him on the dive boat he wanted."

"Okay. I'll be out in a minute."

"Anything special you want for breakfast, honey?"

"No. I don't care. Anything."

"Okay then, see you in a minute, Krissie."

"Sure."

Ann could not get Buddy up for breakfast. She had already started the pancakes and sausage, a calorie-laden meal dating from childhood years, a breakfast associated in all of their minds with warmth and family.

She stopped in mid-batch to awaken Buddy. But he

would not get up. Ann stood staring down at her sleeping son. His big, man-sized body was sprawled face down, crosswise across the double bed. His left leg was flung out of the covers. He'd scraped that leg, Ann noted, on a piece of coral, maybe, while he had been at the beach?

At any rate the wound was raw looking, with little dots and patches of blood clinging to it, oozing up through the skin. Ann shivered and made a mental note to tell Buddy to bandage the leg as soon as he awoke. She didn't want him to get an infection, swimming every day in sea water as he did.

"Buddy," she began, touching her son's arm, "I'm making pancakes and sausage. You'd better get up, or they'll all be gone——"

Buddy twitched and jerked in his sleep, his back arching upward. His mouth opened, releasing a moan that seemed almost driven out of his throat, like the involuntary sound made when a rubber toy is punched. Another thrash of the legs, and he had kicked the sheets off.

Ann saw still another wound on her son's upper right thigh. *More coral,* she thought, frowning. And the injury was fresh too, so fresh that if she didn't know better, she'd think he had gotten it within the past hour or so. But of course, that was nonsense.

Buddy jerked and moaned again.

"Buddy! Bud, are you all right? Wake up!"

For a long shuddering moment the boy lay perfectly still, his body rigid. Then his muscles tightened like the string on a bow. He began to convulse in huge, violent motions.

"Buddy! Buddy, Buddy! Honey?"

Ugly sounds came from her son's throat. He arched his back, one arm flung out. His eyes flew abruptly open, unseeing.

"No . . . no . . ." he began to mutter. "The cave, the cave . . . he . . . the eyes . . . the eyes . . ."

"The eyes? What are you talking about, Buddy?"

"The eyes! They look and they know. They know I was there, they know I was there. THEY KNOW THEY KNOW THEY KNOW . . ."

Buddy's eyelids fluttered rapidly open and shut. His face was a peculiar ashen shade.

"They know! They know, they know . . ."

He thrashed again violently, the muscles standing out like cords on his tightly drawn arms and legs. His limbs were blotchy, Ann saw. And there were more of the bruises, the abrasions or whatever they were. Some on his arm and one on his side. Little droplets of blood and fluid had oozed out of the wounds to stain the sheets.

"Buddy, what's wrong with you? What are those marks on your arms and legs?"

"Mick! Mick, you bastard!" he cried. "You bastard, you left me, you left me there with him . . . HIM . . ."

A short, explosive pause while Buddy gulped for air. Then his hoarse voice again. "The cave. The cave, the cave." Monotonous horror "The cave CAVE CAVE-CAVE CAVE . . ."

"Buddy." From somewhere Ann found the strength to reach out and touch her son's arm. His skin felt cold, clammy. "Son, what cave are you talking about?"

"The needlepoint!"

Buddy suddenly sat up in bed and stared at Ann with eyes widened and horribly blank, his pupils enlarged so that they were like black pits looking into an abyss of horror. "What was it doing down there? WHAT WAS IT DOING DOWN THERE?"

Chapter 18

Lucy Rooten, Ann's former neighbor, was a registered nurse destined to work in doctors' offices because she could not handle hospital emergencies. Every time she saw someone lying on a stretcher with blood pouring from a cut artery or shards of metal protruding from his eye, Lucy had to move her bowels. Only after she had rushed to the bathroom was Lucy able to return and take command of the situation.

Ann felt almost exactly the same way now. There was even a sudden, gripping, dysenterylike pain in her belly. Ice had coagulated in her veins, freezing her whole system. She could not move. Yet this was Buddy, her son, and then somehow she was backing down the hallway, calling for Kristal.

"Krissie . . . Krissie . . . come help me. Buddy's sick . . ."

"What is it, Mom?"

The paralysis had left Ann. "It's Buddy. I want you to help me throw some clothes on him and get him in the car. We're going to drive him to the doctor."

"What doctor?"

"I don't know what doctor, all I know is that he needs one. Go get the— Wait, wasn't there a clinic near the post office? We'll go there. Krissie, come on, let's hurry, let's get him ready." Ann's eyes met Kristal's own horrified ones.

If anything, Buddy was worse. He was still writhing and muttering incoherently. *The cave,* he kept saying. *The cave, the cave.* And something about the needlepoint. Over and over he talked about it, his eyes widening as if he saw something dreadful.

"Hurry," Ann panted. "Get a pair of shorts, Krissie, out of the drawer. That one there, the top one."

Obediently Kristal did as she was told, and together the two women struggled to pull the jean shorts over Buddy's surprisingly heavy legs. As they worked, he kicked and tossed and convulsed, flinging his body from side to side violently.

"M-Mom?" Kristal quavered as they finally got the shorts yanked up over the jockey briefs Buddy wore. "I— I can't get the zipper."

"Don't worry about it. Getting him to the car, that's what we should think about. The two of us . . . are we strong enough? Oh, Krissie . . ."

Ten minutes later, Ann had managed to swerve her car down the hilly streets of Makai Heights to Makai Road. Buddy muttered in the back seat, groaning and crying out. Kristal sat tensely in the front seat beside her mother.

"Mom? What do you think it is? Those marks . . . on his legs . . ."

"I don't know, honey."

"But they're so funny looking, they're bleeding, Mom..." Unconsciously Kristal stroked her own leg through the denim of her jeans.

"Krissie, I don't know. I don't know!"

Ann was sweating with relief that they had been able to get Buddy to the car at all. When had he gotten so heavy? He was built like a grown man and even smelled of dank perspiration like a man.

But once they had managed to swing him to a sitting position on the edge of the bed, he had suddenly loosened his muscles and cooperated with them. He stood up and actually walked, in a zombielike fashion, to the door, down the steps to the driveway, and then to the car.

What they would do when they got to the doctor's office, Ann didn't know. She hoped he'd be cooperative again. If he wasn't, she would have to run into the doctor's office and get someone to come out and help them.

The Makai Road rammed past. It was the resort's one and only main street, lined with hotels and businesses.

The hospital, Ann thought. She should have taken Buddy to the hospital. But she wasn't really sure where the hospital was. It was somewhere in Wailuku or Kahului, she supposed, twenty-five minutes away. And she didn't want to have to take her son there. Surely this wasn't a hospital case. It was the flu of some kind or an infection caused by the coral injuries.

Yes, that was it, an infection. The doctor would give him a shot, prescribe a couple of bottles of antibiotics and send Buddy home. He'd be fine...

Yes, there it was, the small shopping center to the left, its parking lot still mostly empty at this time of morning. She parked as close to the clinic as she could. It was a small cement block building painted yellow and landscaped with white Plumeria and several species of ugly, exotic cactus.

"Buddy?" She spoke into the rear view mirror, seeing a portion of her son's hair. "Son, we're at the doctor's office now, and I want you to get out of the car and walk in by yourself, because you're too big and too heavy for Kristal and me to manage."

From somewhere—God knew where—she had found the strength to keep her voice calm and normal. And now her mind was calculating. Together she and Kristal would help Buddy out of the car and support him, one on either side, up the walk . . .

"Mom? Mom?"

Kristal had turned to look into the back seat.

"Mom? Look . . ."

Ann turned.

Buddy was staring out of the back seat at them. His eyes had the stunned, flattened look of a survivor of a plane crash. But the look in Buddy's eyes was not the worst of it.

Ann quickened her breath and wondered at the ragged sound of the air pumping into her lungs.

Buddy had begun to bleed. From the eyes. From the nose. From the mouth. Blood trickled down his face in slow, red, leisurely, hideous rivulets, one trickle of red flowing down to join another and another.

At Ann's screams, people came running, seemingly out of nowhere, and crowded around the car, staring in at Buddy, then backing away a little.

"Oh my God," someone said. "Was it a car accident?"

"No," someone responded. "They just drove up."

"Buddy! Oh, God, Buddy!" Ann heard her own voice rise above the crowd's. She wanted to go back to that time when her son had been all right and there hadn't been blood running down his face, making his features into a mask and her son into something horrible.

She saw a flash of jeans and T-shirt. Kristal ran toward the doctor's office and began to beat with her fists on the door. *Jesus,* Ann thought. *It's early, I forgot, it isn't even eight in the morning yet. What if no one is there?*

A nurse came trotting out of the door, a slim oriental woman of about fifty wearing a white uniform and black-trimmed cap. She was followed by an aging man wearing a green-printed Hawaiian shirt and a stethoscope around his neck. The doctor. Praise God, the doctor.

Ann pushed her way toward him.

"My son, he's bleeding. I don't know what's wrong with him. I was bringing him to your office, I didn't know he was bleeding like that until I turned around and saw him—" Her voice was breathless.

The doctor had reached the car. Ann saw that he was old, sixty-five at least, with a face tanned leathery from long hours on the beach. His hair was white and silky and fine, bare patches revealing pinkened scalp. His eyes were as blue as those of a sailor.

"What is this?" he asked her. "He's in the car?"

He bent over, leaning forward to peer through the opened door into the back seat. When he withdrew, his face was expressionless.

"Is he a hemophiliac?"

"A . . . No. No, he's not."

"Get him into my office. Will some of you people help?"

And then, calmly, the doctor stood back while a man with a tool belt and another man wearing only shorts pulled Buddy out of the car, slung him between themselves, and carried him into the office. Ann was dimly aware of sounds: bird calls, traffic on Makai Road, a construction vehicle, someone sobbing. She realized that Kristal was weeping.

"Well, Mrs. Southworth, I certainly don't know what to tell you. Not yet."

The doctor faced Ann across his desk. His office was furnished in rattan furniture, grass cloth, and thick green carpet. His name, according to one of the framed diplomas on the wall, was Garrett Hartung. More framed pictures were propped on the big desk: Dr. Garrett Hartung standing on the deck of a charter fishing boat grinning into the camera beside the corpse of a huge marlin. Dr. Garrett Hartung and two other men standing by a row of more fish.

Ann let her eyes travel around the office, soaking up the normality of it all. As long as she could sit here in this cooly furnished office, then everything would be all right. Buddy would be all right. In her mind she made it a prayer. *Let him be all right. Let him . . .*

From somewhere down the hall—she had seen only one examining room, so that was where Buddy had to be right now—she could hear moaning, the sounds of thrashing.

"I don't know what to say," Dr. Hartung repeated. "Obviously he's very sick, but to be honest, I don't know yet what it is. I've never seen anything like this. I'd like to put him in the hospital for a couple of days to run some tests and see what happens."

"But what do you think is wrong with him?"

"Mrs. Southworth, I don't know much yet. All I do know is this. From the history you've just given me, your son seems to be in perfect physical health, other than the abrasions that mark his arms and legs, and of course the facial bleeding. The bleeding stopped as soon as my nurse cleaned him up, and it hasn't been repeated. I found a cut on his tongue, which could explain the blood from his mouth. As for the nose, a nosebleed ..." Dr. Hartung shrugged slightly.

"A nosebleed! You've got to be kidding! There wasn't— There wasn't any—" Ann's voice rose.

"There are a lot of things about this case I don't like, Mrs. Southworth, and I'll be frank about that. Your son has a normal body temperature, no fever whatsoever, he's clean of drugs as far as I can see at the moment, yet he's babbling and incoherent. You tell me he's been absolutely normal up to this point, a good student, a good kid. You said he's been diving recently, so it's possible he's somehow embolized."

The man hesitated. "But I don't think so. No, this doesn't give me that feeling. I'd like to keep him in the hospital ... watch him for a few days, and keep him sedated. Maybe he's having some sort of emotional breakdown, Mrs. Southworth. You told me he lost his father recently ..."

"A breakdown!" Ann snapped. "No, my son is not having a breakdown."

"He was extremely fond of his father, you told me. And you said that he blames you for the death."

"Well, yes—"

Ann supposed that, in giving a medical history, she had told the doctor these things. It seemed logical that she would have done so. But now, she couldn't remember doing any of that. She did know that Buddy's problem was not mental. He was physically ill.

"An infection," she began. "Surely it's an infection from one of those wounds on his legs, those coral scrapes—"

"Maybe those are coral abrasions and maybe they're not," the doctor told her flatly. "Frankly, I rather doubt that they are. I've seen enough of those to know them. I get scuba divers in here all the time. We'll see. Thus far, however, the wounds don't seem to be infected. We're going to give him a tetanus shot and antibiotics—"

Ann sat very still, forcing herself to absorb this information.

"The hospital," she said at last. "I have Blue Cross, Michigan Blue Cross—"

Dr. Hartung rose. "They'll take care of all that in Admitting, Mrs. Southworth. Now I think we'd better get your son ready to travel. You can follow me to the hospital."

An hour later, Ann and Kristal sat in the small, shabby emergency lounge of the hospital. Even at this early hour there were patients waiting to be seen: a wailing two-year old whose barking cough sounded to Ann like croup; a construction worker with a crushed index finger dripping blood onto the floor. Beside Ann, Kristal fidgeted, flipping through the pages of a six-month-old *Reader's Digest*. Ann herself could not read. She could not even seem to think properly.

Buddy, her son, Buddy, was in an examining room now, sick with some malady the doctor had never seen before. What could it be? If not an infection, then what was it? She rejected Hartung's hint that the problem might be mental. She knew her son, he had never had any serious emotional problems. She couldn't imagine . . .

Beside her on the couch, Kristal was crossing and recrossing her legs. Several times she scratched at her thigh.

Would the doctor, Ann wondered, never come out and tell her what was wrong with Buddy? At least tell her *something* so she wouldn't have to sit here and worry like this? What was taking so long?

Time inched by. The two-year-old and his mother were ushered inside to an examining room. The construction worker was seen, too. He came out smiling, joking to the friend who had brought him about taking a day on the beach to recuperate. Ann wished she could have a day off, too.

Kristal tossed aside the *Reader's Digest* in favor of a battered copy of *Family Circle*.

"Krissie," Ann said suddenly, "do you know anything, anything at all that might help to explain this?"

Her daughter hesitated. "I don't know, Mom. He was with Mick and Lisa the other day, and when he came home there was somthing funny about him. Yesterday Mick kept looking at Buddy strange, and whispering to him a lot. I don't like Mick. Or Lisa either."

"Oh they're all right. They're your second cousins ... I think that's the relationship," Ann said automatically. "Susan's my first cousin, so that makes them second ..."

But as she talked, saying anything that came in her head to reassure Kristal, Ann's mind kept clicking. What had Buddy been talking about? What had he and Mick been doing?

Maybe Kristal had been right. Maybe they should have stayed at home, in familiar surroundings, with snow. They could've driven up to her parents, who lived at Higgins Lake, near Roscommon, and taken in some skiing at Boyne. Anything but this agony now ...

"Mrs. Southworth?" Dr. Hartung came striding briskly down the hall, looking exactly like a tourist in his gaudy Hawaiian shirt. "Mrs. Southworth, there's an office around the corner. I'd like to talk to you a minute, if I may."

"Yes, of course."

In the cluttered little office-storage room, Dr. Hartung spoke quickly. "There's nothing I can really tell you at this time. We've sedated your son, he's resting comfortably, we've treated his wounds, and we're going to be running a lot of tests on him. By tomorrow I should know a great deal more." He paused. "I'm also arranging to call in a psychiatrist as a consultant on the case. We have a man here on the island, Dr. John Lung. He's an excellent man in every respect, and I've often referred patients to him."

But Ann had heard only the one word. "A psychiatrist?"

"Now, Mrs. Southworth, don't be alarmed. I've told you, we have a lot of tests to do, and it's only a matter of leaving no stone unturned. Your son is sleeping right now. I'd suggest that you and your daughter go home and get some rest. You can come back this afternoon for visiting hours and bring your son some slippers and a toothbrush, whatever items you think he might want."

"All right." Ann said it slowly, for there was nothing else to do. She certainly could *not* have hysterics here in this junky little storage room under the scrutiny of those blue-blue eyes. Buddy was sleeping. They would do tests. He needed slippers. She could manage. Could and would.

"Thank you," she heard herself reply. "We'll come back later. And doctor, I appreciate the way you came to the hospital with us."

He nodded. "That's all right. I had to make rounds anyway."

Chapter 19

"Mom, what do you think it is?" Kristal asked in the car.

"I don't know what it is, Krissie."

"It was awful, the blood running down his face. Mom, what could have made him bleed like that?"

"I don't know, honey. Calm down, okay? He isn't bleeding now, and they've got him sleeping. Tomorrow they'll know more. They're going to do tests."

Ann was making a beeline for Makai Heights as fast as the traffic on the two-lane road through the cane fields would allow her to go. The sky was a brilliant blue, glittering off the tall grasses, which were paint-box green.

"What kind of tests?" Kristal persisted.

Ann had forgotten to ask. "Oh, blood tests, I suppose. And x-rays, urinalysis, things like that. Tests. You know."

And a psychiatric test, a little voice in Ann added. That too.

"I want to leave the island," Kristal said in a small, hopeless voice. "Mom, we've all got to leave. Now. Today."

"Today? With Buddy sick and lying in the hospital? Don't be silly, Krissie. Maybe it was a bad idea to come here, and we'll go home as soon as we can. But it won't be until Buddy is ready to travel."

"No, I . . . guess not."

Kristal's head swung back and forth in a kind of numb panic. Ann focused her eyes grimly on the road. Kristal was showing the fright that she herself felt. *My little boy, my baby . . .*

When they reached the pole house, Ann ordered Kristal into the kitchen to prepare breakfast for the two of them—the remainder of the pancake batter, eggs, anything that would give them strength and distract her daughter long enough so that the glassy look might leave her eyes.

Mary Tanaka was lumbering through the house doing the dusting, and Ann quickly told her to leave Buddy's room alone. She, Ann, would clean it herself.

Carefully she went through her son's bedroom, looking for signs of . . . what? She didn't even know. She opened up the dresser and poked through each of its four drawers carefully in turn. She found nothing except jeans, T-shirts, Jockey underpants, a copy of *Penthouse.* There was a pile of Maui post cards he had bought at Island Pharmacy. There was a copy of Frank Herbert's book, *Dune;* two issues of *Mad* magazine.

She found the *PADI Dive Manual,* a couple of cone shells, a Maui Tourist Guide, three empty Pepsi cans, a crumpled Snickers wrapper, a scrap of foil from a pack of gum, and a used Kleenex that had missed the wastepaper basket. She found no drugs, no strange letters, no cryptic bits of scribbling on torn scraps of paper, no evidence to say anything other than that here was a perfectly normal sixteen-year-old boy who wasn't particularly tidy and who was on vacation.

But there was also no diving gear in the room, either, and hadn't Buddy been storing his gear bag in the closet?

Ann barely tasted breakfast, so anxious was she to get to the job of finding young Mick Rogers and confronting him. Did he know something about Buddy she didn't? Why had Buddy kept babbling about a cave? Why had he called Mick a bastard? What had happened on that dive that Buddy and Mick had made the day before Christmas?

Mick Rogers was annoyed at being awakened by Ann's pounding on the lower lanai door.

"What is it?" he demanded crossly. "Mom's already left for work, her and Dad, they'll be back after five."

"It's not your parents I want to talk to. It's you, Mick, if you don't mind."

"Me?"

"Yes, that's right."

For an instant they glared at each other through the glass door, a determined woman and a sullen boy. Then Mick glanced downward and slid open the glass door to permit her to enter.

"I was sleeping," he told her. His dark hair stuck straight up in tufts, his eyes were crusty, and there was a red sheet-wrinkle on one cheek. Mick wore nothing but a pair of ragged cutoffs, the front pockets hanging below the hem of the pant legs.

"And Lisa?" Ann asked. "Is she here, too?"

"In bed, I guess," Mick allowed. "I haven't looked."

He was a short, squat boy, with a rich Maui tan, and he was making clear his discomfort. She was an adult, his look seemed to say, a creature unrelated to him in any way. What could she possibly have to say to him?

Mick flung himself onto a flower-print living room couch, and propped one bare leg up on the rattan couch arm. His right hand played with a ragged thread that hung down from his shorts.

"It's Buddy," Ann began, sitting down in a wicker chair. "He's sick, very sick. Kristal and I had to take him to the hospital this morning. We just got back a little while ago."

Mick glanced up with the first sign of interest but said nothing.

"The doctor doesn't know what's wrong with him," Ann went on, "but I'm going to find out. I want to know what Buddy has been doing for the past few days. He's been with you and Lisa, right?"

Reluctantly Mick nodded.

"Doing what?"

"Oh, things. The beach and all that. And yesterday was Christmas." Mick's shrug was casual.

"The beach. I seem to remember that you and Buddy made a dive the day before Christmas. Is that right?"

"Well . . ."

"Buddy mentioned it at home. And his diving gear, it's not in his closet anymore. Where is it?"

Mick shifted uncomfortably. His eyes avoided hers.

Ann felt a spurt of rage so powerful that she wanted to leap out of her chair, spring toward the stocky boy lounging on the couch, and strangle him . . . clamp both hands around that mahogany-tanned neck and squeeze until he choked for breath.

"Mick." Her voice was soft. "Mick Rogers, I know that you took my son on a dive, and I'll bet that his gear bag is still in the trunk of your mother's car. Do you want me to call Susan at work and have her come back with the key and open that trunk? Because I will if I have to. Do you understand that? I'll do anything I have to do to help my son."

She heard her own words with surprise. "You're hiding something, Mick. I'm not a fool and I'm not stupid, no matter what you may think. You're hiding something, and I'm going to find out what it is."

Mick eyed her. His brown eyes were stony. He said nothing.

Ann could feel perspiration on her chest, flowing between her breasts.

"I know Lisa's in the bedroom," she went on quietly. "Did she go on the dive, too, Mick? Did she? Because if she did, I'm going to go and wake her up and ask her about it. And she'll talk. Both of you will talk, Mick, because my son is sick in the hospital, and he might die, and I'm going to find out why."

A pause. A very long one in which Ann could hear all the small mechanical noises a house makes: rumble of refrigerator motor, creak of a board settling somewhere. Outdoors, the pair of myna birds were squabbling on the lanai, and there was the distant rumble of a road grader.

"It was just a dive," Mick said. "A dive, that's all."

"Tell me about it."

He shifted his position on the couch. His fingers yanked at the thread dangling from his jeans and snapped it off.

"There's nothing to tell."

"Oh, I have a feeling there's a lot to tell, a great deal indeed. You see, Mick, Buddy is incoherent, and he's been saying some things. Some very strange things."

Mick stiffened. His hands stopped their movements. "Like what? What's he been saying?"

"He mentioned a cave," Ann told him grimly. "And eyes, eyes looking at him. He said your name several times. He said you left him. What did he mean by that, Mick?"

Mick's tan lost some of the look of robust good health.

"We were just diving, is all. And Buddy, he got scared. He's just a beginner, a scaredy-cat beginner, and he couldn't handle it, is all. You know."

"No, I don't know. I want you to tell me, Mick."

Ann felt like a police inspector questioning a reluctant and guilty suspect. The more she talked to Mick, the more she was sure he was hiding something. But what? What?

"Where did you dive, Mick? Tell me that."

"Off the beach." His eyes glittered defiantly at her.

"Off what beach? Dammit, Mick—" She stood up, making clear her intention to go into the bedroom and awaken Lisa.

"Oh, all right. We were down off Kaunoa."

Ann remembered driving past the entrances to the beach, when she went to Kam Smith's house, seeing the jungle of *kiawe* trees, tents and campers visible among them.

"Where off Kaunoa?" she demanded.

"The lava flow, actually." Now Mick's eyes met hers.

"The lava flow?"

"Yes— You won't tell her, will you?" Mick's words abruptly poured out. "You won't tell Mom? She's mad at Lisa and me, she's just waiting for a chance to send us to school on the mainland. And she'd do it, too; maybe we'd all go to the mainland, Mom's getting tired of Hawaii."

He stopped for breath. "See, we're supposed to tell Mom when we dive and where; that's the only way she'll let us dive at all. And we weren't supposed to go to the lava flow."

"Why not?"

"It's not a beach dive, it's off rock, and the surge can be pretty strong sometimes. It's pretty far away from things down there, too; no one around if you need help. And . . ." Mick hesitated.

"And what?"

"The caves," he said reluctantly.

"*Caves*. So that's what he meant." Ann caught her breath. "What kind of caves are down there, Mick? Tell me about it. Tell me everything you did on that dive, everything. Tell me where the place was and how you got to it and what you did."

Mick sat up, swinging his legs to the floor. He began to fuss with a large floor lamp, picking at the lamp shade with thumb and forefinger. "I can show you how to get there, if you really want to know. But the cave wasn't much. We didn't even go in it."

Again he wasn't looking at her. Again she saw that sheen of fear on his skin.

"Who didn't? Who do you mean by 'we'?"

"Lisa and me . . . we didn't go in."

"And Buddy did? My son did?"

Mick turned to gaze at her, the tan faded from his face, the brown eyes for the first time frightened and pleading. "Yeah, Buddy did. Buddy went in."

Ann questioned Mick for ten more minutes, learning little more than the fact that Buddy had had to make an emergency bail-out, arriving on the surface conscious and able to shout to Mick and Lisa on shore. He'd had to be helped from the water and half-carried along the rough path back to the car. He had appeared to become sick in

the car. Mick and Lisa, alarmed, had hurried him home
and ordered him to conceal the fact that they had been
diving off the lava flow.

"Anything else?" Ann questioned grimly. "I've got
to know, Mick."

Mick looked uncomfortable, but his complexion was
back to a more normal hue.

"The mushrooms," he admitted reluctantly. "We
went and ate some magic mushrooms before we dived.
You know, the mushrooms that you can pick upcountry
in the cow pastures there?"

Ann hadn't known.

"Well, they make you high. Not real high, they
aren't bad, they aren't the psychedelic kind of mushrooms
at all. Buddy wasn't supposed to tell," Mick went on.
"Anyway, he came right out of it, so it couldn't be the
mushrooms. Magic mushrooms don't make people sick
like that; they just wear off after a while, just fade away,
you know? They sure didn't make Lisa and me sick."

Ann could only stare at the boy.

"You won't tell Mom, will you?" Mick questioned
anxiously. "Lisa and me, we didn't mean anything. We
only showed Buddy where the mushrooms were, is all.
Nobody asked him to take any, nobody made him, he did
it all himself. And, anyway, they wouldn't hurt him. All
they do is make you laugh a little. Make you high."

Buddy Southworth lay covered over in sleep, a blue
water sleep as infinite and deep as the ocean. He floated,
suspended, unable to move or escape from the pair of
black eyes that burned at him. Watching him. Watching.
Waiting there just at the rim of his vision. They knew him.
Those angry eyes knew him, *they knew, they knew* . . .

Buddy drifted up and down, in and out of the blue
place where he was. Sometimes he heard voices, felt

objects probing him. *Jesus, he's really out of it, isn't he,* a voice said once. *Wonder what he's been on.*

Then he heard the sounds of wheels rolling and ceiling echos, as if he were in a long corridor going somewhere. Elevator doors opened and closed. There was the smell of cooking. A rattle of trays. Hands on him, sliding him off the stretcher and onto a mattress.

It didn't matter—none of it did—because he wasn't there with the noises and the voices and the hands doing things to his body. He was down below in the blue, fixed under the hard, lonely fire of those eyes. They were Kam Smith's eyes and he, Buddy, knew the secret, he *knew,* and Kam didn't want him to tell.

Time passed. He was lying in bed. Or was he? He writhed. He tossed and turned, struggled in and out of the sleep that possessed him. Tried to get to the top, to the clean sunny air. Tried to talk.

"He ... he ..." He mumbled in his sleep. "He, it's he ... K— K-Ka— Kam ... he ... the eyes ..."

A picture of his mother floated into his mind. Mom, sitting in her chair with the needlepoint canvas spread across her knees, smiling at him. Her face was young and pretty, a little dimple showing at one corner of her mouth, young and laughing at something, full of surprise. Mom ...

He tried to talk, to warn her. "Oh, God, oh, God, the needlepoint. The needlepoint! What was it doing down there? What was it doing? Mom? *Mom, the needlepoint! I've got to tell you! Ohgodgodgod GOD ..."....*

But the noises went on, the interminable noises of voices in hallways and feet shuffling and somewhere a PA system and someone laughing, and someone else groaning. Buddy twisted on the bed, impaled in the blue, where he hung suspended under the scrutiny of those black eyes, and no one heard him. No one heard ...

Chapter 20

Kristal stood in the coolness of the camera shop, trembling so violently that she feared she couldn't stand upright. After she had prepared breakfast for her mother, she had left the house, walked down to the road, and hitchhiked down to Makai Road. She had to talk to Donnie. She had to talk to somebody or she would go crazy. The nightmares. The thing in the bathtub. And then Buddy. They had to leave Maui, and they couldn't, and what were they going to do . . .

Donnie was waiting on a customer, a big fat tourist wearing a strapless terry cloth romper that barely covered the whipped-cream mounds of her breasts. The woman was buying two double packs of Polaroid film for her camera and bitching about the price. Too high, she complained. She could get film in L.A. for a lot less, and who did Donnie think he was, charging such prices?

"This is Maui," Donnie explained politely. "Everything has to be shipped in on the Matson Line or else flown in by air. That's why it costs more."

Deftly he rang up the woman's order, and then moved away to let his father get some change out of the cash drawer. Mr. Perriera was an older edition of his son, his body filled out to muscularity. Worry lines cut deep furrows into his forehead, and his black hair was grayed at the sideburns.

"Dad?" Donnie asked. "Can I take a break? A short break, yah?"

"That's all you want to do. Take a break, take an hour, take a day. You go home, I can find plenty of work for you there, too, the lawn needs work, there's lots of weeding to do. Or you can stay here, the back room needs cleaning—"

"Dad—"

But Mr. Perriera cast a sidelong look at Kristal waiting by the door, and relented. "Well, okay, you take the rest of the day off, yah? Then you work tomorrow night late."

"Okay. Okay, Dad."

"You straighten that stuff in the back before you go. Finish unpacking and put away the boxes."

"Okay."

"The beach," Mr. Perriera said to no one in particular. "Always it's the beaches and the *wahines* with these kids. They think money it grows on trees, for god's sake, they think you can reach out and pick it like coconuts, drink the juice and you're rich. Pfah!" And he turned to wait on two little boys who wanted to buy some post cards.

They walked along the road toward the Makai Burgers, their sandals kicking up little eddies of red dust.

Donnie reached into his shirt pocket and pulled out an 8 by 10 glossy print, waving it in front of Kristal's face.

"Look at that, will you, Kristal? Just look at that!"

Kristal stepped backwards, nearly stumbling on a low spot on the shoulder of the road.

"What is it?"

"The picture you took of your Mom and her needle-point. Remember? I enlarged it. You said you couldn't see what was in the picture, and I said I'd make it bigger."

Kristal nodded. Her face felt frozen, wooden. She no longer wanted to see what was in the picture, because she knew, she *knew*.

"Well? Aren't you going to look . . . after I went to all the trouble?" Donnie's voice sounded funny. Sharp and annoyed and full of excitement, all at once.

"Okay. I'll look."

She forced herself to do so. Ann Southworth sat facing the camera, her face turned slightly to the left. Her cheekbones were in shadow, the pose making her look more like twenty-eight than thirty-eight. Her mother was a very pretty woman. But Kristal stared at the canvas half spilling out of her mother's lap. The last time Kristal had seen it, there had been large blank areas, places not yet filled in with yarn. But now, as if by some spirit hand, the picture had been completed.

Kristal stared at the photograph, swallowing back the taste of nausea. For she had seen all of this before . . . in her dream, alive and vivid.

Evil. Ancient wickedness. It was, Kristal thought slowly, as if neither of them, the woman or the shark, had any control over the monstrous force that possessed them . . .

"Well?" Donnie's voice brought her back to reality. "What do you think?"

"Oh, God. Donnie, I don't know . . ."

As they walked, she told in a breathless voice of Buddy's sickness and hospitalization. Donnie listened attentively. They reached the drive-in, a small wooden structure shaped like a diner. A painted canvas banner in front advertised "Super Burritos and Tacos."

Kristal and Donnie climbed the steps to the open front porch and went up to the order window. Donnie gave their order to the short, brown girl: two super cheeseburgers, two cokes, two orders of onion rings. Kristal shuddered lightly but did not change the order. They sat down at a tiny table to wait for their number to be called.

Donnie was frowning. "Funny, he should be sick like that. I've read things, things about the *kahunaanaana*. They used to do that sometimes. They could make skin diseases happen to people, really bad ones, make their skin fall off, make them stop breathing . . ."

Kristal shuddered. Her arms were itching again where she had scratched them, and her skin felt hot.

"But that's not all," she told him. "I haven't even told you all of it yet."

"You mean there's more?"

"Yes. Oh God, Donnie, I don't think you'll believe me when I tell you. *I* don't even believe it."

"I might. I've got books at home, you know . . . lots of books."

"I was in the bathtub this morning, taking a bath. Then all of a sudden, I was just picked up. *Picked up,* Donnie, and smashed against the wall and then dropped again, soaking wet, into the tub. Have you ever heard of anything like that? And there was sand in the tub." Kristal's voice had risen. "Beach sand. Black, pebbly beach sand, the same kind I found before . . ." Her eyes sought his, implored.

"Picked up." Donnie was thoughtful. "You were just

picked up. Like this?" He reached for a salt shaker, lifted it, dropped it to the surface of the little table.

Kristal nodded. "Only . . . only there wasn't anything there to pick me up, Donnie . . . except this feeling in the air. It was so eery. I'm scared, I'm really scared now."

Another group had come into the drive-in, a family with beach sand crusted all over their feet.

"It's okay," Donnie told her. "It was a spirit manifestation, that's all. In one of my books it tells about a woman being picked up out of the tub and hurled against the wall. Only, in her case there was a smell in the room, a terrible, sickening, sulphury smell. Did you smell anything?"

"No. But there was a . . . a *feeling* in the air. A rumbling, almost, like electricity along a power line. And then it threw me down and the power was all gone. It . . . went away."

Donnie considered. "What were you doing when it happened?"

"Doing! I was taking a bath!"

"I mean, what were you thinking about?"

"I was thinking about leaving the island. I was thinking about telling Mom everything and then all of us jumping in the car and driving to the airport. And then it happened. It . . . lifted me."

"So. It's working through you, Kristal. *He* is."

"He? Working through me? What are you talking about?" Kristal's voice rose. She waited impatiently as their number was called and Donnie went to the pickup window. She dug into her small change purse and fished out enough money to pay her share.

Automatically they opened their cheeseburgers and began to eat.

"What do you mean, working through me?" Kristal demanded after a moment.

"I mean you're a . . . a conduit, a doorway . . . a

message board. I don't know how else to put it. You have a susceptible mind."

"And the picking me up and throwing me down? That's a message too?"

"I guess, yah. There's something in you, Kristal, that lets it happen. That's why you have those dreams and why you take those pictures. You have psi ability. I suppose you could be a medium, if you tried."

"Ugh," she said violently. "I don't want to."

"Well, you have the powers whether you ever use them or not. I'd like to see what would happen if you ever started to play around with a Ouija board."

"I'll never."

"It's probably better if you don't. You shouldn't open up your mind to the spirits like that. Things can happen."

The shudder that shook Kristal started at the core of her belly and convulsed outward to her arms and legs. "That's what I've done, somehow, isn't it, Donnie? I've called him . . . it . . . this shark demon or god or whatever it is."

"Yes."

Kristal's whisper was almost too low for Donnie to hear. "Way back in Ann Arbor, after Dad died, I started having these dreams. I don't know why, they just happened. Dreams of the sea. Over and over, the same thing. And when I got to Maui, *he* got in them . . ."

"Who decided that you should come here to the island?" Donnie asked.

Kristal shook her head. "I don't know. Me, maybe. Or maybe it was Buddy. All I know is that someone mentioned it one day and then we talked about it again and then a letter came from Aunt Susan, and suddenly we had made up our minds we were going. Mom too, she wanted to come. She started doing that canvas, that underwater stuff . . ."

"Your mother is a beautiful woman," Donnie said. It was a simple statement of fact.

"Yes," Kristal whispered. "And ... and, Donnie, I have the awfulest feeling, the most terrible feeling. I think it's her he's after. It's not me, I know it's not. I'm only the one who ... who is the message board. It's my mom he wants. I don't know how I know that, but I know."

Donnie nodded.

"Oh, Donnie, I'm so scared, and I don't know what to do. My mom ... and Buddy, and ... and Kam—" She had turned to him, was clutching his thin, wiry arm beneath the faded Hawaiian shirt. "It's Kam Smith who's the shark god, isn't he, Donnie? Isn't he?"

Donnie's eyes searched hers. They were intense with excitement. "The question now is, what are we going to do?"

"Do?" Kristal stared down at her half-eaten cheeseburger, playing with the paper wrapper in which it had come. There were a few grains of salt on the table. She pushed them around with her forefinger, remembered that they might be sea salt, and withdrew her finger from them as if they had stung her.

"I mean, are you just going to sit around while your brother gets sicker and sicker and your mother keeps on going out with this Kam Smith and God knows what starts to happen? This spirit stuff is nothing to mess with. These shark legends—who knows what sort of fact they're based on? These *are* islands. There *are* sharks in these waters, reef sharks, hammerheads, tiger sharks, great blues. Shark attacks are pretty rare, but they do happen once in a while, the statistics say so ..." Donnie's eyes were glittering.

Kristal stared at him. A strange anger pelted through her. "Are you enjoying this, Donnie? All of this? Look at you, you'd think you were Sherlock Holmes or something, out on a case."

Donnie looked chagrined. "Okay, so I read a lot, yah? I'm interested, that's all. I want to help you, Kristal. I will help. You can't do it alone, I know you can't."

She nodded wordlessly.

"Then? Okay?" Donnie asked.

"All right."

"It's Kam Smith, at the dive shop? You're sure of it?"

A long silence while Kristal probed within herself, focusing her eyes on the tiny, perfect grains of salt that still lay scattered on the table top. She let her mind go beyond them, let it swing loose and free, searching out into the misty blueness, the vast abyss. She remembered the pictures she had taken. Went over them in her mind, one by one. Let them merge with the otherness.

"Yes," she whispered at last. "It's him."

"Then we'll have to prove it," Donnie said. "I've got all the rest of the day, and you have your camera with you, right?"

Kristal glanced down at the battered camera case, which she had laid beside her on the wooden bench. Without even thinking, she had brought it with her. It was as much a part of her as her hair or her eyes. In fact, she thought shivering, in an eery way the camera *was* her eyes, letting her see things visible in no other way.

"Yes, I've got my camera," she said shakily. "And enough film."

"Good."

Driving along Makai again on her way to visit Buddy, some impulse made Ann stop first at the dive shop to see Kam. She parked in one of the parallel spaces in front of the hotel arcade and walked across the grass to the shop.

Kam was waiting on three teenaged boys who were trying on snorkeling gear. Stacks of boxes were piled on the floor amid a litter of black rubber flippers. Kam bent over them easily, his big body graceful.

How handsome he was, Ann had time to think. A beautifully carven man, as comely as the god Maui himself, who was said to have harnessed the sun . . .

Kam looked up from what he was doing. "Hello, Ann."

"Hi."

For a moment something hung between them, discernible even to the boys, who glanced uncertainly among themselves.

"I'll be with you in a minute, Ann," Kam told her. "Let me finish waiting on these customers."

Fifteen minutes later, burdened down with gear, the boys left the shop and Kam turned to her. "I've missed you," he said. "I never did get a chance to see you alone yesterday in the midst of all that holiday cheer."

"I'm sorry," she said quickly. "It's Buddy. He's been sick. In fact, I had to take him to the hospital this morning. I'm on my way back there right now to take him some things. Robe and slippers, his book, things like that."

"What's wrong with him?"

"It's— Oh, I don't know! He has these strange wounds on his skin, like scrapes, as if he'd brushed up against coral. And he's been bleeding . . . from the eyes and nose and mouth. He's incoherent too. Delirious."

Kam was looking at her intently. She fancied for a moment that she saw a glint of satisfaction in those black eyes. But surely that couldn't have been so, for now he was all concern, patting her shoulder, touching her.

"He seemed well enough yesterday . . . a bit quiet, perhaps, but then boys that age can be moody."

"This isn't a mood. The doctor doesn't know what's wrong with him. Kam? It might be an infection from the scrapes, or it might be—" Ann stopped. She took a step forward, and then she was in Kam's arms, clinging to him.

"Oh God, Kam, I don't know what it is, I don't know at all. The doctor talked about getting in a psychiatrist. A psychiatrist!" She broke off to pull away and look up into Kam's face. He was frowning.

"Kam? What do you think it could be?"

"I don't know. But whatever it is, Ann, I'm sure you don't need to worry."

"But I do worry! I'm his mother, and I—" Ann tried to smooth out the shaking in her voice. "Do you think it could have had something to do with the dive he made the day before Christmas? He was mumbling the strangest things."

"What sort of things?" Kam asked sharply.

"Oh . . . about my needlepoint. And a cave. He kept talking about eyes . . . eyes looking at him."

Kam pulled away from her and went to stand at the glass display case, leaning his big body against it. It seemed to Ann that the full-carved mouth was straighter than usual. His eyes were black, burning with some emotion. She felt an instant's swift unease. Outside the shop, the brilliant Maui sun poured down, but here inside the shop it was cool and shadowy. The air conditioning was turned too low, she told herself. That was why she was shivering now.

"Cave," she repeated. "Buddy said he saw a cave."

"There always are caves in coral," Kam told her. "Or at least overhangs where the fish can hide. No doubt Buddy and his friends found one of these. There are some dive sites off Lanai that are quite spectacular in that respect—they are called Cathedrals One and Cathedrals Two. One of the sites actually has a big rock formation that looks like an altar—a sacrificial altar. Very interesting. You should arrange to take a charter out to Lanai before you leave. I'll go with you if you like."

Ann stared at Kam. His voice, with the slightly old-fashioned accent, was perfectly calm. Effortlessly he had steered her away from the topic of Buddy's cave to caves in general, and then to diving off Lanai. And how had he known that Buddy had been diving with friends?

She drew a careful breath. Buddy, Mick, and Lisa had probably gotten their tanks filled here at the shop before making their dive. That was how Kam knew.

As she was leaving, Kam assured her again that Buddy would be all right.

"Will he?" She had to turn toward the door so that he wouldn't see her tears, hot and ashamed. "Oh, Kam, will he? I want him to be. I . . . I have to go . . ."

She fled out of the dive shop, seeing in front of her, like a hideous vision, Buddy's face, his eyes opaque with terror, his mouth moving, as if there was something he was trying desperately to tell her . . .

Chapter 21

At the hospital Buddy had been moved to a semiprivate room and strapped to the hospital bed, its sides up so that he couldn't injure himself. At first Ann did not recognize her son, so red and congested was his face, with huge welts and scratches along his cheeks and a new trickle of blood running from the corner of his mouth to the sheet.

"Cave," he was groaning as Ann entered the room. "The cave! He's looking at me, he knows, he *knows!*"

"He been like that for hours," said the occupant of the other bed.

Ann looked at him. He was a little dried-up Filipino man, immaculately attired in striped pajamas and chenille bathrobe, sitting on the edge of the bed with a paperback book. His feet were clad in clean slippers. Someone had brought the old man a lei made of Plumeria and it had been arranged on the window sill, where it was slowly drying out. The sweetness of the flowers seeped into the room, mingling with the acrid odor of Buddy's sweat.

"Hours?" Ann questioned.

"Ever since they roll him in here. He never let up, not once. They strap him in the bed, he not been still for a minute. And he keep talking. Over and over, the same things. The cave. Something with eyes. Something that keep looking at him. And his mother. Talks about his mother, about some needlework. He clean out of his head, all right."

The little man glanced at Buddy, then down at the book he held. "I'm here for tests," he added. "Prostate tests." He smiled.

"Oh, I'm sorry."

Ann said it politely, inanely. She went up to the bed and took one of Buddy's hands in her own. It was cold and clammy and it clutched at her. For an instant her son stopped his rolling back and forth and clung to her. Then the muttering started again.

"He . . . the cave . . . the cave . . . Mick and Lisa, damn them, damn the bastards, they left me, THEY LEFT ME . . ."

"Buddy? Why did they leave you?"

"Left me— Oh, God . . . oh God, the eel! It's a guard, a guard! Two of them! They guard it, they guard HIM . . ."

The violent thrashing of Buddy's body threw off the sheets. Ann saw his bare arms and legs. Raw scrapes of flesh oozed little pinpoint drops of blood. The sheets, Ann saw, were stained everywhere with blood and body fluids.

And there were more scrapes on his legs. More since she had seen him this morning. How had he gotten them? In the name of God, how? Here in the hospital. And surely he was worse. Oh, much worse. The sedation must have worn off. Or perhaps it hadn't taken effect properly.

Or, she thought to herself with inward suck of horrified breath, maybe this illness, this thing that had possessed him, was so strong that even sedatives couldn't help . . .

"Buddy, Buddy . . . Oh, son." She knelt on the floor beside the bed. "Buddy, what is wrong with you? What happened on that dive? Can you talk to me? Please talk to me."

He did not seem to notice her. His knees flexed up, thrusting at the bands that bound him. The bed shook, its frame and wheels creaking. The old man sitting on the other bed coughed genteely. Ann could hear the sound of a cart being wheeled across tile out in the corridor. Someone was laughing.

"Buddy!" she demanded. "Tell me. Tell me what's wrong. Did you take mushrooms? What happened on that dive?"

"Dive." Abruptly his voice changed, grew almost childish. "Beautiful in there, beautiful. Never . . . never saw anything like it. A world, a world in there. God! God!"

Jerk and tense of muscles. Fear convulsed Buddy's face. "Oh dear Jesus God!"

"Buddy! What is it, what's wrong?"

"The needlepoint! It's there! IT'S THERE!"

Buddy struggled to sit up, fighting the heavy straps. His face was red with the effort, and a stream of blood had begun to run out of his mouth. A crust of dried red in his nostrils showed where he had been bleeding earlier.

Horrible, Ann thought. *Horrible.* Hadn't they done anything, these people here at the hospital? Couldn't they help him, do something, *anything?*

"Are you talking about my needlepoint?" she asked in a low, tense voice. "The canvas I lost?"

"It . . . it . . . the picture! It's changed! Oh, God, it's changed and it's awful. Awful . . ."

Jerking of the body, powerful straining at the straps until Ann was sure they would break off like crepe paper.

"Doing it, they're doing it. Her and . . . him. *Doing it*. God God GODGODGOD. Oh dear Jesus, Mom, mother, oh, please PLEASE PLEASE PLEASE . . ."

"Buddy." Her son's hand flailed in the air, and Ann grabbed it. It flexed with muscular insanity. "Bud, honey, you've got to relax. It's all right. It—"

"WHAT WAS IT DOING DOWN THERE? IN THE NAME OF GOD WHAT WAS IT DOING? OH, GOD, OH, MOM . . . MOM, DON'T YOU KNOW? DON'T YOU KNOW? KAM! KAM!"

"Doctor!" Ann was hunched up to the wall telephone in the hospital corridor, almost screaming into the receiver, shameless of who heard her or what they thought of her.

"Dr. Hartung, he's worse, he's much worse now, he's delirious and they've had to strap him to the bed. He's bleeding again, not as bad as before, but he's still bleeding, and there are more marks on his arms and legs, and I don't know how he could have got them in the hospital! In the *hospital,* Dr. Hartung—"

"Mrs. Southworth . . ." The doctor spoke in a dealing-with-hysteria voice. "Mrs Southworth, I examined your son this morning and I prescribed medication for him. I'll make another visit to him tonight to see how he's doing. There is also a resident at the hospital, a physician in charge, and your son is under the best of care. You mustn't worry, Mrs. Southworth. Tomorrow the psychiatrist will examine him, and I am sure that will be very helpful to us . . ."

"Psychiatrist! My son is not in need of a psychiatrist! He made a dive the day before Christmas with his cousins. I found that they also ate some of those magic mushrooms that grow upcountry. Do you think the mushrooms could have made him sick?"

"Mushrooms. Do you mean *Psilocybe?* No," the doctor went on. "I've dealt with drug emergencies in Makai, and I've never seen anything like this before. Mostly the mushrooms just make them giggly and silly, or else thinking very deep, deep thoughts. In fact, sometimes I think the mushrooms have more of a reputation than any effect based on actual fact."

"Oh—"

"Mrs. Southworth, I'll be up at the hospital around five or six tonight, and I'll see your son again, and I'll see if there have been any significant changes. Meanwhile, I suggest that you try to relax. Go over to Apple Annie's at the Kaahumanu Shopping Center and get yourself one of their strawberry-pineapple daiquiris. They're delicious and very relaxing."

"Dr. Hartung, I can't relax—not with Buddy sick like this!"

"Will it help him if you worry yourself into a nervous wreck?" For the first time, the doctor's voice was sharp. "I'll see you late this afternoon, Mrs. Southworth." He hung up, and the sound of the dial tone buzzed in Ann's ear, maddening.

She walked back down the corridor to Buddy's room. When she opened the door, she saw that a nurse was bending over him, giving him an injection in the buttocks.

"Do you know why he's getting those new marks on his arms and legs?" Ann asked her.

The girl looked up. "I think he's doing it to himself, you know? Digging himself in his sleep. Look at his fingernails, yah? Look how dirty."

Ann was horrified. "Those aren't fingernail scratches!"

The nurse looked away. "He's delirious, yah? Tossing around, hitting the bed, hurting himself, it happens."

"But—"

"Crazy people, they can do things like that." The nurse—young, Oriental, pretty—started out of the room, and then stopped. "You worry too much, yah? I just gave him sedation, he'll be lots better in an hour or so. It just wore off, yah?" Then she was out in the corridor with a swift turn of bare, beach-tanned ankle, leaving Ann to stare after her.

"God, God, God," Buddy was groaning now. "Dad ... oh, Dad, I didn't mean it, didn't mean to take it, meant to put it back . . . Dad! *Oh, God, the cave, the cave!*"

Kristal and Donnie began at the dive shop. They sidled into the store as if they intended to buy something. In fact, Kristal did plan to ask whether the shop had any swim goggles. The salt in the water stung her eyes, and a few days ago Susan had suggested that she try a pair of goggles. Now, today, she and Donnie had decided that that would be as good an excuse as any.

She was frightened. Her camera case was slung over her left shoulder, and she felt as if it were monstrously visible, shouting out her intentions in neon letters. Perspiration formed a sheen all over her body. Would Kam be able to smell the fear on her, sense it as an animal might? He *was* an animal.

God, she thought, trembling. Sharks had amazingly sensitive smell apparatus, they could scent a fish in distress from long distances away. She had read a book about that once, a Cousteau book. Sharks had been called *chiens de mer,* dogs of the sea . . . She was shaking.

They walked in. The shop was filled with sunlight, its air conditioning humming. Scuba gear filled its shelves —wet suits, boots and bags and gloves. A stack of canvas flotation rafts occupied one corner. A hand-lettered sign above them said. "Please Do Not Sit."

"Well, hello." Kam Smith's voice, deep, resonant, seemed to come from nowhere.

Kristal jumped as the dive instructor emerged from a back room, where the sound of some big machine could be heard rumbling and vibrating.

"I was filling tanks," the man explained. His big body seemed to loom within the close confines of the shop. He wore blue shorts and a yellow-print Hawaiian shirt. "I hope you haven't been waiting long."

"No, we . . . we just walked in." Kristal and Donnie did not look at each other.

Kam smiled. His teeth were very white and clean. *And sharp,* Kristal found herself thinking.

Kam and Donnie were making small talk . . . about beaches and snorkeling and the weather, hot for Christmas. Maybe there would be *kona* winds. Nervously Kristal waited. At last the man turned to her.

"Your mother was just here." His dark eyes were focused on her unblinkingly.

"Was she?"

"She said that your brother is sick."

"Yes— Yes, he's very sick. In the hospital. We had to take him this morning."

Kam nodded. "I'm sorry to hear that."

But he didn't sound sorry, Kristal thought.

"We want to look at some swimming goggles," she said. "The water—the salt water—it bothers my eyes." Her right hand slid down to the vinyl of her camera case. She could feel her fingers slide across its surface, wet, slippery.

"Well, we have several types of goggles. Maybe you'd like to try on a few pairs to see which fits your face best."

Kam led them over to the right corner of the shop near the window, where some small items had been clipped to a revolving display rack. Bonine, for seasickness; antifog spray for lenses; small goggles made of yellow plastic.

Kristal picked up a pair at random, two yellow eye-cups. They looked like something a bug-eyed Martian might wear, she thought. She suppressed a nervous giggle.

Her eyes met Donnie's, and he nodded imperceptibly. Then he asked Kam if he had any prescription diving masks.

When Kam, distracted, moved toward the display of masks on the adjacent wall, Kristal reached for her camera case. She slid open the flap, thrust in her hand. The Canon met her fingers, faintly warm from being outside in the heat, familiar to her touch. She slid it out and raised it.

Get him in focus. Get him.

The light streaming in the shop windows would be enough; it would do, if . . . Her mind concentrated on the problem. Automatically she framed him in—Kam with a mask in his hand leaning toward Donnie Perriera, big and dark-skinned and handsome.

She held her breath, snapped the shutter.

Kam looked up.

"Why did you do that?" he asked sharply.

Kristal wondered if her convulsive trembling was visible to him. She eased the camera down, put it back into its case with an air of nonchalance.

"Oh, just testing it," she said. "I got it repaired this morning at Donnie's father's shop, and I wanted to see if it worked. I thought I'd get a picture of Donnie."

"I was the one who was in focus." Kam's eyes were very dark, very black, scrutinizing her.

"I— I suppose— Actually you were both in the picture."

She felt her eyes being pulled to his. Abruptly Kristal realized why her mother was drawn to Kam Smith. There was definitely something about the man. Something that drew you, pulled you trembling into his orbit, whether or not you wished to be there . . .

"We're going to the beach this afternoon, Donnie and I are," she babbled. "That's why I wanted to be sure my camera worked."

"And the goggles? You'll want those?"

"Oh! Oh, yes!" In her fright she had nearly forgotten them. She fumbled at her purse, found her wallet, and grabbed the goggles.

"Which beach are you going to?" Kam asked.

"Lani Beach," Kristal lied.

"Oh, yes, Lani Beach. There is some good snorkeling there. Just go down the sand to the left by the big outcrop of rocks and angle out and to the left. There are some good reefs. But you'd better go right away," Kam added. "Don't dally, or the surf will be up and kicking the sand around, and the visibility will be bad."

"Oh, yes—"

"And be careful where you swim," the man went on, his voice light now and jocular. "Be careful, or a shark might get you."

Kristal saw Donnie give a little startled jerk of his head. She said something—she never remembered what —and grabbed for her change, fleeing the shop with Donnie. The camera in its case banged against her side.

A hundred yards away from the shop, she and Donnie slowed their half-run to stare at each other.

"Did you hear what he said? Did you?" Donnie demanded.

"Did I hear what?"

"He joked. He *joked,* Kristal. Don't you know what that means? The old shark gods used to do it. They'd make a joke about sharks and then when the person would go into the water, there'd be an accident. A shark attack . . ."

Kristal shivered. "One picture," she said dully. "It was all I could get. I think he's suspicious, Donnie. He doesn't like my camera. At our house on Christmas, he acted funny about it, too."

They had started toward the car. "I think we need to get more pictures, though," she went on. "Let's go down to his beach house, Donnie. Mom talked about it. I think I know how to get there. Places. They have feelings around them. I'm sure his house would."

Donnie's mouth tightened. "Okay, if you want to."

"Donnie—" She clung to him. "Oh, Donnie, tell me this is all a dream. Tell me I'm crazy and that you really do want to go to Lani Beach. We could lie on the sand and get a nice sunburn, be real tourists. Okay?"

Donnie looked at her. Cars were whizzing by on Makai Road, and one of them had stopped to pick up a hitchhiker, a bearded man wearing a knapsack on his back.

"Kamohoalii," Donnie said softly. "That's the name of one of the shark gods, Kristal. The one who was supposed to have lived off Maui."

Kristal stared at him. She could feel the blood leaving her face.

"Kamohoalii." She repeated the unfamiliar Hawaiian syllables, the *ah,* the two i's pronounced separately, *ee-ee.* The name had almost a musical cadence. "Kamohoalii. Kam, Donnie. Kam!"

"Yes, it fits."

"Come on," she said, "while he's still at work. If we hurry, we can get to his house and back before he even leaves the shop. And if anyone sees us on the road, we can always say we decided to go to Kaunoa Beach rather than Lani. He'll never know."

"I wouldn't be too sure of what he knows and what he doesn't know," Donnie remarked.

But they got in his car and went anyway.

Chapter 22

The tops of tall coconut palms waved above the roof, and a big clump of banana palms was bunched by one huge glass window. On either side of the beach house, gnarled *kiawe* trees formed thickets, and through their branches could be glimpsed a sea so violently blue it appeared dyed.

Donnie pulled his car halfway up the driveway, found the turnaround, and faced the car back out toward the road, just in case they had to make a quick exit.

He stopped the motor, and they sat there for a minute listening to the sound of the surf pounding the rocks. Somewhere a bird was crying out. *You're purty, you're purty,* Kristal thought it called. Between them in the front seat, her camera waited. It all seemed very unreal to Kristal, the brilliant blue sky and sea, the sun glittering off the wraparound windows of the beach house, her own fear.

"Were we dumb to come here?" she asked Donnie. "What if he comes back early?"

"He won't. The dive shop closes at five, and it's only two now. We've got plenty of time."

Kristal slid the Canon out of its case again and ran quick fingers over its compact shape. Then, impulsively, she brought the camera up to her forehead and pressed it against her skin as hard as she could.

"What are you doing that for?"

She laughed harshly. "I don't know. Power, maybe. Energy. Something crazy. Donnie, do you think it'll work?"

"How would I know? Those other pictures all showed something. These will, too. Then we can show them to your mother and she'll believe you. What other kind of proof could we possibly get?"

"I don't know. Oh, Donnie, I don't like this!" Kristal said as she reached for the car-door handle and slid out of the front seat. Donnie followed her. They walked up the driveway toward the beach house, their feet crunching on uneven bits of gravel and rock. The thicket of *kiawes* loomed toward them, branches misshapen and twisted. One entire tree was a corpse, still propped upright by its mates.

"Widowmakers, that's what my father used to call those dead branches," she told Donnie, shivering.

"Ugly trees," he said. "They've got sharp thorns. They were supposed to have been brought here by the missionaries—to mortify the natives, some say."

They had reached the house, where a path skirted to the left toward the beach.

Kristal hesitated. "Let's go down to the beach first, that ought to be a good place. I . . . I think I can feel something coming from there. *He* would use the beach a lot. If he were really a—" She cut off the rest of the sentence.

They began the walk downhill, their feet skidding on the sand drifting up through the chicken wire that had been laid flat to provide footing on the sandy slope.

"Do you know what I read last night?" Donnie asked. "I was reading a book of Hawaiian legends, and it said that the only time the shark men could make the change from shark to human and back again was when they were touching water. Water was what gave them their power."

They stood at the end of the chicken wire walk, gazing at the tiny, perfect beach. Chunks of driftwood, bleached white by sun and salt, had been tossed up the slope to mingle with a rubble of broken coral. And the sand was black . . . well, almost. Mingled with it were fragments of white coral and shells, chopped to bits by the action of the surf. More rocks were scattered where the surf came plunging in wild, lacy washes.

Kristal picked up a handful of the black sand and let it trickle through her palm. The granules were larger than regular beach sand—pebbly, rougher, and they were gritty, faintly sticky. She was sure that they would smell of the sea.

"This is it, Donnie," she whispered. "This is the same sand—the sand I've been finding in my room!"

"Are you sure?"

"Yes! Yes, I'm sure!" Violently she flung the sand away, wiping her hand on her jeans.

Donnie was exploring ahead and to the right, where an outcropping of rock marked off the edge of the tiny beach.

"Look!" he called. "Look out there, Kristal, at the color of the water. Can you see? There's a deeper blue in the center than there is at the edges."

Kristal came to stand beside him. He was right. The

little inlet was painted with a blue as brilliant as cobalt, but slightly to the right center that blue was more somber. The darker shade seemed to edge outward and then to the left.

"I see it," she said.

"The darker color means deeper water," Donnie said. "I think there's a channel coming through here, almost up to the shoreline. And I think it's deep enough to allow something pretty big to go in and out."

A channel deep enough to allow access to something large.

Kristal's skin suddenly felt very cold. She thought of it, a man walking down that chicken wire path as she and Donnie had done, pausing on the small, perfect beach to shed his clothing, then wading into the foaming surf until it surged at his waist. She could picture him diving beneath the water, to be replaced by a huge form marked with muted stripes. A creature that twisted a massive fin and then was gone, arrowing into deep and misty blue . . .

Her fingers tightened on the camera.

"Well, come on," Donnie urged. "What are you waiting for? Come and get some shots of that channel. Then I'd move back and get the beach from a couple of angles, and maybe even the house too. Just don't wade into the water. I wouldn't do that if I were you."

Kam Smith. Kamohoalii.

Numbly, feeling as if this were another dream from which she would awaken at any minute, Kristal did as Donnie instructed.

Donnie paced around the small beach, calling out to her in an excited voice. He kept pointing to something on the rocks, but Kristal didn't listen to what he said. She was trying too hard to concentrate.

Carefully she photographed the wood-and-glass front of the beach house, focusing on a window to the far right. It was *his* bedroom, she felt sure, although she was not certain how she knew this. And a room where he lived would surely possess more psychic emanations.

But maybe, the thought came to her chillingly, he didn't use the bedroom much. She supposed he didn't, not if he were a— If he were one, then it was much more likely that he went down to the beach at night, waded out into the channel, then swam out into the night sea.

The night sea. Swallowing, she concentrated her attention on the rocks again, and on the slot of deeper water that angled outward.

It was just after Kristal began her second roll of film that she began to get the eery sensation that something or someone was watching her. No, it wasn't that, not exactly. She wasn't being watched, but someone knew she was here. Yes, that was it. *Someone knew she was here.*

She held the Canon with hands gone abruptly shaky. The Maui sun burned down on her shoulders, yet she still felt cold. Donnie climbed about on the rocks, his shoes slipping as he called out to her. But Kristal couldn't hear what he had said, for the wind had come up, and it was blowing the words away from his mouth.

Kristal could feel that same wind tugging at the hem of her T-shirt, slapping it against her midriff as if to scold her. They shouldn't have come here. It had been a mistake, a terrible mistake, for what good would a few pictures be? Suppose that when they were developed, they somehow did show a shark image superimposed on a picture of a beach, or a house, or even Kam Smith himself. So what? What could that possibly prove to a woman like her mother who was normal to the core, who thought nightmares could be cured with hot chocolate, and grief with a trip to Maui?

Even if Kristal waved the pictures right in her face, Ann would not believe them. She could not, for if she did, it would be admitting darkness to her life. It would be acknowledging that there were things that could not be explained, no matter how hard you tried. Ann, Kristal knew, did not like the unknown. The pictures would tilt her life askew, and therefore Kristal thought that Ann would look at them and not see.

The wind was growing very cold. Kristal lowered her camera and started up the beach toward the walkway, her canvas shoes skidding on the granules of dark beach sand. It was then that she turned and saw him . . . Kam Smith, rounding the tongue of rock to the far right, walking slowly, deliberately, as if there were no hurry, no hurry at all.

How had he gotten there? It was Kristal's first thought, full of a dulled panic. *How had he gotten here?* They had left Kam at the dive shop miles to the north, in Makai, and now here he was, emerging from the rocks, and they had not seen his car along the road, nor had they heard one pull into the driveway.

As the man drew closer, Kristal saw another chilling thing. Kam's golden brown skin was wet, running with droplets of water, but his clothing was dry. How could that be? She felt a shiver shake its way along her rib cage. Unless . . .

Unless Kam had walked out of the sea naked, and then had put on dry clothing hidden for him among the rocks somewhere. And weren't these different clothes than she and Donnie had seen him wearing at the dive shop less than an hour ago? She was sure that he'd been wearing blue shorts and a Hawaiian shirt. Now he wore navy blue swim trunks and a yellow "Ocean Divers" T-shirt.

Silently Kam approached her. His eyes were black holes. Donnie, now far out on the rocks and stooping to examine something there, hadn't seen him yet. Kristal took a step backwards, her heart beginning to pound. Black sand oozed up over the tops of her tennis shoes and gritted in on her feet.

"What are you doing here on my beach?" Kam asked in a voice gone as dark and distant as a cave.

"I— I— Donnie and I thought we'd come and take some pictures," she stammered. "Pictures of the rocks and the tide pools and the surf—"

His mouth was as arrogantly carved as that of an ancient Greek statue. Handsome, handsome. It twisted now.

"You can take pictures of the tidal pools at any beach. Why didn't you go to Lani Beach, as you mentioned at the shop? Or to Kaunoa Beach? It's right down the road."

Kristal kept backing up, edging toward the walkway, nearly tripping on a big piece of driftwood. Behind Kam she could see Donnie still on the rocks, bending over, his mouth opening and closing. He was shouting something to her. But she could not hear it, for the wind whipped his words away over the open sea.

"I'm sorry we trespassed on your property," she began. She felt impaled by those piercing black eyes. "But Donnie told me— I mean, aren't all beaches on Maui public? We were just walking along the rocks—"

Kam gestured toward the north, where they could see the yellow sand line that was Kaunoa Beach and the small dots of bathers. "You didn't come over the rocks. You came in a car. It's parked in my driveway. I can see it from here."

Kristal gasped, turned. It was, of course, true. Sunlight glinted off the rear windshield of Donnie's car, giving lie to every word she had said.

"Give me that camera, little girl." Kam walked slowly toward her.

"No. I won't."

"Give it to me, you interfering little bitch. It is your mother whom I have business with, not you."

"My— Mother? Oh, please. Don't hurt her. No. I'll

leave right away. Donnie and I will leave, we won't bother you anymore."

"No, I don't think you will."

Donnie was scrambling off the rocks now, headed toward her, and Kristal saw that he carried a rock in his hand. He brandished it, as if he wanted to show it to her.

"Please," Kristal heard herself beg, her voice seeming to come from a very long distance away. "Please, don't hurt me. Don't make me dream those dreams anymore. I can't stand them, they frighten me so."

"Dreams?" The fathomless eyes, which were thousands of years old and had known the torment of hell, bored in on her. "I gave you no dreams."

"But you did! I dreamed of a— I dreamed of you. It was you, I know it was. I woke up to find sand in my room, black sand."

"I know nothing about it."

Implacably he approached her. And now in the air Kristal could feel the same low, subliminal rumbling that had been in the bathroom. Power. Raw, shimmering, vibrating power, alive in the air all around her. Lifting her up, taking her . . .

The wind grew even colder. It was, she observed, a black wind. It swirled up from the channel in the water and came toward her, enfolding her like a shroud. The power vibrated . . . strong, intense . . . focused on her, and it lifted her up and then dropped her.

The sand came up to meet her. Granules and pebbles and small, sharp lava rocks, reeking with the smell of the sea.

"Kristal! Kristal! In the name of God, what's the matter?"

Donnie was shaking her. He gripped her shoulders

and shook her back and forth as if she had been a mindless doll. Kristal could feel the beach pebbles move and shift beneath her. Dimly she noticed that one of her tennis shoes was touching the chicken wire walkway. The black wind was gone, and the sun was very hot . . . burningly hot, as a matter of fact. She could feel its fire lick up and down her arms, burning her skin like hot wax.

Donnie was agitated. "Kristal! What's wrong? I was calling to you, I wanted you to come and see this rock, it's been burned, melted almost—then suddenly you fell down. Did you faint?"

"Faint?"

She felt unutterably groggy. Reality was slipping away from her. She could feel it go; it was as if she had been tied to life by fragile gossamer threads and now those threads were breaking one by one . . . When the last thread broke, what would happen to her? Where would she go? Would she sink beneath the sea, to that blue-blue world of colors and shadows and things that lunged and fought and killed?

"Kristal! Answer me!"

"Him," she managed to gasp out. "I saw him, Kamohoalii . . . *He* . . . did it . . . the power . . ."

"What're you talking about?" Donnie's voice was frightened. "Nobody was here. I didn't see anybody."

"He— It's my mother he has business with. My mother. He said so, Donnie, HE SAID SO—"

"Kristal?"

"He came from the water, his skin was wet but his clothes were dry, Donnie; he swam here from the shop, don't you see? *He came from the water. Oh, God, oh, God . . ."*

Donnie was crossing himself. "Kristal! What are you talking about? Did you see him? Kam Smith? But how could you? He wasn't here. I was here all the time. I would have heard his car, I would have seen him. And where's your camera? What happened to it? Did you lose it?"

Donnie's voice went on, high, scared. But Kristal could not talk to him anymore, for there was something wet running down her cheeks, something hot and wet and sticky. When she glimpsed the horror in Donnie's eyes, she knew that it was blood.

Ann Southworth sat in the emergency lounge of the little island hospital for the second time that day, her body frozen with alarm. Now Kristal was ill, sick with a malady identical to Buddy's.

Two hours ago she'd been in Buddy's hospital room, trying desperately to read the paperback novel she'd purchased at the drugstore. The print was impenetrable, the complex plot beyond her, and she was turning a page, trying to concentrate, when she heard her name paged on the hospital's PA system. She was to go to the emergency area immediately.

There, strapped to a bed on wheels, she found her daughter, Kristal. The girl was a horrifying sight. The blonde hair streaming out on the flat pillow was reddened and matted with blood, and her face was a mask of blood. Red had poured out of her mouth, some of it crusted and dried on her lips and neck. More blood had streamed from her eye sockets, from her nose, giving her face a wet, red, glistening look.

Her daughter's breath came in ragged gasps; and beneath the thin cotton blanket, she fought the bands that bound her to the bed, fought with a violence that Ann had not imagined those slender limbs could possess.

"He came out of the water . . . the water . . ."

"Kristal? Krissie?" Ann's horror was an actual, physical thing, tasting of acid and bile. "Krissie, honey, oh, baby . . ."

"Mom . . . Kamohoalii . . KAMOHOALII . . ."

The cries and mumbling of her daughter made no
sense, yet in some terrible way they made a very great
deal of sense. Ann's mind was reeling. She stayed by the
stretcher, clutching Kristal's hand until a nurse came to
wheel her into the examining area. Then she sat tensely
waiting in the crowded waiting room, which reeked of
sweat and cigarettes and disinfectant.

"Mrs. Southworth?"

Ann looked up. Donnie Perriera, his suntanned face
bleak, was standing in the doorway of the waiting room.

Chapter 23

"I drove Kristal to the hospital. I didn't know what else to do. I hope that was all right, Mrs. Southworth."

"It was, Donnie . . . it was fine."

"We were at the beach," he told her.

The boy was full of fear, Ann thought, exactly as Mick Rogers had been. He sat beside her on a shabby seat in the waiting room, and he twitched and fidgeted.

"Her camera," Ann asked. "Did Kristal have it with her? Where is it now?"

Donnie hesitated. "I don't know. I couldn't find it. She had it, and she was using it, and then— Then it was just gone. I guess I could go back and look for it."

"Yes, I'd appreciate that. What beach were you at?"

"Kaunoa."

A lie. She knew it, she felt it. She thought of her daughter on a stretcher, tossing from side to side, blood matting her hair. *Think, Ann,* she ordered herself. *Think.* Buddy and Kristal were both sick with the same illness, ugly scrapes disfiguring their arms and legs, their limbs fighting with insane strength at the straps that tied them down. Both of them were muttering things having to do with the sea, with an entity to whom they referred as *he.* *He* ...

Buddy had developed his illness after making a dive in the ocean. Now Kristal, after having gone supposedly to the beach, was also sick. Mick Rogers and Donnie Perriera were both lying, or at least hiding something ... something that terrified them.

Questions vibrated in Ann's mind, to which she could find no answers. There was something, some common denominator to all of this, she knew there was. But what?

Kamohoalii. Kamohoalii.

What a strange thing for her daughter to have cried out. It was a Hawaiian word, of course, the syllables flowing and musical yet somehow ominous with a dark majesty.

"*Kamohoalii.* That's a Hawaiian name, isn't it?" Ann asked Donnie. "Kristal said it. Do you know what she was talking about?"

The boy's facial muscles gave a little jerk. He looked down at the floor, where someone had crushed out a cigarette butt, and answered, "I ... I don't know, Mrs. Southworth."

"I suppose it would be easy enough to find out," Ann said. "I could drive over to the library and get a Hawaiian dictionary, or I could ask the librarian to help me. Do you really want me to have to do that, Donnie?"

His tongue came out to lick his lip. "I guess ... it's just some stories she's talking about. Some old Hawaiian legends I told her."

"Legends about what?"

"Oh . . . shark legends."

"Sharks?" The word seemed to hang in the air for a minute.

"Stories about the old shark gods . . . things like that. They're kind of a hobby of mine. I have a whole lot of books at home. And Kristal had taken some pictures—" He broke off.

Ann stared at the boy who sat beside her. She had heard his words, but somehow they seemed not quite real. Shark gods. Legends. She thought of Kristal's nightmare of sharks, of a needlepoint canvas missing for nearly a week and then found, it seemed, by Buddy at the bottom of the sea.

"We're going to have to talk, Donnie. There's a lot that I think we need to say to each other."

"Yes, Mrs. Southworth."

Donnie Perriera's face looked frightened, but there was none of the hostility she had felt with Mick.

They went to Apple Annie's in Kahului in the Kaahumanu Shopping Center where Ann, taking Dr. Hartung's suggestion, was halfway through a frothy strawberry-pineapple daiquiri, the drink having arrived embellished with a parasol, a maraschino cherry, and a quarter slice of fresh pineapple.

The evening crowd was low-keyed. There were a few families, some tourists, an attractive couple holding hands. Beside Ann in the booth, Donnie toyed with a Coke. He looked uncomfortable and kept pushing his glasses back up on his nose.

"Now, what is this all about, Donnie? I wanted to stay with Kristal, but I felt it was more important just now to talk to you. And I think it's time we did talk. You were lying to me there at the hospital, weren't you? And I don't think you're the kind of boy who usually lies."

"No. I'm not."

The boy stared down at his Coke, stirring it with the long straw.

"Well then, Donnie?" Ann asked gently.

"I don't know if I can tell you, Mrs. Southworth. It's too fantastic, yah? You wouldn't believe it. Kristal knew you wouldn't believe it. That's why we—"

"Why you what?"

"Why Kristal wanted to take the pictures."

"What pictures, Donnie?"

Ann tried to quell her impatience. Donnie was a good kid, a studious and obviously hard-working one; he was polite and terribly frightened for Kristal, and Ann liked him. And he was still afraid to talk to her.

The boy was searching for words. "She was good at taking pictures, Mrs. Southworth. Better than you know. Oh, it's all crazy. I've got books at home with stuff in them . . . I let Kristal read a couple of them, and they're crazy, too. My dad, all he knows is the camera business and taking care of the lawn. He'd get mad if he knew what was in those books. I was going to tell Kristal some of the things I'd found out, some of the things in the legends—"

"What legends? Donnie, I want to understand everything you have to tell me. I promise I'll listen, and I won't get mad at you, and I'll believe it if I can. But you have got to talk to me. Buddy is sick and nobody knows what's wrong with him. Now Kristal is sick, too. They could die, Donnie. Don't you see that?"

He looked at her over the rim of his drink, then said, "Are you sure, Mrs. Southworth? Sure you want to hear this?"

"Donnie—"

"It's the shark gods I'm talking about, Mrs. Southworth. I think there's one on the island now, and I think he's the one who gave Kristal those bad nightmares and left the black sand in her room, and I think he's the one who's making her sick now. I don't know how he's doing it, but I think he's the cause."

Ann swallowed hard. She forced herself to look into the youngster's earnest face, the brown eyes that believed.

"And all this has something to do with the pictures she was taking?"

"Yes."

Again Donnie hesitated. "You see, she— Kristal's different, Mrs. Southworth. She's very sensitive . . . *a* sensitive. If things were right, she could be one of those mediums you read about—you know, the mediums who have seances and call up spirits. She has that kind of ability. She sees things, knows things . . ."

Unconsciously, Ann was nodding.

Donnie went on. "That's why she came to me at the shop that first time. Because this thing, this ability, whatever she has, was showing up in the pictures she took. She kept getting these really strange photos. Superimposed images, things in the shots that shouldn't be there, that she hadn't put there. She wasn't faking, Mrs. Southworth. I may be only seventeen, but I've been using a camera for years. I'm good, too. I think I can tell a fake."

Donnie's words were coming out faster now. He had forgotten his Coke.

"The first shot she took was off your lanai—a photo of the sunset. But the picture came out wrong. She got the image of a shark superimposed over the sunset. There was no way for that to have happened accidentally. No way at all."

Ann remembered the occasion, the furtive way Kristal had seemed to hide the spoiled photo. The way she had acted at Christmas when Kam had found her "goof."

"And she took one on the rocks at Lani Beach," Donnie continued. "There was a cloud in the picture, a kind of misty cloud over the rocks, and inside that mist

was a body, Mrs. Southworth . . . the body of a woman
. . . all chewed up and mutilated. Did you know that four
years ago a dead woman *was* washed up on those rocks?
Those very same rocks. They said she'd been killed by a
shark. I didn't tell Kristal, I didn't want her to know that,
but it's true. And the house in Lahaina, that missionary
house . . ."

But Ann had stopped listening. *It was his girlfriend
who was the last known shark incident on Maui. She got
it in the water, just like that girl in Jaws.* Susan's voice
rang in Ann's mind like an alarm. What did it mean?
God, what did it all mean?

Ann drew a deep breath, gathering her resolve. "Go
ahead, Donnie, tell me about these shark legends and this
shark god, whatever you call him. I want to know everything."

So he told her. About Moaalii and Apukohai and
Uhumakaikai, about Kuhaimoana and Kamohoalii, who
was reputed to be the older brother of the volcano goddess Pele.

He told her of shark forms so huge that they could
inhabit only the deepest channels of the islands, sharks so
huge that they were larger than a grass house, bigger than
two grass houses. Shark gods who, at night, inhabited
deep undersea caverns, mysterious retreats guarded by
pairs of smaller, white-tipped reef sharks, or even by
moray eels.

Ukanipo. Moaalii.

Donnie told her about the fishermen who worshipped the shark gods, prayed to them and made them
offerings of food so that they and their canoes would be
spared. And sometimes their prayers were answered. It
was often told how a man whose canoe had capsized and
who was left to struggle in the viciously choppy Auau
Channel, would be fortuituously rescued by a long, grayish form, ridden to shore on a kingly back.

The shark demons had the power to come ashore disguised as tall, strong, handsome young men. But, Donnie went on, these winsome young men were careful to hide their backs from the sight of ordinary mortals, for upon their backs were marked—like a tattoo—the telltale lines of a shark's opened jaws. This was the one way by which they could be discovered and exposed.

Ann heard Mary's voice. *Ask him why he always wears a shirt.*

Donnie continued, sometimes such a young man would go down to the beach where people swam and surfed and fished. Stopping to be drawn into conversation, he would make a casual joke. "Don't go into the water," he would jest, the sun shining upon his cleancut, strong and beautiful face. "If you do, a shark might get you."

The jest would be taken as simply that—merely a joke, for the Hawaiians were a happy people. Swimmers would wade into the surf anyway . . . and there would be an accident. One of the bathers would be attacked by a shark and tragically killed. Back on the beach, the young man who had joked about sharks would be gone, no one knew where. And the people would realize that he had been a shark god.

Donnie told Ann the story of a woman, many centuries ago, who had fallen in love with such a young man, drawn irresistibly to his strong good looks, his flashing dark eyes, and muscular shoulders. The woman had had a husband and half-grown children. She'd left them all to follow the young man. She had dived off a rock and swum out into the sea to meet him, and she'd never come back again, ever. And there were songs sung of that love, and of the shark man Kamohoalii, and of the loneliness within him that could be assuaged—if only for a short time—by the love of a human woman.

Once, a real young man, a true human being, had

decided to try to kill one of the frightening shark men. He searched all over, visiting many sacred places and consulting with a kahuna of much magical power, until at last he found a sacred spear point, one that had been consecrated by many holy battles. With this spear point, the legends said, he was able to kill the shark man.

Another way to kill a shark god, the legends whispered, was to totally immerse him in fire. If you could keep him away from his mother-sea, which was the source of his strength and power, and if you could fight the hypnotic thoughts that he visited upon you, and if you could burn his flesh absolutely clean, then perhaps you could kill one. Maybe.

For it was known that some of the shark demons possessed powers. One of these was the gift of fire. With the sheer force of his mind alone, a shark god could set the water that washed over rocks to boiling. They could even turn the rocks themselves as red hot as the round stones that were placed inside the belly of a pig to roast it. And if a man happened to be walking on those rocks, he would be burned.

After Donnie had finished telling her these things and more, Ann looked down and found that she had finished her drink, that she had taken the slice of sweet Maui-grown pineapple and crushed it with her spoon, smashing it beyond recognition.

"Donnie— Oh, Donnie, this is incredible . . . all of it."

"The legends are real, Mrs. Southworth. You can look in any book. Go to the library if you want, see for yourself."

"But—" She shook her head. "But that's all they are . . . just legends. I mean, you don't think any of this could be real?"

"I have friends, Hawaiian friends, who talk of a

shark god somewhere off Kaunoa, near the lava flow maybe."

Ann was quiet for a long time. The waitress came, smiled at them, left their check, went away again.

"And you think . . ." The words clogged in Ann's throat. "You think that this . . . this shark god person might be someone we know?"

Donnie's eyes slowly met hers. They were brown and earnest, flecked with specks of amber, and they held fear.

"Yes. Kristal thought it might be Kam Smith."

"Kam? *Kam?*"

Ann felt as though her entire mind were rocking. She clutched the Formica surface of the table at Apple Annie's, grabbed on to it for support. For surely, if she dared to let go of it, she would be whirled away, hurled into the clear, cold maelstrom of terror . . .

Ann's mind fought for control, for reality. "Now, Donnie . . . surely you're not talking about the Kam Smith we know? The one who teaches scuba diving at the Ocean Divers shop?"

"Yes, I am. That's who I'm talking about."

"But— It's ridiculous! Kam is a person just like anyone else. He's a man, a human being, he breathes, he eats, he goes to the bathroom just like any other person—".

Ask him why he never takes off his shirt.

Donnie's mouth had turned obstinate. "Kristal felt it, Mrs. Southworth. She *knew* it. I know it sounds crazy, I know it sounds really far out . . . but one of the pictures Kristal took, it was of you and Kam going into the water. Kam had his wet suit on, but in the picture there were lines—funny white lines—superimposed over the wet suit. *That picture showed the mark of a shark's jaw on Kam Smith's back.*"

"Oh, Donnie—"

"Kam," Donnie said. "Kamohoalii. The names are similar, Mrs. Southworth. Do you think that's an accident? I don't."

Ann felt as if she could barely breathe. "But that's not evidence. That's not enough, Donnie. It's only speculation—"

"Mrs. Southworth, remember Kristal's nightmares? Those bad dreams she had? She found black sand in her room after each of those dreams, sand she hadn't put there. It was black sand, Mrs. Southworth . . . the same kind of sand that's at the beach where Kam Smith lives."

"Black sand?"

"Yes. I— I guess I should tell you . . . that Kristal and I, we weren't just at any beach, the way I told you. We were at Kam Smith's beach house when she got sick. And Kristal said she saw him just before she collapsed. She saw Kam Smith."

Chapter 24

It was two in the morning—or was it three? Ann had utterly lost track of time. She stood by the front sliding doors of the pole house, gazing out at the night view. The moon rode the sky, nearly full, its face mottled. Light splashed down onto the sweep of ocean, setting it afire with pale phosphorescence. Along the curve of the Makai shoreline, she could see the pinpoint glitter of hotel and condominum lights.

She slid open the lanai door and stepped outside. The air was clear and crisp, carrying sound so faithfully that she could hear the sound of a car on Paliuli Street, a distant baby's fretful whimper, the wash of the surf two miles away. Incredible, she thought dully, that she should be able to hear the sea from that far away. But it was true. Susan had verified it.

Susan. Ann thought of her cousin, fast asleep on the

floor below with her husband, wrapped in her normality like a cocoon. At midnight, when she had driven up to the house, exhausted and frightened, Susan had come out to the driveway to greet her.

"God, Ann, is there anything I can do? Both kids sick. This is terrible, just terrible."

"I guess there isn't anything," Ann had replied wearily. "They're both under sedation right now, and the hospital is doing all they can. Dr. Hartung says he can fly them to Honolulu or even the mainland if he has to."

"Do you know what it *is*? I remember when Cliff and I were in South America that time, I had to have an innoculation, and they gave it to me with a dirty needle and I ended up with hepatitis—"

Somehow Ann managed to cut Susan off. She didn't want to hear about uncleanliness in faraway places, she didn't want sympathy or questions or anything else. She had to think.

"Well, remember . . . if there's anything, anything at all . . ." Susan had started up the driveway again, yawning. A few two-inch cockroaches were scurrying on the cement—part of the normal nighttime scene here.

Ann, starting toward the house herself, suddenly stopped. "Yes," she said. "Yes, there is one thing . . ."

Susan yawned again, her jaw popping. "What's that?"

"I was wondering, do you know much about the ancient Hawaiian legends? I mean . . . the old stories?"

Susan laughed shortly. "Jesus fucking Christ, Ann, have you completely lost your mind? Here both of your kids are in the hospital, and you're thinking about legends."

"Yes, I—"

Ann stood very still, the words almost on the tip of her tongue. All she had to do was to say them, tell it all to Susan, and Susan would reduce the fantastic things

Donnie had told her to normality. *What a bunch of bullshit,* she'd say. *Ann, now I know you've lost your mind.*

But her cousin was edging toward the house—a cold December wind had sprung up—and suddenly Ann felt too weary to talk. Susan drank too much and said *fuck* too much and was disillusioned in paradise. No, she didn't want to talk to Susan, she couldn't. They had nothing to say to each other, not really.

She said a quick good night and went into the house.

Coming into the empty house, she had switched on a lot of lights and then gone over to the telephone. It was a wall phone, hung in the kitchen near the refrigerator. Its color was bright, slick yellow, and there was a long cord, some of its coils twisted backward into half-knots. Her hand shaking, Ann dialed Kam Smith's beach house. She let the telephone ring at least twenty times before she finally gave up.

Where was he? she wondered feverishly. Out with friends? Attending the movies at Kaahumanu or drinking in one of the hotel bars in Makai? Or was he out swimming in the dark night sea?

Oh God, Ann, she ordered herself grimly, *don't start that, don't start it.* It was bad enough that Donnie Perriera had told her those shark-god stories, had stared at her with frightened brown eyes that believed.

But she, Ann, didn't believe. Oh, the legends were fascinating, she wouldn't deny that. Maybe they were even beautiful, with their tale of a creature half man, half devil, driven through the centuries by a deep and piercing loneliness. It was, she supposed, the story of Lucifer, the fallen angel, told in another form. But she didn't believe it.

Out on the lanai, she stepped to the railing and leaned over. She looked downward at the panorama of moon and sea. Condominium lights glittered. The Wailea Beach Hotel was an iridescent gem. A car wound uphill, its headlight beams flashing among the *kiawe* trees, which were everywhere. From far away, a steer bellowed. A cattle ranch actually abutted the top increment of the subdivision, Susan had told her. Cowboys here were called *paniolos.*

The Hawaiians were a beautiful people, she thought, swallowing. Their language was lovely. Their legends too were beautiful and warm. But that was all they were, legends, fairy tales, no more. It was, of course, utterly impossible that a man could assume the form of a shark at will.

Facts, she thought, staring down at the pinpoint lights of Makai. *I will think about the facts.*

One fact was that she, Ann Southworth, a new widow grappling with grief and with her own guilt feelings, had met a very attractive man, a man who possessed undeniable physical magnetism. She had been drawn to that magnetism.

The legends had mentioned that, Ann remembered with a queer feeling. *The woman had had a husband, half-grown children, and she had left them all to follow the handsome young man . . .*

Well? Ann thought it with anger, remembering Susan's cautions on Christmas Day. In many ways her cousin had been right. She, Ann, was vulnerable. Her marriage to Bob had been going bad for a long time. His death had been, in a way, a relief. Now here on Maui she had responded to the first attractive man she had met. Was that so wrong?

It was a relationship that probably couldn't survive her leaving the island, she added to herself grimly. She was realistic enough to hold no illusions about that. In two weeks she'd be back in Ann Arbor again, taking up her life there, whatever it was to be now. She'd forget

Hawaii. It would become a post card again, distant and unattainable. That was reality.

Another reality was the fact that Kam Smith was a man born on Maui. He loved the sea. But why shouldn't he? The ocean surrounded him every day of his life, it provided his livelihood. And if he did possess a scar on his back, who was to say that a welding shop accident had not caused it? That was certainly a far more reasonable explanation than Donnie's assertion that it was the "mark" of a shark god.

As for the fact that Kam concealed his back, that, too, could be explained. He was ashamed of the scar's mutilation. She could not blame him for that. People did hide their flaws; were ashamed of their bodies sometimes. It was a part of human nature. And if there were people on Maui who did believe the old legends it was probably because these were part of their heritage.

Ann had begun to pace the lanai. Questions surged about her, would not leave her alone:

What about Kam's other girlfriend? Karen Weeks, the woman who had worked at a local travel agency, and who had been killed by a shark four years ago?

What about Sarah Faulker? Sarah had been the wife of the missionary in whose home Kam Smith's grandfather had been a household servant. Sarah Faulker too had been killed by a shark.

There was also the woman in the legend. She had dived off a rock, swum out into the sea to meet the shark man, and she had never come back again, ever.

Ann looked down at the gem lights of Makai and shivered.

Oh, Mom, Kristal had told her after that first nightmare, *I was under the sea. It was dark down there, but I didn't care, it was beautiful, all muted in a thousand shades of green and blue and gray and purple. . . . I was strong, so strong, Mom, and it felt good going through the water like that, my fin—*

My fin. The frightened childish voice still full of sleep and nightmare. The sea smell in the room, the puddle on the floor that had tasted of salt. The black sand Ann had found; the odd, spoiled photograph.

And hadn't Donnie too mentioned Kristal's pictures? Hadn't he cited them as proof for his wild stories?

And now, at last, Ann thought of something she could do, something more concrete than placing a call to a telephone that did not answer, or simply pacing the lanai, wrestling thoughts that were too much to handle.

She went back into the house and walked down the hall toward Kristal's bedroom. *I've never been the kind of mother who searched my children's rooms,* she thought as she opened the door. *Yet now I've done it twice in one day. First Buddy, now Krissie. And I've got to.*

Her daughter's room was like Kristal herself—neat, dainty, pretty. Even in a house that did not belong to them, Kristal had still managed to add essences of her own personality to the bedroom. A spray of salmon-colored bougainvillea was arranged in a small bud vase. A few seashells and bits of coral sat in a row on the bureau top. There was a swatch of Hawaiian-print fabric, rich with earth tones.

But there were other items in the room that were more disturbing. A wastebasket, shoved against the wall, was filled with unlikely objects: an empty Breck bottle, a pair of garishly painted coconuts, an alarm clock still ticking away. Why? Ann wondered. What had been the purpose in it?

And there had been something else. In the corner by the dresser, there was a spill of dark sand on the carpet. Some of the pebbles were sugar-sized, others were the size of small pebbles. Running her hand along the bureau top,

Ann felt more grittiness. It was as if Kristal had tried to clean up the sand, but had been in a hurry.

Where had that sand come from?

It was late, Ann told herself, nearly three in the morning. She was being over-imaginative. It had been an upsetting day, she was worried sick about her children, and Donnie's incredible stories about shark legends had struck in her brain like a broken record.

She was tired, so weary that she could sit down on the yellow carpet here in her daughter's room, and weep and weep. Ann put her face in her hands and waited until the convulsive shaking of her body had stopped. Then, drawing a quivering breath, she continued her search.

She found the shoe box in the bottom drawer of the dresser, stored beneath Kristal's treasured old University of Michigan sweatshirt with holes in both elbows. In the box, carefully arranged in rows, were the pictures Kristal had taken with her camera over the past two weeks. Tidal pools and rocks and beach scenes. Sunsets, rich with color. The wharf at Lahaina, the hodgepodge of shops, a picture of Ann standing by the huge banyan tree on Front Street. Slowly Ann leafed through the collection of prints, discovering nothing more unusual than evidence of hard work and strong talent.

Then, at the back, she found them . . . the pictures that had gone wrong: a mutated sunset shot in which a creature with dark and baleful eyes glared at the camera; a beach photo of something twisted and broken and dead; and a picture of herself and Kam Smith in full diving gear. On the back of Kam's wet suit, sketched there in funny, wiggly white lines, was the outline of a shark's jaw.

There were more. And nearly all of them had something to do with a shark . . . and, either directly or indirectly, with Kam Smith.

For a long time Ann sat on the floor in Kristal's room, staring out through the sliding glass doors at the Hawaiian night. The moon had been obscured by clouds: darkness had descended, impenetrable as a blanket.

Kam, she thought. *Oh God, Kam.*

Her body felt icy with a terror that had no name, for now she knew what she had to do.

Chapter 25

It was seven-thirty the next morning. The Maui sun was already bright, glittering off rock and filling the air with its intense light. The blue of the sky was rich, sharp, acrylic-hard.

Ann lugged her tank and backpack along the path crushed in the lava debris. Her breath already wheezed in and out of her lungs, although she had come only about 200 yards from the car.

Was this the way that Buddy, Mick and Lisa had come? But she was sure that it was. Mick had been specific in his directions and now, she thought, she was going to find out. She would learn what had happened to Buddy on that dive, what had begun the illness of her two children.

Proof, she thought. Proof lay somewhere in that ocean, and she was going to get it.

She stopped, out of breath, to set her tank down and rest. The damned thing was heavy. She wasn't sure exactly how heavy—fifty pounds maybe. The plastic handle of the backpack, which she had already attached to the tank, cut into her hands. She probably should have worn the tank on her back, but she was afraid of slipping on the rocks deposited here two hundred years ago. Already she had twisted her ankle on the uneven footing.

Ann shaded her eyes to stare at the panorama of the lava flow. It began somewhere up on the volcano's shoulder, its beginnings shrouded in greenery, in *kiawe* and pasture grass. But gradually there was the beginning of a darkened blotch that tumbled seaward, merging into outcroppings of rock, vast fields of it, a flowing now frozen for eternity.

It was in terms of giants that the lava flow forced Ann's thoughts. Collossal, tumbled causeways. Gigantic boulders. Precipitous fissures, rocks heaped on top of lava bombs, their surfaces jagged, cutting, dangerous. Nothing had had time to become worn down by time. Only in a few places had grass managed to sink in roots to soften the jagged magnificence of this behemoth place.

Perspiration poured down Ann's face. Impatiently she wiped it away. She moved the heavy tank a few more yards, then set it down again and yanked at the zipper of her wet suit.

She unzipped the suit, feeling the cool morning air on her bare midriff and at the top of her bikini. She was burdened with straps and equipment, the deflated B. C. vest, the ten-pound weight belt, the mask pushed up now onto her forehead, the flippers carried in her left hand.

But still there was room for a breeze to cool her hot skin. God, but it felt good. She never should have worn the wet suit, it was becoming a steam bath under the stress of her exertions.

She hesitated, eyeing the path that lay ahead. It

angled toward the beach, where waves pounded rock, the loose stones in the water making an eery, rolling noise. The sea would wear the lava down to sand, if it were given centuries enough to do the job.

Was this the place? Was this where the three had dived?

No, Ann remembered. Mick had said it was further, past the first inlet where a tiny stand of *kiawe* trees were trying to make a foothold. How on earth had the kids lugged their tanks this far? But they had.

They were sixteen, with the vitality of the young. Maybe they had shared their load somehow, or made more than one trip. But Ann knew that she herself could not make two trips. She could barely make one. She was thirty-eight years old and only moderately athletic, and she had not gotten much sleep last night. She was desperate now, desperate . . .

She trudged on. Grimly she eyed the cutting rock edges that were on every side of her now. One misstep and she might trip again, cutting her ankle or foot, or even breaking her leg. If that happened, she'd be out of luck. There was not another human being in sight, and it might be days before there would be. She had already gone past the point where the tourists stopped. Beyond here was nothing but primeval rock.

Maybe a lone fisherman, carrying his tackle box and pole, might find her, a week from now, or two weeks . . . She shuddered.

A dot of something white lay ahead, among the rocks where the path toiled upwards. Sweat poured from her as she dragged the heavy tank. Her head was aching, her arms were agony, her breath screamed. How much farther? How much?

When she reached the white dot, she saw that it was a piece of coral, sun-dried and beach-tossed. Someone had put it there, probably to mark the path. Yes, up there ahead lay another one. So people did use this path. Occasionally.

She climbed on. Deliberately she made of her mind a blank. She would concentrate on one thing only: the path. She would take one step at a time and then another one. She would not think about Kam Smith, about the strange, tattoolike scar on his back, a telephone that rang and rang in an empty house . . .

Ann, Ann. Get control of yourself. Don't think. Not now. Just walk.

She discovered that if she put her foot on a large rock, rather than on one of the countless small ones, it would not tip but would provide firmer footing. Rocks were balanced on rocks, hung over fissures, formed grottos and overhangs, and were jagged. The path led her beside a fissure, around lava bombs as big as closets, then toward the sea.

Cliffs. Uncompromising. The trail wound across their brink, over a precipitous drop. *Insane,* Ann thought, her heart hammering. She had been insane to do this.

She set the tank down, regripped it with fingers that were running with sweat, and tried not to look down. Had the three youngsters really climbed this trail? How could they have? Were they fools? Suicidal? No wonder Mick hadn't wanted his mother to know where they had been diving. Ann didn't want to know either. She didn't want to be here.

God, help me. Help me to do this.

There was a place where the rim of the cliffs slid away toward the sea, where she had to scramble to keep her feet from slipping and clutch at the sharp rocks for balance. She prayed. She put the tank down and picked it up again and hauled it a few more feet, and kept going.

She had to urinate. For at least the hundredth time she put down the tank. She peeled down the wet suit, its black neoprene inner surface running with the moisture of her own body. It stuck to her skin, and with revulsion she plucked it away and stepped out of it. Then, impulsively, she hurled it down the cliff.

She saw it, a tumbling spot of orange that smacked against rock, plunged into a white swirl of surf, and was gone. She didn't see where. Well, she would dive without it. It was too hot anyway to wear a wet suit, and all that perspiring was weakening her.

She squatted within the sharp black shadow of a boulder and pulled down her bikini bottom. The smell of urine hissing against rock was sharp, ammoniac. Ann smelled it with an odd kind of pleasure. It was a human smell, it was real, it proved that she was still alive.

She stood up, adjusted her bikini and her equipment, dragged at the tank again, and got going. It was better walking now that she had shed the wet suit. And now she could drop off some of the lead weights too.

There was a place where the rocks were like steps. Abruptly she was at sea level, near a rocky flat. The surf here was milder, the water stained a blue as brilliant as the tube of ultramarine in her paint box.

And here, as if to mark the spot, were the remains of what had once been a pair of Hawaiian beach thongs. Had they been washed ashore here? Left by some previous explorer? Or had Mick or Lisa dropped them?

Ann put down her tank and flexed her aching right arm. It was numb; she felt as if it might fall off at the armpit. Her knees were shaking uncontrollably. She let them buckle and sank onto the rocks.

She rested for nearly forty-five minutes. At last she stood up, turned on her air supply and slung herself into the tank, tightening the straps of its harness. She walked out to where the flat table of rock edged into the waves.

Stooping, she spat into her mask, both lenses, then rubbed the spit all over the glass. She dipped the mask back into the water to rinse it. Now the lenses would not fog up while she was underwater.

She pulled on the mask, made sure her hair was not breaking its seal, and adjusted the head strap. Then she bent awkwardly to pull on her flippers one at a time. She had forgotten her gloves, but it didn't matter. She certainly wasn't going back for them.

She popped a little air into the buoyancy control vest to float her until she made it to deeper water, and then put the mouthpiece of the regulator into her mouth.

Sssssssssss.

She could hear her own first breath, dry and raspy now because the rubber diaphragm had not moistened. But there was no reason to panic, as she had done on her first dive. The diaphragm would moisten, and then her breathing would be deep and slow. Hadn't Kam Smith, in the classes, assured her of that? If nothing else, Kam could teach diving. And now, ironically, she would use the knowledge he had given her.

She started swimming. Some instinct made her angle to the right, and after a few minutes she stopped, hanging on the surface to stare down.

The lava had, of course, kept on flowing directly into the sea. Here too it had hardened, and marine animals had made their homes on the rocks, softening them until they had made a jungle, a garden of color and life.

There were promontories, underwater cliffs, sloping fissures, bridges and overhangs, all of it sized to fit a giant. And it was lavishly beautiful.

Breathing easily into her regulator, she began her descent. As she had been taught, she cleared her ears every few feet, and as she sank downward, she looked about her.

This was a very private world, full of colors that few human beings would ever see. There were growths of tan-yellow coral, where small reef fish darted in and out.

There were butterfly fish of the same type she had seen at Molokini, scraps of graceful yellow.

Coral: rich rust-reds. Beige and tan and yellow and white. Little patches of sand so clean-washed and perfect that they might have come fresh from the hand of God.

Her gauges had been mounted on a console that hung to her left along with a small diving light. Carefully she consulted it as she swam deeper into this coral world.

Thirty feet.

Forty, forty-five.

Sunlight glinted on the bottom, forming moving chains of light. Ann turned and headed toward a big coral-covered dome. It was a huge outcropping, as big as a building, formed when the lava had erupted into the sea. Sometimes, Ann had read, these formations could be hollow. The outer edges, cooling faster than the molten core, formed a crust, and when the hot lava drained away, it formed a cave.

This was such a formation. She knew it as soon as she saw the first aperture, almost beneath her flippers, a hole reaching downward into the cave and admitting light to it.

She swam down to stare into the cavern.

Buddy had babbled of a cave. *The cave. The cave, the cave.* Monotonous horror. *The cave CAVE CAVE CAVECAVE...*

She could enter here, she was almost sure. Yet she hesitated. The tank she wore on her back was bulky, and there had to be room for it to go through the opening. She could not allow herself to be trapped, for she had violated all the rules of safe diving. There was no companion to free her, or if she ran out of air, to buddy-breathe with her.

She decided to keep on swimming, to see if she could find a bigger opening. She angled lower, swam past two more apertures, odd little crannied, coral-dripping windows. Then she found it, the big wide mouth, big enough to drive a car through. It admitted the sunlight so brilliantly, she would not even need a light.

She swam into the cave.

She was just beginning to wonder whether she ought to use the underwater light anyway—after all, she had brought it—when she spotted the first moray eel. From a crack in the rock, the creature lunged at her, its beak snapping viciously.

Ann reared back, suppressing a scream into her regulator. What a huge, coiled-up, snakelike creature it was, fat and brown-spotted and undulating. It looked like some prehistoric monster, its beak opening and shutting, its little eyes savage.

As Ann edged away, she felt her heart hammer. Was the animal capable of swimming out of that crevice and coming after her? Could it sense her fear?

The regulator was wheezing now with her quickened breathing, and she felt the full, flowing spray of air. Then she caught a movement out of the corner of her eye.

ANOTHER EEL.

A second eel—yellower, fatter, and larger than the first one—protruded from the wall on the opposite side of the cave entrance. Its jaws menaced her, its eyes little holes of fury. An eel could snap a man's hand off at the wrist, Kam had told them in class. He personally knew people who had lost fingers, chunks of their arm.

Guards, Buddy had whispered over and over. *Guards, they were guards, they guard him . . .*

The legends, they had said that too.

Frantically Ann finned past the eels and was inside the cave. She looked about her, almost forgetting to breathe in her wonderment. The cavern was gorgeous, almost cathedral-like, all shadows and misty blue and openings that admitted bars of sunlight. Reef fish were like swimming flecks of gold. To her right the cave seemed to penetrate into the sea floor itself, and here the shadows were deeper.

Ann gasped. For an instant—one shaking instant—she had thought she saw something move, far back in the shadows. Something that shifted a long body and turned so that sunlight gleamed on dark eyes.

She whirled about.

Her heart had begun to slam again. But nothing happened, and at last she began swimming up the left wall of the cave, her eyes searching out the coral. Ahead of her a small opening admitted a triangle of sun and a flotilla of little silvery fish.

Gradually Ann's heart slowed its frantic pounding. She finned through the cave, searching for she knew not what. The underwater lantern—which she had managed to switch on—cast a pale tunnel of light.

She spotted a pair of feelers protruding from underneath a ledge and flashed the light at it; abruptly the slipper lobster, bright and angry looking, scuttled away. Another ledge revealed a nest of them, at least five. A pity they wouldn't be having lobster dinner tonight; a shame Buddy wasn't here with her to enjoy this. Buddy . . .

She was transferring the light from her right to her left hand, about to start exploring the other side of the cave, when she felt it.

Pressure.

It felt as if something huge had slapped the water, sending vibrations through it. Then she saw him, aimed at her like a projectile, monstrous in his size, his body streamlined, planed down, and beautiful. His sides were mottled by faint stripes. His low-slung jaw hung open, revealing sharp, irregular teeth. *A shark!*

He came toward her in a quick thrust of his powerful tail, plunging so close that she could feel the pressure of his movements in the water. His eyes were black, black as ink, as death, holding her, mesmerizing her as a snake would a bird.

Terror spurted through her. She tried to swim backwards, kicking out with her flippers, but the huge grayish body rammed forward again. *Something was happening in the water. A terrific, whirling energy.*

The eyes . . . familiar . . . tried to possess her.

Ann, Ann. I want, I want I WANT I WANT I NEED, I AM SO LONELY, I MUST HAVE . . .

"No . . . " Ann tried to scream into her regulator, her voice coming out as a ragged choke.

The shark made another lunge. Ann closed her eyes and cried out. Force boiled in the water, huge power. She was helpless, whirled about, tossed . . .

Chapter 26

Something stopped it.

Something . . . she didn't know what, but whatever the reason, the thing, *he,* had gone.

Ann clung to a piece of coral, grasping it with bare bleeding fingers. She sucked on her regulator in agonized gasps. She was sure that she had only a little air left now, and she almost didn't care.

What had it been? Had it been . . . him? Kamohoalii?

Huge shudders racked her, and there was a sensation in her groin, molten and moistening and frustrated. Her bikini bottom, she noted dully, had nearly been torn off. It hung from her right thigh only by a piece of elastic.

She still was not sure exactly what had happened. He had come at her, the huge shark, and there had been the awful power in the water, the deep, subliminal, incredibly thrilling vibration that had sent little shock waves through the water and into Ann's body, probing every orifice of her. Oh God . . . God . . . oh, *Jesus,* and the shudder gathered in her, and then she had felt her body surrounded by something. A form huge and hard and rippling with the supple musculature of a snake.

Vibrations. Some hugely sexual force pulling at her, melting in her, spreading her, this wasn't happening, it wasn't . . . oh God! *Dear God, oh— Oh—*

Then, as suddenly as it had begun, the thing was finished. Or, rather, left unfinished, for the powerful form had uncoiled itself from her and sliced away into the darkness of the cave. One of the apertures had abruptly darkened with its passage, and Ann knew that it was gone.

Jesus Christ. Sweet, sweet Jesus.

Ann hung exhausted, clutching the piece of coral and waiting for the strength to come back to her so that she could leave the cave. The coral was as rough as a Brillo pad, abrading the water-softened pads of her fingertips, and Ann wished for her gloves. She clung, forcing her breathing back to normality. *One . . . two . . . breathe, Ann, breathe slowly. Don't use up all your air; you've got to conserve it.*

Breathe slowly. Breathe . . .

At last she was calmer. Water surrounded her, chilly now, for without the wet suit, her body had begun to shiver. Raised goose bumps were hard along the surface of her arms and legs. Trickles of water had begun to leak into her mask, and quickly she cleared it as Kam had taught her in the dive class. *Kam.* Oh God.

She took another long, slow breath and then pushed off from the coral and began to swim upward, puffing a little air into the B.C. vest to help her ascend. She'd seen one of the openings big enough to swim through and at least that way she'd avoid the moray eels.

Then, glancing downward, she saw the scrap of white. No, it wasn't quite white, there were patches of color. Blues, greens, a blotch of yawning black.

Ann paused in her upward swim. The goose bumps on her arms and legs prickled her like pins. She focused her eyes on the square of white. What was it? Then she knew . . . knew with a freezing core of dread. It was the needle point canvas. The canvas that Buddy had babbled of in that hoarse agonized voice she had barely recognized. *What was it doing down there? What was it doing down there?* She would never forget the terror in that cry.

And Buddy had been right. Why *was* it there? There was no logical way the canvas could have found its way more than forty feet beneath the sea to an underwater lava cave. But it was here.

Ann's mind struggled to explain it. She finned downward to scoop up the canvas. She felt the texture with her fingertips. The white cotton threads of the canvas were softened by water, their sizing gone, the wool itself squashy from soaking. But the colors had held true. She recognized part of the design: the scuba diver, the free-form shell she had stitched in the lower left.

She held the canvas out to examine it more closely. It had changed. Someone, *something,* had finished it.

Ann stared at the canvas, her mouth drying. Yes, the picture had been completed. Everything that Ann had begun—the diver, the cave opening, the other fish shapes —all of it was altered now, as if the stitcher had donned a pair of horror-film glasses that gave everything seen through them a twisted, macabre, evil cast. That was exactly it, Ann thought. The canvas had become evil.

Yet it also held terrible magnificence, for now all of the areas, all of the yarn, was filled in, the work as exact and careful as Ann's own. There was a cave mouth exactly like the one Ann had entered only moments ago. The scuba diver on the point of swimming into the cave was a woman. A naked woman.

Ann recognized the flying blonde hair, the curve of hip and thigh and buttock. Herself, nude, her breasts floating free . . . *Herself*. And in the cave, just inside the entrance and lying flat, all the curved, vicious length of him, was . . . *he*. The shark.

Ann's breath caught. Shuddering, she expelled it again. In her shock she was having trouble maintaining her buoyancy. She had unknowingly floated up more than ten feet. She must breathe, she knew. You could not hold your breath while using scuba, for if you rose even a few feet, the compressed air you took into your lungs could expand and kill you.

Breathe, Ann, she ordered herself. *Don't hold your breath.*

There was more. There had been another picture to the upper right of the canvas, a shape with which she had been struggling for days, for she had not yet known clearly what it was to be. Now this too had been finished.

A woman was entwined sexually with the form of a huge shark, her spine arched back, her pelvis tilted forward against the muscular tail. On her face was etched a look of joy and agony.

> *How can those terrified vague fingers push*
> *The feathered glory from her loosening thighs?*
> *And how can body, laid in that white rush,*
> *But feel the strange heart beating where it lies?*

Oh God, Ann thought. That damned poem. She pushed back nausea. Did a shark have— How could it . . . ? They . . . they *can't be*—

The shark had been stitched as semihuman in appearance (*like an Indian frieze*, Ann realized), with huge, dark, agonized eyes. Clasped about the woman, penetrating her with the appendage at the base of his tail, he was a performer in a monstrous parody of human sexual intercourse. And something in the expression of the shark showed that he knew this. That he suffered, as the woman was suffering.

Yet there was . . . more. For, looking at the picture, Ann could almost feel the sexuality throbbing in the water about the writhing pair. And she knew one other thing, knew it with a sickening, visceral twist in her belly. The shark was huge. The woman was small and vulnerable, her muscles already shrieking with the pain of her physical penetration. She would not be able to survive this monstrous coupling. This hideous and frighteningly beautiful love would be ephemeral. It would last only the space of moments, a lifetime crammed into a few heartbeats, a few ecstatic thrustings.

Soon, very soon, the terrible joy would seep into the water like lymph fluid. The clean, incandescent flame burning the woman would turn to agony. She would fight and gasp for air. The shark, turned animal now, would voraciously lunge toward her again, and— The ecstasy would be over. Rushing into pain now, into shocked ugly hurting, a slam of power, and then . . .

A body was lying on the tumbled sea-washed rocks, blurred and shielded by the odd misty cloud in Kristal's photograph, but still clear enough so that Ann could see it all. The hair floating in the wash of surf as loose as grass, no longer combed, no longer living. Nipples pointed upward, shriveled, dead. Limbs sprawled like thrown things, like old rags, loose and vulgar, both legs gone just below the thighs. Strings of flesh hanging in gobbets and pieces, chopped-up musculature like badly butchered beef . . .

Ann was vomiting. She spewed forth her insides into the regulator, heaving and choking. She backed away from the cave wall, letting the needlepoint canvas drop from her fingers to fall, as softly as a leaf, to the clean sand below.

Bury it here, she thought. *Leave it here, let it be forgotten.* Then she was finning upward, kicking hard, frantic in her need to get to the surface.

It was nearly two in the afternoon now, the air hot and breathless, as if all of the forces of nature were gathering. Ann was in the bathroom of the pole house, staring at her own naked body in the vanity mirrors that abutted each other. She still was not sure how she had managed to get home. Half crawling, half walking, she had managed to drag herself back onto the rocks. There she had sunk down to lie pressed to sun-warmed lava by the weight of her tank.

For long moments the world seemed to turn about, tilting crazily. She gasped, sobbed, nearly gagging. But at last she was able to sit up and managed to unstrap the backpack so that the tank rolled heavily to one side. She yanked away the rest of the equipment, letting it fall. Then she just lay there, nearly naked, trying to stop the convulsive shivering of her body.

Kam . . .Kamohoalii . . .

At last she staggered to her feet and found her tennis shoes where she had kicked them off. Her bikini was a shambles; her bare skin was beginning to burn in the hot sun. But there was a pair of shorts and a T-shirt in the car, and it didn't matter anyway. No one would see her here on the lava flow: never had she been so alone, so far away from other humans.

She abandoned her equipment where it was and stumbled back up the path, fighting waves of exhaustion that threatened to topple her.

Facts, she said in her mind grimly as she walked. Think about the facts . . . if you can.

Shark gods were known to possess a mark on their backs, a scar in the shape of an opened jaw. Kam Smith had one. She herself had seen it.

He hid his scar, just as the shark men were supposed to have done. In fact, Kam had had no girlfriends since Karen Weeks until herself—was this because sexual intimacy meant that he would have to reveal his telltale scar to a lover?

Shark men sometimes joked, telling people not to go into the water or a shark would get them. Hadn't Kam Smith made that very joke the first time she and Buddy had walked into the Ocean Divers shop ? She could still remember Buddy's glower at the inappropriate humor.

Two women connected with Kam Smith or with his family, Karen Weeks and Sarah Faulker, had died grisly deaths from shark attacks. Kristal had dreamed of sharks. The black sand that Ann had found in her daughter's room was exactly like the sand at the beach in front of Kam's home.

The illness that her son and daughter both suffered from— What if Kam Smith were somehow the cause of it?

As for the mind, Ann, that too can be a very powerful instrument, Kam had said that day as they were sitting around the pool at the Hawaiian Beach Maui after making a dive. *What if impulses can be transmitted from one brain to the unconscious center of another? What if that second brain could be told to tell its muscles to slow down, or even to mutilate its own body?*

Hadn't the little nurse at the hospital implied that Buddy might be abrading his own skin, mutilating himself? Dr. Hartung had hinted at that too, by wanting to call in a psychiatric consultant.

Images flashed in her mind. Kam Smith, once before a dive class, carefully putting a pop can from which Buddy had drunk on a shelf. What if he had saved it in order to have a sample of Buddy's saliva with which to work a spell?

Had he taken something from Kristal too at the Christmas party—maybe, when the girl had been showing him her photographs? *Didn't Kam tell her once that he had studied the magic of the kahuna, the Hawaiian magicians?* God. What if . . .

Her thoughts hurried on. *The needlepoint.* Kam had told her that one day it would be completed. And now it had been. Hideously, obscenely. Just how had that been accomplished? The stitching, she recalled with a tremor, had been as careful as her own, indistinguishable from her own work.

What if it was her own work? What if Kam—Kamohoalii—had somehow transmitted impulses to Ann's mind and fingers telepathically so that—unconsciously, like spirit writing—she had actually *completed the canvas herself?*

Impossible! Or was it? Her mind raced. All those nights when she had slept poorly, had awakened exhausted and with sore fingertips, as if she had been working for hours in her sleep. And the maid, Mary Tanaka. What if impulses had been transmitted to the fat woman so that she stole the canvas *without even knowing that she did so?*

Terrified by her thoughts and the abyss to which they led her, Ann fled the lava flow and drove home.

She had parked the car in the driveway, seen that both Cliff and Susan were still at work, and stumbled indoors like a wounded animal seeking sanctuary. It was early afternoon—nearly two now—and she had to go to the hospital yet, and there were other things she wanted to do, as well. Things which, yesterday, she could not have imagined herself doing. But now they were necessary. She must do them. *She must know.*

She headed toward the bathroom, stripping off her shorts and T-shirt as she went. She threw the torn bikini into a wastebasket. First, a shower. She needed to get the salt off her skin, she needed the cleansing warm spray of water on her, the normality and the comfort of a steamy bathroom.

But instead of getting into the shower right away, something made her pad, nude, back out to the kitchen and dial the Ocean Divers shop.

"Hello? Ocean Divers, Gordon speaking."

It was Gordon Begrin, owner of the shop and Kam's employer. Was Kam there? Ann let the question form in her head but did not speak. She stood clutching the receiver of the telephone.

Was Kam there? He could be, probably was. And, if so, what did that prove? According to the old legends, a shark man could go into the water and assume the form of the shark at will. Just as easily, he could switch to his man-form again.

After he had encountered her in the cave, all Kamohoalii had to do was to swim back down the coast to Makai. There was a beach directly across the road from the dive shop; the beaches were everywhere on Maui, you could not get away from them. Unseen in the waves, he could resume his human form, retrieve a hidden bathing suit, walk to the dive shop, and tell Gordon Begrin he had taken a scuba class out, gone for a short swim or a break, whatever lie he chose to tell.

A shark, with its powerful musculature, could swim miles of sea without the slightest effort, did it daily. Kam Smith could have made that transition in only a few minutes. No one would ever suspect. Why on earth would they? This was 1980. This was the age of gasoline shortages and television sets and Johnny Carson. Legends weren't real.

Would Susan Rogers believe Ann's story . . . assuming that Ann were to pull her courage together and tell her cousin, mincing no words? *Susan, I think Kam Smith is really a shark man. He walks around on land as a handsome young man, and sometimes he changes into a shark. A big one.*

Ann could hear Susan's reply now. *Jesus God, Ann, what the fuck is happening to you? I think you've had about ten daiquiris too many. I told you Kam Smith was the beach boy type, but I think this is carrying it a bit too far, don't you?*

Well, then Cliff Rogers ... she could tell Susan's husband.

Slowly Ann replaced the receiver of the telephone, hearing its click, and stood there thinking. Tell Cliff? Susan's husband was certainly sensible and as prosaic as a piece of shoe leather, as a slice of calves' liver, or the daily newspaper. He had no imagination whatsoever. To him, Maui's lava rocks were something to be rooted out with a bulldozer and replaced by shrubbery and sod. He wouldn't believe her story, would feel uncomfortable even listening to it. He would reject her with a sour remark, as he rejected his own wife. No, she could not talk to Cliff Rogers.

Buddy and Kristal? They were in the hospital, helpless under sedation. They certainly could not help her. Mick Rogers then? Or bouncy Lisa, with her puppy fat and vacant chatter? No.

Dr. Hartung. Now, there was a thought. But the man was a physician, had spent his life listening to fantastic stories from people who looked otherwise perfectly ordinary. *Dr. Hartung, they tap my telephone. Doctor, she hits me in bed after I'm asleep ...*

Ann had a feeling that Dr. Hartung was tired now. He had come to Maui for the beaches and for the deep sea fishing. He had a light medical practice. Soon he would taper it off even further; he would retire. He did not want to think about strange legends, about men who could change their bodily form, about a shark that harbored a hunger for the love of a human woman . . .

Ann walked toward the bathroom again, absorbed in her thoughts. Donnie Perriera then. Donnie was really the only one, she thought. He would listen. He was young, his mind was still flexible, he'd have ideas. He already believed and could believe more. He could believe as much as Ann now did.

But first she needed that shower. And there were some other things she had to do before she could go to the hospital and visit her children—proof.

A sense of urgency possessed her. There was time— it was only two o'clock—but she would have to hurry.

It was in the bathroom, turning herself in front of the mirrors, that Ann saw the mark on her back. Her body was covered with injuries and scars from her ordeal, most of which she had not even noticed at the time but were now beginning to throb with pain. Her ankle, which she'd twisted on the rocks, had begun to swell. There were cuts on the sides of her feet from the rocks. The coral had cut her fingertips. Her back and thighs had been scraped by the shark's body as it lunged past her.

But, narrowing her eyes into the mirror, Ann saw something else. *Oh, no,* she thought, *it couldn't be,* but it was.

The mark was faint, barely noticeable to the eye . . . and it didn't hurt. Ann would never have known she had it if she hadn't been inspecting herself for other damage. Yet there it was, delicately etched in shadow, the mark of the shark's opened jaw.

Chapter 27

Ann was in the car again, driving with desperate speed, for it had somehow become two-thirty, and there was much to do. She had let nearly the whole day fleet past her. There was no time to think or to give way to the horror that filled her.

She, Ann Southworth, had a mark of a shark's jaw on her back *exactly like Kam's*.

Oh, yes, the Devil's mark, the frantic woman at Kaahumanu Shopping Center had shouted at her. She had approached Ann, menacing her. *You have it, his mark, his! The devil, Beelzebub, oh my god, yes, he comes in many forms, my lady. Fish forms and fire forms and eel forms and slime forms . . . and when he puts his mark on your back, then you are his. You are his!"*

Was she? Oh God, *was* she his? Ann's fingers squeezed the steering wheel until her bones hurt.

The travel agency was located in one of the small hotel arcades that were common in Makai. The arcade had a delicatessen, a little newsstand stocked with paperbacks, a real estate office, a bathing suit shop.

Ann stepped inside the travel agency and felt the air conditioning chill her like the touch of a hand from a sarcophagus. The office was small, carpeted in burnt orange and furnished with furniture of a type Ann had seen in the window of Rattan Art Gallery. There were three desks.

"Yes? May I help you with something today?" A redhead looked up. She was about Ann's age but had evidently spent hour upon hour baking herself in Maui sun. Her skin was creased with hundreds of nearly invisible, papery little lines, so that you could see upon her face the ghost of the old lady she would someday be.

"I don't know," Ann said. "I suppose you'll think this is strange, but I would like to ask you something. Did a woman named Karen Weeks ever work here? About four years ago? I was told it was an agency in Makai—"

The redhead's face had changed. "She's dead, now. But, yes, she did work here. She was assistant manager."

"I know I have no right to ask this, but would you mind coming to have a cup of coffee with me? I'd like to talk to you about Karen."

The woman's eyes questioned. "All right. I guess I could. I'm rewriting a ticket, but it can wait. Would Dongo's be all right? It's close enough to walk."

Her name was Elyse Chow, she had grown up in Morton Grove, Illinois, and had met her Hawaiian husband while vacationing at Waikiki. The couple had moved to Maui, and now she worked at the travel agency and he ran a car-rental business. For fun, they went backpacking in the crater of Haleakala and did a lot of spear fishing.

Ann liked Elyse immediately and felt that under other circumstances they might have been friends. But today she felt too urgent for anything except the questions she must ask.

"I'm trying to find out about Karen; she's my step-sister," she said after the waitress had brought their coffee. "My family always thought there was more to her death than people were telling. I was vacationing here on Maui and I thought— I mean, she did work here, and I thought you might know something—"

Elyse nodded. "I don't know how much anyone knows. It was horrible and I'd rather not think about it. I mean, my husband and I are in the ocean nearly every day, and there are some things you'd just rather not put your mind to."

Ann knew.

"Could you tell me about it? And about Karen too, of course," she rushed on, covering herself. "I mean, the way everyone here knew her. What she was like here. Karen had grown kind of distant from the family."

Elyse frowned. "Oh? But I thought Karen said— She did hear from her mother pretty often, she used to get letters—"

"Was Karen well liked here?" Ann asked quickly.

"Oh, yes. She was a quiet kind of person, quiet and friendly, and she was devoted to Laurie. She'd have done anything for her. It was a damned shame when Laurie had to be sent back to the mainland; she'd done so well here, she'd almost gotten over her troubles—"

Laurie? Who was Laurie? But Ann was afraid to ask, she'd only get herself more tangled up in her lies.

"Troubles?" she allowed herself to question cautiously.

"Why, the asthma." Elyse was staring at her. "That little girl was in a pretty bad way when she got here to the island, but of course the sun and all that swimming helped her. A funny little thing she was, all bright-eyed and full of stories. She was always dreaming funny things too. Dreamed in color, she said. She'd come down to the office sometimes and talk to us."

Always dreaming funny things. Had Laurie Weeks dreamed of sharks? Ann felt her fingers freeze on the china handle of her coffee mug.

"The accident," she blurted. "Tell me about that."

Elyse Chow hesitated, some of her friendliness gone. "Well, none of us knew much about it. Karen kept to herself pretty much, I told you that, how quiet she was. A nice, romantic kind of person, you know? She'd been all wrapped up in her boyfriend and a bit upset—I think she had some worries that she wasn't talking too much about . . ."

Ann sat very still. Karen Weeks had been upset, worried about something. Her boyfriend had been Kam Smith. But what sort of worries could she have had? Feelings, strange intuitions that all was not right with the man she loved? Questions about him that could not be answered?

"Anyway, Karen took to going to the beach a lot, on her days off. She was quite a swimmer, always had been. She'd go down to Lani Beach, or Pulelelua, and swim just out beyond the surf—oh, she'd go a mile, at least. And it showed, too. She had a beautiful body and looked ten years younger than her age. I wish I could say that for myself."

Elyse's hand flicked up to her own cheek, then came down again to toy with a coffee spoon.

"Did the . . . attack happen while she was swimming?"

"We think so. You see, her body was found one morning by a couple of tourists . . . a father and a little boy. They'd been out snorkeling in front of the hotel where they were staying. They found her washed up on some rocks there. She was—" Elyse swallowed. "She was dead, of course, and they said— The doctor said she'd been attacked by a shark. She must have bled to death in the water, both of her legs had been—"

Elyse's hand fluttered again at her face.

"After she died, Laurie just went crazy. She had to be sedated and put on a plane for the mainland. She kept talking funny, really queer things, and I think they got her out of here just to hush her up. The tourists, you know, they don't like . . ."

"What was she saying?"

Elyse had stiffened. Again there was a tiny pause before she spoke. "Oh, what I'm trying to say is that here on Maui we get thousands and thousands of visitors and it isn't good to alarm them. Because shark attacks are so rare, you see, people swim here all the time, *all the time,* and it's safe. But they said Karen went swimming just as the sun was setting, and the water was cloudy that day because a lot of sand had been kicked up by the surf. The visibility wasn't good. They say you shouldn't go swimming at night or when you can't see in the water, because if there are any sharks, that's when they come out to feed, and—"

Elyse shoved her coffee cup away. "Well, now you've got me started thinking about it again. Karen and I were friends, I liked her. She was too crazy about Kam. I'd told her that, told her he would never be serious about anyone, but she believed in true love and didn't listen to me. And, anyway, it didn't matter, did it? Because she died, and it didn't make any difference."

But it did make a difference, Ann wanted to shout. But Elyse Chow was sliding out of the booth, smoothing out the skirt of her Hawaiian print sundress.

"Which doctor did the autopsy?" Ann blurted, getting up, too.

Elyse Chow's face tightened. "You're not Karen's

stepsister, are you? You didn't even know Laurie was her daughter. Are you from some insurance agency, some welfare office or something? Karen didn't have any insurance, she didn't have anything. She was one of the nicest women you'd ever want to meet, and she didn't deserve what happened to her."

"I know. I'm sorry. I—"

"You can go talk to Dr. Hartung if you want. He'll tell you the same thing. Karen was a good person and that little girl, Laurie, she was the best. I hope she's all right, wherever she is. I hope she got well. That's all I hope."

Ann hurried after the redheaded woman.

"You hope she got well? Was Laurie sick when she left Maui?"

"Sick? She had some skin disease, I guess. A nasty one. The doctor said it was brought on by grief. And her breathing, it had gone bad. They shipped her right to the hospital in L.A., I heard."

They were at the door now, by the little newsstand offering copies of the Maui *Sun*. Elyse had started to stride ahead fast, trying to get away from Ann.

"Elyse. Please. Just one more thing. Could you tell me if Karen ever did needlepoint? Embroidery, needlework, anything like that?"

Elyse Chow turned to stare at Ann as if she had started to strip off her jeans in public.

"No, she didn't do needlepoint, she painted on china. And, anyway, what do you care? You're a ghoul, they all are; all they ever cared about was the blood, and the shark."

In the car again—it seemed that was her refuge, her thinking place—Ann drove hard. She was sweating. Moisture ran down her sides and down the backs of her knees: she could feel its slow trickling. Karen Weeks, who had dated Kam, had been warned away from him just as Ann had. Karen had had some worries she would not discuss with her friend. Karen had painted on china.

And Laurie, bright, winsome, little Laurie Weeks, a child who dreamed in color. What had Laurie talked about, after her mother's death, which had been so threatening they "got her out of here just to hush her up"? Had it been a shark man she talked of? And what of Laurie's strange illness, which so closely resembled Buddy and Kristal's?

Oh God, Ann thought, and she swerved to avoid a fat woman pedaling along the road on a battered moped.

She didn't deserve what happened to her. Elyse's face had gone funny when she said that, sort of stiff, as if she had opened up a closet door to find an obscenity hanging there.

Why? Why had Elyse's face looked like that? It had been more than a shark attack, Ann was sure . . . because you got one look on your face thinking about a grisly accident and another look when you thought of the unspeakable.

Drive, Ann, she ordered herself. *And hurry,* because Buddy and Kristal are sick, and those marks, those skin scrapes or whatever they are, they can come out of thin air and he doesn't even have to be near you. All he has to do is exert his mind power.

Power, power vibrating in the water, rumbling, subliminal, as if she'd been hurled to the center of some enormously powerful generator . . .

Twenty minutes later she was again sitting in the office of Dr. Hartung, her eyes fixed on the portrait of the doctor taken beside the corpse of the large marlin. The man shuffled some papers.

"Mrs. Southworth, I have only a minute before I

must go to the hospital. We've had an accident in Makawao, and they're doing emergency surgery. I have to
assist."

There are others more in need than your children, he
was telling her indirectly. Ann flushed.

"I— I won't take your time, and I am sorry to
bother you, but it's my children I've come about. You
see, there's something, something I have to tell you—"

"Mrs. Southworth, I really do have to leave."

"No!" Desperately she stood up, tears welling in her
eyes. "Dr. Hartung, I want to know about the death of
Karen Weeks. I know it sounds crazy, but I must know. I
can't take the time to explain now, but it's important.
Urgent—"

"Karen Weeks?" His face showed no expression. "I
don't believe I remember her."

"She died of a shark attack about four years ago."

"Oh. That one." And now the doctor's face did
show a reaction. A slight dilation of the blue-blue eyes, a
congealing of expression.

"I don't know much about autopsies," Ann plunged
on. "I don't know if they are a matter of public record,
and I certainly don't want to intrude on Karen's privacy.
But I know there *was* an autopsy and that you did it, and
I think this is all related to the children's sickness." She
sat down again and leaned forward. "Dr. Hartung . . .
please. Tell me what you learned in that autopsy?"

The man's face was carefully blank. He said nothing.

"Dr. Hartung, wasn't there a report made of that
death? I mean, accidents *are* a matter of public concern. I
could go to the county courthouse in Wailuku and get
copies of that death report. I could ask a lot of questions,
Dr. Hartung, and I will ask them. Buddy and Kristal are
my children, and they're sick!"

The doctor steepled his fingers and blew through

them. "All right," he said. "Yes, I did it, I was the one. It wasn't a very pretty case, Mrs. Southworth, and there were things connected with it that— well, I've never seen them before and I don't want to see them again, ever."

Things. Ann could imagine what things. She felt the perspiration begin to flow again, down her sides from her armpits. She wondered if she had remembered to put on deodorant after her shower.

"There was more to it than just a shark attack, wasn't there?" she demanded.

"Yes. There was. I was never sure, Mrs. Southworth, exactly what did happen to that woman. The evidence of her body—well, no explanation, no rational explanation, was quite enough to explain it. She'd been attacked by a shark, that was very clear. The shape of the chunks taken out of her flesh indicated that it was a very large animal. I even found a tooth in her. And when we sent the tooth to Honolulu, they sent back a report verifying that it had come from a large tiger shark."

"But there's more." Ann said it flatly.

"There was a mark on her back— I'd never seen anything like it. And she'd been— I don't know how to put it —abraded. It was as though the animal had toyed with her, brushing against her over and over again. Sharkskin is sharp, it's rough, and when it's rubbed across the human body, it can tear it exactly as a file can rip away flesh.

"And there were other things . . . another indication. And that one I couldn't understand because . . ." Dr. Hartung stopped.

"She was sexually violated, wasn't she, Dr. Hartung?"

"Yes. Something had penetrated that woman's vagina and virtually ripped out her insides. It was as if she'd been raped by—" He struggled for words, found none, and stopped.

"I kept that autopsy quiet. Didn't let anyone see it, except the ones who had to. And even they were not fully aware of what it all really meant. I'd put the language into the most esoteric of medical terms so that they couldn't understand. I didn't want them to understand. I didn't want anyone to know, anyone. Because— You see, I found some objects embedded in her uterus, high up, very high up, where nothing should have penetrated. Nothing should have gotten that far—nothing."

"What did you find?" Ann whispered.

"I found portions of shark denticle, unmistakable. I sent those to Honolulu, and they were positively identified."

It was as if the doctor had forgotten her presence, as if he sat once more in his office on another day, staring down at a dry written report held in shaking hands.

"Pieces of sharkskin, Mrs. Southworth—pieces of sharkskin. Do you know what that means? *That goddamned shark was inside her.*"

Dr. Hartung stood up. His face had gone papery, the blue eyes burned. "I'm sorry, I really have to get to the hospital now. That splenectomy won't wait. I shouldn't have told you those things. I hope you'll keep them quiet. And I pray that your children—" Then he looked at her, ducked his chin a little, and left the office quickly.

Chapter 28

Ann sat at a table in the public library in Wailuku. She was out of breath, for there were only forty-five minutes before the library was to close, and she had hurried to get here. But she was here now, and she could be damned efficient when she chose.

The library, located across from the courthouse, was an oasis of dingy tranquility. There was a linoleum tile floor, dulled cream walls, and jalousied windows opening to a view of lush palms. Through the windows sifted the sound of traffic, a child's high-pitched, joyous shout. Inside the library, someone coughed hollowly. There was the persistent hum of a fan. The librarian, seated at her table by the door, talked in a low voice to a man who was checking out books.

Ann stared at the stack of books in front of her. One

was a greenish paperback; the others were cream-colored paper-bound books printed by a small local press. She could check out the book on sharks, the librarian had told her, but not the others, for they were a part of the library's private collection of Hawaiiana and were housed in special locked shelves. Duplicates were available for checking out, if she wished, but sadly, many of the duplicates were out or had disappeared . . . she did understand, didn't she?

Ann nodded, wishing only that the woman would finish her speech and leave her alone. There wasn't time. Urgency gnawed at her, making her heart race.

Quickly she opened the shark book, flipped through its pages. *General Form. Anatomy. Food and Feeding Habits. Fresh-Water Sharks.* All of the prosaic details of a beast shimmering in its savagery.

She turned to the index and paused, fascinated. *Shark Arm Murder, Sharkfin soup, Shark repellants, shark-sucker (remora)* . . .

Ann's eyes searched the columns of the index until she had found what she wanted; then she switched back to the beginning of the book. Page forty-three, all laid out for her in scientific language.

In all male selachians the inner edge of the pelvic fins is modified to form an elongate clasper, an erectile organ used to transfer sperm to the female during copulation. The claspers . . . during copulation are bent forward and are swollen. They may be armed with one or more hooks . . . or covered with denticles, presumably both to rupture the female hymen and to secure a firmer hold . . .

Clasper. So that was that it was called. Jesus, sweet, sweet Jesus.

Her eyes took in the print, tried to digest it, failed, and tried again. She forced herself to finish the page, to turn it and go on to the next. Page after page she skimmed, looking for what she knew she must find.

Sharks held captive in the tank had been observed. It had all been written down by one of the attendants lucky enough to be passing by at the precise moment.

The 27½ male had seized a slightly larger female by the left pectoral fin and was firmly holding on to her with his mouth. Shortly after, the male was able to manipulate his body so that his tail was over her back immediately in front of the second dorsal fin and, using the latter as an anchor and with her pectoral fin still firmly in his mouth, he was able to thrust his right clasper into her vent. The fishes copulated for about half an hour, the female remaining passive and the male making a gentle, rhythmic motion with the hind part of its body . . .

Ann stopped, laid the book down, and sat staring across the room at the file drawers of the battered card catalog. She blinked her eyes rapidly and tried to quell the nausea that rose in her as powerful as the surf itself. She must not be sick . . . she must not be sick . . .

Slowly the feeling of sickness went away. She discovered that she was sitting with her legs clenched rigidly, her thigh muscles tight.

Across the room the librarian checked out books to a small Japanese boy. Ann could hear her asking him if he had enjoyed his reading over the holiday vacation. She could not hear the boy's reply. Outdoors, a car horn honked, and there was the distant sound of an ambulance siren. The hospital was nearby, and life went on, or tried to . . .

Her hands shaking, Ann reached for the other stack, the booklets printed up by the historical society. *Missionary Days on Maui: Josiah Faulker,* was the title of one of them. Ann opened its pages and began to read.

Sarah Faulker had kept a diary. She had embraced life with a joy that could not be restrained by the rules of religion or by the isolation of the island village in which she lived.

Although much of the booklet reprinted letters and observations made by the severe Josiah, along with his careful statistics on converts, there was a twelve-page section of excerpts from the diary of the missionary's wife. This part of the book was prefaced by a portrait of Sarah herself. Ann stared intently at it, drawn by some quality in the pretty woman of thirty who posed for the camera with her hands loosely folded in her lap.

Sarah Faulker had a face almost square, with a full mouth and wide cheekbones. Her eyes, set within a delicate slant of bone, faced the primitive camera with a smoldering passion. She wore a plain black dress, but even its severe style could not hide the lushness of her figure. Wide, graceful shoulders sloped downward to rounded bust and slim, strong waist.

According to Kam, Sarah Faulker had been a strong swimmer, and Ann could believe it. In fact, she could almost picture Sarah jumping up, once the picture was taken, to fly with long graceful steps out of the house and down the dusty road to where the surf pounded the beach. Stepping behind a jut of lava rock, Sarah would quickly strip the black cambric dress from her body and then would jubilantly stride into the surf . . .

There were other pictures too. Josiah Faulker, patriarchal in full beard and mustache, his mouth stern with the pronouncements of God. What had it been like between Josiah and Sarah, at night when the candles were blown out and they lay together in their bed with the jalousied windows open to the Maui breeze? Did they whisper together and laugh? Did they hold each other tight and hot, twining their bodies together, until neither could tell where one ended and the other began?

Ann's thoughts, distracted, began to slide away. She felt tears burn the backs of her eyes, although she wasn't quite sure why. No, she didn't think it had been that way for Josiah and Sarah.

Her thought of Kam came with piercing intensity. Could it ever have been that way for them? Once, just once, she longed to be loved with fierce joy, to blend herself utterly with a man, to lose herself in him . . .

Ann forced her attention back to the leaflet. Sarah's diary.

Our little household here is small but cozy. We are a bulwark against the paganism (Josiah says) of this farflung island. There is Josiah and myself, of course, and the children, Mary, Patience, and Fortitude. Ah, my little Tudie, such a secret joy she is to me with her bright laughter and winsome dreaming . . .

More entries followed, selected by the historian seemingly at random to provide, Ann supposed, a mosaic picture of missionary life. Yet, disjointed as it was, scraps of Sarah's life came through.

Kamo took me to the beach today, and we swam among the rocks searching for crabs. He was able to snare four ono with his spear, he is very good at fishing and can talk about the sea for hours. Each day he learns more English and sounds more and more like a fine Eastern gentleman, most amusing, since he is in appearance a wild and beautiful primitive man, quite at home here on these wild rocks and promontories . . .

Kamo had to have been Kam's grandfather, of course. He was mentioned several more times, each time in the same breathless manner. *A wild and beautiful man.*

Had Sarah Faulker been in love with Kamo . . . or merely attracted to his vitality, such a contrast to that of the dried-up missionary?

Ann noted that Sarah's references to religious matters were few and quickly penned, as if they meant little, and she cursed the unknown compiler, for the entries held little continuity. Sarah and her children had taken a picnic to the Iao Valley, where they had swum in a mountain pool. They had cooked fish over an open fire, had spent a joyous day riding in one of the big Hawaiian outrigger canoes. A daughter of their cook had fallen ill with belly pains and Sarah had spent an agonized five days trying to nurse her. Still, the child had died.

A few entries were disturbing:

My little Tudie has been unhappy these days. She has awakened screaming almost every night with such frightening nightmares that I do not know what to do for her. And we have found bits of black beach sand in her room, most strange, for her room is cleaned most thoroughly, despite what Josiah, in one of his tempers, insists. I wake up and brew Tudie some hot milk mixed with tea, but it does not help much . . .

Another entry:

My daughter has scrapes and bruises on her arms and legs of a most distressing nature, and babbles in her sleep of uncomfortable things. I have mislaid my embroidery . . .

Maddening, maddening, for now the entries—were they out of sequence?—went back to matters of everyday living. A pig hunt. Another fishing expedition, the making of soap, the picking of mangos, for it was mango season and Josiah Faulker had imported some trees for the delectation of his family.

One final entry:

*Fortitude continues her nightmares unabated. I am
fearful for her, wondering if it is some tropical fever
she has picked up. She dreams of sharks, it is most
ugly, and I am wondering how a fragile child of
twelve can know such horror. Josiah tells me to
pray, and not to worry, but I cannot follow his
advice . . .*

The librarian was flicking the lights, signaling that
she was ready to lock up. Frantically Ann leafed through
the rest of the booklet, hoping to find something more.
Another entry referred to beach sand. A notation mentioned the severe illness of one of the Faulker children,
but the compiler of the booklet had left out the para-
graphs that would have told which daughter and what the
sickness had been. Ann burned to know, but the diary
was silent.

The booklet ended with a brief notation of Sarah
Faulker's death. Sarah had simply gone down to the sea
late one afternoon and never returned alive. Her body
had been found several days later washed up on the
rocks—what was left of it. The historian did not give
details of that particular grisly discovery and Ann was
glad of it, for she could well imagine.

*Pieces of sharkskin. Pieces of sharkskin. Do you
know what that means? The goddamned shark was inside
her.* Dr. Hartung's voice echoed in Ann's mind, scalding
her thoughts.

Just as the librarian was impatiently flicking the
lights again, Ann found another picture at the back of the
book. It was a photograph of the man known as Kamo.
Ann studied it with fascination. Kamo had been a big
man with powerful musculature and a raw, powerful
sexuality that leaped out of the grainy photograph like a
flame. The picture showed him clad in a black suit similar

to the one that Josiah Faulker himself wore. Kamo's dark eyes seemed to stare right off the page and into Ann's heart. Something in her chest twisted.

It was Kam Smith's face looking at her out of that photograph of the 1860s. There was the same jaw line, the king-look to him, wild and free, the compelling little line at the corner of his mouth, the deep chin cleft and bold nose. Kam Smith.

Of course, Ann reminded herself with another odd little twist in her belly, it was not Kam, it couldn't be. Hadn't Kam himself told her about his grandfather who had been a servant of Josiah Faulker's, to whom the missionary's wife had taught proper English? And surely it was not unusual for a man to resemble an ancestor, especially here in Hawaii, where bloodlines were often intermingled. Still . . .

She stared again at the arrogant, beautiful face. Those eyes, so like Kam's . . . surely they were touched with the same devouring loneliness. *They were Kam's eyes.*

Kam Smith, she thought. It was a ridiculous name for a Hawaiian to own, a name totally foreign to Maui. Where had he gotten *Smith,* from one of the missionary's books or papers?

Ann caught her breath. Suppose— Just suppose that Kam's resemblance to Kamo was more than just coincidence? Suppose that Kam Smith and Kamo were *one and the same man?*

That would explain the oddly archaic rhythm to Kam's speech: he had learned it in 1860!

Ann's head was whirling, and when the librarian cleared her throat loudly, she did not hear.

What if Kamo had not died but simply left the employ of the missionary and gone elsewhere, eventually assuming the name and identity of the Kam Smith whom she now knew?

Ann thought of Karen Weeks, with her beautiful swimmer's body; Sarah Faulker, with a vibrant figure even a sober black dress could not entirely hide; and herself. Her own slim, size-10 figure. She too liked to swim, had been attracted by Kam, had embraced the sport of scuba diving, listened to his talk of the sea.

I have mislaid my embroidery . . .

She, Ann, had mislaid her needlepoint.

Ann's shudder was a deep one. Was she herself to be the next woman to disappear into the sea?

The rattle of dinner trays and the smell of roast pork filled the elevator and seeped into the hospital's corridors like a miasma.

Miasma, Ann thought dully as she left the elevator and started down the hall toward Kristal's room. Wasn't that supposed to be the poisonous vapor once thought to rise from swamps and marshes, causing disease in humans?

Plague, consumption, diptheria, even measles. Once these had all been mysteries, sicknesses terrifying because no one knew how they happened. But man, with his curious, restless mind, did not like a mystery. So thus had risen the story of the putrid rotting vapors that rose out of dank water to make people sick.

Legends too, Ann thought, had grown from the same urgent need. Man could not exist in the terrifying natural world without something to explain it all. Gods, totems, trolls, witches, demons, devils . . . man had invented them, he'd had to, in order to justify the unspeakable.

But what if man had *not* invented those things? What if gods and demons and devils were real, had always been there, waiting to be acknowledged? What if—

Stop, she begged herself. *Stop, oh stop, don't . . .*

Tray carts rattled. At the end of the hall, three local

girls in white giggled together over the steamy kitchen smells. Ann wondered what they would think of a shark man, if they had ever thought of such a thing at all. Probably, she thought, they hadn't.

She reached Kristal's room and went in. A third bed had been wheeled into the room, and someone's dark hair was spread upon the pillow. In the bed by the window, an elderly woman was sitting up to eat her supper, her face yellowed by either a fading suntan or jaundice. Ann didn't know which. The third bed, Kristal's, was empty. Made up, a cotton spread pulled taut over the mattress, a flat pillow geometrically arranged.

Empty . . . Kristal's bed was empty.

Ann stood very still in the doorway, rough chunks of clay seeming to clog up her midsection, ramming themselves down her veins until she stood paralyzed. *Kristal's bed was empty and ready for another patient.*

The kitchen girls were still giggling in the corridor, and the elderly lady started to cough and choke on something she had swallowed. She beat feebly at her chest until she had her spasm under control. The girl in the extra bed moaned and whimpered and turned on her other side. There was a bandage, Ann saw, on her forehead.

"Kristal," Ann began in a voice so low that it was barely a whisper. "My daughter." She tried to speak louder. "My daughter was in this bed."

"Her. Oh, her." The old lady laid down her fork onto a plate that contained a soupy mess of potatoes, gravy, and colorless meat. She looked like a cleaning woman Ann's mother had once had, all beaky nose and wattled neck and flyaway white hair. "They took her out of here a couple hours ago, down to intensive care."

"Intensive care?"

Ann's foot scraped something. She looked down.

There was a grit of sand on the floor. It was black and pebbly: beach sand. Black volcanic ash . . .

Ann stood stock still, wondering why she could not move, why everything seemed to be happening so slowly. The old woman's mouth gobbled like a turkey's. There were holes where her upper molars were missing. She had small blackbird eyes, and she was enjoying being the center of attention, the bearer of bad news.

"Did you say *intensive care?*" Ann whispered, stunned. "What— What happened?"

"Her breathing, is all I know. Lord, Lord, she scared me with all the tossing around and crying she done. *Him,* she kept calling. *Him, him.* She cried out a lot of other things too, some of them dirty things, real nasty. About a woman and some shark, it was. Terrible dirty, and not no kind of thing to be coming out of the mouth of any decent young girl, I'll tell you that. No, sir."

The old lady shook her flabby chins and scooped up another forkful of pork.

Ann still could not move.

"Them cuts of hers, they got bloody again, and then she started acting real funny. Gasping, you know, like she couldn't breathe. Passed right out. I'm the one called the nurses," the old woman announced proudly. "I'm the one. They come running right away, and you shoulda seen 'em, getting her the oxygen and like that. Dirty," she added, "dirty things she said. A pretty young thing like that. Oh, it's a shame."

Chapter 29

I am wondering how a fragile girl of twelve can know such horror ...

Sarah Faulker's words—they were a cry, really—filled Ann's mind. She ran down the hall to the nurses station, her thoughts exploding in the quick logic of terror.

Fortitude Faulker, Sarah's little girl, had been ill with unexplained scrapes on her limbs. Laurie Weeks had been sick when she left Maui. Now Kristal was sick.

All three of the girls had had a tendency to have strange dreams. According to the diary, Fortitude too had dreamed of sharks. Was Kamohoalii afraid of those dreams? Afraid of what a young girl might learn about him? *Was that why he had made them sick?*

Ann had reached the nurses station. A dark-haired nurse was sitting at a desk, scrawling something on a chart. A mug of steaming coffee sat beside her. A Hawaiian name had been hand-lettered on the cup. "Leilani."

Ann stopped. Thoughts pelted her like bullets.

If people knew what Kamohoalii really was, they could stop him. Yes ... Kamohoalii could be stopped. Because if he couldn't be stopped, then it wouldn't matter who knew about him or what they knew, because that wouldn't make any difference.

But if you were vulnerable, if you were destructible, then you had a reason to destroy those who suspected the truth about you, even if those people happened to be no more than innocent children ...

Yes, she thought feverishly. *Yes.*

"My daughter," she began, speaking to the nurse. "Can you tell me where she is? Please, I must see her right away—"

Both Buddy and Kristal had been moved to the hospital's intensive care unit and lay like still-living corpses attached to tubes and machines, something out of a science fiction movie.

"Five minutes," the nurse had told Ann. She could have five minutes with her children and no longer.

"It's their respiration, Mrs. Southworth. Something has paralyzed it. Now, I don't want you to be frightened when you see them, but we've got them both on ambubags, it's just to help them with their breathing, support them a little ..."

"But, nurse ..." Ann's voice was a cry. "What's wrong, what's wrong with them? Both of them the same —"

As if she didn't know. As if she didn't carry the knowledge like a lump of clay at the center of her belly. Kamohoalii. He had transmitted telepathic impulses to the breathing centers of her children. He had done it because they suspected who he was, and he was afraid they would expose him.

If he was afraid, then he had something to fear. There was some way . . . some way he could be destroyed . . .

Five minutes. Five short minutes.

Ann crouched between the beds, near the two nurses who were hand-operating the bags, wondering why, now that this moment was at hand, she couldn't cry. Her eyes felt hard and hot and dry, burning in her head. Her heart was a stone. But the tears would not come.

How vulnerable they looked. They were both unconscious. Buddy, flat on his back, was passive now, his arms loose at his sides. He wasn't fighting the straps now, he wasn't doing anything. The ambu-bag looked like an ugly black football, the airway going into her son's mouth, taped to his face. The bag made an ugly, obscene sound: *whooh-too . . . whooh-too.*

There was an intravenous line taped to her son's neck, more lines coming from each arm, and small plastic bags of medication piggybacked to it. A urinary catheter protruded from the sheet, filling up a container with dark, deep yellow.

Buddy. His hair was rumpled, it stuck up in wisps at the top of his head, absurd little-boy tufts. Ann longed to reach out and smooth his hair, kiss him, assure him everything would be all right.

The nurses, one middle-aged, one Japanese, sat quietly, not saying anything, letting Ann have her privacy, her precious minutes.

Buddy's mouth twitched. His eyelids fluttered once, then relaxed. His jaw was very square, and muscles were knotted at its prominences. He was clenching his teeth as the machine breathed for him. Fighting it. Thank God, fighting it.

In the other bed Kristal was a fragile sleeping beauty, her skin bleached to palest porcelain, lashes curved on her cheeks. The breathing tube attached to her was an intrusion of the grossest kind. *Whooh-too . . . whooh-too.* Was it Ann's imagination, or did her daughter's breathing seem slighter than Buddy's? There seemed—Ann was sure—less life force coming from her than from her son. Kristal was fading away.

Her daughter was dying. Buddy was dying, too, but he was fighting his death and he was strong and he might yet win. Kristal would not win. Ann knew this deep within the core of herself. Her daughter was too fragile, she had been under attack too long and could not keep on battling, and she was letting go, little by little. In a matter of hours, at the most maybe a day, then even the most sophisticated of machines would not be able to save her, for Kamohoalii would have accomplished his aim.

Perhaps—Ann drew shuddering breath of her own —perhaps the shark man was in her daughter's head at this very moment, probing the vulnerable young mind, causing dreams to sprout there like swamp mushrooms . . .

"Kristal? Krissie?" Ann's whisper seemed too loud. The Japanese nurse looked at her, then looked away. "Krissie, can you hear me?"

The oval face carved out of pale stone did not move or turn. The breathing did not change. Of course she could not hear, Ann thought. She was far away now. Perhaps she was in a sea-dream again, swift murderous dream of things moving and lunging and killing. *It was beautiful, all muted in a thousand shades of green and blue and gray and purple . . .*

"Krissie, oh, Krissie—"

I love you, Ann wanted to whisper. She wanted to fling herself upon her daughter, to embrace her fiercely. I love you, oh God, I love you. I bore you and I bore

Buddy. I gave birth to both of you in pain and you are part of me in a way that nothing else, no one else, can ever be. I am you and you are me, and always, always, it will be that way, my love for you will always be there . . .

Buddy, Krissie, don't die. Don't . . . God. I'll give anything, do anything . . . if only you'll let them live.

Fight, Krissie, fight. Dammit, don't just lie there like a sleeping princess. Life is too precious to let it slide away. If you want life, you must grab it in your two hands. You can't let yourself freeze up inside and do nothing. You must never do that. God, didn't I learn that? At Washtenaw . . . Why, why can't we ever give what we learn to someone else?

Live, Krissie. Buddy you were always a fighter, weren't you? You didn't give up, not even at the shopping center when I did . . .

There was a noise. A choked sound coming from deep in the throat. Ann was not even certain if she had heard it. She glanced at Kristal. The girl lay flat and pale, ethereal, letting the life force slide out of her. The colorless lips, partly obscured by the breathing tube, had not moved.

"Buddy? Son?"

The sound came again. Her son's eyelids fluttered. His knees convulsed, his hands flailed the air, then came to his mouth. The Japanese nurse got to her feet. Buddy jerked up, pulled at the breathing tube, yanked it out of his mouth.

"Young man! Young man! You must—"

"*Mom?*" Her son's voice was a hoarse cry. He pushed at the nurse, shoved her away.

"Yes, yes, it's me. I'm here, Buddy. I'm with you. Don't struggle with the bag, it's for your own good, it's to help you breathe. It's going to be all right, honey."

"No . . . no, it won't . . ." Hoarse whisper, implacable. Buddy's eyes stared at her, dark brown and full of adult knowledge. Her son was rational, Ann realized. For the first time, he wasn't babbling or delirious.

"Buddy? What are you talking about? Of course it's going to be all right! What's happened? Do you know what's wrong with you?"

"It's him. *Him,* Mom. Kam . . ."

"I know, Buddy. I know."

"Mom?"

A pause, while her son breathed painfully. The Japanese nurse had gotten up and was running off down the hall. A very long silence filled the room, mingling with the ticking of the wall clock and the sound of Kristal's ambubag. There were only a few minutes left for her visit. Then they would make her leave, and she couldn't go yet, she couldn't possibly. She had to stay with her children. Had to . . .

"Mom, are you afraid?"

Mom, are you afraid

The words held awareness, and Ann knew that it had been an adult question born of grown-up compassion and knowledge.

"Yes, Buddy, I'm afraid." Her hand found his, felt the coolness of his skin and underneath it, the erratic pulse. "But it doesn't matter, son. I've already felt all the fear there is; I don't think I can feel any more. I don't think there *is* any more. And it doesn't matter now. I have something to do. I think I can do it."

There were sounds in the hallway. Buddy's mouth twitched, and there was a faint glaze of moisture in his eyes.

"Mom?"

"Yes, honey?"

"You can . . . kill him."

"Yes."

Her son's eyes had fallen shut. His mouth was tight,

his jaw clenched, his chest heaving with the effort to draw air. A mumble came from him, a sigh. He was back in that other world. He had gone from her, was off somewhere fighting his demons unassisted.

No, she thought. He wasn't unassisted. She was here, she, Ann, his mother. She had fought his dragons when he was five years old, she had frightened away boogie men for Kristal too. How many times had she done it for both of them, a hundred, a thousand? Well she'd still do it. She'd fight anything, anyone, for these children of hers. She was their mother.

Two nurses were back, reinserting the ambu-bag tube in Buddy's trachea. He was unconscious now, so it was easy for them.

"Buddy," Ann whispered, although she knew he couldn't hear her now, might never hear her again. "Buddy . . . son, I'm going to help you. I'm going to stop him. I don't know how, but I'm going to. You've got to hang on . . both of you. You must keep breathing, you must keep on living for just a while longer.

"Do you hear me? You've got to keep on breathing. Don't stop. Don't stop for anything."

She was beside Kristal now, shaking her, weeping over her, pressing her face to her daughter's pale one, kissing her, kissing.

"Krissie, Krissie, *live*. Live a little longer. Don't give up, don't let it all slide away, because I'm going to stop him."

How? How was she going to help them? In the name of Christ, how?

Ann was back in her car again, hurtling along the road through the cane fields as if the devil himself powered her car's engine. Lights flashed at her: oncoming traffic. Darkness had fallen, dropping over the jagged outlines of the West Maui Mountains like a shroud. Later there would be a moon, nearly full. One could read the headlines of a newspaper in the Hawaiian moonlight, Ann had been told. Its glow was full, clear, pale, unutterably cold.

But what else could you do in the moonlight? she wondered. She steered grimly for Makai. Could you kill a shark man?

Because that was what she had to do. Oh, God, that was her only choice. Because as long as Kamohoalii still lived, he could maintain his connection to the minds of her children and soon, soon, they would both be dead.

And whatever must be done, she had to accomplish herself. Certainly she could not go to the police: her story was far too fantastic. A tale of a man who could enter the sea and change his bodily form to that of a tiger shark? A being who could project thought-impulses into the minds of others, who could cause children to grow sick and die . . .

No. No one would believe her, not the police, not Dr. Hartung or Susan Rogers or Susan's husband, Cliff, no one except Donnie Perriera.

And she knew that whatever she did, she must do tonight. For Kristal did not have long to live, she was drying up as a plucked flower petal crumples in the sun. A few hours, a day perhaps, and Kristal would be gone forever.

Donnie Perriera. Donnie knew about the shark man!

The thought pelted into Ann's mind like a BB shot, panicking her. She had rammed her foot down on the gas pedal, speeding the car up to more than ninety miles an hour. *Oh, no,* she thought. *No.* She could not bear to think of yet another young person stretched out on a hospital bed attached to machines and tubes.

She had to find Donnie, and she had to do it fast.

Get his help or help him, whichever had to be done. Maybe it was not too late. She prayed it was not.

The camera shop was still open, lights blazing. Ann opened the car door, got out, went running across the pavement.

Inside, a man was dusting off a glass counter, his face lined with weariness.

Ann stopped, dismay plummeting through her. It was Donnie's father. Somehow she had expected to see Donnie here at the shop. But what if he were not? What if he was at home or lying beside the road somewhere, already sick? She would have to go into the store and ask, and let the father think what he would.

She walked inside and heard the door jingle. Oriental bells had been tied to it; they made a pleasant tinkling sound like old candy shops. The man looked up. His smile was tired.

"We're closing in about five minutes. But could I help you with something? Camera film, maybe?"

"No, I— Well, yes, I'll have a pack of film for my Polaroid, two packs," she babbled, giving herself time. While Mr. Perriera reached for the film, she darted her eyes around the shop. Maybe Donnie was in the back, developing film or something. Maybe while his father was ringing up the sale, Donnie would come out and she could speak to him unobtrusively.

She handed Donnie's father a twenty-dollar bill and waited for him to bag the film and give her change. Donnie still did not appear.

"I'm Mrs. Southworth," she said at last. "Kristal Southworth's mother."

The man looked at her but did not seem to recognize the name.

"My daughter— Your son—"

"Oh, yes, I'm glad to meet you. I hope you're having

a nice vacation here. It's been sunny, hasn't it? Not much rain, a good holiday. But I heard on the radio that we might get some wind, yah? The *kona* winds are coming up, it could get a little rough, yah?"

All the while he talked, Perriera was tidying up, dusting film packs and display cases, rearranging a display of books on photography. Ann kept looking around. Where was Donnie? Not here, evidently. Urgency filled her. She would have to ask.

"Mr. Perriera?"

"Yes?" He did not even look up from his dusting.

"I don't suppose— Is your son Donnie around?"

"Donnie? Has that kid done something wrong?"

"No. No, he hasn't done anything at all. It's just that— I wanted to give him something . . . a book he loaned to Kristal. My daughter is sick, and she asked me to give it to Donnie, she said she'd promised to return it—"

"A book. Oh." Mr. Perriera said it heavily. "That boy is always fooling with books. Well, he's home right now. I could take it to him if you want. He isn't feeling so good either."

Ann's heart sank. "He's sick?" she managed.

"Went home right after supper, looked peaked. After he said he'd work, too . . . promised me he'd come into the shop and work tonight. Well, that's kids for you. Tell you anything so they can get some time to go to the beach, yah?" Perriera made a sound of contempt in his throat.

She drew back. "The book's in the car. Mr. Perriera, do you suppose I could give it to Donnie? I mean, give it to him myself? There's something that I have to talk to him about."

"Talk?"

"Yes." Her eyes met his flatly. Let him think her Mrs. Robinson. Let him think any damned thing he chose. There wasn't time for games. "I've got to see him, Mr. Perriera. It's important."

"Oh. Well . . . we live on Loulu Street, it's about a mile up the road and to your right." He gave her the address. "You can't miss the place, it's got a big mango tree in front of it and a bunch of Yamaha cycles. My son, my other son, Donnie's brother, he's fixing bikes for the whole neighborhood now." Perriera laughed dryly. "He doesn't want to come into the shop either; he'd rather fix cars and bikes and lie around on the beach and think about going into the Navy. The Navy, for God's sake, the *kamaaina* Navy. Didn't I have enough of the service in Korea, didn't I sweat my butt off for the government, yah? Now I got one boy who wants to be a damned sailor and one that wants to go to college on the mainland. Nobody wants to work in the shop . . ."

Ann whirled out on the litany of complaint, jangled the door bell, ran to her car and jumped in. She heard a shout coming from the camera shop. She had forgotten her film.

She backed out of the lot in a crunch of gravel.

The house where the Perrieras lived was made of cement blocks. Its tropical shrubbery was immaculately tended. An outdoor light was on, illuminating dozens of hanging-plant baskets suspended on chains from the roofline of the carport. Inside the carport was parked a disabled van, three or four motorcycles, two surfboards, and a huge assortment of lawn equipment and household junk. Two more cycles were parked in the driveway.

Ann pulled up behind the Yamahas and hurried up to the front door. The sound of rock music screamed from the house, its beat loud and insistent. She could not imagine Donnie liking such music: the other brother must be home, she decided. She pressed on the bell, hoping that Donnie was all right. She hoped—

"Mrs. Southworth!"

Donnie was at the door, wearing nothing but a pair of cutoffs, his chest bony and sunken. There were bruises and welts on his shoulders and on his right arm, scrapes of flesh bleeding in small pinpoint dots of blood as Buddy's wounds had done. Donnie's eyes stared at her with animal fright.

"Donnie! Donnie, you're sick, too."

"I guess so."

The rock music blared, and Ann had the feeling that their conversation came straight from nightmare. Young male voices laughed somewhere in the house: Ann could smell beer.

"I've got to talk to you, Donnie."

His eyes flicked. "Where?"

"God, I don't know. Out in the yard, away from that music? Please, Donnie, we've got to hurry, this is important."

He followed her down the steps to the walk and then across the well-manicured grass to the right of the carport, where a fanatically trimmed hedge formed a cul-de-sac. The beat of the music followed them.

"My Dad is coming home from the shop soon, it's almost closing time. He always closes up right on the dot."

"Yes, I know. He told me you were sick."

"How's Kristal, Mrs. Southworth? How is she?"

Donnie stood blended in with the shadows, one hand rubbing the welt on his shoulder. He looked very young, and Ann felt a terrible misgiving. She had counted on Donnie—she guessed that she had. All the way over here, she'd been thinking about him, planning in her mind what she was going to tell him, counting on his belief, his intelligence, his enthusiasm.

"Kristal isn't good, Donnie. In fact— Well, she's pretty sick. I've got to do something. I've got to."

They looked at each other. Their eyes met and locked.

"It's Kam," she said softly. "Kamohoalii. He's the one who's making them sick. He's making you sick, too, Donnie . . . because you know about him, and he knows that you know. If we don't do something, it's going to get bad. Very bad."

The boy nodded.

"We have to kill him, Donnie. You understand that, don't you?"

"I— I guess so. Yes."

"I need your help, Donnie. I'll do it, but I need to ask you some things."

A car was pulling down Loulu Street, its headlights flashing in the road.

"Yah." Donnie nodded again. He did not have to ask her what things. He knew. Instinctively she pulled him further back into the shadows of the shrubbery.

She spoke quickly. "You told me the things that would destroy him."

He looked at her, licking his lips. "Sacred spear point. But we don't have it. God, we could look around Maui forever and never find it. That was probably two hundred years ago, and the spear point is probably in some museum in Honolulu right now—if it's anywhere."

"But . . . but fire," she whispered. "You said he could be destroyed if he were totally immersed in fire, Donnie."

He stared at her, his face frozen. "Oh, but—"

"Donnie! Donnie, you said that! I heard you, we were in the restaurant at Kaahumanu, Apple Annie's, and you said that."

"I said it, but—" He looked at her. "Mrs. South-worth, you're a woman, a mother. Don't you know what he could *do*? I was down there on that beach. I felt it, his power, it was in the air like smoke. And the rock . . . the melted rock, Mrs. Southworth. They can make rocks turn to fire, Mrs. Southworth; they can pull you with their mind—"

"Can you help me figure out a way to burn him?"

"I don't know, I don't know, Mrs. Southworth—"

"Can you, Donnie?"

Somewhere a night bird was calling repetitively. The rock music stopped, then started up again. Someone had put on a new tape.

"I . . . I could. Yes."

"Well then. I know you don't feel well, but you'll have to do it right now, Donnie. This very minute. Kristal is dying. You may be dying, too. You must help me."

He nodded. He padded barefoot toward the house, a thin, gawky, tall figure in his cutoffs. "I'll get my shoes, Mrs. Southworth. And I have to get some things out of the carport. My Dad has a lot of yard junk in there."

"Okay."

The car in the road hadn't been Donnie's father's. But he would be arriving home any minute. Ann hoped that she and Donnie could get out of here before then. She stood waiting outdoors in the Hawaiian night and looked up at the sky. The moon was rising. It floated on the horizon like a silver disk, impossibly lovely.

God, she prayed in her mind, *God, please, if you are up there, if you are anywhere at all, please help us. Please help.*

A cloud slid toward the moon and enveloped it. Shadows sifted down as soft as death. Ann shivered.

Chapter 30

They jounced down Kaunoa Road. The wheels of Ann's car spun off lava rocks, sending one hurling into a *kiawe* thicket. The moon had gone into a blanket of clouds, and the road was dark . . . *as dark as a tunnel into hell*, Ann thought. Beside her Donnie sat wearing shorts and a frayed T-shirt, his hand rubbing nervously at a welt on his right leg, a welt that—she was sure—had not been there when they'd left his house twenty minutes ago.

In the back seat things rattled. Garden equipment that Buddy had filched from the carport, metal containers and segments of plastic hose. Liquid in one of the containers sloshed. Resolutely Ann closed her mind to the significance of that liquid and tried to concentrate on her driving.

At night Kaunoa Road was like a roller coaster. Steep hills crested, so that when you pulled your car over the rise of one of them, you seemed to hang for a moment suspended in blackness.

They had hurtled past the Makai Golf Course. Sprinklers had been running, spraying water into the dark. Ann could picture golfers riding up and down hills in their carts, their clubs rattling in the back. She hadn't had a chance to play the Makai course. She wondered if she ever would.

They drove further into the black tunnel that was the road. *Kiawe* thickets. Prickly pear cactus, tall and ghostly in the car's headlights. Ann began to think about what they would meet when they finally arrived at the beach house. She tried to recall every detail of the place in her mind. The driveway. Hadn't it been shaped in a big curve, with a crude turnaround? She'd have to remember to park so that her car was headed outward again. She'd want to drive away fast.

A big lava rock the size of a basketball lay in the road. Ann swerved to avoid it. A white face looked out of blackness, its eyes shadowy holes. Ann jerked the wheel again and suppressed a scream.

"Hitchhiker," Donnie said, scratching. "Must have been down at Kaunoa Beach. They're here all the time, they camp out and live on the beach. Bums, hippies, college kids, tourists, you know."

Yes, Ann did know. Maui's easy life. She felt like sagging with released tension.

Car headlights illuminated more trees. Another pair of phosphorescent green eyes glared at them from the side of the road.

"Cat," Donnie said. "They run wild here, they're all over."

"Well, I hope that one wasn't black. All we need right now is for a black cat to run across the road in front of us—"

Metal cans sloshed in the back seat as they bounced

over a pothole, swerved and dodged to avoid hitting another one.

"This road gets worse," Donnie told her. "There's a place, Akolu, it's only a few feet from the water there, you could go off on the rocks real easy if you don't know the road. My brother and I, we go there snorkeling."

"Oh—"

Grimly, barely listening, Ann negotiated the road and watched out for cats and said her prayers, over and over in her head. *God, help me. Help us. Take care of Buddy and Kristal, don't let my children die . . . God, are you there? Are you out there?*

The sky was dark and there was only the road, weaving ahead of them into the night.

Kiawe trees loomed in the headlights as Ann pulled up the driveway to Kam's beach house. As she did so, something small ran across the drive in front of them. A mongoose? A coconut rat? It seemed a night for small and furtive things.

She pulled the car into the turnaround, backed it up, and headed it toward the road again, as she had planned. She tried not to give way to the frozen ball of horror that clogged her midsection. She would accomplish this, one small step at a time. She would let nothing stop her. Nothing.

"We're here," Donnie said inanely. She could hear the sound of him shifting about on the front seat, his breathing ragged. She wondered if he were in pain from those ugly welts on his skin, but there wasn't time to think of that now. There was only the job they had to do.

"Yes," she said. "We're here. And now I think we'd better take that stuff out of the car, hide it in the shrubs somewhere. I was thinking about that on the way over here."

"All right."

"You'll have to move fast, Donnie . . . before he comes outside and finds us."

They got out and then Donnie was hauling objects out of the back seat and setting them on the rocky ground. The moon had partially come out from its barrier of clouds, casting a weak, cold light. Plastic hose clinked against metal. They could hear the pound of surf on the beach, only a few hundred yards away. Powerful, a ceaseless wash of water over sand and rock.

A light gleamed from the beach house. It was a thin yellow, coming from somewhere behind glass and wood. Ann wondered from which room the light came. His bedroom? A hallway, the kitchen?

"Wonder if he's home," Donnie said.

"I don't know."

"Only one light on, and that's not very bright, yah? You couldn't even read by it. Unless he's watching television or something."

Ann shivered, for she had remembered something that had been missing from the house. "He doesn't have a television set."

Donnie forced a laugh. "Wow. Anyway, can you imagine him watching *Mork and Mindy?* With a big can of Olympia in his hand?"

The laugh ended in a cracked whisper of sound, and Ann did not reply. She was still staring at the house. What if Kam were not at home? What if, despite all their efforts, they could not find him in time? Kristal would die. It was as simple as that. She was sinking rapidly into respiratory failure, and she would not be able to survive very far into tomorrow. If they did not hurry, it would be too late.

"Well we'd better go up there and knock," Donnie said. "Get it over with."

"All right."

"Remember," Donnie said, "make it sound good; make it sound real good, or he won't come with us. I've got to have that equipment or nothing is going to work. We can't do anything without it. And remember to keep refilling."

"Okay. I know, God, you don't have to tell me."

"I mean, nothing is going to work if we don't have those sprayers handy."

Donnie got out a flashlight. It made an eery cone of light as they crunched up the path toward the house. Ann felt as if she were living some old midnight movie on TV. Nothing was real, nothing seemed to connect. Smells assailed them: the faint breath of the sea. Dust. Green things, plants, and flowers. The cloying thick sweet smell of Plumeria.

Hadn't there been a pair of white Plumeria blooming on the lawn? Ann couldn't remember now.

The moon had crept again out of the clouds, its face mottled.

They were at the door now. Ann remembered the day when Kam had come out of it to meet her, tall and muscular and impossibly good-looking. His eyes had been like something from her most secret fantasies, fixing her in their gaze so that she could not look away.

"Go ahead," Donnie ordered. "Knock."

"I— All right."

The rap of her knuckles echoed against wood, seemed to reverberate in the air. They could hear the surf pounding the beach. Nothing else. They waited, but no sounds came from within the beach house.

"I don't think he's here," Donnie said at last. There was relief in his voice.

"But he's got to be, he's got to be here!"

"Mrs. Southworth, he's a shark god, remember.

They go into the sea most nights; that's where they live. He's out there." Donnie pointed beachward. "That's where he is."

"But . . . Kristal and Buddy! And now you, you're sick, too. He's making you that way, I know he is. He has *kahunaanaana* powers, he told me. Right here at this house he told me that. Donnie, what are we going to do?"

"Wait until tomorrow. That's all we can do."

"But we can't! It'll be too late!"

Ann fought tears. She tried to picture herself confronting Kam Smith in the humdrum atmosphere of the Ocean Divers shop, walking into the air conditioning, hesitating among the display of masks and tanks and goggles before asking to see Kamohoalii the shark man. The owner, Gordon Begrin, would surely look at her as if she had gone mad . . . as perhaps she had.

Who, Ann wondered desperately, would believe her story anyway? If any sensible person could see her at this very moment, armed with what amounted to a flame thrower, standing here pounding on the door of an empty house, they'd think her insane. Obsessed.

"We'd better go, Mrs. Southworth. Go back home. He's not here."

"But he's got to be!"

"I told you, he isn't. He's out there, out in the sea."

"Yes, but he's got to be here," she repeated foolishly. Donnie was right, of course. Tears of frustration burned her eyes. To have forced herself to come this far for nothing—to let Kristal die, and Buddy . . . to let her children slip from her grasp, all that was important and dear in the world to her. No, she wouldn't let it happen. She'd think of something, anything.

"Mrs. Southworth," Donnie urged her, "please come

back to the car. We'll get the stuff and go. This was a bad idea, it was a terrible idea. He isn't here. We'll go to the police or something—"

"The police? The Maui Police Department?" She could weep with her frustration. "Donnie, are you crazy? Donnie, we can't leave yet, we— We'll call him, that's it. I'll call him."

"Call him? How?" Donnie's voice was thready, uneasy. Ann realized that he had been caught up in the eery spell of this black night. Donnie was afraid, frightened deep in his gut.

Well, Ann thought, so was she. But it didn't matter anymore, her fear. It didn't matter at all.

"I don't know," she said. "Just be quiet for a minute, will you, and let me think? I've got to think."

"But Mrs. Southworth, you can't—"

"Just give me a minute. Please. I'll think of something."

Ann started to pace. Donnie turned and began to walk back toward the car, playing with the arc of the flashlight, making wide curves into the dark.

Call him, she was thinking. *I've got to call Kam somehow. Make him come to me. But how? How can I?*

She tripped, stumbled on a lava rock—they were everywhere—and caught her balance.

The beach, she thought. *I've got to go down to the beach.* Donnie's right. *That's where he'd be if he were anywhere, not up at the house. This isn't a real house anyway, it's only a shell.*

She thought of the way it had been when she had first visited here. The furnishings impersonal, lifted straight from a store; the refrigerator empty except for the meal they had been going to eat that night. No, Kam Smith did not live in the house. It was only a façade. His real home was the sea.

She'd go to his home. She'd go down to the beach
. . . and there she would think of something, some way to
draw him.

"Donnie," she called sharply, "go get the equipment
and help me carry it down to the beach."

"The beach?"

"That's where he'll be. Hurry, Donnie, hurry . . . before he sees us."

"He won't come. He's far away."

But Donnie's voice did not hold full conviction, and
his movements were jerky as he picked up the two garden
sprayers. He put them down again to make the sign of the
cross.

"Come on," Ann ordered. "Hurry."

Ann shivered as she made her way out onto the
rocks, her tennis shoes slipping on the damp places where
the spray washed up, making the footing dangerous. She
had taken the flashlight from Donnie—he was waiting for
her on the sand—and now shone it ahead of her. There
were little pools caught in the low spots of the rocks,
where spiny urchins clung and small fish darted. Crabs
scuttled over the rocks, too, naked in the gleam of the
flash.

And always there was the wash and pound of the
surf. The sound made Ann think of the way the world
must have been three million years ago. Was that when
Kamohoalii had been born? Somewhere in the spume of
prehistoric seas, rising up full of his loneliness and abyssal
need? Over the centuries, how many women had he lured
into the sea, to mutilate them in a wild travesty of
love?

Ann caught her breath. *It wasn't a very pretty case,
Mrs. Southworth. Something had penetrated that woman's vagina and virtually ripped out her insides. . . . That
goddamned shark was inside her.*

No, she couldn't think of that now, or she would turn to jelly. She had to make her mind soft and smooth and calm and beckoning, she had to wrench all fear out of herself, for her terror would betray her. She must use her mind to call Kam.

She stepped gingerly over a large boulder, her feet nearly slipping. The flash beam wavered, and she dropped it as a huge spume of spray smacked against the rocks.

She was at the end of the spit of rock now, facing directly outward toward the horizon. The moon had risen a little higher now, lighting a block of clouds from behind into silver brilliance. Carefully, watching her balance, Ann found a rock with a flatter top than the others and sat down on it.

For long moments she sat there, letting the night surround her. The air was moister here, down by the beach. She could smell the salt spray, warm sea things, sun and weed and urchin and shellfish. Surf pounded up to spend itself on rock. Spray dampened Ann's legs as she put her head in her hands and tried to concentrate.

Why? she wondered. *Why am I here? What is there in me that made me a prey for him?*

I'd led such a damned dull life. I wanted romance and loving and losing myself in a passion for a man. I wanted to join myself with someone physically and spiritually. I was so goddamned vulnerable. And he sensed it. He knew. That's why, out of all the women on Maui, of all the woman anywhere, he found me. Because I wanted. I too needed.

Karen Weeks had been a quiet sort, maybe she had fantasized love, too. Heaven knew Sarah Faulker probably had. Sarah had been married to that dried-up missionary—

She forced the thoughts out of her mind. She had to make her mind receptive, not jumping with a thousand recriminations and fears. She must blank her thoughts of everything except wanting him. She must want him.

She must want him very much, must desire him with every particle and fiber of her being, must put longing into her mind and nothing else, longing so strong that it hurt. Then he would sense it, wherever he was, and he would come to her.

He would come . . .

She didn't know how long she sat there on the rocks. She had lost track of time utterly, aware only of the wash of the surf and a naked, silver moon rising higher in the sky, stripped of its clouds now.

Kam. I want you. I need you. I want to go with you. Wherever you want me to go, I'll go. I love you, Kam. I love you.

Truth? A lie born of desperation? Ann did not dare to look too deeply into herself.

Time had stopped, and there was nothing but herself and the moon and the surf. She stared out at the metallic wash of sea. For a moment she had thought she saw something dark break the surface of the waves. Then the object disappeared into the water again as if it had never been.

Kam, she projected. *Kam, please come. I need you. I need to see you. I want to be with you. Kam . . .*

And then she heard it, the sound of a loose stone falling against the rocks behind her. Something in the dark night seemed to pause, to turn slowly over. Or was that just the sudden terror in her own belly twisting there like a stiletto?

Ann whirled about and saw nothing at first, nothing except damp, spray-washed rock. Then she saw him. He came walking out of the *kiawe* trees to her right, just past the outcrop of rocks. He wore nothing but a bathing suit and T-shirt, a yellow Ocean Divers shirt that glowed in the moonlight. And, yes, didn't his skin, wet with glistening droplets, seem to glow, too? There was a faint greenish shine to him as if he were one of those phosphorescent night creatures.

He strode toward her. He was big and impossibly handsome, and his eyes were two black holes. They drew at her with a force as strong as Satan, pulling her up, pulling her stumbling over the rocks toward him.

"Ann. Why, Ann! What are you doing here on my beach at this hour of the night?"

"Kam," was all she could say.

She was in his arms, and she felt the warmth of his arms around her, the human warmth. And she smelled him, too; he smelled of night and damp and sea salt. Time had run down, it seemed forever that she was clasped to him. She could feel the full, hard length of his body, the powerful sheaths of muscles, the flat hardness of his chest and belly, the erect bulge of his masculinity further below.

"Ann," he said in his low-timbered, thrilling voice that was like something out of Ann's past, "what are you doing here? I went for a swim. I didn't expect to see you. I didn't expect to see anyone."

She was gasping, crying, burrowing into him, the humanness of him. He was a man, a human man, his body thrusting toward hers eagerly. Her hands slid around his back, clutching at him through the fabric of the T-shirt. Under the cotton fabric (*dry,* she thought wonderingly), she could feel the raised ridge outlining the scar on his back.

"I had to come," she told him. "Buddy and Kristal are sick, and I was so worried. I . . . I had to see you."

The half-lie poured out. She thought of Donnie waiting for her only a few hundred feet away, by the chicken wire walkway, along the route she and Kam would have to take back up to the house. Then, with a spurt of fear, she erased the image from her mind. He would sense her fright, he would read her mind.

"Oh, God." She clung to the maleness of him. She could feel herself softening inside, moistening. She could not imagine this man a shark god, could not picture it. "Oh, Kam . . . Kam . . ."

"Ann, what's the matter with you? Is something wrong?"

"No. Yes. Oh, it's Buddy and Kristal. I'm upset. They're very sick, in the hospital. Respiratory failure, they're on breathing machines. I came down here, drove here, I had to see you—"

Her words were coming out in unplanned gasps.

"You shouldn't have driven so late on that road. Kaunoa Road is nothing to fool with at night."

"I know. I— Do you mind? I just wanted to see you."

"I know. I know, darling, I know."

Insane talk, utterly insane. She felt Kam's arm go around her shoulders and then he was helping her off the rocks and back toward the soft and yielding black sand where, hidden in the shadows, Donnie Perriera waited with the homemade flame thrower they'd rigged up.

Jesus God in Heaven, Ann thought. What if they'd made a mistake? What if all of it was a terrible, terrible mistake?

She would be committing murder then . . . cold-blooded, grisly, horrible murder.

Chapter 31

She and Kam walked back up the beach, toward the chickenwire walkway.

Get him away from the water, Donnie had instructed her. *You've got to get him away from the water, Mrs. Southworth, because that's where he gets his power, that's what makes him strong.*

Now, as she walked with Kam Smith through the granular black sand, the same sand she had found in Kristal's hospital room, she fought her doubts. His arm across her back was warm. Human-warm, man-warm. She could hear the sounds of his breathing. Kam Smith breathed, respired his air in and out exactly as she did, as Donnie Perriera did and everyone else, everyone human.

"Kam." She stopped dead in the sand so that he was forced to stop, too.

"Yes, Ann?"

"There's something I want to talk to you about. I don't quite know how to say it—"

"Yes?"

"Are you—"

She stopped. Incredible. No, she couldn't even say it, because if he wasn't, if he was only a human being, after all, a real person— No, it was unthinkable to say the words aloud. Yet she had to find out.

"There is something on my back," she went on in a dead, dull voice. "Something. An odd mark, a scar, really, just like yours. I want you to look at it."

She turned and lifted up her T-shirt so that he could inspect her back in the clear moonlight. She could feel the cool sea wind on her skin.

"There," she said. "Look."

"I don't see anything . . . except a very lovely back."

"There's a mark," she told him grimly. "A mark almost exactly like the one you carry on your own back. Why, Kam? Why do I have it?"

Silence. Kam stood facing the ocean. In the moonlight his skin still held a faintly phosphorescent tinge.

"There isn't anything on your back, Ann. It's all your imagination, nothing more."

"Is it? And what about that scar on *your* back?" Her voice was beginning to shake. "I saw that, I saw it at Molokini. You said you got it in a welding shop, but I've never seen any shop injury—*any* injury—that looked like that, exactly like a shark's opened jaw—"

"You're talking nonsense, Ann." Kam's voice was cold, and its archaic accent made Ann think again of the missionary family from whom he had learned his English. Kam Smith, she thought with a jolt of terror, had learned English more than a hundred years ago.

"Am I speaking nonsense?" she demanded. *"Am I?"*

"Ann, Ann . . . what am I going to do with you? You're being silly and foolish, my lovely, lovely Ann . . ."

He was holding her again, filling her with that electrical thrill that penetrated her whole body, every cell and fiber of her. He had tilted her head back, was gazing down at her with eyes burning with all the grief and sorrow of a hundred centuries . . .

"Ann," his voice whispered, beguiling, "come with me."

He was still erect. She could feel him against her, hard, male, potent. There was an answering melting, moistening, longing deep within her own groin. She knew that she wanted to follow him wherever he went, to do whatever he wished, without holding back. She wanted to belong to him, to be his, whatever that meant . . .

"Kam . . ." Her voice was weak. She felt drained of all strength, all will. "Kam, tell me about Sarah Faulker. Was she very beautiful?"

"Sarah Faulker?" His eyes drew hers. "What would I know about a woman born in 1830?"

"I . . ." She stopped, had to swallow. Her mouth was dry, the flesh of her throat like cotton cloth. Buddy and Kristal seemed very far away. "I think you know a great deal. I think you know everything there is to know. She loved you, Kam, didn't she? Only you weren't Kam, then, you were Kamo, and you were a beautiful wild man. She wrote that in her diary. She was attracted to you, you took her spear fishing, you taught her about the sea, as you taught me—"

Kam said nothing. His eyes, dark pools of need, drew Ann into them. Her will receding, she felt herself giving in to their power. He wanted her and she wanted him. She longed to feel close to him, to yield herself to him, give herself utterly.

Kristal. Kristal struggling for breath. Buddy's jaw

clenched into knots as he fought the unseen death which stalked him. And Donnie Perriera, bleeding, frightened, waiting for her in the shadows.

Somehow Ann managed to wrench herself back, just a fraction . . . managed to look clearly at that beautiful face, to pull herself out of the hypnotic gaze.

Her voice shook as she accused him. "You took Sarah into the sea, didn't you, Kam? You took her down into the water with you and you made love to her. You loved her and your love destroyed her . . ."

Hot tears burned from Ann's eyes, sudden ones, and she didn't know why.

"Ann . . ." Kam's words were as soft and alluring as the touch of silver moonlight. "It wasn't what you think, it wasn't like that at all. Ann, darling, come with me into the sea. Come with me as Sarah did. I love you. I need you. I want you to be with me. We will give love to each other in a way that is given few to know . . ."

"Kam—I *can't.* You know I can't. My children . . ." She was shaking. All over, convulsively.

"Ann. You are so beautiful, so lovely, and the sea will be good to you, I promise you that. There will be beauty . . . beauty . . ."

He had turned. His arm still about her, Kam was urging her back toward the circlet of beach bound on either side by rock. Waves pounded against small stones, foam spilling up onto the sand to wash seaward again.

"I've been waiting for you such a long time, darling. Come with me. Come into the sea with me."

Kam began to strip off his shirt. His chest gleamed bare in the moonlight, glowing and beautiful like that of a young and handsome god. Kam's eyes glowed at her, too, a force radiating out from them. It was powerful, shimmering, electric, and it connected the two of them like a steel cable.

She belonged to him. She was his.

And she clung to him, her body arched against the strength of him, and felt her thighs spread and her pelvis grind against his. Then it came, the penetration, a force filling her like nothing she could ever have fantasized in her wildest dreams. Filling her, FILLING HER, with the piercing joy that was beyond joy, that was beyond everything, beyond all imagining. Pleasure exploded upward and outward. She was a star and he the sun—OH GOD, OH DEAR GOD . . . THEY WERE JOINED . . . THEY HAD BECOME ONE, INCANDESCENT . . .

Thoughts.

Strange sexual images swirled in her head, vivid, achingly real. Yet there was an alien feel to them, as if they didn't come from her own mind at all, but from somewhere else. *From him.*

He was pulling her toward the beach, toward the shore where the waves piled in. And unprotestingly she stumbled with him. She was barely able to walk now, for she felt so weak, so yielding, so totally his.

In a moment he would scoop her up and carry her. She would revel in the strength of him, the powerful muscles strong beyond human strength . . .

And in the water, once they were in the waves, it would be even better. For then she would see him in his real form. She would know his power and maleness, huge, beyond anything she had ever known. He and she would go on a wild journey to the very source of love . . .

They were almost at the water's edge now. Water surged in, splashed among sand and rocks, dampened the sand, curled foam in delicate patterns. Ann walked with Kam, letting him support her, for she had no strength. She loved him, needed him. Would go anywhere with him, anywhere at all. Foam curled, waved washed at sand.

"Mrs. Southworth!" Donnie Perriera screamed.

"Mrs. Southworth! What are you doing? Don't! *Don't go in the water with him!*"

The night seemed to jerk around Ann, changing its colors from faded, moonlit gray to the sharpest focus. She could feel her entire body shudder as she drew back from Kam.

"Mrs. Southworth! Mrs. Southworth! Get back! Get back from him! Don't you see what he's doing to you?" Donnie's voice shrieked at her.

"Donnie?"

She took a step backward, feeling thwarted, interrupted, just as if she had been stopped in the middle of sex before reaching orgasm.

"Mrs. Southworth! Get away from that water! Get away!"

"Ann, come into the water. Strip off your clothes and come with me."

Soft, his voice was, and alluring. It pulled at her, offering worlds of persuasion in every syllable. Beauty, he had said. And in her mind she knew it was true. Just as in the picture on her needlepoint canvas, there would be joy, unbearable glory of a kind so rare that most women had never known it. But she, Ann, could know it. All she had to do was to go with him.

Kam—Kamohoalii—loomed in front of her, magnificently big, a beautiful man. Beautiful wild man. Yes . . . oh, yes . . . His skin rippled with muscle, and his eyes burned at her like star light.

"Mrs. Southworth! I'm getting the stuff, the cannisters! I'm bringing them down. Mrs. Southworth, you've got to wait. Don't! Don't go with him yet!"

"Ann. Come with me. Come."

"Kam—" Her voice shook. "Kam, I can't. You're him, you're . . . Kamohoalii."

Black eyes sucked at her, knew her. "Ann. Come.

Come now to the sea. It will be beautiful. Beautiful . . ."

She shuddered. "No— No, oh God, no, I can't . . . please don't make me . . ."

"Ann . . ."

"No!"

She staggered backward, tripping, falling, scrambling to her feet again. Gritty black sand clung to her knees. Donnie had rushed across the sand to her, was thrusting something into her hand. Something hard and cold and metallic—a compressed air sprayer attached to plastic garden tubing. They had filled it with kerosene.

"Ann Southworth." How beautiful his voice was. Soft, persuasive, compelling. "Ann, you must not do this thing. You must come into the sea with me where you belong. We should be together. It will be beautiful there, hauntingly lovely beyond anything you can ever imagine. We will experience it together."

"No— No!"

Her mouth was dry. She clutched the metal spring-handle of the lawn sprayer. Cold hard steel. All she had to do was squeeze it and she could send out death in jets of fire. She took a step away from him, and then another one. Fear had left her now, washed from her mind, leaving it utterly clean and free.

"Kamohoalii," she heard her voice intone as if she were a priestess. "You are Kamohoalii. I know you. I know you."

"Mrs. Southworth, Mrs. Southworth, use the lighter and start it. You've got to hurry. Hurry!"

Donnie Perriera danced at the edge of her vision, jumping up and down in his impatience. The moon filled the air with eery pale light.

Donnie's voice harried at her. "Hurry, Mrs. Southworth, hurry!"

"Ann, Ann, you must not do this. Ann, I love you, I

adore you, and I want to take you with me. I want to show you the beauty, I want to take you far beyond anything you have ever known . . ."

"Mrs. Southworth!"

"Ann . . ."

Ann's hands tightened on the sprayer pump. She could feel its metal as hard and real as the beach sand that gritted beneath her feet.

"Do it, Mrs. Southworth! Do it! Do it!"

"Ann." His eyes looked into hers, filled with unholy light. Deep pinpoint flashes of fire burned in their pupils. Power surged out of them, a power directed at her. And there was something in the air now, growing stronger with each passing second.

Energy. Sheer, utter, vibrating energy, filling the air like a summer storm. It was as if they were at the center of some massive generator, at the heart of an electrical transformer. Buzzing glowing vibrating filling up all the spaces of the air.

Ann began to shudder with the building of it, the force concentrating in her, growing, unbearable . . .

Donnie's voice ripped at her. "Mrs. Southworth, you've got to start it, you've got to do it now

DO IT MRS. SOUTHWORTH

DO IT

NOW

NOW NOW NOW NOW

Ann's right hand clenched the handle of the first compressed air sprayer, which Donnie had stolen from his father. She closed her fingers and squeezed, and then her left hand went into her jeans pocket for the Bic lighter Donnie had borrowed from his brother.

And then flames. Flames spewing out, spraying, whooshing, red. Fire-light killing the moonlight, drawing all the dark to it and vomiting it out red.

Flaming onto Kam. Onto Kamohoalii.

"Ann. Ann. You must not do this. Oh, Ann."

Eyes dark pits of sorrow, grieving in their burden of centuries of suffering. *And flames shot through the night in red rivers, spraying all over that beautiful phosphorescent body . . . Red red red.*

Kamohoalii was burning. His skin was engulfed with licking tongues of flame glowing around him like a coat of light. His shorts were smoldering, being consumed. His hair had turned to red, was going up now in a hiss of fire. His mouth was opened, his lips were moving, was he screaming? Oh, God, was he screaming?

If he wasn't, Ann was. She felt as if she could not bear this any longer. She could hear her own terror cut the darkness, but she did not dare to stop the flame thrower. She braced her legs wide apart in the sand and she held the cannister like a bucking horse and she aimed the red jet at the burning figure.

She sprayed, sprayed and saw the river of red, the flowing of fire like the heart of white-hot steel, like crematories and hellfire and explosions and napalm—

The black eyes held hers, holes of loneliness, grief, agony. *Ann, Ann,* his voice said in her head. It was huskier than she remembered, heavy with sorrow. *Ann, are you really doing this to me?*

She was sobbing. "My children— You're killing them— I can't help it—"

Ann, you don't understand.

"You're Kamohoalii! You're him, Kamohoalii!"

He burned . . . red-sheeted, eery. He was a torch, a living, burning torch, and still his voice spoke in her head.

Ann, you would do this to me, to the one that you love?

"I don't love you, I don't!"

You do love me, Ann. You always have. I was in your dreams when you were a little girl, you fantasized me all through your married life. You betrayed your husband with me. Oh, yes, Ann, you have loved me all of your years. Why do you want to kill me now?

She was spraying him, she didn't stop, he was redness now, with only black eyes in the midst of the flames to beseech her. His face was disintegrating, the shorts, his flesh wrinkling and darkening like incinerated paper. He had begun to stagger backward, in the direction of the crescent of beach and the twin spits of rocks that enclosed it on either side.

"I have to kill you, Kam," she wept. "I have to. For Kristal, for Buddy, for all of us. Oh, don't you see? Kam . . . Kam . . ."

Ann. He was suffering. She had never imagined that any creature could suffer so much. *Burning, Ann. I am burning. You are burning me.*

Suddenly the air around Ann seemed to waver, and it was as if *she* were Kamohoalii, she was the one who was burning. Pain seared her. Excruciating, white-hot hot HOTHOTHOT— Oh, God please, it was a pain that was almost an orgasm burning BURNING . . . the very sand beneath her feet had begun to burn, searing her. Nightmarishly she could see herself, Ann Southworth, from Kam's eyes. Her face was white and set, her eyes wide with horror as she braced herself in the sand with the sprayer. Behind her Donnie rushed up with the refill sprayer, dashed off with the first one to fill it again.

HOT. AGONIZINGLY HOT, HER SKIN WAS SEARING OFF, PEELING AWAY, SHE COULD FEEL HER BONES MELT AND SAG, HER BLOOD BOIL IN HER VEINS STEAMING AND BUBBLING AWAY. Screaming filled her ears, her own, Kam's, Ann didn't know, she didn't even know whose body she was in now.

"Dear God in Heaven." She forced her burning lips to form a prayer. "If ever I believed in You I believe now.

I believe You can help me. Please . . . I don't care about me, just save my children. Save them. Save them . . ."

Eerily she was back again in her own body. Perspiration covered her, a cooling river of moisture. Kam still burned.

Ann, Ann, Ann, his voice intoned in her head. *Ann, you love me. Come to the sea with me. Come.*

"No," Ann screamed. "No, oh, please, Kam, no—"

Come, Ann.

Ann. Ann. The voice in her head was hypnotic in its plea. For a shimmering second Ann wavered. She was inflicting torture, she was killing a mind, a soul that was alive and could suffer, a soul that had loved her . . .

"Mrs. Southworth, watch out, watch it, he's moving, he's trying to get to the water!" Donnie screamed a warning. He ran toward her with another canister, shoved the spray handle into her fist.

"Burn him," he hissed in her ear. "You can't stop now, you've got to burn him before he gets to the water. He'll change there, he'll *change himself back*—"

Ann felt sick. She knew instantly exactly what Donnie was trying to tell her. Kamohoalii was lunging toward the water, and once the shark man could get a part of his body into the sea, he could sink beneath its coolness and extinguish the flames. He would be Kamohoalii again, he would swim downward through night waters to his cave, and all would be as before. He would survive . . .

The burning figure staggered, fighting for balance. It had managed to move three feet closer to the water, charred feet sliding on roughened lava rubble and shards of smashed coral, chunks of driftwood. He stumbled. Fell.

And still Kam inched toward the water with desperate animal strength, dragging himself on all fours now, but still moving. His blackened skin hung in shreds, bone showing under the nimbus of fire. And—oh, God—didn't she see a melting of him somehow? A wavering of the image that had once been Kam Smith?

For a moment it almost looked as if his arm were a fin. In the pale moonlight she caught a suggestion of the sinuousness of shark muscle, a trace of scales, of silvery mottled skin— And his mouth, opened in a soundless scream. Weren't there teeth? Not human teeth, but ragged, jagged, sharp ones, a whole mouthful of them. And the mouth where it hung open was underslung and gaping, a shark's mouth.

HE WAS TRYING TO CHANGE NOW.

Trying, but not succeeding, not yet. That would have to wait until he reached water. If he got to the sea, then he could douse the flames and dive deep into his shark form, and he would live . . .

I cannot let you kill me, Ann. I will not.

Vibration. Power. The sand seemed to buck beneath her, hurling her. Ann looked downward in horror to discover that the black lava pebbles were smoking. The rubber soles of her tennis shoes were white hot. He was melting the sand beneath her feet. She leaped backward with a shriek.

A rock came hurtling toward her. It was red, molten as lava. Ann dodged, ducked the viscous red-melting blob, dodged from another one. Horror prickled her skin, jammed in her chest. Wasn't Kamohoalii supposed to be the elder brother of the volcano goddess, Pele? He could melt rocks beneath a man's feet— He could burn her alive.

Another molten boulder came flying toward her, hissing so close to her arm that she could feel its heat sear her skin. Ann jerked back from it, grabbed the sprayer handle, her lips moving soundlessly. She crossed herself as she had seen Donnie do. God, god, help me. Help my children.

Ann. Ann. You will not kill me.

The voice in her head had changed. It was fainter, blurrier, as if the syllables had been spoken by something that could not articulate quite clearly.

Another molten rock flew toward her, but fell short in its trajectory.

He was losing his control. He was dying.

"Mrs. Southworth! That's almost empty, you'd better take this."

Donnie thrust a refill at her again. Something in his voice had been strange. Ann glanced quickly at him. The boy's welts were bleeding, his face had become a raw, red mask of blood. Rivulets of red funneled down from his eyes, from his nose and mouth, his forehead, from the very pores of his skin.

See, Ann, what you have made me do? If you do not stop I will have to kill you too.

And now Ann saw that her own arm was covered with a raw scrape. Little pinpoint dots of blood oozed to the surface, blood trickling down her arm. She could feel something hot and moist and oozy on her face. Something was flowing down her cheeks ...

She was sobbing, retching.

"Mrs. Southworth." Bleeding, Donnie had fallen to his knees beside the empty canister. His breath came in desperate wheezes. "Get him ... before he goes in the water ... before it's too late ... get him ..."

Ann's own breath had begun to come short now. She gasped, pulling oxygen into her starved lungs. Dimly she glimpsed Donnie sprawled on the sand like a discarded puppet. He was a tumbled mass of bleeding arms and legs and rumpled shorts. One arm was stretched limply toward the spray cannister. Was he still breathing? She couldn't tell.

Kamohoalii was inching toward the surf.

There was a huge, silvery log of driftwood lying near the chicken wire walkway, and desperately, with her last strength, Ann grabbed for it. She hefted it in her hands to prod at the thing crawling on the beach, the creature she must destroy or die herself, along with her children and Donnie Perriera.

Painfully, agonizedly, the burning thing crawled a few more inches toward the waves. Ann beat at it with a stick, pounded it until she sobbed in frustration.

God— God help me—

Ann, why are you doing this? Why?

She sobbed, weeping out her horror and revulsion. She braced herself and wheezed for air and smacked down at the crawling mass. She forced it into the sand face down.

Or did it have a face? Wasn't there a blunt, heavy nose with burning black holes for eyes and wide snapping jaws—jaws that snapped and lunged, at the stick, at the rocks, at her own legs? Kamohoalii seemed to melt and merge from one form to another. First he was man, then shark, parts of his body fading and blending. Fin . . . arm . . . splayed burning charred hand . . .

Ann Ann I love you I need you I won't let you kill me

And still the fallen shark man struggled toward the waves. He was only a few feet away from them, just a few feet, and desperately Ann brought the stick up, pounded it down on him. Again, again. She rushed back for the sprayer, pushed the squeeze nozzle. Pumped it again frantically. Empty. The sprayer was empty!

More kerosene? *Was* there more? She would have to fill the cylinder herself, for Donnie was lying unconscious or dead. Was there time? He was dragging himself, by wild, stubborn, inhuman strength. An inch, another inch . . .

Desperately, gasping for air, almost at the point of fainting, Ann scrabbled at the air-compressor pump. She poured the fuel into it. God, God, why couldn't the stuff pour faster, why was it so terrifyingly slow? Then she rammed on the lid and began the pumping process. Pump, Ann, pump the air in, pump for your life. Faster, faster, her heart slamming, her lungs searing with pain. She jammed the air in until the pressure grew hard and her own chest was squeezing.

The burning shark man had almost reached the edge of the damp place on the sand where the waves crept at their highest flow. It would be only a matter of time, a few seconds perhaps, before another big one poured in, foaming and beautiful, to touch the charred hand-fins groping in the sand. Water would flow in and pick him up. It would float him outward and he would be free . . .

Ann yanked at the heavy cannister and secured its top. She fumbled with the Bic and relit the spray. Red fire spurted out in a wide hosing jet stream of death. She aimed it at the struggling black figure.

Ann Ann let me go out to the sea
Ann it would have been beautiful
I would have loved you

Words, thoughts, growing fainter, disappearing like smoke in the moonlight air.

Ann
A . . .

The moon lit it all with cruel intensity. He was dead. A charred, blackened mound of still-smoking flesh. It was impossible to tell what the thing had been—shark or man—for it was only a dark shape now, sprawled on the edge of the waves, one hand-fin stretched toward the curling lace of surf as if in supplication.

Kam. Kamohoalii. He was really and truly dead. Ann could barely believe it.

The wash and suck of the surf had grown higher now as a new set of waves came rolling in, four-foot high walls of water surging up to crash on the sand. The air was heavy, thick with the smoke of Kam's burning. Behind Ann, still lying inert on the sand, Donnie Perriera had begun to moan and retch.

In a moment Ann would go to him. Meanwhile, something held her there at the surf line beside the body of the creature she had killed. She was shaking, her whole body gripped in a spasm that would not let her go. Slowly, her tennis shoes slipping in the sand, she walked closer to stare down at the unmoving form.

She hadn't meant that he suffer so much. Oh, God, she would never have done such a thing if there had been any other way, if he hadn't been threatening to kill herself and Donnie and her children . . .

She gazed down at Kam, puzzled. Surely his body was lying closer to the water line than she had first thought. Or was it only that the waves were bigger now? Yes, she saw, looking out. The wall of surf was higher now as the waves pounded in.

A curling head of foam washed over the sand toward them. It arched up over pebbles, seemed to hesitate infinitesimally, then hissed on again toward the black outstretched hand. It touched what had been the fingertips.

Ann stared at Kamohoalii, what remained of him. How still he lay.

The wave swept back again, toward the sea, and Ann, her eyes fastened on the body, thought she saw it move. There was a twitch of the hand, a little shudder galvanizing its way through the burned tissue.

A movement of the water had caused it, of course. Kamohoalii was dead, how could he be anything but dead? Hadn't she burned him, charred him, COOKED HIM? She had used at least five containers of kerosene on him. She had reduced him to carbon and shards of skin and bone, a black ugly mass that had no shape other than that of death. And yet . . .

Another wave came rolling in. It was even bigger than the last, its face vertical, foam spilling as it came. She saw that it was going to ride further up the sand than the other one had; at least up to Kam's wrist and possibly to his midsection. It was going to lift him a little . . .

The wave flowed in inexorably. As it did so, Ann took an involuntary step backward. She saw that the part of Kam that once had been his chest was heaving, that his arms were pushing now, struggling at the sand . . .

The water came. It lifted him and pulled him partly down the slope toward the surf line. He moved with the wave, flowed with it, something, some energy, gathering in him.

"Kam? Oh God, my God . . ."

Ann's words were not really words, they were little outcries of horror. She was backing up, stumbling away.

HE WAS STILL ALIVE. SHE HAD NOT KILLED HIM, AFTER ALL.

Kam was moving into the full boil of the surf now. The sea had taken him back, the sea that gave him his strength and power.

Chapter 32

The moon overhead was a huge cold coin, light spilling down to illuminate the beach. Rocks cast shadows of jet black. Sand furrows were etched in relief. The barbed wire was a pattern of diamonds cut by some demon jeweler.

Behind her, Donnie Perriera had stopped his retching. The waves kept crashing on the sand, their roar magnified in Ann's ears until she thought she would go mad with the nightmare of it.

Kamohoalii was still alive, and it was all over, everything she had fought for. Her children—they would die. Donnie too. All of them . . .

"No!" She screamed it. "No, oh God, no! NO! YOU WON'T DO THIS TO ME, KAM!"

Her shriek was sucked away into the moist sea air,

swept out over the cresting waves to where the ghostly islands of Molokini and Kahoolawe rode the night horizon. The dark shape of Kamohoalii was being carried rapidly outward now, picked up by the outgoing waves and swept toward deep water.

Was he changing even now as he flowed seaward into the glimmer of phosphorescent moonlight? Did she see fins? A suggestion of blunt heavy head, underslung tooth-filled jaws?

Ann stood rooted in the sand. Exhaustion and despair washed through her. She had sprayed Kamohoalii, she had washed him down with fire and it hadn't done any good. She had lost. Now Kam was moving on the surface of the water, his body altering form, growing larger, longer, more sinuous . . .

There was no more fuel for the sprayers. But, she knew with dull sick despair, even if there had been plenty of kerosene, she could not have waded out into the surf to use it. It was too late. Kamoalii had returned to his own element now. She could not harm him.

Ann. Ann!

At first the voice in her head was so low that Ann didn't realize it was there, for it blended so subtly with the wash and flow of the surf.

Ann. Listen to me.

The voice knew her mind, could slip itself into the crevices of her thoughts with the familiarity of a hand in a pocket.

"Kam? Oh, my God—"

Her voice didn't seem to belong to her. The sea was empty. There was nothing now, not even foam, to indicate where he had been. There were only the empty canisters to throw jagged shadows on the beach, and the flattened trail on the sand where he had crawled.

But the waves— The water— Oh, surely the place

where Kamohoalii had disappeared into the sea was brighter, as if all the cold moonlight had beamed down like a laser onto one area.

Ann, you must take off your clothes and come to me. Come.

The moonlight glittered and danced on the water. The surface of the waves was roughened with whitecaps, and Ann thought she saw something come to the top. It was dark and shaped like a fin. There was a swift flick of the surface, and then it was gone again.

He was waiting out there for her. In the sea.

And his strength was growing. She could tell it, sense it in the eery increasing glow of moonlight, in the very feel of the air around her, beginning to throb with energy. Yes, the air was full and charged, vibrating with power.

He was out there.

Ann, take off your shirt. Take off your jeans. Come to me. You belong with me. You know that. You know it.

"No!"

She was sobbing. Had she been crying all along? Was that why her chest felt so aching and splintered, her breath catching raggedly in her throat?

He was alive, and in the water, which was his natural home. Which meant he would survive. Which meant he could continue to manipulate the breathing centers of her children with his mind. Which meant... Oh, God, Krissie, Buddy... Her mind could not carry the pictures any further.

Ann. You must come. I command you to come.

"No!" she screamed. "No, I won't! I won't come, damn you!"

You will. I command you.

"I *won't!*" Tears geysered in her, a wild aching raging flow of them. She took a jerky running step forward and scooped up a jagged lava rock. She hurled it into the sea. At him.

The rock fell short of its target. Laughing and crying and choking, Ann reached down and grabbed another and another, hurling them until rock scraped her palms and bled them raw.

The rocks sailed out into the surf, and some of them were obliterated by the big wave-walls. Some didn't make the waves but died on the damp sand, and none of them reached their mark.

"I hate you," she panted. "Kam, I hate you, I won't let you kill my children, I WON'T—"

Rage. Sheer, insane rage. She threw the rocks and she cried and the stinging abrasions on her hands only fueled her fury.

"TAKE THAT, YOU BASTARD— YOU DAMNED BASTARD—"

The last rock landed in the middle of the surf line and was instantly sucked away by the water. Then she sensed it in her mind, the laughter.

You are very foolish, Ann. Do you really think that rocks can stop me?

Her spine abruptly sagged. The strength left her. Ann's knees were shaking as if she had been ill for weeks. There was a terrible lassitude creeping through her now.

"No . . . I don't suppose they can. Rocks. My God."

And now, because she had no more energy, she knelt down on the sand. Her thigh muscles were twitching uncontrollably. She was weak, trembling, and the tears flowed blindly down her cheeks. It was all over. Everything.

Ann. Take off your shirt. Obey me.

Trembling, she found the buttons of the light cotton plaid shirt she had thrown on over her jeans earlier today when she had dressed after her shower. That seemed a hundred years ago. It had all happened to some other woman in some other time; it had nothing to do with her now, nothing at all.

That's it. That's it, Ann. Satisfaction colored the words that spoke in her mind. But was there a tiredness too? A soft grief, a sorrow?

Methodically, Ann's fingers managed the buttons of the shirt, slid it off her shoulders, let it fall to the sand. She wore nothing beneath, and her bare breasts caught the silvery brilliance of the moonlight.

And the jeans, his voice ordered. *The shoes. Go on, Ann. All of it.*

She obeyed.

Her arms belonged to a puppet, an automaton that had no choice other than to do as it was told. She found the snap at the front of her jeans and parted it. Got to her feet in order to climb out of the jeans and then to step, with slow hypnotized tread, out of the tennis shoes and the bikini panties.

She was naked now. Moonlight glimmered over her body, warming it. She was surrounded by warmth now. It was as if the moonlight had somehow ignited the rocks around her, for they glowed like dull coals, forming a path that pointed toward the circlet of beach. A path she was expected to use.

You are beautiful, Ann. Lovely beyond my imagining.

The voice in her head wooed her and played with her and persuaded her and commanded her.

Come, Ann. Come to me. I want to love you. I want to love you as no one has ever loved you before on this earth.

The path stretched before her, lit on either side by the glowing rocks and pebbles. The moon overhead seemed bigger, closer than she had ever seen it before, impossibly brilliant.

Energy surged in the air around her, a rumbling

vibrating power. It was as if she were at the center of a generator, a volcano, or even the sun itself. The trembling in the air was irresistible; it vibrated into the very cells of her body, every pore and crevice and orifice, until she could feel it everywhere—her arms lungs belly gut vagina throat anus mouth eyes breasts clitoris.

I want you, Ann. I need you

The path lay before her. Ann began to walk. Her legs were weak, trembling, their strength gone, yet still her muscles functioned, as if something had come into her body and was making her obey.

The damp sand gave under her feet. She heard the roar of the surf as it sucked back. When it hurled itself forward again this time, it would wrap itself around her bare legs and thighs.

She walked. There was the hissing, susurating flow of water as it came toward her, bubbles of foam seeking, and then she felt the wash on her legs. The water curled high, higher than she had expected. It sent little cold tendrils of wetness as high as her hips, snaking moisture into her very body itself, the secret, innermost places of her.

Ann. For a second, the voice seemed to change slightly, as if its strength was fragile and could not be held forever. But quickly it regained control. *Ann, you are coming to me. You cannot stop now.*

He was right. She could not stop. She began to stride forward, into the washing roiling sweep of the water. Small rocks gave beneath the soles of her feet as the water sucked outward again, pulling her with it.

Ann. Ann . . .

She walked through the wall of surf. It did not knock her over but permitted her to pass through it. Salty fingers of water caressed her like a lover. The energy was everywhere now, in the air, the sea, at the very center of her own bones.

At first there was no sign of Kamohoalii.

Ann swam out into the little bay much as she had swum with Kam that night (was it only a few weeks ago?) when she had come to have dinner with him here at the beach house. She remembered noticing then that the water seemed deeper in the center of the inlet, almost as if it had been scooped out by some giant bulldozer.

Now, as if by instinct, she swam along that same channel. The big moon seemed to grin at her, tonguing the surface with phosphorescent licks and curls of foam. When she opened her eyes in the water, she could see downward to the dim, barely discernible mounds of coral, the underwater world to which Kam had introduced her.

She stopped swimming and began to tread water. A sob caught in her throat. It was really over now. Over at last.

First Kamohoalii would love her as he had once loved Sarah Faulker and Karen Weeks, spending himself in her in one destructive frenzy. There would be a few uterus-piercing moments of agony; then it would be finished for her. If she were lucky, she would die of drowning, before Kamohoalii scented the blood and fluids in the water, reverted to his shark heritage, and devoured her.

In a few days her body—parts of it—might be found on some Maui beach to be stared at in sickened horror by the tourists. But at least, she told herself, Buddy and Kristal wouldn't be among those to experience *that* nightmare. For they would be dead then, too. After her own death Kam would finish them off, and Donnie as well. Then there would be no one left to tell the story of the man who could change his form to that of a shark. It could all begin again, somewhere else, with some other woman.

She continued to tread water, gasping as the foam-topped breakers tilted toward her as if they would crash over her head, then lifted her up instead so that she continued to bob on their surface.

The sea was empty, lit only by the evil moon. She was alone, surrounded by the energy-charged air, the force building in the water . . . Then she saw it. The swift slash of a fin at the surface. At the same time, she felt the movement, the passing of a big shape only feet away from her. He was here.

God, oh God. It wasn't a prayer, exactly, just a wild, quick thought. *God, are you anywhere?*

Ann. Do you see me?

She gasped another breath of air and lay face down on the water, opening her eyes against salty wetness. Dimly she saw the huge body undulating through the water, snakelike, fluid in its power. And yet, wasn't there a waver for an instant in the way that tail moved? It was as if the big shark was having to make a massive effort.

Ann, I am here. Come to me. Come.

Ann kicked and raised her head for a gulp of air, then floated on the rolling surface of the sea and looked downward again. He was still there, angling now to her left, then swinging around with arrogant power to ram toward her again. Bold, strong, the King, in full command of his environment.

And yet . . .

Ann. I need you. I must have you must have

There it was again, that cry inside her head that came from him. It ached with need and with that curious note of sorrow.

The huge shape . . . how big it was, how coiled with massive power—the big body swept toward her. Ann's widened eyes glimpsed the skin as he came close, the hide that had been carbonized . . . ravaged. There were black places, peeled away to cartilage. Raw hunks of flesh hung down, spurting out little bits of fleshy materials and fluids to stain the water. He was a bulky ruined mass of flesh: would the water, would anything, ever heal him?

Ann, you burned me. You burned me.

There was a terrible flowing surge of the energy-force in the water, yet Ann could sense the emotion there, too. The pain, deep-ripping and intense.

A man, she thought numbly, as Kamohoalii, with one flipping surge of strength, jammed his dorsal fin against her, shoving her under the surface of the waves. After all he is partly a man too. *Partly human.*

The thought had a meaning—a significance so important that nothing else meant anything. But Ann's mind could not keep hold of it as she was forced underwater by the diving shark.

Deeper, deeper he pulled her, until her eardrums were nearly bursting with the depth pressure. Her heart was hammering, and she knew that she would soon feel the tight hot need of her lungs to breathe. Kamohoalii was undulating like a huge snake, his skin dripping with tattered shreds of flesh as he twisted for position. And she could already see it, the *thing* growing, growing at the base of his tail. Huge, erect, throbbing, obscene. And big. She had never seen anything like it.

Ann Ann . . . His voice split her mind. Feverish, thrumming with excitement.

Oh— she thought. *No.* He wasn't going to— He couldn't—

There were pounding vibrations in the water as the shark lashed about, maneuvering for position.

Ann's mind was going now. She could feel her thoughts sliding out of control, disintegrating into the panic of the need to breathe. Her lungs were getting tight. Hot. Hard.

He was going to fuck her with those claspers. Ram her, immolate her, gut her.

Her chest hurt now. Her rib cage was being savaged into iron bands, her lungs, her eyes. And she knew that worse was coming. When he rammed *it* in, she would be skewered, ripped right up through her cervix as if it were butter.

The pain. The pain would be excruciating. But how much of it would she really feel? Would she be dying by then, strangling as the water rushed into her lungs; would her eyes be popping out of her head?

Beautiful. His words breathed in her mind, full of enormous urgent sexuality. *So beautiful. I don't want— Lonely—*

She was drowning now, she knew, had started her death spasms. She knew what was happening and could not stop it, the tight hard hot agony, the clawing panic. He was in position now; he filled the water with huge slapping waves of power as he gripped her with one huge fin.

The clasper, armored with row upon jagged row of denticles, abraded her upper right thigh. The savage pain scraped along her nerve ends as if she had been slashed with many knives.

In a moment, he would be inside her, thrusting past the sensitive vaginal lips, the soft moist vagina, the . . .

NO. DAMMIT, NO.

Rage poured into her again, a primeval fury stronger than any anger that she had ever known. Fury flamed through her, torching her mind, becoming one with the white-hot pain of her lungs and chest, the shrieks of her nerve endings.

She convulsively twisted herself away from the clasper. Fins thrashed. A tag of his flesh hung almost in her face, dangling obscenely.

Then, like beads sliding on a necklace, Ann's thoughts suddenly came together. Partly man. Yes, that was it. Kamohoalii was partly human, had known pain and loneliness, had been desperately hurt by the burning she had given him earlier. She still had a few seconds left, a tiny space more of life. If he could speak into her brain, THEN SHE COULD SPEAK INTO HIS.

The rage still filled her, and now she could feel a change in it, a sharpening and a purpose. She flung a prayer—only a word—out into the void, and then she pushed on the fin that held her, forcing herself to face the shark's head. It was hideous, the low-slung mouth grinning with teeth and charred now, like a disinterred corpse.

YOU BASTARD! She let the incredible energy fill her head. YOU FUCKING BASTARD, YOU'LL KILL ME FOR NOTHING! FOR NOTHING, DO YOU HEAR ME?

He was surprised, she could sense it. Hadn't expected this from her. She knew she had to hurry, because her chest was tighter, almost bursting, and the added depth pressure was pressing on her ears with vicious strength.

THIRTY SECONDS, THAT'S ALL WE'LL HAVE. UNTIL I DROWN. THEN YOU'LL BE ALONE AGAIN.

Silence.

IT'LL ALL BE FOR NOTHING BECAUSE YOU'LL STILL BE ALONE. YOU'LL *ALWAYS* BE ALONE, YOU BASTARD. CAN'T YOU SEE IT?

The silence was deeper now, terrible, brooding.

KAM! NOTHING CAN HELP YOU.

No. NoNoNoNoNoNONONONONO

Water crashed around her, rolling in thunderous wave motion as the big body thrashed, filling the molecules with the savage screaming of its psychic pain. He convulsed away, then rammed back toward her again like an express train hurtling.

God, Jesus, he was coming back and she could see it, the distended clasper, and it didn't seem to matter much now because she was drowning, she really was, hard hot pain exploding her, *bursting her*.

She fought for consciousness. She fought to keep her chest, her lungs, from exploding, and she projected the thought, forcing it out toward him, her desperate last attempt.

IT WON'T WORK, KAM. BECAUSE . . . BECAUSE WHEN THIS IS OVER, YOU'LL STILL BE ALONE. YOU'LL BE ALONE FOREVER, KAM. FACE IT.

Anguish in him. Huge violent despair ripped at her mind, tore at the delicate structures of her thoughts, the white-hot bursting heat of her dying. Blackness closed in.

ACCEPT IT, KAM . . . ACCEPT . . .

And then the spasms in the water were gone and she was beyond thought; she was simply floating at one with the water. The soft, encompassing sea water that was like a lover and a pillow and a bed.

Gasping, choking, gagging, spitting out the salty water, vomiting it . . . she was on the surface now, totally unaware of how she had got there. Had she clawed her way upwards even as she was in the last convulsive throes of drowning? Or had he, Kamohoalii, somehow lifted her here?

She didn't know. Didn't care. All she did know was that she was somehow alive, sucking in the moist, salty, life-giving air, weeping with relief. The moon, overhead, was partly covered with clouds now and somehow it seemed farther away, more normal. It was back now to the sort of moon you might see hanging over any Hawaiian resort.

Ann bobbed on the waves, being pushed at by the whitecaps that lifted her and shoved her on again like floatsam. A current was taking her in the direction of the lava flow, and slowly Ann began to kick, to move her arms in the motions of swimming. To her left, car headlight gleamed along Kaunoa Road, and she could see the yard lights of a house.

It was then that she saw it—or sensed it, really, the violence in the water only a few hundred yards away from her. Dark shapes boiled the surface. Things moved fast in the water, big things full of ramming, frenzied violence. They slashed in on some central target and then cut back out again, a lusting, twisting, savaging mass.

Sharks, Ann thought. *Many sharks.*

Cautiously, so as not to attract their attention, she began swimming toward the yellow lights that gleamed on the shore.

They were lying on the beach called Mahinipeopeo, gazing out at a view of sky and hazy islands floating at the horizon like a glimpse of paradise. Noon sun glittered down on them, and there was the rich smell of coconut oil. They had their things with them: woven beach mats, lotion, paperbacks, towels, a cooler of pop and fruit juice, combs, car keys and money.

Buddy spoke lightly to his sister. "God, that stuff stinks, Krissie, that suntan stuff you've got. It smells like you squashed a whole coconut."

"I think it smells great," Kristal murmured. "And you'd better put on a little yourself or you're going to get burned. After all that time in the hospital, you're white as a ghost. We've got to catch up on our tan, or nobody'll ever believe we were in Hawaii."

"Buy a T-shirt. *Here Today, Gone to Maui,*" offered Donnie Perriera. He too had lost his tan, was thinner, gawkier than ever. "That'll make 'em believe you. We're selling 'em at the shop now, twenty percent off. Good bargain, yah?"

Buddy and Kristal laughed. Ann was smiling, too.

She sat with her arms folded about her crossed legs—the scars there had nearly healed—and stared out at the ocean.

How peaceful it all was. It was hard to believe that she had returned two days later to the beach house to find nothing left. For the *kona* winds had come, whipping up the surf into powerful roiling twelve-foot waves, and all of it had been swept away. The air sprayers, the empty cans of kerosene, the flattened indentation in the sand where the blackened thing had pulled itself so painfully toward the sea.

But up at the back of the beach, caught on a corner of the chicken wire amid a litter of storm debris, there had been something. It had looked like a jaw bone, or at least part of one, huge, blunt, with sharp and ragged teeth. Was it *his*?

Ann swallowed back sudden nausea, thinking of the dark shapes she had seen savaging the water near where Kamohoalii had been. Sharks, she recalled, could scent a wounded animal from miles away and unerringly zero in on their prey. Attracted by leaking bits of food and flesh, they could go into a wild feeding frenzy . . .

Had Kamohoalii, accepting what Ann had told him, somehow called his own brothers, to be at last devoured by them? Or had it only been, after all, the inevitable savagery of nature?

Well, Ann guessed that didn't matter now. The sea had come in, the mother-sea, and she had taken back what was hers. Kamohoalii, perhaps, rested now.

Kristal, fussing with her camera, interrupted Ann's thoughts. "Hey, wow, look at that." She was pointing at the cloud-washed profile of the island of Lanai. "What do you think, maybe a time study of the way the light comes in and hits the island? Or the surf. I love the way the foam curls in, it's so primitive, don't you think?

Primitive.

Donnie was agreeing with Kristal, their two heads close together, a blonde one and a dark one. Buddy turned lazily over on his stomach, the frown lines relaxed from his face. He looked sixteen again, sixteen after all.

Ann, looking out to sea, suddenly stiffened. She thought she had seen something out there, a fin slicing through the waves, perhaps. But then it was gone and she decided that she had seen only the shadow of a wave crest glittering on the surface. She lay back on the beach mat and put her paperback over her eyes against the sun glare, thrusting all thoughts out of her mind.

THE BEST OF THE BESTSELLERS
FROM WARNER BOOKS

DEAD AND BURIED
by Chelsea Quinn Yarbro   (91-268, $2.50)

He thought dead men told no tales. The murders were bad enough but what Sheriff Dan Gillis couldn't understand were the newcomers to Potter's Bluff, and their eerie resemblance to people he had seen DEAD AND BURIED. Was he imagining things? Or was something evil preying on the sleepy town of Potter's Bluff—something as shadowy as the faceless killers who roamed the land.

RAKEHELL DYNASTY
by Michael William Scott   (95-201, $2.75)

This is the bold, sweeping, passionate story of a great New England shipping family caught up in the winds of change—and of the one man who would dare to sail his dream ship to the frightening, beautiful land of China. He was Jonathan Rakehell, and his destiny would change the course of history.

P.S. YOUR CAT IS DEAD!
by James Kirkwood   (82-934, $2.25)

It's New Year's Eve. Your best friend died in September, you've been robbed twice, your girlfriend is leaving you, you've just lost your job . . . and the only one left to talk to is a gay burglar you've got tied up in the kitchen. "Kirkwood is a fine writer, and keeps the suspense taut all the way."
—*The New York Times Book Review.*

ACT OF VENGEANCE
by Trevor Armbrister   (85-707, $2.75)

This is the true story behind one of the most frightening assassination plots of our time: the terrible corruption of a powerful labor union, the twisted lives of the men and women willing to kill for pay, the eventual triumph of justice—and the vision and spirit of a great man.

ALINE
by Carole Klein   (93-526, $2.95)

She was an eminent theatrical designer; he was an unknown. She was a 44-year-old sophisticated New Yorker; he was a 25-year-old hillbilly from North Carolina. From the moment he glimpsed her "flower face," their fiery relationship grew, ripening and exploding into one of the most turbulent and passionate love stories the world has ever known. "A richly detailed portrait of the woman and the many worlds through which she moved . . . a rare and unforgettable personage."
—*New York Times*

ROMANCE...ADVENTURE...
DANGER...

THE BEST OF SUSPENSE
FROM WARNER BOOKS